LONGARM HELD UP
HIS HANDS IN SURRENDER.

Jessie, laughing, pushed him down so that she could stretch out on top of him. She ran her fingers through his thick brown hair, and began to nibble kisses along the strong line of his jaw.

Longarm slid his hands beneath the blanket, gliding his palms down along Jessie's shivering spine, to caress the satiny mounds of her bottom beneath the tantalizingly sheer gauze pants. Jessie pressed her mouth against his for a lingering kiss. Longarm flipped her over so that she was lying on her back...then nudged apart the silk kimono...

TABOR EVANS

LONGARM

AND THE LONE STAR VENGEANCE

A JOVE BOOK

LONGARM AND THE LONE STAR VENGEANCE

A Jove Book/published by arrangement with
the author

PRINTING HISTORY
Jove edition/July 1983

ISBN: 0-515-07085-8

Chapter 1

Ask any experienced lawman—the hardest part of the job is learning patience. Any dumb jasper can make a move, Longarm knew. The trick lies in knowing how to wait for the right time to make that move. . . .

Longarm had been waiting two weeks. He and all the other available deputies had been ordered by their boss, the Chief United States Marshal of the First District Court of Colorado, to set up undercover stakeouts. Marshal Vail's district was being plagued by a particularly ornery band of murdering bank robbers. The marshal had scattered his deputies in and around Denver, trying to do his best to see that every bank was covered. This meant that the marshal had no choice but to spread his forces mighty thin; Longarm, pretending to be a teller, was the only lawman in the massive central office of the city's First National Bank.

For two weeks now, Longarm had been forced to give up his usual garb for the boiled shirt, starched collar, and blue pinstriped suit of a junior clerk. Why, he'd even had to give

1

up his name! Vail had quite rightly pointed out that the legendary Custis Long, known as Longarm to friend and foe, was going to find it hard enough to blend into the bank's tan marble walls and oak woodwork without having his real name trumpeted about the place.

Billy Vail could be a stubborn old coot, but when he was right, he was right. Longarm could don a teller's clothing, but there wasn't much he could otherwise do to make himself look like a teller. Oh, these bank clerks were nice enough fellows, but there weren't many of them who stood well over six feet tall, like Longarm, or had his lean, muscled body born of thirty-odd years spent in the saddle, and not perched upon a high stool inside a teller's cage. Longarm had brushed back his tobacco-brown, closed-cropped hair, and he'd waxed his long-horn mustache with some sweet-smelling gunk that would've set the coyotes laughing for miles in every direction out on the open range, but there wasn't much he could do about his skin, burnished copper by the prairie sun. Why, he looked like an Indian next to these pale tellers who spent all of their days indoors. There wasn't much that Longarm could do about the look in his blue-gray eyes, either. They were the eyes of a man-tracker, not a paper-pusher. Finally, there wasn't much he could do about his big, callused hands. Oh, his hands were nimble enough to count out money with dispatch, but there was something about Longarm's agility that told the wise watcher that here was a man whose fingers were trained to handle a weapon a hell of a lot more lethal—if less powerful in the long run—than twenty-dollar silver certificates.

Longarm knew that despite his pretty clothes, he stuck out like a turd in a bakery window. That was why Billy Vail insisted thay he use an alias. There was just one thing that stuck in Longarm's craw. Why had Billy insisted that his undercover name be—

"Ah, Noah? Noah Dick! Come here at once, I need you!" the head teller ordered, turning his scrawny back before Longarm could reply. "And hurry it up!" the little fellow added.

"Coming, sir," Longarm said politely, doing his best to sound like the sort of poor son of a bitch whose livelihood might depend upon pleasing this little asshole. As Noah Dick, Longarm had made himself a few friends during his fortnight

2

at the bank. The tellers had been quick to confide their loathing for their supercilious supervisor, Morton Crisp.

"Dick!" Crisp fairly screeched. The other tellers snickered helplessly, even as they offered Longarm sympathetic glances of apology.

"I said I was coming," Longarm growled. Crisp shot him a startled look, and Longarm cursed Billy Vail and his warped sense of humor for sticking him with a moniker like Noah Dick! It was hard enough for him to keep hold of his temper, without folks braying like a pack of damn mules every time he was summoned. . . .

Longarm left his cage and hurried past the other tellers, who were all preparing themselves for the noon rush, an hour from now. The First National was Denver's largest bank, and this branch was located right at the foot of Capitol Hill. The bank was pretty much empty at the moment. The heels of the few customers in the place clicked upon the marble floors and echoed off the sandstone walls and high, gilded, cathedral ceilings of the mammoth bank. In fact, right now the place seemed more like a church, what with the hushed murmuring of its employees and the soft flicker of its ornate gas lamps. Come lunchtime, the bank would be jammed with clerks who'd left their desks in the various municipal and state government offices up on the Hill, in order to conduct their financial transactions during the only free time they had during the business day.

"Ah, there you are, Noah," Crisp said, rubbing his hands together the way a horsefly fiddles its forelegs. "I want you to help my assistant in the basement," the head teller explained, smacking his lips. "There are some rather heavy boxes of files to be rearranged, and a strong back is what's needed," he sneered.

Longarm stared down at the little fellow. Crisp stood five feet six inches tall. He'd come by his five feet honestly enough, but he got the last six inches by piling his thick mass of black hair into an elaborate configuration that was cemented in place by the kind of lilac lard that the barbers on the wrong side of Cherry Creek liked to peddle. "Maybe you ought to get someone else—" Longarm began.

"What!" Crisp said, astounded. "Why, how dare you, Dick!

3

I'll give the orders around here! Now you get your tail into the basement, and fast!" With that, he turned on his heel and strode off.

Longarm stood where he was, uncertain as to what he should do. He didn't mind the idea of rolling up his sleeves and doing a little physical labor; his muscles, unaccustomed to the inactivity of working behind a desk, were yearning for some exercise. The problem was, he couldn't very well stop a bank robbery if he was stuck in the basement. The other thing was that his weapons—his double action .44-40 Colt Model T and the sawed-off, double-barreled, twelve-gauge shotgun he'd figured might come in handy—were both clipped beneath the counter in his teller's cage. Longarm had his derringer in his vest pocket, but he'd been forced to cache his Colt beneath his desk, since a bank clerk couldn't very well go strutting about with a holster strapped around his waist. A shoulder holster wouldn't have worked; all the other tellers made it a habit to drape their suit jackets over the low backs of their high stools and work in their shirtsleeves. If Longarm kept his jacket on, it would draw too much attention to him. Besides, he was certain that the robbers spent some time casing the bank they were going to raid. An experienced man, no matter which side of the law he was on, could spot the bulk of a shoulder holster beneath a suit jacket. Each minute that Longarm spent away from his teller's cage was a minute in which the bank was a sitting duck for the robbers—if they were ever going to show up. . . .

Of course, Longarm could explain none of this to Crisp. Billy Vail had no way of knowing just how the bank robbers operated. The fact that an employee of the bank could be bribed or threatened into cooperation with the outlaws meant that no one beyond the bank's highest officers could know Longarm's true identity. Crisp had been hoodwinked into believing that "Noah Dick' was a nephew of one of the bank's vice-presidents. The air of nepotism around the new clerk had done nothing to smooth over his relationship with the head teller. Indeed Morton Crisp had gone out of his way to make Noah Dick his personal whipping boy.

Longarm shrugged miserably, and went around the wooden

railings toward the double doors that led to the basement stairway. It wouldn't do to go getting himself fired—not today. During his two weeks in the bank, Longarm had occasionally noticed an odd-looking fellow with a big, black, bushy beard, tanned skin, and elaborately stitched, high-heeled Justin boots. The fellow spent a lot of time over at the writing desk in the center of the bank's public area, but never seemed actually to get around to conducting any transactions. The man wore a city slicker's black wool suit, but it was always dusty, as if he'd ridden in from out of town. The man wore no gunbelt around his waist and no pistol in a shoulder harness, as far as Longarm could tell. Now, lots of people in Denver didn't bother to carry a gun; the city had become a fairly civilized place now that the depression of the seventies was over, and President Rutherford B. Hayes was near completing his first term, which he'd captured by promising prosperity, law and order.

Yep, Longarm thought to himself as he began to descend the steps that led down into the bank's basement. In Denver, in 1880, a lot of folks no longer bothered to carry guns, but Old Blackbeard wasn't the type.... Call it a hunch, or call it intuition born of being a deputy U.S. marshal for close to ten years, but Longarm had a funny feeling in the pit of his belly. If something was going to happen in this bank, it was going to happen today.

The double doors at the top of the stairs had been hung to close of their own accord. As they did, the noise from the main floor of the bank was cut off.

Just great, Longarm moped as he glanced up at the doors. *The entire Cheyenne Nation could be rising up and surrounding the bank just now, and I wouldn't hear it....*

Well, the thing to do was to get this job over with and get back upstairs as soon as possible, Longarm decided. He passed into the warren of filing areas and storage rooms, looking for Crisp's assistant.

As Longarm searched, he detected an odd scent in the air, one that overpowered the smell of stale air and mildewed paper. It was a familiar scent, one that froze the lawman in his tracks.

"Well, I'll be . . ." he chuckled to himself, closing his eyes and inhaling deeply. It was an illusion, of course. He couldn't

5

actually be smelling it, but just now, Longarm could swear he was inhaling the blessed aroma of one of his very own two-for-a-nickel cheroots!

Not being able to smoke during the day was the toughest part of this damned undercover assignment. He kept a cheroot in the breast pocket of his suit jacket next to his wallet, inside of which was pinned his silver-plated federal badge. Unfortunately, though, he couldn't smoke his cigar until he'd left the bank at the end of the day. Lunch for the employees was a measly half hour spent in a dingy back room. The management of the bank supplied its workers with coffee and tea to drink with their brown-bag lunches, but smoking was expressly forbidden.

Longarm had tried to quit smoking a number of times, so he was no stranger to the tricks a man's tobacco-starved mind could play. A fellow might smell smoke at the damnedest times! He remembered an eventful evening spent with a young lady in a San Francisco bathtub when—

Once again Longarm froze, but this time the smile faded from his expression as his eyes narrowed. His hand instinctively reached for his Colt, but then he remembered where he'd left it, and fingered his derringer out of his vest pocket instead. The little brass gun held two .44 rounds. He palmed the derringer and moved forward silently.

The smoke he was smelling was no illusion. Somebody in this basement was puffing on a stogy. The only person supposed to be down here was Crisp's assistant, and it *couldn't* be the assistant—

"Hello . . ."

Longarm was slipping his derringer back into his vest pocket even as he turned toward the person greeting him. "Linda!" he chuckled, his blue-gray eyes crinkling at their corners as he grinned at her. "Just what do you think you're doing, gal?"

Linda held up the cheroot. "Want a puff?" she giggled. "I figure it's only right that we share it, since I swiped it out of your coat upstairs, when you left your teller's cage, earlier this morning."

Longarm, shaking his head in mock anger, took the cigar from her fingers for a blissful drag. "A good smoke is the finest pleasure on this earth, except for one," he teased, delighting

6

in the pink blush he'd brought to her pretty face. She was a cute little brunette with a buxom hourglass figure, a set of pouty, bee-stung lips that looked as red as cherries and twice as sweet, and big eyes about the size of robin's eggs and just as blue. Longarm knew that she was a single girl, both from the lack of a gold ring on her finger, and from the way she looked at him during the day. A single man himself, he was quite attuned to the magnetism that jolts between a pretty girl and an available fellow when the two pass each other in a corridor. The saucy tilt of her hips as she flounced past him during such times had put some very devilish thoughts into Longarm's mind. . . .

But thoughts were all they were, and thoughts they would remain, Longarm had firmly told himself. He was no prude; he knew that most women enjoyed a good roll in the hay as much as any man, but men didn't have reputations to worry about. A fellow could go around sowing his wild oats and be thought all the better for it by his peers. But if a female got caught, she was likely ruined for life. This cute little Linda, with her dark curly hair, her fine breasts straining against the high, modest front of her gingham blouse, had a tough row to hoe: she was a woman trying to succeed in the man's world of banking. Longarm was not about to spoil her chances by taking advantage of her.

"When Mr. Crisp told me to sort out these files, I told him I'd need somebody to help me move the boxes around," Linda explained. "I knew he'd send me you," she smiled bashfully. "I mean, with your muscles . . ." She reached out to caress Longarm's biceps tentatively with the tips of her fingers, then quickly jerked her hand back, as if she'd been burned.

Longarm leaned against a waist-high stack of cardboard file boxes. He took back the cheroot and puffed a couple of smoke rings into the air, watching as Linda perched her bottom on a rickety old stool, hiking up her skirt and exposing her shapely ankles in the process. She was just now close enough to snatch the cheroot from Longarm's lips, which is what she did.

Longarm watched her smoke. "Why, you're not fooling, are you?" he laughed, amazed. "You really enjoy that cheroot!"

"Do I!" Linda blushed. "I've been smoking on the sly since I was ten years old," she confessed. "I used to swipe my daddy's

7

pipe and puff away out behind the barn. My husband was a smoker too—"

"Whoa!" Longarm gasped. "Slow down. You mean to say you're a married woman?"

"I mean to say I was. I'm a widow now," Linda told him. "But that's got to be our little secret," she added quickly. "You see, I was married when I was thirteen, to a boy not more than sixteen. I'm from eastern Tennessee. My husband got himself killed during the War."

Longarm nodded. "You sure don't have a Tennessee accent," he remarked, adding, "Give me back that stogy. It's my turn."

"I left the mountains right after the war," Linda said, handing him the cigar. "I settled in Denver, and worked hard to complete my education and lose my hillbilly tongue. It turned out I had a head for figures. I started with First National as a teller in one of their branches. Pretty soon they gave me a spot here in the main branch, and I worked hard to get to be the assistant head teller," she finished proudly.

"Linda, I do admire you," Longarm smiled. "You're pretty as a picture, smoke like a trooper, and have the cunning to beat all those fellows upstairs at their own game."

"Ah-hah!" Linda crowed in triumph. "All *those* fellows, that's what you said! You didn't include yourself."

Damned if she hadn't set her trap and pounced on him right and proper.

"W-why, I meant to include myself," Longarm fumbled.

"I don't think so," Linda said meaningfully. "I've been in banks long enough to know how a man acts when he intends to pursue the money business. You could care less about this job, Mister whatever-your-name-is." She paused to lick her lips as she looked Longarm up and down. "I call you that, because it's plain to see that you're not the type of man to be labeled 'Noah Dick.'"

"You can't judge a book by its cover," Longarm said, trying his best to keep a straight face.

"Are you going to arrest me?" Linda suddenly asked.

"What?"

"I mean, for stealing your cigar," she explained innocently. "You see, I know what I did was dishonest, but I was simply *dying* to lick its wrapper like this." Her pink tongue darted out to moisten the tip of the cheroot. "And then I was *dying* to put it in my mouth and puff away until I had it all fired up and blazing." Her eyes never left Longarm's as she held out the cheroot. "Your turn," she smiled.

Longarm shook his head. "A man would have to be a fool to fiddle with his own cigar when he's got a woman like you do to it for him," he remarked.

"So you won't arrest me?" Linda teased.

"Now, you listen here. I'm just a bank teller," Longarm began.

Linda waved him quiet. "Oh, no you're not. You see, while I was fishing around in your coat pockets, I came up with this." She pulled open the top drawer of a file cabinet and displayed Longarm's wallet. His silver badge glittered in the feeble gaslight. "You're a federal deputy marshal. Now just what are you doing in this bank?" she demanded keenly.

Longarm thought about it for a moment, and then shrugged. By discovering his badge, Linda already knew most of it, so he might as well trust her by telling the rest. "You've got me dead to rights, Linda. My name's Custis Long, and I *am* a lawman. . . ." Longarm quickly filled her in on the particulars of his undercover mission in the bank.

Linda listened to it all with wide eyes. She gulped when he'd finished and said, "And you suspect that this bank might be robbed?" She shook her head. "You know, Custis, ever since I got my first teller's job, I've always thought about the possibility that I might be involved in a holdup, but never *seriously* . . ." She frowned. "I mean, you always think it won't happen to *you*."

"First of all, you won't be involved," Longarm said firmly. "Not if you have any sense in that pretty head of yours. If trouble comes, you do just what the robbers tell you to. Only a fool would risk getting killed over money." He paused, and smiled. "Only a fool, or a lunatic who makes his living taking such risks, like me."

"Am I?" Linda asked dreamily.

"Are you what?"

"Pretty?"

"Did you hear a word I said?" Longarm demanded sternly.

9

"Of course I did. You said, 'that pretty head of yours . . .' So am I? Pretty?"

"You sure are, Linda," Longarm smiled. "Probably the prettiest banker in these United States," he couldn't help adding.

"Oh, you!" she pouted. She'd let the cheroot go out, and now she set the stub down on top of the file cabinet, next to Longarm's wallet. "Tell me true if you think ah'm pretty. . . ." she begged, her childhood years in Appalachia creeping back into her speech.

"I think you're a very pretty woman indeed," Longarm said softly.

Linda's blue eyes glinted merrily. "Let's have a drink on it!" she laughed. She pulled open the second drawer of the file cabinet and extracted a bottle of whiskey. "I smuggled this down here a couple of days ago. Hope you don't mind bourbon."

Longarm took the bottle from her, pulled the cork with his strong teeth, and sniffed. He nodded approvingly and took a long swig. "I'm a rye drinker, usually," he said, "but I never have minded good bourbon."

Linda reached for the bottle and helped herself to a healthy swallow. Tears welled in her eyes and she coughed a couple of times, but as soon as she had her voice back, she managed to squeak, "Hmmm, that's smooth."

"You say you brought this down a couple of days ago?" Longarm was puzzled. "But you only discovered my badge this morning."

Linda took another sip of bourbon, as if she were trying to drink up some courage, and then shrugged. "I had a hunch then that you weren't really a teller, but no matter who or what you did for a living, I knew I'd find a way to get you down here, and all to myself," she confessed. "You know, my having been married and then widowed so quickly, taught me to grab a good thing while it was available." She slid off of her stool took a single step forward, and then forthrightly nestled her hand in Longarm's crotch.

"Ooooh, Custis!" she crooned. "I was right." She gave him a little squeeze. "This is a very good thing, indeed!"

Longarm could feel himself stiffening in her hand. "Ah, Linda . . . this isn't . . . I mean . . ."

"You just hush," she ordered softly, keeping a firm hold on Longarm with one hand and beginning to unbutton her blouse with the other. "We're as safe as home in bed down here," she giggled. "Although I *do* wish that was where we were. I know Crisp's schedule, being his assistant. He's nicely occupied in a meeting with the vice-presidents right now. You know how thick those doors are at the top of the stairs. Nobody could possibly hear us."

Her blouse pulled apart to reveal her round, creamy breasts spilling over the top of her tightly cinched corset. Longarm gave the undergarment a slight tug downward, and out those breasts popped, revealing aureoles more palomino-tan than pink, and sweet nipples that sprang to attention as Longarm's tongue did its dance down along the warm, silken fragrance of her cleavage.

His erection was now throbbing as she stroked it lightly through his trousers. "We'd better get you out of those pants before you split them," she teased.

"Don't reckon you have any more surprises in that there file cabinet?" Longarm said huskily. "Like a four-poster bed, maybe?"

"I thought about swiping your handcuffs," Linda admitted. "But I thought that would be rather brazen, this being our first time and all."

Longarm stood up to embrace her as her fingers undid the last of the buttons of his trousers. His erection popped free through the slit in the front of his longjohns. Linda's fingernails scraped lightly along the underside of his jutting member, causing him to moan with pleasure.

"There's an old desk back there," she hissed urgently as Longarm unbuttoned the waistband of her skirt. Her skirt fluttered to the ground and she stepped out of it as she led him to the desk deep in the shadows of the basement. Her snug, lacy pantalets were cinched about her narrow waist by a pink ribbon. As they kissed, Longarm toyed the ribbon loose. Linda had to do a little shimmy to wiggle the clinging undergarment down past her hips. As she did so, Longarm ran his palms over the high, firm mounds of her backside, just now pressed up against the ledge of the wide old desk.

Linda kicked herself free of her pantalets, and then said,

"Now that I'm bare, its your turn, Custis." With one smooth yank she had Longarm's trousers and longjohns down around his ankles. She hopped up, resting her bottom on the desk, and spread her legs wide.

"Oh, put it in me!" she whispered as her tongue darted into Longarm's ear. "I'm ready. I've been ready for you since last week!"

Longarm needed no further urging to slide deep inside her. Her legs cinched around him and she leaned back, supporting herself with her arms as Longarm moved to pleasure her, slowly at first, but faster as Linda began to gyrate her pelvis, grinding herself against him.

"Slow down, woman," Longarm chuckled, planting kisses along her damp brow. "Take your time and have your fun."

Linda seemed not to hear him. In any event, she certainly didn't need more time. Her arms gave out, and she fell back in a heap, shuddering and groaning with pleasure. She might well have cracked her skull if Longarm hadn't caught her in his strong arms and lowered her gently to the desktop.

"Thats was wonderful," she sighed.

"We're not done," he growled thickly, and once more began to slide in and out of her. Her legs rose up so high that her ankles were pressing against the back of his neck as Longarm let himself go. Her little yips and yelps became one long, guttural moan from the depths of her soul as Longarm finally came. It was long and sweet and turned his knees to rubber. Now it was Linda's turn to catch him up as he collapsed in her arms.

She rocked him gently, murmuring endearments into his ear as he fought to get his breath back. When he did, he smiled down at her. "I think that's the nicest deposit I've ever made in a bank."

Linda laughed richly, and then, quite suddenly, wiggled out from underneath him. "Back to work!" she said cheerfully.

Longarm grimaced. He was still half-erect, and the cool air of the celler was not a totally pleasurable sensation on his glistening, sensitized member. He watched ruefully as Linda bustled about, gathering up her clothes. *Old Son,* he told himself, *here's a woman who knows what she wants, gets it, and then moves on to the next thing.* He supposed that she had to be cool and calculating to succeed in the hard-as-nails world of banking, but he was a trifle miffed by the way she had shut herself off. After all, they had just made love; there was no call for her to pull away from him so abruptly. . . .

Linda was just then bending over at the waist to pick up her pantalets. Longarm couldn't resist. He hitched up his trousers, step forward, and planted a sharp smack with the palm of his hand square across her backside.

She yelped like a hound, and jumped a foot in the air. She spun around, rubbing her behind, to demand angrily, "What was that for?"

"Have you had any experience in investing in long-term bonds?" he asked.

"Yes, so?" she pouted.

"Well, then, you know there's a penalty for early withdrawal." He pointed down at his flagging erection.

"Oh, Custis, I'm sorry," Linda murmured shamefacedly. "It's just that I've been a widow woman for so long, and my job has been my life for so long, and . . ."

"Well, give me a kiss and then we'll get back upstairs," Longarm chuckled. As they hugged, he said, "You know, I bet you'll be president of this bank someday."

"Oh! Do you really think so?" she cried happily, clapping her hands. "That would be just wonder—"

"Quiet!" Longarm commanded sharply. He strained his ears. "I thought I heard . . ." He glided off, toward the staircase.

"Darling!" Linda giggled. "I'd finish pulling up my pants before going out on the main floor, if I were you!"

Longarm nodded absently, buttoning up his trousers. His attention was focused on what he sensed was going on in the bank. He took the stairs two at a time, and at the top he pressed himself against the double doors, pushing them open a crack.

His field of vision out into the main floor was severely limited, but he was able to see several bank customers lying facedown on the floor, while a man with a revolver in his hand stood over them. The bank was being robbed!

Longarm hurried back down to Linda. He snatched up his wallet and folded it in half, backwards. When he tucked one half into the waistband of his trousers, his silver badge hung down, clearly visible.

Linda, watching him, suddenly paled. "Oh, my God! Do you mean the bank's being robbed right now?"

Longarm picked up his half-smoked cheroot and clenched it in his teeth angrily. "Yep, and I'm stuck down here." He shook his head, drawing his derringer from his vest pocket.

Linda stared at the little gun. "But how could you have heard anything? *I* certainly didn't—"

Longarm shrugged impatiently. "Maybe I didn't hear, maybe I *sensed* that something was wrong. In any event, now is the perfect time to rob the bank, when you think about it. The place is still fairly empty. It's another twenty minutes until noon. This way, there aren't so many customers for the crooks to keep an eye on while they empty the vault."

"How many of them are there?" Linda asked.

"Don't rightly know. I only saw one, but witnesses have said the gang is four men."

"Custis!" Linda gasped. "Is that little gun the only weapon you have?"

Longarm sighed. "My other guns are upstairs, hidden in my teller's cage, where I was supposed to be when this happened."

"Oh, Custis . . ." Linda trailed off. "I've gotten you into a terrible fix."

Longarm's stern visage softened. "Hey, you didn't get me into *anything* I didn't *want* to get into," he reassured her, laughing.

"Thank you for that," she smiled. "But what are you going to do now?"

"Go up there and try to bluff my way through this thing," Longarm muttered. "Maybe I can take them all without anybody getting hurt. If push comes to shove, I'll try to get the closest one with this little peashooter, and somehow make it to that jasper's guns in order to take on the rest."

"That's crazy," Linda said adamantly. "Four against one are terrible odds, even if you were well armed. Going against hardened criminals with a derringer is suicide."

Longarm tilted up Linda's chin in order to stare into her eyes. "I've got no choice. I've got to play the hand I've been dealt in this little game."

"Well, I got you into this," Linda frowned. "The least I can do is help you get out of it."

"You're going to stay down here, out of harm's way," Longarm began.

"Listen to me," Linda said urgently. "What I'm going to do is put on my pantalets, tuck my titties back into my corset, and—and—" Her voice began to quaver, but she stiffened her back and said with resolve, "And make enough noise so that they'll know I'm coming, and then walk right out onto the main floor in just my undies."

Longarm nodded slowly, a smile playing across his features. "I get it. Every eye in the place will be on you. That will give me a chance to duck low and scoot behind the row of tellers' windows to my own cage, where my guns are." Longarm gave her a big hug. "I think it might work. Not even a bank robber would shoot a girl in her undies."

"Especially with my figure," Linda beamed.

"Just make sure you make enough noise so that they don't shoot you out of reflex when you barge through those doors," Longarm warned her. "And you hit the floor when I take over. "There'll be shooting, most likely."

"You be careful," Linda pretended to scold him. "Don't go getting yourself killed. I'm sacrificing a lot to keep you healthy. Like my reputation, and my job." She smiled wanly. "There's no way that prude Mr. Crisp will let me stay on, not after I make this spectacle out of myself."

Before Longarm could reply, she'd turned away to scoot up the stairs. He stayed close behind. "Make noise!" he hissed as she pushed through the double doors.

"Hello!" he heard Linda call out brightly. "Don't shoot! It's only me, and as you can plainly see, I'm totally unarmed!"

Longarm slid through the doors, bent low and hidden from view by the tellers' desks in their long counter. He moved as quickly and quietly as he could behind the stools of the tellers, who were all sitting with their hands up in the air.

"What the hell?" Longarm heard a gruff male voice mutter.

"Holy cow! Lookit them tits!" another man gasped.

Longarm had to grin. He could well imagine how delectable Linda must look to the outlaws, her considerable physical charms straining against the thin lace of her snug-fitting lingerie.

He hurried along. His teller's cage was the last one in the line, and Longarm figured he didn't have more than a few moments to get to his guns before the outlaws quit their ogling, gathered up their wits, and got back to the business at hand. Longarm had not chanced peeking above the counter to get a fix on where the robbers were, but from past experience in such matters, he knew that one or two of the outlaw band would be guarding the doors of the bank, with the rest getting the customers herded together and under control before proceeding on to the bank's vault. One thing was certain, none of the robbers had yet come behind the counter into the tellers' area. That was a stroke of luck; this central branch of the bank was so large that the robbers were still busy gathering up the customers and bank employees scattered about the place.

"You're a sight for sore eyes, girlie," Longarm heard one of the robbers laugh as he finally reached his cage. "But tits or no," the robber continued, "you lie down on the floor with the rest of these folks."

"Yes, sir," Longarm heard Linda reply meekly. *Good girl!* he thought as he pocketed his derringer, snatched free his double-action Colt with his right hand, his double-barreled twelve-gauge with his left. He snicked back the twin hammers of the stubby shotgun as he vaulted over the counter to land in a crouch. "Federal Marshal! Don't anybody move!" he called out.

"Jesus Christ!" yelled one of the outlaws. He, along with his partner, was standing over the customers huddled on the floor. They were about twenty feet away from Longarm, on his left. A third man was standing at the far end of the row of tellers' cages. He was about twenty feet away, on Longarm's right. The fellow Longarm had spied earlier in the week, the one with the big, black, bushy beard, was guarding the bank's door. The fellow was still wearing his black wool suit, but today he had a gunbelt strapped around his waist. Still, Black Beard was over sixty feet away, which made him a low-priority target. Unless the outlaw was either a crack shot or very lucky, Longarm doubted that the man could hit him with a revolver at that distance.

The outlaw at the far end of the row of tellers' cages swung his pistol around toward Longarm and fired. His shot echoed in the cavernous interior of the bank as Longarm crabbed sideways, pointed his Colt like a finger, and squeezed off one round, hitting the outlaw in the chest. The mighty impact of Longarm's .44 slammed the outlaw back against the counter, rattling the bars of the tellers' cages. The man's pistol went cartwheeling off into the air as the outlaw himself crumpled to the floor like a marionette whose strings had been cut.

Longarm saw none of it. As soon as the man had dropped his gun, the tall deputy had switched his attention to the duo of crooks standing watch above the trembling, customers.

"There's three of us left, lawman," one of the robbers muttered. He and his partner both had their revolvers trained on Longarm. "We got you cold," the robber continued, but there was uncertainty in his voice as he stared into the twin barrels of the twelve-gauge.

Longarm held the shotgun rock-steady. He was aiming precisely between the two robbers. Out of the corner of his eye he saw Black Beard take a step toward him. Without shifting his gaze from the duo close by, Longarm pointed his Colt in the man's general direction and called out loudly, "You trade pistol shots with me like your dead buddy did, and I'll send you to hell along with him!"

Black Beard glanced at the man Longarm had shot, lying still and cold in a puddle of blood. He shook his head and suddenly turned around to dash out the bank's doors.

Longarm let him go as one of the man's buddies screamed out, "Bert! Come back, you damned coward!"

"That makes it two to one," Longarm said evenly. "And with this scattergun on you, I'd say the odds are now in my favor."

"You don't scare me," the robber replied. "He was a short, fair-haired man dressed in tan trousers and a green corduroy jacket. His nickel-plated Smith & Wesson was cocked and ready to be fired. His partner was of average height, dark-complexioned, and dressed in worn denims and a tan flannel shirt. The hammer was down on his Colt Peacemaker, which was a single-action weapon.

"Maybe I don't scare you," Longarm said mildly. "But this here scattergun ought to. It's loaded and ready to send a brace of twelve-gauge big boys into you guts to find out just what it was you had for breakfast."

The man with the Peacemaker tossed his weapon over his

shoulder and put up his hands. "I'm stepp'n out of this," he muttered as he began to edge away from his partner.

"Wise choice," Longarm agreed. "Especially since you'd still be fumbling to cock that thumb-buster of yours about the time this scattergun would be cutting you in half. Just keep your hands where I can see them, and you'll come out of this all right."

"That still leaves me, Marshal," the man in the green corduroy jacket said quietly.

Longarm heard the edge to the man's voice, and knew that this one was not going to back down. There was going to be at least one more killing in this bank. "Then make your move, mister. You think your pistol can beat my twelve-gauge, go ahead and find out."

Seconds ticked by. The man did not lower his Smith & Wesson, but neither did he fire. He seemed mesmerized by the gaping muzzles of the shotgun. Longarm began to feel more confident. There came a time in a showdown when a man either took his chance or didn't. Just now, the deputy sensed that this fellow had let his moment pass him by.

"Either shit or get off the pot, old son." he said softly.

The robber smiled thinly. "You win," he chuckled. "We'll try this some other day when you've left your scattergun home, lawman." He began to lower his revolver. One of the prone customers began to sob with relief.

The doors of the bank's entrance crashed open as the first of the office workers down from Capitol Hill on their noontime lunch break entered the bank, chatting among themselves. *Damn!* Longarm thought as his concentration was momentarily diverted by the customers' noisy arrival. *I should have remembered that when Black Beard ran off, the doors were left unguarded. . . .*

It was the head teller, Morton Crisp, who chose that moment to leap to his feet in hysteria, shrieking shrilly, "It's a robbery! Get help! Get help!"

The fellow in the tan shirt swung his revolver back up in a flash, taking advantage of Longarm's distraction. He fired a shot that gouged chips out of the counter behind Longarm as the deputy crabbed sideways to make sure Crisp was not in his field of fire. Then Longarm pulled both triggers of the shotgun. There was a deep double *BOOM!* immediately followed by a high-pitched scream from the man in the green jacket as Longarm's double load of buckshot blew a dinner-plate-sized hole through the outlaw's torso. He hit the floor as limp as a rag doll, and as dead.

"Now it's your turn, Deputy," the dark-complexioned man in the tan shirt growled. He'd left his Peacemaker on the floor, but during the confusion he'd managed to come up with a derringer—and a hostage. He was not pointing his pocket pistol at Longarm, but had it pressed against Crisp's head. "Try anything and I'll kill him, Marshal," the outlaw swore nervously, at the same time tightening his forearm choke-hold across Crisp's throat.

"That little man's a mite small for you to be hiding behind," Longarm observed as he tossed aside his empty shotgun. His Colt was still in his right hand, but pointed down at the ground so as not to panic the outlaw.

"He's big enough to get me the hell out of this, Deputy," the outlaw grinned wolfishly. "Now here's what I want you to do. First of all—"

Longarm brought up his Colt and shot the man in the face. There was a look of surprise in the outlaw's eyes as Longarm's .44 round drilled its black hole right between them. Then the man's eyes glazed over, and his derringer clattered to the stone floor. Crisp toppled over in a dead faint. The outlaw also toppled, just plain dead.

Linda was on her feet and wrapping her arms around Longarm a split second later. "You were wonderful!" she gushed. "I've never even *dreamed* anybody could shoot like that!"

A door to the rear of the tellers' area opened and out came William Fletcher, a tall, good-looking man in his early forties. He was the vice-president who had been Marshal Vail's contact in placing Longarm undercover. "Deputy, what's happened?" Fletcher demanded. "We were in conference when we heard the shooting." The bank officers peeking out from around the door nodded in agreement.

"These fellows tried to rob your bank, and I stopped them," Longarm said tiredly, tucking his Colt into the waistband of his trousers, "Marshal Vail will send you a copy of my report."

Fletcher nodded dazedly. "Miss Thorp," he addressed Linda. "Why, you have no clothes on!"

"No, sir," Linda pouted. "B-but I c-can explain—"

"Dick!" screeched a revived Morton, jumping to his feet, fueled by rage. "Dick! You could have gotten me killed!"

"My name's Custis Long," Longarm told the little man.

"I don't care what your name is!" Crisp shouted. "You're fired!"

"You jerk," Longarm said mildly, "I'm a deputy U.S. marshal, here undercover. I don't really work for you."

Crisp looked ready to explode in frustration. "Well—well, *she* does!" he crowed, pointing at Linda. "Miss Thorp! You're standing there in your unmentionables like some wanton lady of the night—"

"Watch your tongue now, Crisp," Longarm growled.

The head teller hurried backward, to stand beside Fletcher. "She's fired! Fired, I say!" he screamed. "Get out! Get out now, you brazen hussy!"

"Hold on." Longarm commanded. "First of all, one of you fellows back there hand me my suit jacket," he ordered the tellers behind the counter. The jacket was handed over to him, and Longarm draped it over Linda's scantily clad, totally dejected form. "Linda here saved your bank, Mr. Fletcher."

"How so, Deputy?" the vice-president asked. He seemed unable to tear his eyes away from girl.

"She and I were trapped in the basement when the robbery began," Longarm began. "We were both sent there by Crisp, I might add."

"Is that true, Crisp?" Fletcher demanded, frowning. "I *told* you this man was not to be removed from his post as a teller."

"B-but, s-sir, I, I—" Crisp stuttered miserably. "She said she needed . . . I m-mean—"

"Well? Spit it out, will you, man?" Fletcher cut him off.

Poor Crisp was crestfallen. "I forgot."

Fletcher looked away in disgust. "Continue, Deputy," the vice-president said to Longarm, even though he was looking— and smiling—at Linda.

"Well, sir, there I was, weaponless, and not at all sure how I was going to tackle these hombres, when Linda here came up with the brilliant idea of taking off her clothes, and risking her life to distract the outlaws, giving me a chance to reach my guns," Longarm explained.

"I see . . ." Fletcher nodded, still gazing at Linda.

I guess you're seeing plenty, Longarm thought wryly, *but not as much as I got to see.* . . . "Anyway, if it wasn't for the quick thinking of this young lady, ready and willing to sacrifice her reputation for this bank, I would have been killed, and your vault stripped clean as a whistle," Longarm concluded triumphantly.

"Well, this puts things in an entirely different light," Fletcher mused. "Miss Thorp, you are most certainly *not* fired. Indeed, I think you should be promoted!"

"Oh, thank you, sir!" Linda smiled shyly.

"Yes, indeed!" Fletcher grinned. "Such cunning, Linda— May I call you Linda?"

"Oh, yes, sir," Linda nodded demurely.

"Such quick thinking!" Fletcher continued. "Why, I never realized you had so much talent concealed beneath the surface—"

Longarm bit his lower lip hard to keep from laughing. "Uh, Mr. Fletcher, I've got to be moseying along to Marshal Vail's office to file my report. I'll have some town constables sent along to take away these bodies."

"Hmmm?" Fletcher was still staring into Linda's big blue eyes. "Oh! Yes, of course. You do that, and thank you, Deputy Long. Thank you very much!" the vice-president added warmly. "You did a marvelous job. I shall commend you to Marshal Vail."

"Couldn't have done it without Linda here," Longarm added, just for the hell of it. He knew from personal experience that Linda was a sweet enough cake to do without the icing.

"No, we can't do without Linda," Fletcher laughed. He turned to the girl and said, "Why don't you gather up your clothing, my dear? After you've made yourself, er, decent, perhaps you'd like to come to my office. We've much to talk about. Your new position, for instance." He glanced at Crisp. "I believe the position of head teller will soon be vacant."

"Really?" she said breathlessly, looking up wide-eyed at Fletcher and letting Longarm's jacket fall open just slightly, as if by accident, giving the vice-president a prize view of her high white breasts.

Fletcher reddened and cleared his throat, then turned and walked toward his office. Linda winked slyly at Longarm, and he winked right back, and then she went to retrieve her abandoned clothing.

In a few moments she returned, now fully dressed, and handed Longarm his jacket before sauntering off to Fletcher's office. The lawman thought it was entirely likely that Linda and Fletcher would strike up an agreement that would be beneficial to both of them...

As Longarm turned to leave, Crisp, who was standing nearby, watching Linda's swaying bottom as it receded toward the vice-president's office, turned to him and said, "She's going to get my job, I just know it!"

"Cheer up," Longarm said. "I know of another job."

"Really?" Crisp brightened. "Where"

"Shit shoveler at the livery stable," Longarm laughed. "You ought to fit right in."

Crisp sputtered incoherently, trying to think of a reply. Longarm dug the stub of his cheroot out of his vest pocket, jammed it between his teeth, and strode for the door. The grin settling in beneath his longhorn mustache was a mile wide.

★

Chapter 2

Longarm, his shotgun cradled in the crook of his arm, made a slight detour before heading up Capitol Hill to Marshal Vail's office. His rooming house was about a ten-minute walk away, and he figured his report could keep until he'd had a chance to change out of these dumb banker's duds and back into his own clothes.

He did flag the first constable he came across, a portly fellow in one of those blue uniforms that Denver's town coppers had taken to wearing.

"Howdy, Longarm," the officer said as he nodded in greeting. "Who'd you kill today?"

"Three old sons who were trying to rob the First National, back there at the foot of the Hill," Longarm said without batting an eyelash.

The constable's lower jaw dropped a foot. "Huh? Really?"

"Yep, and if you get on over there real quick, you can cut yourself in on some of the credit with your desk sergeant," Longarm suggested.

"I'll do that!" the constable said, hurrying off. "Thanks, Longarm!"

Longarm continued on, leaving the sandstone sidewalks of Colfax Avenue behind as he crossed the little sandy wash of Cherry Creek. Now his banker's low-cut shoes were treading upon cinder paths, for Longarm's rooming house was located in an unfashionable part of town, as befit a man who drew a deputy marshal's salary.

It was now well past midday, and the house was quiet as Longarm mounted the stairs to his small corner room. Before unlocking his door, he checked to see if the broken-off match stick he'd wedged into the jamb was still in place. It was, which meant that he'd not unwittingly played host to visitors while away. Longarm wasn't worried about burglars, as he didn't own anything much worth stealing. A federal lawman did have a way of making enemies, however. Longarm always liked to make sure some owlhoot from his past wasn't lying in wait underneath his bed in order to settle old scores.

Inside, he dropped the shotgun on his sagging brass bedstead. The weapon was the property of the marshal's office, and Longarm figured to let the armory personnel have the chore of cleaning it. He set his Colt down on the dresser top, and swiftly stripped off the blue trousers and vest and that danged boiled shirt with its scratchy starched collar and sissy bowtie. In their place he tugged on his own brown tweed trousers that fit like a second skin over his lean hips. Next came a gray flannel shirt and the silly black shoestring tie that the new regulations said a federal lawman had to wear. Longarm couldn't understand the sense of it—a U.S. marshal had to be quick-thinking and quick on the draw, but who gave two shits whether or not he looked dignified?

"Rules and regulations," Longarm muttered to himself as he turned away from his dingy mirror, figuring his tie was as straight as it had to be. He didn't need to shave, having taken care of bathing and scraping his beard off his lantern jaw early this morning, before reporting to "work" at the bank. At least *that* charade was over and done with! Linda's female scent was still rising faintly from him, but Longarm figured that anybody who got close enough to sniff it deserved what they got. He

24

sat down on the bed and stomped his feet into his low-heeled stovepipe boots. Next he turned his attention to his Colt.

He fetched his cleaning kit from out of the dresser and spread an old towel across the mattress to protect the bedspread. Then he emptied his gun of its two spent rounds and three live ones. Longarm always let the hammer ride on an empty chamber, for safety's sake. More than one poor fool had blown off his toes—or worse—by hopping down off a horse with a fully loaded sixgun strapped to his hip.

Once Longarm had scrubbed away the gummy black-powder deposits with kerosene and lubricated his weapon's action with sperm oil, he reloaded his Colt and slid it into its waxed and heat-hardened holster. The Colt had its barrel cut down to five inches, eliminating the front blade sight, which was useless in most situations anyway, and could be a hazard if it snagged on the lip of an open-toed holster.

Longarm moved back to his mirror, in order to position his holster until his Colt was riding butt forward, high on his left hip, just the way he liked it. To make sure, he reached across his belt buckle with his right hand, drawing the revolver in a whip-fast, rock-steady, single motion.

Returning his gun to its place on his hip, Longarm next shrugged on a vest cut from the same tweed cloth as his pants. He connected his brass derringer to the long, gold-washed chain of his pocket watch, and tucked the Ingersoll watch into the left-hand pocket of his vest and the derringer into the right-hand pocket, letting the chain drape between the two.

He dug his brown frock coat out of the closet and slipped it on, filling one pocket with spare .44 cartridges and transferring his wallet, badge, handcuffs, and keys to the others. He gathered up some matches and a couple of fresh cheroots, lifted his snuff-brown Stetson off its nail in the wall, and set it dead-center on his head.

He took one final look in the mirror, and grinned. "Yep, that's me, Custis Long. Nice to have you back, old son."

On the way out of his digs, Longarm grabbed the sawed-off shotgun in order to return it to Vail. After locking his door, he wedged a fresh piece of match stick between the door and the jamb.

The midafternoon sun was high in the sky as Longarm approached the Hill, and it made the gold dome of the Colorado State Capitol glitter fit to blind a man. That yellow dome almost, but not quite, stole the show from the Front Range of the Rockies, a bare fifteen miles to the west. Longarm made his way into the Federal Courthouse building, and mounted the stairs to Vail's office.

The oak door at the end of the marble-floored corridor read UNITED STATES MARSHAL, FIRST DISTRICT COURT OF COLORADO. Inside, Longarm found his boss standing above a harried-looking clerk who was pounding away at a typewriter.

"Took you long enough to get here, you bastard," Vail scowled. "Where the hell you been since you wiped out those bank robbers?"

"Wanted to go home and change into my own clothes, Billy," Longarm replied. He set the shotgun down upon the clerk's desk, eliciting an angry glance from the young man. "This here's for you, sonny," Longarm said.

"You clean that scattergun?" Vail demanded.

"I just shoot them, I don't clean them."

"Bastard," Vail muttered, shaking his head. "Well, come on into my office. We gotta talk."

Longarm followed his boss. Vail wasn't more than fifteen years older that Longarm, but he'd let himself run to lard. His bald scalp had taken on the baby's-ass-pink flush of a man who'd spent too much time behind a desk and bellied up to a bar. He was dressed in a rumpled and baggy gray suit, a light blue flannel shirt, and a black shoestring tie similiar to the one worn by Longarm. Hanging low beneath Vail's beer-swollen gut was a gunbelt from which dangled an old .45-caliber Walker Colt. It was a heavy hogsleg of a firearm that threw out a thumb-sized piece of lead. As Vail was fond of saying whenever he'd drunk himself a snootful, 'Old Captain Walker ain't the fastest around, but he sure is one of the most thorough.'

Personally, Longarm thought that Vail should have traded in the old cannon years ago, but he'd learned to keep his opinions to himself where Vail was concerned. Anyway, if Vail wanted to hold onto his relic, what was the harm? These days, about the only thing the deskbound marshal got to shoot were dirty looks at his deputies.

Longarm sat down in the red morocco chair in front of Vail's flat-topped mahogany desk. The desktop was covered, as usual, by an untidy blizzard of paperwork. As Vail settled his wide butt into his creaking swivel chair, he swept a pile of papers onto the floor so as to be able to catch a glimpse of his deputy. "All right, tell me about it," the marshal growled.

Longarm stuck an unlit cheroot into the corner of his mouth so as to have something to chew on as he filled Vail in on what had gone on at the bank. He left out the part where he and Linda had scratched each other's itches down in the basement. As he spoke, his eyes strayed to the banjo clock ticking away on the oak-paneled wall above Vail's file cabinets. The marshal had promised him a vacation after this bank stakeout job. Another couple of hours and he'd be able to claim full pay for today, and start his off-time tomorrow. . . .

When he'd finished, Vail said, "Don't worry about that bearded fella getting away. We'll keep after him, and alert the town constables here and in the outlying territories."

Longarm shrugged regretfully. "Guess I just don't like any loose ends when I finish a job, Billy."

Vail nodded. "I know what you mean, Longarm, but look at it this way. That son of a bitch didn't have the balls to face you down, which says to me that he won't have the balls to go breaking any laws now that his buddies are on ice." He grinned wickedly. "Of course, he might try to backshoot you someday."

"Thanks for setting my mind at rest," Longarm scowled. He stood up. "Now, if you're done with me, I'll be starting that time off that you promised me."

Vail was shuffling papers around on his desk. "Sit down," he said. "I *ain't* done with you."

Sighing, Longarm did as he was told.

"Ah, here it is!" Vail announced triumphantly, waving a sheaf of papers in the air.

A sickening feeling began to form in the pit of Longarm's stomach. "Billy, you're not going to stick me with another case, are you?"

"Can't help it, Longarm," Vail said gruffly, averting his

27

eyes to avoid his deputy's stricken gaze.

"Dammit! You promised me a vacation after this bank stint—"

"Well, you can take your vacation later," Vail cut him off. "This is a big case, and I'm going to need every available man. Now quit your sobbing and listen up!"

"What the Justice Department expects of its deputies is criminal, if you ask me," Longarm glowered. "Well, go on. What have you got for me this time?"

"Ever hear of a jasper named Wilson Barston?"

Longarm thumbed back his Stetson and scratched his head. "Seems to me I've read about him in the papers. Ain't he a congressman or some such? From Texas, as I recall?"

Vail nodded. "Yep, he's a Texas congressman, all right. A member of the United States House of Representatives. You recall *why* you've been reading about him in the papers?"

"Not rightly, Billy," Longarm said slowly.

"Representative Barston had been making noises about giving President Hayes a run for his money, come the next presidential election. Barston's the son of a cattle baron who left his boy a fortune when he died. What with all that money, his dead daddy's network of powerful, influential cronies, and his good looks, this Barston fellow won his congressional seat hands down. And he's only about your age."

"That's young to take on the job of the United States President," Longarm said doubtfully.

"Constitution only asks that a man after the job be at least thirty-five," Vail pointed out.

Longarm nodded. "Think this jasper has a chance?"

"Don't know and I don't care," Vail said flatly. "I'm not keeping you on duty to jaw politics."

"Why *are* you keeping me on duty?" Longarm asked.

"To keep Wilson Barston alive."

"Why don't you start at the beginning?" Longarm sighed.

Vail leaned back in his swivel chair. "A town in Texas is holding a down-home whoop-dee-do, a county fair. The center attraction is going to be a shooting match, the first prize being two thousand dollars—"

"Holy smokes!" Longarm gasped. "Two thousand! Hell,

Billy, I just may enter that contest, win the money, and turn in my badge—"

"You know a federal lawman ain't allowed to participate in something like that," Vail glowered.

"Just joking, old son," Longarm smiled. "Well, go on."

"Barston, being from Texas, and priding himself on being bred from cattlemen's stock, has announced that he intends to win his home state's match, giving the money over to charity if he takes it, of course."

"Of course," Longarm echoed dryly. "Hell, two grand must be ass-wiping money to a fellow like him, I'd reckon."

"I reckon," Vail chuckled. "Anyway, he ain't in it for the money, he's out to win himself some publicity for the upcoming campaign season. The problem is, there's going to be a lot of sharpshooters—both professional and amateur, both on the right and on the wrong side of the law—who *will* want to enter that shooting match for the money. Longarm, you know how a shindig like a county fair can attract all sorts of riffraff—pickpockets, cardsharps, gunslicks." Vail counted them off on his pudgy fingers. "Outlaw bands of every description, rowdies—"

"I get the idea, Billy," Longarm interrupted. "I take it you want me to be Barston's nursemaid."

"You got it," Vail agreed. "Barston travels with a personal bodyguard, but his late daddy's cronies have put in with the Justice Department to make sure that nothing happens to their native son during the shooting competition."

Longarm shook his head sourly. "Why me, Billy? I'm plumb exhausted. I haven't had a vacation in a long while. Why, there's any number of deputies who could play babysitter to this Texan."

Vail replied, "Most of my other men are scattered all across my jurisdiction. I told you before that I need every man I've got on my force, and I mean it. I myself am going to be leading a posse of the rest of my available men." The marshal's face grew thoughtful. "Rumor has it that Wink Turner's gang is headed for that fair."

Longarm frowned. "Hell, Billy, that's trouble."

Wink Turner was a murderer who'd gotten his name from

29

the fact that half of his face had been burned away in the very fire that Turner himself had started in order to escape from prison. According to the grapevine, the federation of outlaws that rode with Turner these days numbered close to forty. Turner himself was based somewhere in Texas, but at any one time small bands of his men might be rustling cattle in Texas, robbing miners in Nevadas, or busting banks throughout the Dakotas. "If Wink and all of his boys ride together, he'll have the biggest force in the state, next to the Texas Rangers."

"Don't I know it," Vail said uneasily. "And I've got to ride with no more than nine men to try and stop that outlaw army."

"Billy, that's plumb stupid," Longarm declared.

"What? What did you say to me, Deputy?" Vail barked quickly, his bushy eyebrows lowering like storm clouds.

"Simmer down and listen to me, boss," Longarm said firmly. "You've got nothing to prove. In your day, you rode against all manner of owlhoots and Indians, and lived to tell about it, everybody knows that."

"Damn right!" Vail declared.

"Well, I mean no disrespect, Billy, but all that was a decade ago." Longarm shook his head. "Let's face it, you haven't ridden anything but that damned desk chair for a lot of years now."

"I know that, too," Vail muttered. "But me and Captain Walker here,"—he patted his holster—"we still got some bite left in us."

"Of course you do, Billy," Longarm soothed. He thought for a moment. "Tell you what—why don't you take on the job of bodyguarding Barston, and I'll lead that posse to intercept Wink Turner?"

Vail stared hard at his deputy. *"You* giving *me* orders?"

"I'm trying to keep you from getting killed!" Longarm shouted, his temper flaring. "You got yourself a nice wife! You want to make her a widow before her time?"

The marshal's usually flushed face grew beet red, and his jowls began to quiver with rage. His jaw began to work, but no sound came out of his throat, save for a low-pitched, constant snarl.

Longarm, watching his superior, thought to himself, *Old*

son, this time you may have overplayed your hand. It just could be that you're going to find yourself on an extended vacation, after all. . . .

But Vail's nail-chewing expression softened abruptly. He leaned back in his chair and chuckled to himself. "Custis, I do believe you're worried about the old marshal," he beamed.

Oh, shit, Longarm thought. The only thing worse than an angry Vail was a sentimental one! "Why don't we just exchange jobs, boss?" he said plaintively.

"I can't do that," Vail said quickly. "I'll tell you true, Longarm, I wish I could, but I can't. I'll not let it be said about me that I sent my men into a tough situation while making sure that I was safe and sound." Vail peered at his deputy. "Can you understand what I'm saying? If I was a lot younger, or a lot older, I could most likely talk myself out of the need to test my gumption. But I'm at that age where I still have to know if I've got what it takes."

"Enough said, Billy, and well put," Longarm grinned. "Well, how's this? You assign one of your other deputies to guard Barston, and I'll ride *with* you against Wink Turner—"

"Noooo," Vail sighed. "I already thought of that. The problem there is that all my other boys have a tendency to spit on the floor and not care if their breakfast is splattered across their shirtfronts." He winked. "Everybody knows that you're my best deputy marshal, but you also know how to talk like a gentleman, and not eat your peas with a knife. You change your clothes when they're dirty, and take a bath once a week, whether you need one or not. This Barston fellow made it real clear to *my* bosses at Justice that he doesn't want any sodbuster with hay in his hair queering his style." Vail shrugged. "You're *it*, Longarm. As of today, you're assigned to Barston. I'd rather have your gun alongside of mine when I go up against Turner, but what I want and what my bosses want are two different things."

"If that's the way it's got to be," Longarm said.

"That's the way," Vail replied firmly.

"You could call out the Texas Rangers to help back your play." Longarm pointed out.

"I thought of that," Vail groused. "You're starting to try

my patience, Longarm. Just 'cause I'm old doesn't mean I'm stupid. According to Justice, the Rangers have been cleared out of the general area surrounding the fair and its host town."

"But why?" Longarm was mystified.

Vail shifted uncomfortably in his seat. "You can't imagine how this gets my dander up, Longarm, but the Justice Department somehow got the idea that the Rangers are just a bunch of rowdy roughnecks with some peculiar ideas about law enforcement. Justice figures they can't be trusted with a job like protecting the fair from the likes of Wink Turner and his army. Apart from Congressman Barston, there's some powerful folks involved in this shindig, and the powers that be in Washington have decided to keep things under control their own selves. Which means you and me, old son."

"I can see how that would piss you off," Longarm conceded, "since you used to be a Ranger yourself, just after the War. Hell, I've had my share of dealings with the Rangers. Apart from being mighty proud and proddy when it comes to matters of jurisdiction, they're some of the best lawmen I've ever worked with."

"You better believe it," Vail said. "But that's Washington's decision, and there ain't a damn thing I can do about it. There won't be so much as a solitary Ranger within two hundred miles of Sarah."

"Sarah!" Longarm sat up straight in his chair. "This fair is being held in Sarah, Texas?"

Vail nodded silently.

"Why, that's Jessica Starbuck's cow town. . . ."

"She's the one throwing the fair," Vail explained. "Seems her business holdings have prospered real well since she took over as head of Starbuck operations. This here county fair is her way of celebrating."

Longarm grinned. "Just like that woman to throw the world's biggest party. I guess this publicity-hungry fellow Barston went and invited himself to Jessie's celebration," he added confidently. "Ain't that just like a politician?"

"That's not exactly how it happened," Vail said uneasily.

Longarm's eyes narrowed. "Something tells me you've got something to say, Billy. Why don't you just spit it out?"

"I heard you were a little sweet on this Starbuck gal," Vail said, watching his deputy.

"Say what you've got to say, dammit!" Longarm demanded.

Shrugging, Vail picked up a newspaper clipping from the pile of papers on his desk. "This here is a story from the society section of a San Francisco tabloid. It tells about how Jessica Starbuck invited Barston to her fair as the guest of honor."

"That makes sense," Longarm mused. "Her being considered society in the City by the Bay, I mean. Jessie lives on her spread in Texas, the Circle Star cattle ranch, but her late father's import-export business to the Orient is based in San Francisco. But what does Barston have to do with—"

Vail reached across his desk to hand the clipping to Longarm, and watched uneasily as his deputy scanned the article. "Just remember, Longarm, that's a gossip column. They don't necessarily print the truth—"

"Billy!" Longarm cut him off. "It says here that Jessica Starbuck and this Barston fellow are going to get *married!*"

"It's just a gossip column, Longarm," Vail soothed. "Keep calm boy...."

Longarm shrugged. "I'm calm, Billy. It's just that Jessie and I had some fine times together, and I'd always thought since then that—" He paused. "But, hell, it's been a long while since I've seen her. You remember? You sent me to investigate her father's murder?"

"Sure. You did a right fine job of busting up that conspiracy to take over the Texas cattle industry," Vail grinned.

"I haven't seen Jessie since, and there's no law that says a woman can't change her mind," Longarm mused. "She wants to get hitched to this rich, good-looking politician, who's to blame her? I'm calm." He nodded to himself. "I'm calm...."

"That's good," Vail beamed. "I've got your travel vouchers right here—"

"Dammit, Billy!" Longarm suddenly exploded. He crumpled the newspaper article into a tight little ball and snapped it away. It sailed in an arc over Vail's bald head, to land smack in his wastepaper basket.

"Hey...I *need* that!"

"I always get the dirty jobs," Longarm growled. "If this

ain't the orneriest case you've ever sent me on—"

"That's right. I've explained to you why I have no choice." Vail tossed a manila envelope into Longarm's lap, and pointed at it. "That there contains your travel chits and a dossier on Congressman Barston, with a physical description, so you oughtn't to have any trouble recognizing each other." Vail looked at the banjo clock on his wall, then back at Longarm. "You'd best hustle, Deputy. Your train pulls out in less than an hour. You're scheduled to link up with Barston and his entourage at Grassy Bow, a little jerkwater stop in New Mexico, about eighteen hours outside of Sarah—"

"I've been there." Longarm nodded sourly, rising up out of his chair and heading for the door. "When are *you* leaving?"

"Not for another day," Vail replied. "I'm still waiting for the last two of my men to ride into Denver. They should be here by tonight." The marshal began to busy himself with the papers on his desk. "Now get out of here," he snarled. "I got work to do."

Longarm yanked open the door. "If this don't beat all. Congressman Wilson Barston has set his sights on marrying Jessica Starbuck, and I've got to keep him alive so he can do it!"

"Get going!" Vail bellowed.

Longarm got, slamming the door shut behind him. Slamming it *hard*.

Three days and several train changes later, it was a tired, dusty Longarm who sat waiting outside the lean-to that served as the Grassy Bow train station. It was a humid, breezeless afternoon. One of those dog days of summer when the only things that seemed to be moving were the horseflies that inflicted those hard, flat, itchy bites and filled the still air with their ceaseless droning.

Longarm leaned back against his McClellan saddle, and began fiddling with his Winchester .44-40 rifle, more to occupy the time than anything else. After leaving Vail's office, he'd hurried back to his rooming house in order to gather up his things for the journey to Sarah. This had been just about the shortest notice the marshal had ever given Longarm before

34

sending him out on a case, but fortunately, he kept all of his stuff packed and ready to go on a moment's notice.

The next stop—after telling his landlady that he'd be gone for a while—was the stable where he kept his McClellan saddle in storage. Like most working men in the West, Longarm had never owned a horse. It was a hell of a lot cheaper—and faster—to travel by rail, renting a horse when you got where you were going. Not even drovers owned their own mounts. When a cowboy went to work for a cattle spread, the head wrangler issued him a mount, usually a different one each day, from the ranch's stable. Whenever Longarm could manage it, he rented an army mount. They weren't any smarter than your average cowpony, but they had been trained not to run off as long as their reins trailed on the ground, and not to be gun shy. It was Longarm's opinion that those two things were just about all you could ask of a horse, an animal not much smarter than a cat, and a hell of a lot dumber than a dog. About the only thing a horse could do for a man—besides providing short-haul transportation—was alert him to the fact that he had unexpected company. A wild horse's best defense lay in tear-assing it away at the first sign of danger. Even the most docile saddle mount's behavior would turn a mite skittish at some unexpected smell or sound too faint for a man to perceive. Longarm made it a point to study up on his mount's personality, so that he could detect that change in the horse's behavior if it came. More than once, that knowledge had saved his skin. . . .

He'd take any sound horse he could rent, borrow or, occasionally, steal, but when it came to gear, Longarm was more particular. Whenever he could, he brought along his own army-surplus McClellan saddle. The McClellan had brass fittings all over it to fasten stuff to. Right now his Mexican bridle, saddlebags, and bedroll were tied to it, along with the leather boot that protected his Winchester while keeping it handy once Longarm was mounted up.

Longarm slid the rifle back into the boot, and dug out his pocket watch to check the time. It was a quarter to four. The Texas & Pacific train that would carry him to Sarah was due in on the hour.

From behind him came the amused cackle of the stationmaster, an ancient geezer with a grizzled, week-old growth of beard. "Young fellers like you is always peekin' at your watches, while us old boys, we hate to look!"

Longarm twisted around to face the railroad employee. He believed in being polite to oldsters, and besides, it wasn't like he had anything else to do. "She's due in at four, right?" he asked.

The stationmaster took off his worn, patent-leather-visored cap and fanned himself with it. He was sitting on a crate in a tiny cubicle nailed against one corner of the lean-to. A single, jagged, floor-to-ceiling opening hacked out of the cubicle served as both ticket counter and door into and out of the box. "Yessir, she usually is, except when she's late!" He once again began to cackle.

Longarm turned away. He believed in being polite, but everything had its limits. The town of Grassy Bow, such as it was, existed mostly to supply an army remount station located nearby. Both town and station were about twenty minutes' walk away. Longarm hadn't bothered to make the stroll, as he'd only had an hour-and-a-half layover. Now he was beginning to regret his decision to stay put. A cool beer would have tasted mighty good. . . .

"You aimin' to go to that there big fair in Sarah, Marshal?" the stationmaster asked.

"Yep." As usual, Longarm had his badge in his wallet, not pinned on the lapel of his frock coat, but his government travel vouchers had identified him to the stationmaster. "Have there been a lot of folks passing through on their way to Sarah?"

"Yessir!" the old man nodded. "Been busier than all hell the last week, but it's slowed down now. You and that other feller snoozing over yonder is my only passengers since the day afore yesterday."

Longarm glanced down the length of the rickety station, to where his fellow passenger lay stretched out with his head resting on a carpetbag, and his hat over his face. "He going my way?"

"Yessir. Bought his ticket to Sarah right after you," the stationmaster informed him.

Longarm stared at the fellow for another moment, then shrugged. There was something about the man that seemed familiar, but Longarm couldn't quite put his finger on it. As far as he could tell, the man was just a drover on his way to cattle country. Probably he was looking for a ranch job. That would explain his canvas pants, plaid flannel shirt, and high-crowned Stetson. It would also explain his cowboy's pride and joy: elaborately stitched, high-heeled Justin boots—"

Fancy-stitched Justin—

Longarm sat up fast, his right hand reaching for his Colt. He relaxed when he realized that the man ten feet away from him was not just playacting, not keeping his Stetson over his face to avoid being recognized, but was truly asleep. *Son of a gun,* the deputy thought to himself. *You shaved off your black beard and got rid of your black wool suit, but you just couldn't bring youself to part with those fancy-stitched Justins. . . .*

Billy Vail's grim jest had turned out to be an accurate prophecy. Bert, the bank robber who had run away, was now tailing Longarm, and most likely doing his best to work up his nerve to backshoot him.

Longarm hadn't noticed the man on the train, but then again, he'd kept pretty much to himself during the long journey, not moving around outside his own car. It wouldn't have been hard for old Bert to keep track of him without being observed.

"That fellow down there is wanted, eh, Marshal?" the stationmaster asked eagerly. "I seen how you went for your pistol," he added slyly.

"Nope," Longarm fibbed. "He looks something like the fellow I'm after, but he ain't the one at all. . . ."

The stationmaster looked disappointed, but he paid the man at the far end of the platform no further mind. That was exactly how Longarm wanted it. Old Bert might not be the brightest outlaw around, but once he awoke he would have to be jackass dumb not to notice the way the stationmaster would be staring at him, and then smiling at Longarm. Bert would know the jig was up as soon as he opened his eyes. Longarm would most likely be forced to shoot the bank robber, and that was one thing he did not want to do. . . .

The gang that Bert had ridden with, and that Longarm had wiped out, had robbed a dozen banks before running out of luck at Denver's First National. There was no way the four men could have spent all the money they'd stolen, which meant that the loot had been cached away somewhere. Bert had to know where that money was, and Longarm was determined to find out that information in order to return the money to its rightful owners.

But not even Custis Long could get a corpse to talk. That meant Longarm had to figure out a way to take Bert *alive*. . . .

"You sure that jasper ain't wanted?" the stationmaster sighed. "Been a coon's age since we had any excitement."

"Sorry," Longarm chuckled. "Say, I'm mighty thirsty. You wouldn't happen to have a bottle somewhere about, would you, Uncle?"

The stationmaster chewed on his lower lip. "Against the rules, Marshal. Railroad employees can't do no drinking on the job. *You* know that," he chided.

"Wel-l-l-l," Longarm winked. "I ain't no rail inspector, *you* know *that*. I just figured that a fellow stuck in an out-of-the-way place like this would consider himself his own boss. I thought you might have a bottle handy. Not in your office, of course," Longarm added hastily, gesturing toward the crate-furnished cubicle. "That'd be plain dumb. But maybe hidden down beneath the raised floor of this lean-to?"

The stationmaster blushed like a little boy caught with his fingers in the cookie jar.

"Of course, I meant to *pay* for my swallow," Longarm continued, jingling the coins in his pocket.

"Damn, but you're a smart one, Marshal," the stationmaster laughed, a trifle uneasily.

Longarm did not reply, but tossed the stationmaster a dime and a nickel. The most expensive whiskey around cost no more than five cents a shot, but Longarm wanted the old coot to hurry up and disappear in order to dig up his bottle. Time was running out for Longarm to successfully pull off what he had in mind. His ploy would be spoiled if the train were to pull in, or if Bert were to waken. Longarm didn't trust the stationmaster to keep quiet if he was allowed to watch.

"Be back in a minute," the stationmaster promised. He snatched up the coins and hurried out of his cubicle. He carefully lowered himself to the ground and tottered around to the back of the rickety structure to burrow beneath the lean-to's raised floor.

Longarm was already on his feet and silently moving toward the napping Bert as the old man disappeared around the corner. As Longarm approached the stretched-out bank robber, he kept himself ready to draw his Colt if need be. What Longarm wanted to do was to neutralize the outlaw without actually taking him prisoner. It would have been a simple matter to snap the cuffs on Bert while he snoozed, but that would have meant that Longarm would be hampered with a prisoner when he met Barston. He would have put up with the nuisance if Bert were a particularly dangerous wanted man, but Longarm was pretty sure that the only person he'd be placing in jeopardy by allowing Bert his freedom would be himself.

Bert was snoring away as Longarm bent over him. Remembering what an experienced pickpocket had taught him, the deputy waited for Bert to build to his crescendo of snoring, and then smoothly pulled the man's pistol from its holster as Bert's breath rattled out of him like thunder.

The gun was nothing fancy, just a single-action .45 with a cheap, blued finish and worn black rubber grips. Longarm checked the weapon's action. It was dirty. Bert seemed to neglect keeping his pistol clean. Longarm smiled to himself. Bert's laziness would be to Longarm's advantage.

He cocked the single-action weapon and jammed a couple of matchsticks down where the firing pin met the base of the cartridge. Longarm broke off the two matches' excess lengths, and carefully lowered the revolver's hammer.

Perfect—the bits of wood were wedged far enough into the gun's action so as to be invisible to casual inspection, and the revolver's hammer almost, but not quite, rested in its correct position. A careful man—a man like Longarm—would notice that something was wrong, but the condition of Bert's gun testified that Bert was not a careful man.

Longarm slipped the gun back into its owner's holster, and was leaning back against his saddle when the stationmaster reappeared, with his bottle in hand. Longarm enjoyed his drink. He felt quite confident about the way he'd managed to rig things.

Bert's own thirst for vengeance would keep him close to Longarm as effectively as any pair of handcuffs. But Longarm hadn't forgotten how Bert had backed down, turned tail, and run during the holdup. The outlaw was not the sort to jump into the act of killing a man. He was probably napping so deeply now because he'd been unable to sleep the previous night, tossing and turning with worry over just how he was going to throw down on Longarm and manage to come out of it alive. Longarm figured he could count on Bert to dog his footsteps for some time to come. The only real danger lay in Bert's trying to backshoot him, as Billy Vail had so aptly pointed out. The outlaw would have to be rather close to try it with a pistol; he wasn't carrying a rifle. Longarm decided that Bert's jammed pistol would give him enough time to get the drop on the outlaw if and when he tried to make his move.

Until then, Longarm could concentrate on his priority assignment, bodyguarding Congressman Barston. Old Bert—and the bank loot he'd inherited from the rest of the gang—was like a piece of fruit, ripe for the picking, when Longarm was ready to return to Denver.

A low, mournful train whistle sounded in the distance. "That'd be it," the stationmaster said, pointing to the bend in the track around which the train would appear.

"Well then, she's not too late," Longarm said agreeably. He took another sip from the bottle and handed it back to the stationmaster, who quickly corked it and hid it behind the crate that served as his chair.

"I can't risk the chance of havin' this particular conductor catchin' me wettin' my whistle," the stationmaster explained apologetically. "He's the sorta prick who don't know that rules are made to be broken."

Longarm nodded noncommittally. His attention was on Bert, who was just now sitting up and stretching—and surreptitiously glancing at Longarm out of the corner of his sleep-swollen eyes.

The stationmaster mistook Longarm's silence for anger. "I knows that you ain't drunk no fifteen cents worth, Marshal—"

"Keep the difference, Uncle," Longarm cut him off. "I couldn't take more than two sips of that rotgut, anyhow." Now that Bert's hat was off his face, Longarm was able to get a good look at him. His big, black, bushy beard had covered up his lack of a chin. The beard had also hidden a long, thin scar down Bert's left cheek. Longarm shook his head. If it hadn't been for those fancy boots, he never would have recognized the outlaw.

"My whiskey is pretty strong," the stationmaster was chuckling. "I make it myself, you know."

"In that case, two sips *has* to be my limit," Longarm laughed. "I *need* my eyesight."

"Ah, go on," the old-timer laughed back good-naturedly. "I knows my business. Ain't no poison in my mix." He winked conspiratorially. "Got me a still around back, near my digs. I make whiskey when I ain't got nothin' else to do, which is most times, I'm afraid."

"Thanks for the drink, Uncle," Longarm said, shouldering his saddle as the train rounded the bend.

"Come back anytime, son," the stationmaster cackled. "I owe you another drink."

The train belching black smoke, jerked and jolted its way to a stop, more or less in front of the primitive station. Sparks flew from the friction of the train's locked wheels screeching against the rails.

Longarm spied the bored-looking conductor sticking his head out from between two cars. "All aboard!" the man called out once, and then disappeared back inside the train.

Longarm waited for Bert to choose his car. He watched the outlaw hurry toward the rear of the train before swinging himself up and out of sight. Nodding in satisfaction, Longarm stepped up into the car in front of him. It looked as if Bert was not planning to backshoot him for the moment.

The car was half empty. Longarm glanced at the few passengers on the off-chance that Barston was in the vicinity, but nobody looked the least bit like the description Vail had given him. There wasn't a rich, handsome son of a bitch in sight.

Good, Longarm thought. He swung his gear up onto the luggage rack, and slid into a vacant bench seat. He stretched out as best he could across the thinly padded, red velvet upholstery and closed his eyes. The stationmaster's home brew had made him drowsy. He figured there'd be no harm in his catching forty winks before searching out Barston. After all, the man was traveling with a personal bodyguard, as well as who knew what other sorts of assistants. They'd all be safe enough until the train pulled into Sarah, about ten tomorrow morning. They probably even wanted their privacy. There were all those upcoming campaign strategies to puzzle out. . . .

And marriage plans to make. . . .

You might as well get that burr out from under your saddle, old son, Longarm mused sourly. *If he and Jessie aim to get hitched, you'll smile and congratulate her, like a good sport. Hell, what did that newspaper article call them both? Oh, yeah . . . 'The prince and princess of Texas . . .' Well, if the prince and princess want to get married, that's a damn sight better match for a rich girl like Jessie than some down-and-out deputy marshal who's got nothing but his gun, boots, and saddle to call his own.*

Longarm's eyes shot open. "Whoa, old son," he muttered hastily. "You're talking like a man who has already asked for her hand, or was going to. . . ."

Longarm clamped shut his eyes once more, willing himself to sleep. *You need the rest, old son. That geezer's whiskey has gone and made you lightheaded.*

The constant, rhythmic sway of the slow-moving train rocked him to sleep. The next time he opened his eyes, it was dark outside. He hauled out his pocket watch and checked the time. It was 10:00 P.M. He'd slept for six hours!

The long, lean muscles of his back and legs had cramped up during his nap in the uncomfortable seat. Longarm heard himself creak as he stood up and stretched. He noticed that the car was now empty. The few passengers sharing this car with him had evidently disembarked during the many stops the train had made while he slept.

Longarm made his way along the lantern-lit aisle to the rear of the car, and stepped out onto the open platform. The clatter of the wheels was noisy out here, but the night was cool and clear, and the sky was filled with stars. Longarm's conscience nagged at him. He knew he ought to find the congressman and report for duty, but linking up with Barston would just make Longarm brood about Jessie. He didn't like the fact that the woman was so much on his mind. It always spelled trouble for a lawman when he spent more time mooning over a damned female then he did listening and watching. . . .

To hell with Barston, Longarm decided. *He can wait another hour or so.* Longarm would enjoy the evening breeze in private, and maybe have himself a smoke out here.

The railroad had provided a bucket of fresh water and a dipper hanging from a bolt for the refreshment of the passengers. Longarm drank deeply, rinsing out the foul taste in his mouth. Next he removed his hat and leaned over the edge of the platform to spill ladles of water over his head, soaking the last cobwebs of sleep from his mind.

He shook his dripping head like a terrier, sending drops flying, and then straightened up—

To feel something cold and hard pressed firmly against the back of his ear. *Oh, shit,* Longarm thought.

"Just keep that hat of yours in your right hand," a nervous voice hissed.

"Hello, Bert," Longarm said.

"Jesus Christ!" Bert gasped. "How'd you know? Jesus H. Christ—"

"Calm down, old son," Longarm soothed. "Don't forget, *you're* the one with the gun on *me.*"

"That's right," Bert said shrilly. "Don't you forget that, neither! How'd you know, lawman?"

"I recognized you back at the Grassy Bow station. Us marshals are trained to recognize wanted men. We know how to see past the old ruse where a fellow shaves off his beard, or grows one, for that matter," Longarm fibbed. Instinct told him not to let on to Bert that his boots were a dead giveaway. If the outlaw managed to make his escape, the fact that he was wearing those boots would be like a sign around his neck alerting other lawmen to pick him up—assuming, of course, that Longarm managed to live long enough to wire Bert's description to the marshal's office in Denver, so that they could forward it to the various local lawmen in the surrounding areas.

"If you recognized me back at Grassy Bow, why didn't you arrest me?" Bert asked suspiciously.

He's not as dumb as I thought, Longarm mused. "All right, Bert," he sighed. "You've seen through me. I didn't collar you because I want to make a deal."

"Really?" Bert hesitated. "What kind of deal?"

Yep, he's that dumb, after all, Longarm decided. "I know

43

that you know where all that stolen bank loot has been cached. I figured to propose to you that we split it. I was going to wait until the time was right, but you turned out to be just too fast for me."

"That's right, I am," Bert snickered. "I'm so fast that I'm way ahead of you, lawman. For instance, what's in it for me to split the money with you? I got you dead to rights. You're as good as dead. Why should I—"

"I'd tell you why, Longarm interrupted the outlaw's long-winded harangue. "I'd tell you, but it's kind of hard to talk, what with that gun of yours pressed against my skull," he whimpered meekly.

"All right, then," Bert laughed, his confidence growing by the second. He let up slightly on the pressure of his gun against Longarm's head.

"Thanks. That thing drilling against my skull was damned uncomfortable," Longarm said truthfully. What he neglected to add was that he was now quite certain that Bert's gun was still useless. Longarm figured that Bert was the kind of fellow who'd by now have trumpeted gleefully that he'd discovered the matchstick wedges in his pistol.

"Go on, then. Why shouldn't I kill you here and now?" Bert repeated. "The car behind us is empty, and by the time some of those folks in the car in front got up the nerve to investigate the shot, you'd be lying by the side of the tracks, and I'd be in my seat, two cars behind this one."

"You could do that," Longarm agreed. "But what would it get you? Whether or not they ever pinned my killing on you, you'd still be wanted for bank robbery. Sooner or later, some lawman somewhere would recognize and arrest you—"

"Shhh!" Bert hissed. "I think—" He glanced behind him anxiously. "I thought I heard someone come into the car behind us."

"See anyone?" Longarm asked, resisting his automatic impulse to disarm and get the drop on the distracted, amateurish outlaw.

"No . . . I guess I'm hearing things," Bert muttered. "Talk fast, lawman! My trigger finger's getting itchy!"

The last time anybody said a line like that was in an issue

of *Ned Buntline's Wild West Magazine*, Longarm thought to himself. "Here's my plan. Let's say I sent in a report saying *you* were the one shot, and that *your* body was the one lying alongside the tracks. My boss would take my word for it that you're dead, and he'd issue a bulletin to that effect."

"I get it!" Bert said excitedly. "Officially I'd be dead. The search for me would be called off!"

"All I ask is a fourth of the loot," Longarm said.

"Just a fourth?" Bert asked, surprised.

"Sure, I ain't greedy." Longarm chuckled. "Besides, you ain't the first bank robber I've worked this deal with!"

"You old fox, you!" Bert laughed, lowering his pistol. "It's a deal!"

"All right then," Longarm said, turning around. "You ever been to Sarah, Texas?"

Bert shook his head. "This'll be my first visit."

"Well, I suggest you lay over at the next stop for a few days. You don't want to hang around Sarah until this fair blows over," Longarm warned. "The town will be crawling with lawmen."

"Oh! Right!" Bert nodded. "I'll keep out of town for a few days, and link up with you where?"

"There's a right nice saloon on Main Street," Longarm replied. "I don't recall the name, but you can't miss it. It's the biggest one in town. We'll meet there."

"Sounds fine!" Bert began. That was all he got out before a shot pitched him forward into Longarm's surprised grasp. "You bastard!" he gasped. "You stalled me until your partner could shoot me in the back!"

Before Longarm could reply, Bert tore away from him and leapt from the platform of the slow-moving train. Longarm caught a glimpse of the outlaw tumbling down a slope, before he lost sight of the man in the darkness. Longarm himself had gone down into a crouch, his Colt in hand.

"You all right?" a voice called from the empty car Longarm had previously occupied. A man straightened up from behind the seat he'd been using for cover. He was a tall, blond-haired, clean-shaven fellow, dressed in black denim trousers, a white shirt, a black vest, and a suit jacket cut from soft, brown leather.

45

He held his short-barreled, nickel-plated, .38-caliber Smith & Wesson pointed lazily at Longarm's feet. "I *asked* if you were all right."

"I'll be fine when you put away that peashooter of yours," Longarm growled.

The man laughed, tucking away his pistol in a belly holster inside the waistband of his trousers. When he pulled the points of his black silk vest down over the gun's pearl grips, he appeared to be unarmed. "I noticed that man had a gun on you when I wandered into this car a few minutes ago," he explained.

"Then you ought to have noticed that he'd *lowered* his pistol," Longarm said quickly.

"That was what I was waiting for," the blond man grinned. His teeth seemed startlingly white against his tanned skin. "Didn't want to take a chance on blasting him while he had a gun pointed at your head. Who was he, Longarm? An escaped convict? A cow thief?" The man's voice was thick with disdain, and his green eyes sparkled mockingly.

Longarm stared at the man as he slid his Colt back into its holster. "You know me, but I don't know you. Now why is that?"

"Just be glad I came by when I did to get your ass out of the sling it was in, Deputy," the man said, backing away.

"Who are you?" Longarm demanded, hurrying into the car. "Hold it right there!" he ordered, but the leather-jacketed fellow was already disappearing through the far door.

The train chose that moment to begin climbing a steep grade. Longarm cursed loudly as he lost his balance and landed hard on his butt. He got to his feet and used the handholds built into the seatbacks on both sides of the car's narrow aisle to haul himself up the sudden incline.

The man in the leather jacket was nowhere to be seen by the time Longarm reached the next car. This one had some passengers in it, most of whom looked up inquiringly at Longarm as he rushed by them, making him feel like a fool.

Four cars later, Longarm spotted the man. He was leaning against the far door. He had his arms folded across his chest, and that same, taunting grin was still on his face. Longarm was scowling as he approached the leather-jacketed fellow.

This time he was determined to get some answers out of him.

A hand shot out, grabbing Longarm by his sleeve. "Deputy Long? Where the hell have you been?"

Longarm stared down into an angry face that obviously belonged to Congressman Wilson Barston. The congressman looked exactly like the description Vail had given Longarm, though it did not do justice to the man's piercing blue eyes, or his thick, tousled mass of coal-black, curly hair.

Barston stood up and stepped out into the aisle to shake hands with Longarm. He was six feet tall, and moved with the easy grace and economy of movement that characterized an experienced rider and cattleman, as did his thick arms, and his barrel chest straining against the seams of his finely tailored, gray three-piece suit.

"Marshal Vail furnished us with your description, Deputy," the congressman explained. "I'd like to introduce my secretary, Leo Tompkins," he continued, indicating the short, thin, balding man in a brown suit who had been seated next to him. "And this is my assistant—"

"The name's Thorn," the leather-jacketed man nodded with amusement. He kept his arms crossed.

"Thorn and I have already met," Longarm said wryly. He did not bother to offer his hand to the man. "You're a mite quick on the trigger, ain't you, Thorn?"

"Thorn's in charge of my personal safety," Barston cut in impatiently. "I sent him to find you. From what he tells me, his fast shooting saved your life!"

"It's just that he cost me a prisoner, Congressman," Longarm began. "I was investigating an important case—"

"You weren't supposed to be capturing prisoners," Barston said sternly. "You were supposed to be finding me! Where the hell have you been?"

"I figured you were safe enough for the present."

"*You* figured?" Barston shouted. "You're not supposed to 'figure.' You leave that to myself and Thorn here, got it? You do as he tells you. You're not paid to think, you're paid to protect me or at the worst, stop the bullet that's meant for me with your own body. Do you hear?"

Longarm noticed that Tompkins had looked away in embarrassment. Thorn, however, seemed to be vastly entertained by the dressing-down Longarm was suffering.

"I asked you if you heard me, Deputy!"

Longarm stared Barston in the eye. "Reckon I'd have to," he replied evenly, "the way you're spitting your words into my face."

This time, even Thorn looked away as Barston's rugged features drained of color. "You—you—" he sputtered, and then took a deep breath to calm himself. "I guess that federal badge doesn't mean very much to you."

Longarm shrugged. "You ain't the first politician who's threatened to have it taken away from me, Congressman, and it's still in my wallet. In any event, I'm not about to belly-crawl in order to save it. When I first signed up as a deputy marshal, I thought I *was* being paid to think. If the job's changed. I'd just as soon hand in my star."

Barston stared hard at him for a long moment, and then, abruptly, his rage left him. "I guess we got off to a bad start there, Deputy Long." he mumbled, smiling thinly. "Let's just say that you're expected to follow orders, and leave it at that, eh?"

"Let's just say that we got off to a bad start," Longarm smiled back politely. "And let's leave it at *that,* shall we?" He slid into an empty seat across the aisle from where Barston had been sitting. As he did so, he noticed that Thorn was now frowning uneasily as he glanced back and forth between Longarm and his boss.

At least I wiped the smile off that joker's face, Longarm congratulated himself.

Still, he felt uneasy. There was no question that Barston could have him fired if the congressman put his mind to it. Longarm figured that it was simply a matter of time before just that happened. One thing was for sure—there was no way he'd take orders from a backshooting gunslick like Thorn. No way at all.

He was also disturbed by the way Barston had lost his temper. Like most scions of wealthy Texan cattle-ranch dynasties, Barston had obviously grown up in a sage-brush empire where his family's word carried the full weight of law.

Men like Wilson Barston were not used to being crossed. When they were, they didn't know how to handle such defiance, short of crushing it beneath their heel. . . .

Longarm pondered Jessie Starbuck's proud spirit, as uncontrollable as a wild mustang. *Poor Jessie,* he thought. *What have you let yourself in for, this time?*

★

Chapter 3

Jessica Starbuck waited with Town Marshal Farley outside the Sarah train station. It was a bright, beautiful day, and Jessie was looking forward to showing off the town her father had built and then named in memory of her late mother, to the fair's guest of honor, Wilson Barston.

"Sure do appreciate you inviting me to meet the congressman," Farley said shyly. He was a big-bellied, thick-necked man, with sparse yellow hair worn close-cropped at the sides and brushed back on top. His face was seamed and roasted pink by the Texas sun.

"I'm glad you're here to keep me company," Jessie confided nervously. "Our mayor was doing too much business to leave his general store."

"The town sure is bustling on account of this fair," Farley muttered.

"Why, Marshal, you don't sound exactly happy about it," Jessie noted. She brushed back her long honey-blond mane tinged with a glint of copper, and fixed her lovely hazel eyes on the old family friend who'd been the town's chief law officer for so many years. "Come on," she coaxed. "Why, I remember when I was a little girl, and I used to beg you to bounce me on your knee so that I could tell you my troubles, Joe Farley! I do think I could listen to yours for once!"

Farley gazed at her lovingly. "Jessie, I do remember those happy times when your daddy, God rest his soul, was here with us. And I remember holding you on my lap, too, even if it was twenty-odd years ago! I couldn't do that now."

Jessie giggled. "No, I guess it would cause talk." She slid her arm through his. "Shall we run away together?" she whispered conspiratorially.

Marshal Farley turned several shades redder than usual. "Why, miss! I only meant that you're too big—"

"Yes, I suppose I am," Jessie pretended to pout. "I hardly have to stand on my tiptoes to tilt back your hat and give you a kiss on your forehead," she added, doing just that.

Farley turned even more scarlet, if that was possible. He looked around, scandalized, and only relaxed when it was clear that nobody had seen him being kissed. "Jessie, you're too pretty to go around kissing men!" he scolded. "What would your daddy have said?"

"Oh, Marshal," she laughed.

"And Alex wouldn't have liked all that spicy talk coming out of you, young miss," Farley continued, building up a head of steam. "I mean no disrespect, but your daddy was my friend when you were still a little babe, sucking at your mama's—" Farley froze. He turned his stricken face away from the extremely amused and extraordinarily shapely woman standing before him. "Now why did I have to start riding down *that* trail?" he mumbled miserable.

"More like a valley than a trail, I'd think," Jessie said, looking down at herself.

"See what I mean?" Farley demanded. "Spicy talk!"

Jessie, seeing that the Marshal was truly angry, became instantly contrite. "I'm sorry."

"I don't know where you learned it, miss," Farley muttered. "Maybe you picked it up in San Francisco, or all those other places you've traveled to, while minding your daddy's various businesses."

"Yes, sir," Jessie said noncommittally.

"Your daddy's probably looking down at us from heaven, and he's probably glad I'm speaking to you this way, miss."

"Yes, sir," Jessie repeated, this time more adamantly, so that Farley wouldn't suddenly become embarrassed over reprimanding her, just because she was one of the richest, most powerful people in the United States. *Business is business, but friends are friends,* Jessie thought to herself. She knew what was truly valuable. She'd much rather that Farley think of her as that little girl bouncing on his knee, someone he cared enough about to bother scolding when he was worried, than have him standoffish and timid, just because she headed up the Starbuck empire, a mammoth chain of business holdings that stretched across the nation and abroad. "Although, sir, I seem to remember that my father had a right salty tongue," she couldn't help pointing out to the marshal.

"I ain't saying yes, and I ain't saying no," Farley frowned. "But if he did, it was only because he started out in life as a seafaring man. Anyway, it's all right for a man to talk spicy, because—" Farley paused, thinking hard. "Because he's a man!" the marshal finished in exasperation.

Equality between the sexes was one thing Jessie did believe in enough to argue about—but not with dear old Marshal Farley. "Yes, sir," she smiled. "Now let's get back to what's bothering you," she said firmly.

Farley stuck his thumbs in his gunbelt and looked down at the toes of his scuffed boots. "I know that these folks coming here are good for business and all, and I know that this fair is your way of giving this territory a celebration, but the last couple of nights, things have been mighty rowdy along Main Street."

Jessie nodded thoughtfully. Sarah *was* bursting at the seams. Even the train station's no-nonsense cattle pens and loading ramps—now empty, but the real reason for the existence of any cow town—had been gussied up with pink satin ribbons to welcome the visitors flooding in for the fair. Every hotel room along Main Street was booked, and some enterprising folks who owned homes in Sarah's residental neighborhood were making themselves a few extra pennies by renting out their spare beds to boarders. Hungry and thirsty customers crowded the town's several saloons and cafes in order to spend money. The town's boardwalks were lined with people enjoying the spectacle of vendors, drummers, and other carnival-type folks riding through on their way to the fairgrounds, located just outside Sarah.

Jessie enjoyed watching the arrival of various jugglers, musicians, and other entertainers—most especially the professional sharpshooters who had come to compete for the two-thousand-dollar prize in the target competition. Some of the more famous professional shooters had appeared to Jessie like characters out of a fairy tale!

Two-Gun Leroy Kingsley had ridden in on a huge white stallion. The horse's embroidered trappings and fringed stirrups all but swept the ground. Kingsley himself wore a suit of bright red satin. The silver filigree of his holsters glinted in the sun as he tossed candies to the adoring children following in his wake, while doffing his hat to the cheering adults lining Main Street.

If there were a prize for spectacle, Two-Gun Leroy would have won it hands down, Jessie thought to herself. And the runners-up would have been the Cling Sisters. Jessie had never heard of them, but their covered wagon was fancy enough. It was pulled by a pair of prancing pinto ponies, its wheels and bed were painted bright blue, and its canvas top was dyed a pale pastel pink, Emblazoned on each side of the wagon were a pair of crossed pistols and the words:

AGGIE & DOT CLING
"THE GEORGIA CLING PEACHES"
!!!SHARPSHOOTING TOAST OF EUROPE!!!

Jessie figured the reason the Clings were unknown to her was that they'd been spending so much time touring overseas. They certainly was as pretty as peaches, and twins to boot! Aggie had waist-length blond hair, and Dot had hair just as long, but as red as strawberries. Or maybe it was the other way around; Jessie doubted that the sisters' own mother would be able to tell them apart, except by the color of their hair.

Marshal Farley seemed to be following Jessie's train of

thought. "This shooting match is a fine idea, miss, and the professionals aren't giving me a lick of trouble," the marshal added quickly. "But—",

"But somebody is," Jessie finished for him. "Tell me about it. This fair is special to me, and I don't intend to let anyone spoil it." Her eyes, as green as Texas grass when the Lone Star State welcomes spring, were now sparked with fire.

"I see a bit of your daddy's temper in you, Miss," Farley grinned.

"It goes with my salty tongue," Jessie heard herself saying, despite the fact that Marshal Farley would think her wicked. "Now, will you *please* tell me what's bothering you?" she demanded.

"It's like this," Farley began, growing serious. "I've got two deputies to patrol the town. Usually that's enough manpower, but now I've got to watch the fairgrounds as well! Like I said, the professional shooters are as orderly as can be, but this shooting match has attracted a lot of would-be gunslicks." He shook his head. "These fellows are quick to rile, and quick on the draw. It seems that they're too impatient to wait for the start of the match tomorrow."

"I see," Jessie nodded. "There haven't been any shootings, have there?" she asked in concern.

"No, but there have been a couple of close calls," Farley grumbled. "And the fair hasn't even offically started yet. Folks haven't really begun to get liquored up the way they do during these kinds of celebrations. My two men and I can't be everywhere at once," he finished plaintively.

"Well then, why don't you swear in some more deputies for the duration of the fair?" Jessie suggested. "I'm sure the town would authorize their payment for these few days."

"I could do that," Farley smiled. "And I'd thought of it, but the question is, who could I get?"

"I'll ask some of the drovers at my spread to work for you temporarily—"

"Begging your pardon, miss," Farley interrupted. "I'm sure your cowboys are a fine lot, but that doesn't make them candidates to uphold the law."

"I don't understand."

Farley glowered. "I know that there are *some* towns where they'll let anyone who's willing wear a badge, but not here, not in Sarah," he groused. "Leastways, not while *I'm* in charge."

"Well then, I really don't know how I can help—" Jessie paused, and smiled. "I bet you want Ki!"

"Well, I . . ." What began as a shrug ended up as a nod. "Ki and I have had our disagreements, " Farley said. "But despite the fact that he's a stubborn son of a—" The Marshal hesitated. "—stubborn *fellow*, I respect him."

"But as a deputy?" Jessie asked. "He's not the most *patient* man around."

Farley stroked his chin. "I know what you mean, and I certainly wouldn't want him working for me on a permanent basis. But considering the situation at hand, I think he's the best man for the job of temporary deputy."

"Well, it's all right with me if it's all right with him," Jessie said.

"I was kind of hoping . . ." Farley trailed off.

"Oh, no! Not me, Marshal," Jessie laughed. "If you want him, you ask him!"

"But he'd agree immediately if *you* asked him," Farley insisted.

"I want this to be his choice," Jessie replied. "And you should want that, as well. Besides, Ki will respect you more for asking him yourself." She scrutinized the marshal. "You're not *afraid* to ask him, are you?"

"Me?" Farley grumbled. "Afraid? Hell, no!" A perplexed look crept across his beefy features. "I just never know how to talk to him. He's such a *peculiar* critter. . . ."

"In any event, you've got my permission to ask him. Whether he agrees or not will be up to him."

A long, low whistle blast from the approaching train ended the conversation. Jessie stood on her tiptoes to catch the first glimpse of the locomotive pulling into town.

"Here she comes," Farley said excitedly. He peered at the star pinned to his chest, and gave it a final polishing with the cuff of his flannel shirt.

Moments later the train huffed to a halt. Wilson Barston was among the first to get off, followed by Thorn and Tompkins. Jessie, with Marshal Farley in tow, hurried to intercept them.

"Wilson," Jessie called out, smiling. "Hello! Welcome to Sarah!"

Barston's handsome features split into a grin that stretched from ear to ear. "Jessie, darling! How's my little filly?" He ignored her proffered hand, and scooped her up in a bear hug. "Ah, I've missed you so, Jessie!" Barston roared, while Tompkins, counting the number of townsfolk who'd gathered to witness the display, positively glowed with approval.

"Put me down, Wilson," Jessie said mildly. She planted the palms of her hands against Barston's broad chest, and pushed to give herself some breathing space.

Barston, taking the hint, set her lightly on her feet. "Jessie, let me introduce my traveling companions," he began. "This is Leo Tompkins, and this is Mr. Thorn."

"Pleased to meet you both," Jessie smiled politely. "And this is our town marsh—" She froze, her mouth and eyes wide, as she glanced past Barston to see who else was stepping down from the train. "Custis!" she shrieked, elbowing the surprised congressman aside in order to rush toward the deputy marshal.

Longarm just had time to drop his McClellan and the rest of his gear to the ground before he found Jessie in his arms. They hugged tightly for a long moment.

"Hey, lady," Longarm said. "It's been a while."

"Yes, it has," Jessie said, wiping away a tear that had appeared in her eye for no apparent reason. "Oh, you look *wonderful!*" she gasped.

"That's my line," Longarm chuckled.

"I take it you two know each other?" Barston asked stiffly.

"Oh, yes, we're old friends," Jessie gushed.

Longarm couldn't help winking at the bewildered congressman as Jessie embraced him a second time.

Tompkins, checking the crowd uneasily, whispered something in Barston's ear. "Jessica?" Barston called out. "I'd like a word with you."

"In a moment, Wilson," Jessie sighed against Longarm's chest.

"I didn't hear that."

"She said in a minute, Wilson," Longarm drawled to Barston, who was obviously trying to control his fury.

"What in the world are you doing here, Custis?" Jessie asked.

"Well, I'm—"

"Deputy Long is working for me," Barston thundered. "Long, you fetch my bags—"

"I will do that," said a soft male voice.

Longarm turned to see a tall man in his early thirties, dressed in snug-fitting denim jeans, a blousy collarless shirt of cotton twill, and a loose, many-pocketed, black leather vest. The man had almond-shaped brown eyes and straight, nearly blue-black hair, which he wore longish, just brushing his shoulders. At first glance, many people took him for an Indian, which he was not.

"I knew that wherever Jessie was, you couldn't be far behind," Longarm said warmly. "How are you, Ki, old son?"

"Quite well, thank you," Ki said pleasantly. "And you, my friend?"

Longarm just shook his head, glancing at Jessie. "He's just the same. What do you say, lady?" He put his arm around Jessie's shoulder. "Is Ki glad to see me or not?"

Jessie glanced at Ki quizzically as she leaned against Longarm. "Oh, of course he is. Didn't you notice the way the corners of his mouth lifted once, a few moments ago? That was Ki's way of smiling," she teased.

"I see no reason to caper like an ape in order to express my pleasure at once again greeting an old friend," Ki said evenly.

"Yep, he's just the same," Longarm laughed. He looked Jessie up and down. "And you haven't changed a lick either, praise be. Same long hair the color of honey, same big green eyes . . ." Longarm trailed off, taking in her long-legged figure and full, high breasts. Her clothing was expensive. The green tweed riding jacket and matching skirt fit so well that they accented rather than camouflaged her heart-stopping femaleness.

The top few buttons of Jessie's silk blouse were undone, allowing the sheer material to gape open, but Longarm tried not to stare at her cleavage. Instead, he fixed his keen eyes on her smiling face.

Tompkins, meanwhile, was staring in awe at Ki. "What a strange-looking fellow," he said. "Is he an Indian?"

"Ki is half Japanese," Barston explained.

Tompkins nodded, then shook his head, sending a pained expression of confusion in Thorn's direction. The leather-jacketed bodyguard merely shrugged before looking away.

"Hello, Ki!" Barston said heartily.

Ki merely nodded once in Barston's direction. "I will see to the bags," he said, and scooped up Longarm's saddle as he left.

Longarm watched Ki walk away. *He sure didn't smile that time*, Longarm thought with satisfaction. It had taken Longarm a while to begin to understand the peculiar relationship between Jessie and Ki. Ki, Longarm knew, was a born warrior, trained in the skills of the samurai as well as more arcane and deadly arts. When he'd first come to America, he'd pledged himself as a servant to Alex Starbuck. When Starbuck was killed, he'd vowed revenge on his master's killers and loyalty to Starbuck's daughter and only child, Jessie. It made sense that Ki would dislike someone who threatened to steal Jessie away, Longarm thought. But then, Jessie herself had hardly given Barston a second look.

Marshal Farley was tugging at Jessie's sleeve. "Oh, I'm sorry!" she chuckled. "Gentlemen, this is Joe Farley, our chief lawman in Sarah."

"Real pleasure to meet you, Congressman," Farley enthused. "And you, Mr. Tompkins. My two deputies have set up a platform where the congressman can say a few words, just like you wanted. It's in front of the Cattlemen's Association building."

"Very good," Tompkins smiled. "Congressman? Perhaps we should be getting over there?"

Ki returned and informed them that the baggage had been transferred to the Starbuck wagon.

"Well, then!" Jessie said brightly. "Why don't we head over to Main Street?" She glanced at Farley. "Why don't you and Ki catch up to us?"

Ki looked quizzical.

"I've got something I'd like to discuss with you." Farley said hurriedly.

Ki cocked one eyebrow. "I can hardly wait," he said dryly.

"I'll hang back a moment as well, if you don't mind, Congressman," Longarm said. "I've got some business to take care of at the telegraph office. It's just around the corner, unless I'm mistaken."

"It is," Jessie replied. "You've got a good memory."

"Yes, I do," Longarm nodded, a ghost of a smile making its appearance beneath his mustache. "About a lot of things."

Blushing, Jessie made a face at him, and then led Barston and his associates toward the speakers' platform. The congressman whispered something to Thorn, who paused in front of Longarm.

"If you know what's good for you, you'll hang back real permanent-like where Miss Starbuck is concerned," Thorn said meaningfully. He doffed his hat to Ki, and sauntered off to rejoin his boss.

Ki looked at Longarm. "That one . . ." He shook his head.

"He's a punk, sure enough." Longarm's voice was light, but his gunmetal blue eyes were flat and hard. He turned to Farley. "I'm here to make sure no trouble comes to Barston. I'd count it a favor, Marshal, if you kept an extra keen eye on him until I can rejoin the group in front of the Cattlemen's building?"

"I will, Longarm," Farley smiled. "Good to see you again."

"Marshal Farley, what is it you want of me?" Ki asked.

Farley shot an anxious eye at Longarm, who took the hint. "See you two gents later," he said, and strolled off.

"Ki," Farley began as soon as they were alone. "I don't rightly know how to ask you this—" He glanced up into Ki's face, thinking about how the man had gotten his height and build from his Yankee father. The only Japanese aspects about Ki were his coloring, his eyes, and his temperament. *Careful,* Farley warned himself. *You never can tell how he's going to react . . .*

"I am waiting," Ki said, a trifle impatiently.

Farley took a deep breath. "I'm badly short of manpower to keep the peace during this fair. I've talked to Jessie, and she's given me permission to ask you if you'd consent to being sworn in as a deputy. Just for the next few days," he added quickly.

Ki pondered the marshal's request. "I agree," he said simply. "This fair is important to Jessie. I would be doing all I could to assure that it runs smoothly, in any event. Having a badge will help."

"It'll mean your staying in town instead of out at the Starbuck spread," Farley warned.

Ki nodded. "That is acceptable. Normally I would not leave Jessie unprotected, but since a deputy U.S. marshal is a guest at the ranch..." Ki smiled. "I will stay in town and assist you."

"That's great," Farley laughed in relief. "The pay's—"

"Excuse me, Marshal," Ki interrupted. "I am volunteering my services. While I am consenting to be a deputy, you should understand that I will not consider myself under any obligation to follow any of your orders."

"Well, if that's how it's got to be..." Farley grumbled.

Ki nodded "That is how it must be."

"Come on along with me to the office, and I'll swear you in and give you a badge," the marshal said. "Say, I don't suppose you'd consent to wearing a gun?"

"Under the circumstances, no," Ki replied. "It is easier to keep the peace when one is not dressed for war."

Sighing, Farley hurried to keep up with Ki's long-legged, purposeful stride. *Nope,* the marshal thought to himself. *You never can tell how he's going to react.*

The Western Union telegraph office was located behind the stockyards. Longarm found the key operator inside the shack. The man was sitting with his feet propped up on the counter, trying his best to pick out a few chords on an old banjo. The chords seemed to be doing their best to elude him.

"I'd like to send a wire," Longarm said.

"Your face all screwed up tight like that 'cause of my music or the smell of the stockyards?" the operator asked good-naturedly.

"Both," Longarm replied.

"We get most of our business from cattlemen checking stock prices over the wire," the man shrugged. "We've got to be near them, and they like to be near their cattle. Cows don't smell like roses."

Longarm nodded. "And what's *your* excuse?" He winced as the operator plucked out a particularly sour note. "Give it a rest, old son, at least until I can write down my message and be out of here."

He tugged a pad of yellow paper out from beneath the operator's boots and walked over to another counter, where stubs of pencil poked out from a mason jar.

He addressed his wire to Marshal Billy Vail, in Denver, even though he knew that Vail was likely on the trail of Wink Turner by now. He suggested that a new bulletin go out on Bert the bank robber, including the facts that the newly clean-shaven man could be recognized by the scar on his cheek, the seemingly minor gunshot wound he'd suffered, and his fancy-stitched Justin boots.

Longarm paused, thinking hard, before writing the next part of his telegram. He was about to make an "advisement," and that required some responsibility:

MY OPINION SUSPECT IS NOT REPEAT NOT DANGEROUS, Longarm wrote. USE CAUTION BUT TAKE HIM ALIVE SO THAT STOLEN BANK MONEY CAN BE RECOVERED—

He read the wire over, trying to think whether he'd forgotten to add anything. When Bert had the drop on Longarm, he'd mentioned that he'd been sitting two cars back. Longarm had slipped away from the congressman one final time in order to locate and search through Bert's carpetbag. Inside the luggage was some dirty laundry and a newly purchased shaving kit, but nothing to hint at where Bert had been, or where he now might go.

Damn, Longarm thought to himself. *If Thorn hadn't come along when he did, or if he hadn't been so trigger-happy, I'd be looking forward to my rendezvous with that dimwitted jasper and his stolen loot. I guess Thorn thought he was doing me a favor....*

"Or maybe he just *enjoys* killing—or trying to kill," Longarm muttered beneath his breath.

"What's that?" the key operator asked.

Longarm shook his head. "Send this," he said.

The operator tabulated the cost of the telegram, which Longarm paid out of his own pocket, knowing that Vail's office would later reimburse him. He watched the operator toss his message into the wire basket beside his key set and then go back to strumming tortured sounds out of his banjo.

"I paid for a telegram, not a night wire, old son," Longarm pointed out.

The operator yawned. "I got me a kid coming in a couple of hours from now. He never sent anything official like this. Want him to get the practice."

Longarm considered the situation. Vail was away, but his clerk could easily enough relay the message to outlying lawmen, and a couple of hours delay could make the difference between old Bert being caught or getting away.

"I'd like you to send it now, please," Longarm said. "It's important, and—"

"I *told* you when I aim to send it, Deputy—" The operator snatched up the sheet of yellow paper to read the signature. "—Deputy Long. You may catch crooks, but *I'm* the key operator. Company policy allows me to decide how to traffic messages, and I got six hours to set here and practice my banjo before the night rates start. If you don't vamoose, I'll hold this up for the full six, not just a couple of hours," he smirked.

"Is that your last word on the subject?"

"It is," the operator nodded. "Unless you want to come back here and send it yourself," he added insolently.

A smile spread across Longarm's face. "You shouldn't have invited me back there like that, old son." He walked to the end of the counter and kicked open the gate.

"Hey, you can't--" the operator started to protest.

"You invited me, old son." Longarm shrugged. He sat down at the key, tapped out "CQ" to open the line, waited for a response, then tapped out his name, the name of the town, and his telegram's destination. As the operator looked on, openmouthed, he quickly sent his message and sat back to wait for the acknowledgement.

"You know Morse?" the operator asked timidly.

"Yep," Longarm replied, his back to the man. When the acknowledgement came over the wire, he signed off and stood up.

"You just bought yourself a lot of trouble, Deputy," the key operator said. "I'm reporting this—"

Longarm jerked open the man's accounts drawer. *"You* just

63

bought yourself the price of this wire," he laughed, taking the money he'd paid the man out of the cash box.

"Don't do that!" the man yelped. "That money's been logged already. You can't take it out of the till! It's got to be accounted for!"

"I told you, old son, I expect you'll make it up out of your own pockets," Longarm said. "After all, I did your job for you; you can't expect me to pay you, as well!"

"Your boss in Denver is going to hear about this," the operator vowed. "I ain't paying that fee! You'd better—"

"Shhh," Longarm ordered. "Your yapping is worse than your banjo playing. You want to report me, go right ahead. Meanwhile, I'll be informing Western Union that they got themselves a man in Sarah, Texas who tells folks to send their own messages."

"Let's just forget all this," the operator smiled uneasily. "Maybe I was a little rude."

"Maybe you were a *lot* rude, and lazy to boot." Longarm went back through the gate and began to amble out of the office. "Make up that shortfall of money in your accounts, or not, old son. It's up to you. But I've heard tell Western Union's mighty tough on employees who can't balance their ledgers. And you wouldn't want to have to try to make your living playing that banjo. . . ."

"Dammit! Paying for that telegram is going to break me until payday," the operator groaned as Longarm went out the door. "Dammit—"

Longarm let the door swing shut, cutting off the rest of what the nasty little jerk had to say. He headed back toward the train station, and then past it, towards Main Street, pleased with himself for controlling his temper to the extent where he'd not bashed the man over the head with his own banjo. Longarm considered himself an easygoing kind of fellow. He knew how to take a joke or even an insult in stride. Still, the Western Union clerk had not only been impolite, he'd been *wrong* as well. Longarm knew the company's regulations decreed that a wire should go out as soon as possible. Maybe the clerk would remember how his pocket had been emptied, the next time he got the sadistic impulse to bully around some customers.

The last and only time Longarm had been in Sarah, the Cattlemen's Building, a magnificent three-story mansion, had been burnt to the ground by a band of marauding outlaws. Longarm, along with Jessie Starbuck and Ki, was able to bring that gang to justice, and now the deputy was curious as to how the town's showpiece had been rebuilt. . . .

I should have known, Longarm chuckled to himself. He was still two blocks away, but already he could see the tall, gilded steeple of the new Cattlemen's Association headquarters. The building's pale blue paint looked as fresh as the morning sky after a downpour. Longarm guessed that he didn't have to look to know that the interior of the building, along with its furnishings, would be just as ornate as the inside of the original had been.

As Longarm got closer, he could see a small crowd of about twenty-five spectators standing in the street. He was still too far away actually to hear what the congressman was spouting off about, but he could see Barston up above the crowd, gesturing from a wooden platform just in front of the Association building's golden oak double doors.

He was a block from the platform when the shot was fired. He heard it, and actually saw the round splinter the railing of the platform, sending chips of whitewashed wood up into the air just inches from Barston's head, but Longarm did not see where the shot had come from.

Two more shots were fired in rapid succession. The bullets chewed at Barston's heels as he scurried toward the steps to the rear of the platform.

Longarm was already dashing toward the scene, anxiously searching for Jessie among the frightened folks milling about the base of the platform. He was relieved to see that she'd had the good sense to throw herself flat to the wooden sidewalk, about ten feet away from the platform. Ki was not around, but Longarm figured she'd be safe enough; for a change, nobody was shooting at *her!*

Farley was nowhere to be seen, but his two deputies were back-pedaling toward where Barston was cowering, furiously firing their revolvers at the rooftop across the street as they did so. The deputies looked panic-stricken as they tried to form a barrier around the congressman. One of the lawman kept screaming, "Keep down! Keep down!" to the spectators crouched in the street.

Longarm knew that in crazy situations like this, the greatest danger lay in the law officers accidentally shooting each other. He left his gun in its holster and stook stock still, holding his wallet so that his badge was prominently displayed. He waited for the deputies to notice him, and when they did, he quickly motioned to himself and then the rooftop.

He was making his way toward the rear of the building, his Colt ready in his hand, before the deputies had completed their nods. Longarm fully expected that he'd have to kick in a back door in order to get inside and in that way gain access to the roof. He was surprised but not pleased to see that there was an outside staircase for use in case of fire. If he could get up and down from the building's roof so easily, so could literally anybody else in town....

Longarm threw himself up the stairs, head up, ready to shoot at anything that peeked over that ledge. At the top, he vaulted over the low wall and onto the flat roof. He just had time to belly-flop behind a few inches of tin chimney as Thorn, who was already on the roof, whirled and shot at him.

"Thorn, hold your damn fire! It's me! Custis Long!" Longarm shouted as Barston's bodyguard let loose with two more shots. Longarm resisted the urge to knock Thorn off the roof with one of his own .44 rounds.

"Long! Is that you!"

"Yeah . . ." Longarm got to his feet— cautiously—keeping an eye on the trigger-happy bodyguard all the while.

Thorn had his stubby-barreled, pearl-handled .38 in his right hand, and a Winchester in his left. "You ought to warn a fellow before you come up behind him, Deputy." He offered Longarm a wolfish grin. "Else you're going to get yourself shot up." He pushed his gun into his belly-holster.

"You'd better start counting to ten before you pull that trigger," Longarm said. "That's twice now you've sent lead my way without making sure it was necessary. If it happens again, I just might forget myself and and shoot back." He ran the barrel of his Colt along Thorn's left-hand lapel, stopping about where the man's heart would be. "I'd hate to ruin your fancy leather coat by putting a hole in it. . . ."

Thorn batted away Longarm's gun. "I heard you behind me, and I figured you were the shooter, all right?" he snarled. "I figured maybe the fellow had ducked inside the building somewhere along that damned fire escape." He gestured at the staircase with his rifle. "I heard your footsteps and realized I was a sitting duck. In a situation like that, I tend to shoot first and ask questions later."

"You should have realized that a lawman would be on his way up—" Longarm began.

"A lawman takes the time to identify himself before rushing in on a fellow," Thorn snapped back. "You should have realized that a man like me would beat you up here, lard-ass."

Longarm resisted the urge to take a swing at Thorn. For one thing, the man had a point; Longarm should have realized that somebody else might have beat him to the scene of the shooting. "It's just that I saw Farley's deputies down below, and forgot about you." he sighed.

"Next time you forget, don't blame me if you get shot," Thorn smiled, and began to walk past him toward the stairs.

"Wait a minute," Longarm demanded. "I've got some questions. Did you see anybody up here? Did you find anything?"

"Fuck you, and your questions," Thorn spat, not bothering to turn around.

Longarm moved fast to block the man's way. Thorn either misunderstood Longarm's intentions or lost his temper. He swiveled around, swinging the barrel of his Winchester at Longarm's head. Longarm managed to duck beneath the arc of the rifle. He straightened up, using his leg and belly muscles to add momentum to his short, hard right jab to Thorn's solar plexus.

Thorn gagged. His Winchester dropped to the roof as his legs turned to rubber. He was fumbling for his Smith & Wesson when Longarm clipped him hard on the chin. Thorn's head snapped back, and his hat went flying. The bodyguard sagged to his hands and knees. He stayed that way, his head down, his blond hair hanging in his face.

"No more questions," Longarm said, and was immediately

ashamed of the way this two-bit gunslick had goaded him into a fight. Knocking down Thorn had accomplished nothing except to further alienate Barston, should the bodyguard complain to the congressman.

On second thought, Longarm doubted that would happen. For one thing, Thorn would probably think twice before letting on that he'd been bested in a fight.

Nope, all you've really done is made sure that Thorn is your enemy, Longarm decided. *And what the hell, he probably already was your enemy, so that was no loss....*

Longarm was grinning as he helped the dazed bodyguard to his feet. One thing was for certain, knocking down Thorn had been a great deal of fun!

Longarm bent to pick up the Winchester. He was surprised to feel that the barrel was warm. He sniffed the rifle. It had been fired recently.

Thorn saw him checking the weapon. He reached out for it. "Gimme..."

"You shoot at the ambusher with this?" Longarm asked as he handed back the weapon.

Thorn looked as if he were going to say something nasty, but evidently he thought better of it. He glared at Longarm.

"This here standoff is going to stay our business, right?" Thorn demanded.

I wouldn't call getting your ass beat a standoff, Longarm thought. "Sure," he said. "No hard feelings," he added sincerely. "We *are* both on the same side." He stuck out his hand.

It might just as well have been a diamondback rattler from the way Thorn looked at it. He turned and began to make his way down the stairs.

Longarm shook his head. He would have liked to pursue the matter of just when Thorn had found occasion to fire his Winchester. The bodyguard was using his handgun when Longarm had reached the rooftop. Up here, in this close-range situation, a pistol made more sense than a long gun. Longarm would also have liked to ask Thorn why there were no spent casings either from his own rifle or the would-be assassin's weapon. Damn it, he still didn't know whether Thorn had caught a glimpse of the attacker!

Well, I might as well forget about pumping the man for

information for the time being, Longarm thought as he made his way downstairs to the street. Any chance of cooperation between himself and Thorn had been lost during that fistfight. From now on, even the information that Thorn might volunteer would be suspect. Longarm would have no way of knowing whether Thorn was lying to him out of spite.

Farley and Ki had arrived at the scene, Longarm saw. Ki was standing protectively by Jessie. The tin star pinned to Ki's leather vest seemed incongruous when one considered his quiet, unassuming stance, and the fact that he carried no gun. Longarm, of course, knew better; he'd seen the samurai in action.

"You find anything up there?" Farley asked him.

Longarm glanced at Thorn, who was sulking in the background beside Barston, and shook his head. "Whoever it was didn't stick around," he shrugged. "Is the congressman all right?"

"Yes, I am," Barston said coldly. "No thanks to you." He glanced at the handful of reporters who were standing around busily scratching away at their notepads. "The attempt on my life was foiled by the heroic actions of my assistant who singlehandedly rushed the rifleman," he announced loudly.

"Thank you, Congressman," Tompkins said quickly, apparently nervous about losing control over the reporters' access to Barston. "Mr. Thorn, perhaps you'd like to say a few words to these good men?" Tompkins suggested firmly. The bodyguard was smiling as he sauntered over to the reporters.

One of the reporters asked, "Mr. Thorn, did you get that bruise on your chin grappling with the assassin?"

Barston grabbed Longarm and steered him away from where the press was grouped. "All right!" the congressman hissed furiously. "Where the hell were you? And your excuse had better be good!"

"I was here when the shooting started," Longarm said evenly. "Where was *your* man? I didn't see *him* up on that platform, blocking any bullets for you."

"Don't you be insolent!" Barston thundered. Several of the reporters, overhearing him, perked up their ears. "You're lucky the press is here," he whispered hoarsely. "I don't want to foul up a good story by firing your ass out of here—"

Longarm's eyes widened. "A good story is right, Congressman. You know, it's funny, but I didn't find a sign of anybody up there, except for Thorn, of course. . . ."

"Keep your voice down!" Barston ordered anxiously. "Just what are you getting at, Long?"

"Where was Thorn when the shooting started?" Longarm asked pointedly, keeping his eyes on Barston's face.

The congresssman looked away, shrugging. "He was circulating among the crowd. He often does that, trying to nip any potential trouble in the bud."

"You're not fooling me with this phony assassination ploy," Longarm said softly. "This was all a set-up, wasn't it? To get yourself some favorable publicity for your campaign."

"You repeat that false accusation to anybody else, and I'll do more than have you fired, you bastard! I'll—"

"Wilson? What's going on here?" It was Jessica. "I overheard you shouting."

"Jessie, honey, everything's fine!" Barston said heartily, putting his arm around her. "Isn't that right, Long?" His eyes narrowed in warning.

"Whatever you say, Congressman," Longarm said.

Jessie looked from one man to the other, trying to figure out what was happening. She finally realized that she wasn't going to find out. At least not just now. "Let's go, Wilson. I'm sure you've had enough excitement for one day."

Tompkins picked up the cue. "That's all for today, boys!" He wove in and out of the pack of reporters, moving them along the way a collie herds sheep.

Longarm began to walk away, disgusted. He felt eyes on the back of his neck, and turned to see Ki staring at him fixedly.

"Leo! Give us a break," one of the reporters begged Tompkins. The correspondent was a barrel-bellied, middle-aged man wearing a dove-gray derby and a red crushed-velvet suit. "Are the two foremost families of the Lone Star State gonna mingle their brands, or what?"

Tompkins smiled slyly. "No comment on that for the present, boys," he said. *You cagey bastard*, Longarm thought. *Just let'em draw their own conclusions, eh?*

"Wilson, please," Jessie murmured, a troubled expression on her pretty face. "This could become embarrassing—for both of us."

"It doesn't have to be," Barston whispered to her. "Think how happy your dear old father would be if it came to pass!" He embraced Jessie roughly, and managed to press a kiss upon her before she broke away.

"That's quite enough, Wilson!" she said firmly.

"That's plenty, Miss Starbuck!" a reporter yelled, provoking laughter from his colleagues.

"This way to the wagon," Jessie muttered. She began to lead the way, but was intercepted by Ki.

"I must stay in town," he told her solemnly, gesturing to the star pinned on his vest.

Just then, Farley passed by. "Deputy, I've got a job for you," he said.

Ki offered Jessie a private, rather subtle smile, one the samurai reserved for her alone. "Duty calls," he murmured, gesturing with his thumb toward Farley's departing form.

Jessie hugged her oldest and dearest friend. "I'm very proud of you for the way you're helping him out." She stood on tiptoe to peck a kiss on his cheek.

"Hmmm, I thought you had a soft spot for fellows who wore a badge," Ki teased. "Perhaps I should take up cigar-smoking, as well?"

"Oh, hush!" Jessie begged, blushing a bright pink. "At least you won't have to worry about me being unprotected," she sighed. "Between Longarm and Barston, I think I'm going to be too busy to get into any trouble!"

Representative Barston was still taking his bows before the press. "See you tomorrow, boys!" he said jauntily. "The first day of the fair, and the beginning of the target match. We'll see who tries to assassinate me when I've got my pistols in hand!"

"Thank you, Congressman!" Murmuring their approval, the reporters headed off en masse to the Western Union office to wire their stories to their newspapers.

Longarm thought about the kid that the banjo-playing key operator had said was coming on duty. *He'll get his practice after all.*

The newspapermen would battle to get their wires out first in hopes of scooping their rivals on the big "assassination attempt." The more Longarm thought about it, replaying the incident in his mind, the more convinced he was that Barston had rigged the whole thing. It was his guess that it had been Thorn, blasting away at the congressman from the rooftop. That explained how even the poorest rifleman could manage to miss the target so many times from such short range. . . .

Longarm wandered around behind the platform Barston had been standing upon. *Something* had stopped those bullets, since the congressman's body had not. . . . He found what he was looking for in the thick oaken doors of the Cattlemen's building. Longarm stooped to examine the bullet holes, and then took out his pocket knife to pry free one of the rounds embedded in the wood. It was a .44.

Longarm thought as he held the misshapen bit of lead up to the light, *That's the same caliber as the Winchester that Thorn was holding when I found him up on the roof. . . .*

Longarm slipped the bullet into his pocket. By itself it proved nothing. After all, .44 Winchesters were common; Longarm himself owned a Winchester in that caliber. And even if he had an eyewitness to swear that it was Thorn who'd been pretending to try and kill Barston, whom could he take his story to?

Billy Vail would just laugh at Longarm for being a naive son of a bitch. "What did you expect of Barston?" Vail would say. "You know all these politicos are as crooked as the day is long. . . ." Longarm knew that deep down, Vail would be just as shocked at what Barston was trying to get away with. Vail would never admit to that, however, because if he admitted he cared, he'd be put in the position of having to do something about it. Vail didn't have that kind of power. No lawman did, when it came to U.S. congressmen backed by powerful friends.

Should he tell Jessie?

No way, Longarm told himself firmly. *No goddamned way!* Jessie might well lose all of her respect for him if she chose to doubt his story. She might think that Longarm was trying to ruin Barston's reputation out of jealousy.

The Starbuck wagon was waiting for them at the rear of the Cattlemen's building. It was a buckboard, with several rows of wooden bench seats before the cargo area began. The wagon was pulled by a team of two horses handled by a young wrangler from the Circle Star spread.

Jessie and Longarm found themselves standing together as the others settled themselves into the buckboard. "How about it?" Longarm whispered to her. "Are you and Barston mingling your brands?"

Jessie's sea-green eyes glinted with fire. "Oh! Not you too?" she demanded angrily.

Barston reached down to help her into the wagon. She sat next to him, and he put his arm around her protectively. "You sit up front with the hired hand," Barston ordered Longarm, who obligingly hauled himself up into the seat next to the wrangler who was handling the reins.

"How're you?" the cowboy smiled pleasantly.

"Good," Longarm remarked. "How're you?"

The wrangler nodded, and clucked the horses into a walk. Longarm leaned back to enjoy the ride, musing on the pleasure that little exchange had brought.

We asked straightforward questions and gave straightforward answers. That's the first time that's happened today. It was funny how a man never missed a thing until it seemed gone....

Like a good and honest answer—

Behind him, Barston whispered something to Jessie that made her giggle.

Or a good and honest woman, Longarm thought regretfully.

Chapter 4

Sarah's main thoroughfare became a dirt trail outside the town's limits. It cut across Goat Creek a few times, and for that reason the folks in this part of Texas had taken to calling it Goat Creek Road.

If a traveler stayed on Goat Creek Road he'd eventually reach the Circle Star spread, but there were many cutoffs before the Starbuck holdings began. Some of these secondary trails led to other spreads, and some led to wooded, unsettled areas used as communal pastures by the ranchers hereabouts. One of the cutoffs—dubbed Keg's Way for some reason buried deep in local history—led out to the reasonably level field being used as the fairgrounds.

Ki reached Keg's Way a little more than an hour after Jessie's homeward-bound buckboard had passed the turnoff's white-painted stone marker. Ki had waited until Jessie left town, and had then headed over to the town marshal's office to saddle up one of the horses that were kept in a small stable to the rear of the jailhouse. The chestnut gelding that Ki had chosen was a good horse. Like all of Farley's mounts, it had been trained to stay put where a man left it, and not to spook at the sound of gunfire. Just now, Ki talked softly to it as he guided the mount onto the cutoff. As he rode, Ki used the pressure of his knees more than he used the reins to control the mount; he used his will as much as his muscles. The goal was not to dominate the steed, but to become one with it. This was true *bajutsu,* the art of horsemanship, one of the thirty-four *kakuto bugei,* or fighting techniques that a Japanese warrior had to master before his teacher would confer upon him the rank of samurai.

Once, while browsing through the Starbuck mansion's extensive library, he had discovered a book on Greek mythology and culture. In the back was a drawing of a creature with the head, arms and torso of a man, and the body and legs of a horse. Ki had not cared very much for the philosophy expressed in the book's text. The Greeks put too much emphasis on the mind at the expense of the body. This was a mistake, Ki believed. He wished he could have explained to the book's author about the rabbit that chased his own tail, around and around, until his futile exertions had carried him to the side of a pond. Glancing into the still surface of the water, the spinning rabbit had seen that his endless chase had bowed his body into a perfect circle. *A circle has no beginning and no end,* the rabbit realized, *a circle is an endless whole....* The rabbit then stopped his silly attempt to catch himself, and in that way became a tiger....

On the other hand, the Greeks, who seemed as though they had become locked in that endless chase after their own tails, had managed to imagine the half-man, half-horse creature called a centaur. To Ki this proved that they at least had a glimmering of what *bajutsu* was about....

It was a hot day, so Ki keep the gelding at an easy walk. The fairgrounds were still a good five miles away. Five miles! And all around there was not a soul in sight. Just a vast, grassy prairie dusted with wildflowers and studded with woodlots of pecan, walnut, and hickory, lorded over by tall oaks. Of course everywhere he looked, Ki could see cattle in the distance, looking like russet smears upon the green landscape. These were the magnificent herds of the Lone Star State, the steers that had long since replaced the bison as the meat of the nation. The grass, warm sunshine, and open spaces were just right for raising cattle. Thousands of steers might have been fattened up in the holding pens of the Midwest before being slaughtered at points even farther east, but those calves were *born* in Texas, the cow nursery of the world.

But what impressed and awed Ki more than the majestic herds was the way Texans built their sprawling ranches and then separated them by vast stretches of empty space, so that the home spreads were like tiny islands dotting a vast sea. There seemed to be enough room here in Texas so that people never had to feel crowded, never had to bump elbows with their neighbors. How different a situation than in his homeland of Japan, where people were so crowded together that elaborate rules of etiquette had been devised to keep peace between neighbors.

Ki's father had been a New England sea captain, his mother a Japanese woman of noble heritage. His parents died on the eve of the family's departure for America. His mother had already been shunned for marrying a "round-eyed barbarian." Ki, a five-year-old orphan, was treated as an outcast by society. He lived in the streets, wore rags, and was near starvation when he was taken in by the great master warrior Hirata, who'd recognized the warrior's spirit inside the little boy. Ki spent long years under Hirata's stern tutelage. He was a young man well into his teens when the day came that he was pronounced ready to join the ranks of the samurai. There was only one problem. The very meaning of the word *samurai* was "a warrior who serves;" Even Hirata, the greatest master of them all, had gone from being a samurai to being a *ronin*, a "wave-man," one blown here and there like the waves of the ocean, belonging to no one, serving no lord. This was because the feudal lords of Japan, who had employed the samurai class in the many wars they fought for territories and thrones, had now all been vanquished by those forces in the island nation that had embraced the West.

Proud Hirata had committed *seppuku*—suicide by ritual disembowelment—in protest against this turn of events in Japan. Training Ki in the samurai's arts had been his last act of defiance against a world that had changed too rapidly for him. Ki, remembering how he'd been mistreated by Japanese aristocracy because he was a half-breed, decided that he would serve no nobleman, but would become a samurai fighting for the cause of the common man. His parents had meant for him to grow to manhood in America, a land where one was judged by one's capabilities, not by the color of one's skin or the cast of one's eyes.

Ki stowed away on a clipper ship bound for the Pacific coast of America. The ship he'd chosen belonged to Alex Starbuck. Ki knew the name, for Starbuck had become a fabulously wealthy man through the import-export trade. Ki wandered San Francisco's wharves until he found the waterfront Starbuck offices. He pushed his way past the clerks until he was standing before Alex Starbuck himself. Ki had learned English from his father, but he spoke to Starbuck in Japanese, a language the businessman had learned during his early years in the Orient. The proud, teenaged *ronin* told his story to the magnate, including his desire to use his warrior talents in the cause of justice.

Starbuck had earned a reputation for commitment to that same goal. If this was truly so, then Ki wished to pledge his allegiance to the Starbuck cause.

Alex Starbuck accepted the young man's oath of service and devotion. Ki was a *ronin* no longer. *Now he was a samurai....*

Ki reined his horse to a stop at a narrow fork in the Keg's Way trail, about halfway to the fair grounds. The fork led to a large pond fed by Goat Creek. The pond would be cool and inviting; on a hot day like this, Ki was sorely tempted to go for a swim.

Marshal Farley would not like it if he did take the time for a refreshing dip, Ki knew. Farley liked things to be done scant moments after he'd thought of them. There were times when haste was important, of course, but Farley had merely asked him to make a routine check of the fairgrounds.

Anyway, what Farley liked or disliked was of no concern to Ki. He had agreed to help the town marshal keep the peace as a favor. He had sworn no samurai's oath of fealty to the marshal; he had sworn only to uphold the law. And the fairgounds could be just as routinely checked an hour from now.

"In other words," Ki murmured to the gelding, "we shall enjoy going swimming." Ki kneed the mount onto the fork that led to the pond. Perhaps the horse was thirsty, for as soon as it smelled the water, it quickened its pace of its own accord.

The pond was long and wide and somewhat kidney-shaped. Lush vegetation all along its banks extended out several feet over the water, so that a swimmer at one end of the pond could not see around the bend in the water to the other end of the pond, approximately sixty yards away.

Ki let his mount's reins trail, knowing that the horse would be content to stay where it was, drinking its fill and then nibbling at the tender shoots of waterside plants. He quickly stripped off his clothes and then dove headfirst into the cool, clear water. The pond was quite deep. Ki swam beneath the surface for a full minute, the movement of his body more resembling that of an otter or seal than of a man. When he surfaced in the middle of the pond, just before the bend in its shape, he was not at all winded.

Ki had once held his breath underwater for five minutes. At the time he was clad in armor, and had to swim one hundred yards while weighted down in the suit of metal. Such ability in the water was called *suiei-jutsu,* and was a part of a samurai's training.

Ki relaxed to back-float for a while, enjoying the way the sun warmed his face and turned the surface of the water to molten silver. Above him, the dragonflies hovered and darted, and below him, tiny perch rose up to nibble at his toes. He grew so still that a kingfisher, perhaps mistaking his long, lean, tanned body for a floating log, landed on his knee in a flurry of wings. Ki did not move a muscle, but merely opened one eye to peer at his visitor. The bird, attracted by the slight movement of Ki's eyelid rising, cocked its own head to stare back, clearly intrigued by this new kind of log that had an eye. Eventually the kingfisher flew off.

He was about to quit the pond when he heard a distant splash and a feminine shriek of delight at the cool temperature of the water. The noise had come to him from around the bend. A woman had quite obviously decided to go swimming in the far side of the pond. The sound of her voice made Ki think that she was young; the fact that she'd gone into the water at all made Ki think that she thought she was alone. Ki was swimming in the nude. Chances were, she was naked as well. . . .

Now, Ki realized that the proper thing to do was to leave immediately so as to afford the young lady her privacy. The Japanese part of him positively demanded that he do this. But Ki was only half Japanese.

He smiled devilishly. *What would be the harm in ascertaining for myself that the girlish voice I'm hearing does indeed belong to a young lady—perhaps a very attractive young lady in the nude? There is no dishonor in spying upon her as long as I don't cause her embarrassment, as long as she doesn't know I'm there. . . .*

Ki took serveral deep breaths, inhaling and exhaling from his belly as opposed to his chest, in order to clear his lungs of old air and fill them with new. Then he dove, plummeting what seemed to him about fifteen feet below the surface. Now the sounds of the woman's strokes in the water came to him like muffled, distant thunder. He swam towards that sound, around the bend, just skimming the waving tips of the water grass growing like long, green, silky hair from the pond's stony floor.

Above him, the surface of the pond was a mirrored ceiling. He swam, glided, and turned in the water as if he were a gilled creature. He did not make a movement that wasted either energy or the air in his lungs.

Ki saw a monster catfish nosing along the murky bottom. The green-tinted water distorted distances and dimensions, Ki knew, but he was still prepared to wager that the cat was at least five feet long, with a girth as wide as a man's. The cat's whiskers wiggled like worms in the silt, and the sharp barbs cresting the fish's meaty back rose and fell like a mighty warlord's battle flags.

How old are you, noble one? Ki thought as he lazily kicked his legs to match the bottom scavenger's slow crawl. *How many anglers have you outsmarted to grow so large?*

Ki's shadow must have fallen across the catfish's angle of vision. One moment it was there, and the next there was only a wake of mud as it flew through the water with sharp slaps of its thick tail. The samurai let the natural buoyancy of his body take him up in search of the female swimmer. As he rose he noticed a snake—a water moccasin—undulating upon the surface. The snake's long body formed an endless, lazy S-curve as it swam. The water moccasin could afford to take its time and swagger. Like a gunslick in a cow town, the poisonous reptile was confident that it could rely on its lightning-quick speed and the lethal potential of its weapon to get it out of trouble.

Ki had been under for several minutes now, and decided that there was no point in pressing his endurance to the limit. He could no longer hear the sound of the woman's splashing, and thought that perhaps she was floating quietly—assuming that she hadn't taken a quick dip and then left the water, of course.

He kicked upward with powerful thrusts of his well-muscled legs. As his head broke the surface, movement caught his eye, and he barely had time to gulp some air and note the graceful rise and fall of a woman's arm as she cut through the water, before he once again sank below the surface.

He dropped down about five feet, and hovered motionless to watch her swimming along. Fortunately she was heading in a direction opposite to that of the water moccasin.

She was a small woman, not more than twenty years old, Ki guessed. Her legs were long for her spare height, and like her arms, back, and belly, they seemed sculpted from solid muscle and then softly upholstered with creamy skin. Her large, round breasts were tipped with nipples as dark as cherries. Her breasts floated free and bare, as did the rest of her. Her rather endearingly plump, pear-shaped bottom was a creamy shade of vanilla, in startling contrast to her sun-honeyed thighs and calves. Beyond discerning the difference between light and dark, it was almost impossible to judge colors underwater, but Ki thought that the sassy, furry thatch between her gracefully kicking legs was several shades lighter than her long, dark hair trailing in the water.

Ki felt himself growing hard as he watched this water sprite make her way expertly across the pond. He rose up to swim beneath her on his back, almost but not quite within touching distance. To touch her was unthinkable, of course. The woman was totally unaware of his proximity; she had suffered no embarrassment. Ki, however, was beginning to feel embarrassed himself by the way his body was reacting to the sight of her. Viewing her on the sly was one thing. Lusting after her without her knowledge struck him as being somehow dishonorable. The high-spirited Yankee blood coursing through his veins may have lured him here, but it was his mother's Japanese sense of decorum that was now firmly telling him to leave—

Ki slowed, and somersaulted away from her fast-moving form. He made his way back to his side of the pond before rising for a breath of fresh air. As his head broke the surface, he heard the woman's plaintive cries coming to him from across the dappled, rippling expanse of water. He was too far away to make out what she was saying, but the pleading note in her voice was clear enough. Next he heard the laughter of several men....

Ki glanced behind him. It would take too long to swim to where he'd left his clothes, he decided quickly. The woman was naked; totally vulnerable to the men's advances. If he was to prevent a tragedy from taking place, he would have to move *fast*.

He struck out toward the far end of the pond, plowing through the water as efficiently as the water moccasin. As he rounded the bend, he paused to get a fix on the woman's location. She was standing huddled in waist-deep water, with her arms crossed protectively across her breasts. Ki caught a glimpse of her garments draped from a bush on the pond's bank. He also saw the three men who were preventing the helpless woman from reaching her clothing.

Ki swam underwater, angling himself toward a point about fifty feet to the right of the men. He moved quickly and silently, and was able to leave the water and conceal himself in the thick undergrowth along the shoreline without being seen. As he'd suspected, the men's eyes were glued to the voluptuous nudity of their victim, and the woman was oblivious to everything but the menacing actions of her tormentors.

"Come on out of there, honey!" one of the men shouted.

"Listen, you make us get wet, and you'll be sorry," another threatened and then giggled nervously.

Ki moved closer, circling around behind the trio of bullies. Now that the samurai could make out their features, he recognized them as laborers from the stockyards in town. They were big, hulking men who earned their livings through the strength of their backs, but they were not particularly dangerous as long as a fellow knew enough to stay out of reach. None of the three was carrying a gun, but Ki suspected that they had a knife or two secreted in the pockets of their baggy denim overalls. The three passed a bottle around as they taunted the woman.

"I seen a lot, but I ain't never seen nothing like you, honey!" one of the men leered. He wore no shirt beneath his overalls. A long, livid scar from some past battle meandered its way across the tanned and meaty slope of his shoulder.

"You know what's gonna happen, dontcha?" a fellow with curly black hair and a thick mustache warned menacingly. He kicked off his lace-up work shoes, and began to roll up the bottoms of his trousers. "I'm coming to getcha!"

"Please . . ." the woman whimpered, panic-striken. She took several faltering steps back into the water. The warming sun had slid behind a blanket of clouds. She began to shiver, her skin rising up in goosebumps. "P-please," she begged as her teeth began to chatter.

"We'll warm you up!" the third man laughed. He had thinning red hair, freckles, and a massive beer belly. Ki had seen the man at work, however. He knew that there was nothing soft about that belly, or about the arms and chest that stretched the faded chambray of the man's work shirt.

"Fetch her for me, Mikey!" the red-haired man said.

"Fuck you," growled the mustached man who'd waded up to his knees in the water. "Finders keepers!"

"I'll go last," the bare-chested man announced cheerfully.

Ki sighed to himself, shaking his head sadly. He knew that these three were fully capable of brutally raping the hapless woman in the water. Afterward, they would merely clap each other on the back in celebration of their good fortune, while wondering what all of the woman's fuss was about. More than likely, they had never done anything like this before, and had set out today merely to enjoy a swim. But now that they had come upon the woman, and they were not about to relinquish their prize.

"I told you to stay still!" roared the man who'd gone into

83

the water. The woman froze in place, literally too frightened to disobey.

The red-haired man nodded in anticipation. "Now we got fun—"

"No, you do not," Ki said, standing up from behind a waist-high hedge growth.

"Jesus Christ!" gasped the bare-chested man, spinning around in surprise.

"What do you want?" demanded the red-haired man.

Ki pointed toward the pond. "The woman."

A sly smile spread across the other's freckled features. "Oh! Well . . . all right, friend. You can be fourth."

Ki just stared at him.

"Hey! Fourth or nothing!" the man argued. "We saw her first! We'll have our fun and—"

"You will let her go," Ki cut him off. "You will leave here, and allow the woman her privacy so that she can put on her clothing."

"Like hell we will," the man snarled. *"You'd* better leave, or I'll bust yer hole for ya!"

"Easy, Dan," the bare-chested man warned quietly. "I've seen him in town. He works for Jessica Starbuck. Folks say he's somethin' special in a fistfight."

"Yuh? He looks a mite skinny to be able to dish out a man's portion of bare knuckles," the red-haired man huffed. He turned his attention back toward Ki. "What do you say, fella? You gonna leave, or do I have to break yer back?" He raised his fist into the air like a club.

Ki only smiled wistfully. He'd entertained a faint hope that the arrival of a witness on the scene would cause the trio to abandon their plan. Obviously this was not to be. The three men were too liquored up to think clearly. They'd drunk too much courage out of their bottle, and had already goaded each other to a fever pitch. Ki resigned himself to the inevitable.

"You will leave now," he warned quietly.

"Son of a *bitch!*" the red-haired man swore. He moved toward Ki with his shoulders hunched and his big hands balled into fists. The man who was shirtless flanked him, while the fellow who'd waded into the pond gave up his pursuit of the woman in order to back his buddies.

Ki stepped out from behind the hedge.

All three of the men advancing upon him stopped dead in their tracks.

"Jesus," the red-haired man breathed, gaping at Ki. "The bastard's stark naked!"

"As a jaybird," the shirtless man agreed in baffled surprise.

The red-haired man let his fists drop an inch. "Don't know if I can fight a naked fella," he said uneasily.

Ki took advantage of his momentary indecision to take several steps forward and deliver a roundhouse kick to the redhead's chin. Dazed, the man spat blood and staggered a bit, before crumpling to the grassy bank.

"See? I told you! I told you!" the shirtless man swore. His face was set in an expression of grim determination as he advanced upon Ki. The man kept his fists spaced widely apart. As he got within range of the samurai, he began to throw a series of windmill rights and lefts.

Ki ducked and swerved as necessary, expending no particular effort. He'd seen this style of fighting before: two bull-like specimens of manhood stood with their stump-thick legs planted solidly in the earth, trading sledgehammer blows until one or both dropped unconscious.

It is a style, Ki said to himself as he avoided the grunting man's jabs and crosses, *but it is not my style—*

"Stand still, you bare-assed bastard!" the man groaned in frustration. "Stand still and fight—"

"Very well," Ki said brightly. He executed a *mae-geri keage,* or forward snap-kick, directly into his opponent's groin. The fellow's thoughts of rape were doubtless forgotten as he bent over and clutched at himself. Ki merely stepped aside as the man, mewling in agony, waddled off to inspect the damage.

Ki turned his attention toward the man who'd waded after the girl in the pond. As Ki had expected, this one had managed to find a knife in the pockets of his damp overalls. The mustached man held his blade out in front of him like a divining rod as he approached warily.

Ki reached for one of his *shuriken* throwing blades before he remembered that they were cached in the many pockets of his leather vest—and that his vest was with the rest of his clothes, on the far side of the pond.

No matter, Ki thought. His reaching for the blade was an impulse he would not have followed through on, in any event. These three men were not warriors, but clowns. They might have been too much for a woman to handle, but to a samurai they were merely boisterous cubs who needed disciplining, but not killing. Indeed, to kill them would be a dishonorable act. . . .

The man with red hair had recovered sufficently to attempt to attack Ki from behind. The samurai waited until the man's big hands had slid about his throat before driving his elbow back into his adversary's solar plexus. The man retched, and as his fingers slid away, Ki delivered the strike twice again, pacing his blows to tattoo his opponent's throat and eye as he sank to the ground. The man with the knife was just closing in as Ki sank all his weight upon his rear leg, resting the toe of his forward foot lightly upon the ground. This was the *neko-ashi-dachi*, or cat's-foot stance, and while in it, the samurai could move in any direction and still be ready to deflect his opponent's knife blade.

The mustached man chose to thrust low with his glinting knife. Ki's downward forearm block swept the blade away from his belly. The impact of Ki's focused strength on the other's thick wrist caused the knife to fly from his fingers, landing with a tiny splash in the pond. Ki sent a short, hard kick into the man's belly to take him out of action, and then turned to confront the attack of the bare-chested man who was still holding his groin, but now seemed to have recovered his strength.

"Hold off," the red-haired man mumbled hoarsely through bloodied lips. He was rubbing his throat, and one of his eyes had been swollen shut by Ki's elbow strike. "What we'll do is rush him all at once," he commanded, producing a knife.

Nodding agreement, the other two joined their leader in a circle around the samurai. As the three charged, Ki defended himself with a flurry of blocks and kicks. He caught the mustached man with a backhand strike that dropped him flat on his back. The stiffened edge of his palm against the bare-chested man's neck sent that opponent wheeling away in agony. The samurai was dodging the knife thrusts of the red-haired man when he heard a sharp, metallic *click!* The red-haired man dropped his knife and clapped his hand to the side of his face, wailing in pain.

Ki spun around to see the woman from the pond standing naked beside the bush where her clothes were hanging. She was still dripping wet, and was holding an odd-looking pistol in both hands. One of the would-be rapists—the bare-chested man—started for her. She aimed at him and squeezed the trigger of her weapon. Once again there was a loud *click!* This time Ki saw that the gun had fired some sort of pellet at her attacker, who cried out and spun away.

"Git! All of you!" the woman cried out in furious indignation. She quickly cocked her single-shot weapon, slid another pellet from the palm of her hand into its open breech, and fired at the closest of the three laborers—still the shirtless man. This time her projectile—whatever it was—caught him behind the ear.

"Ow! Jesus!" the man cried out running away. "Let's git! Ow!" Another of the girl's shots had apparently struck home.

With both Ki and the wrathful girl advancing upon them, the remaining two laborers turned tail and ran off as well. Ki watched until they'd disappeared into the bushes, and then turned to face the woman—who was pointing her pistol at him.

The samurai quickly raised his hands, but then, remembering that he was naked, decided that it would make more sense to place his hands over his lap. The woman, misunderstanding his gesture of self-protection for one of modesty, lowered her pistol and shook her head.

"Here now, I've got six brothers and once got cozy with a boy named Beauford, so you haven't got anything I've never seen before." Her eyes widened as Ki lowered his hands. "Just more of it . . ." she murmured beneath her breath.

"You are naked," Ki reminded her politely.

The girl smiled. "I know I'm naked! I was swimming, so of course I was naked!" She put her hands on her hips and looked Ki in the eye. She seemed to be not in the least bothered by her lack of clothing. "Swimming's my excuse. What's yours? Or do you make it a habit to parade around in the buff?"

"I was swimming as well," Ki smiled back. "I heard your cries for help and came to investigate."

"Naked like that, and with no gun?" The girl was amazed. "You must be mighty sure of yourself—not that you didn't mop the floor with those three. Where'd you leave your duds?"

"Over yonder." Ki pointed to the far side of the pond. "Around the bend. My horse is there, as well. I was on my way to the fairgrounds when—"

"That's where I was going, too!" the girl cried. "Why don't you circle around to your clothes and get dressed. I'll do the same and then ride over to meet you. We can continue on to the fairgrounds together." She hesitated. "I'd lend you something to wrap around your waist, but I don't have very much. . . ."

Ki nodded wryly. The clothing draped on the bush did appear rather scanty.

"Maybe my horse's blanket?" she began.

"I will swim across," Ki said. He started toward the water. "You will come?" he asked.

"'Course I will," she reassured him. "Said I would, didn't I? I don't lie, Mr.—?"

"My name is Ki, just Ki," the samurai told her.

"That's nice . . ." She smiled. "My name's Phoebe. Now git! And let a girl get dressed!" She pretended to menace him with her gun.

"You are quite interesting, Phoebe," Ki mused. "And so is that weapon."

"So's *your* weapon!" Phoebe giggled. "And its interest has been rising for quite a while!"

Ki blushed as he glanced down helplessly at his raging erection. He threw himself hurriedly into the pond.

"See you in a little bit!" Phoebe called after him, laughing gaily.

Ki turned around to catch a glimpse of her creamy backside wiggling its way up the slight embankment to her clothes. He began to swim in a lazy crawl toward his own clothing, the sound of her laughter in his ears, and the sight of her pert, upturned nose, her wide, sensual mouth, and her big blue eyes in his mind.

He was dressed and waiting for her on horseback as she rode around the bend of the narrow path that encircled the pond. Her hair was still damp from the swim, and she had combed it back and twisted it into a long braid that hung down her back. She seemed to be bursting forcibly out of her plain blue cotton dress, which, judging from its faded and somewhat threadbare appearance, she had owned since before her body had begun to blossom into the lush roundness it now possessed. Several buttons had already popped down the front, exposing a rather wide expanse of her ivory breasts. From this, and from the way the frayed hem of the dress was now hiked up past her knees as she sat her horse, Ki could tell that she wore nothing under the single garment. The cumulative effect was staggeringly feminine, and she was even more sexually alluring than she had been when swimming completely naked. A jarring, decidedly unfeminine note was provided by a pair of beat-up, mud-encrusted work shoes she wore on her bare feet.

"Is that the sort of outfit women wear on farms?" Ki asked.

Phoebe blushed. "I know," she said with a pout. "I likely deserved what you saved me from for being dressed so daringly." She paused, then asked, "How'd you know I'm a farm girl?"

He shrugged. "Your earlier remark about your brothers, your matter-of-fact ease with your own nudity and mine, and the red field mud still clinging to those farmhand's shoes of yours."

Phoebe smiled brightly, "I'm starting to be glad those brutes were bothering me, otherwise I never would have screamed, and you never would have found me." She stared searchingly at Ki. "Hey, what are you chuckling about?"

"Nothing," Ki said, trying hard to keep a straight face. Time to change the subject, he decided. "I don't wish to appear prudish," he began, "but you shouldn't dress like that around here."

"I wouldn't have, but as I told you, I'd left the fairgrounds to ride here for a swim and a little target practice. This part of the trail seemed so deserted, I never dreamed I'd run into anybody." Phoebe looked down at herself. "This is what I usually wear when I'm working my mama's farm in Ohio. My brothers never paid me no mind, and I guess they kept strange fellers from sniffing around like he-dogs in the spring."

"What about Beauford?"

"Oh, *him*," Phoebe laughed merrily. "I sorta think I did *him* more than he did *me*. I put the idea in that sweet boy's head, that's for sure," she explained. "A girl growing up on a farm gets to see all kinds of critters *doing* it—like you said. Well, I sorta wanted to know what it felt like, so I found out. . . ."

Ki kept silent, regarding her expectantly.

"Don't you go giving me that look of yours, mister!" Phoebe scolded. "It felt damned good, if you'd like to know!"

"I *was* curious." Ki murmured.

"Why, ain't *you* ever tried it?" Phoebe demanded wickedly. "Let's ride!"

Ki had his vest folded over the horn of his saddle. Now he shrugged it on, and kneed his horse into a walk beside hers.

"Oh, you're a lawman," Phoebe said, noticing his badge.

"Not really," Ki replied. "You see, I live around here, and I agreed to help the town marshal keep the peace during the fair. A lot of riffraff have been attracted to this territory—"

"Like those three back at the pond." She shivered. "I guess I should have realized that a girl alone wouldn't be safe."

"You mentioned that you were planning to practice your shooting," Ki remarked. "Are you entered in the match?"

"You bet I am!" Phoebe said proudly. "And I'm planning on winning it, as well! I rode all the way here from Ohio, and I aim to ride back with that two thousand dollars in my saddlebags."

"You had better be good, in that case," Ki warned. "The most famous shootists in the country have converged upon Sarah for the competition."

"Well, I don't like to boast, but I figure I *am* good," Phoebe said seriously. "My papa died in a blizzard when I was just a little tyke, you see. All us kids had to grow up fast. When I was nine years old, my brothers taught me how to shoot, just in case I could get lucky and bag a rabbit for mama's stewpot. We had a whole bunch of rabbits messing around the garden. Anyway, it turned out that I had a way of hitting any target I aimed at. I don't rightly know why, but the Good Lord saw fit to make me a natural shootist, just like some folks are naturally good at drawing pictures or playing the fiddle. My talent is shooting guns."

"Is this your first competition?" Ki asked.

"Hell, no!" Phoebe laughed. "I won just about every contest I entered in Ohio. Of course, all I got for my trouble was a bunch of plaques that aren't worth spit. But it was fun to win." She shrugged. "Anyway, when I wasn't doing that, I was out hunting game. We'd ship the meat to Cincinnati by stagecoach. The money I earned paid off the farm's mortgage," she finished proudly.

"You certainly handled that pistol of yours well back at the pond," Ki complimented her.

"What? *That* little thing?" she scoffed. "Hell, *anybody* can shoot one of *them.*" She reached behind her into one of her saddlebags, and took out her odd pistol. "This here weapon operates on a spring mechanism," she explained, handing the gun over to Ki for his inspection. "It's a cinch to aim, because there's no recoil. It fires hardened wax pellets. It doesn't make much noise, and you don't have to worry about a stray shot doing any real damage to people or property."

Ki nodded, handing the gun back to her. "You will need a real six-shooter for tomorrow's competition," he warned.

"I know that," Phoebe told him. "I brought along a damned *lovely* Smith & Wesson to use. My pellet gun's just for target practice. I like to get in a couple of hours worth of shooting a day," she confided. "That's a lot of rounds. At that rate, even .22 rounds would be much too expensive."

"That makes sense," Ki agreed. They were now close enough to the fair's site to hear the music of the strolling musicians who earned their livings by playing a listener's favorite tune for a few pennies. "Do you have a place to sleep?" Ki asked his companion. "Somewhere safe, I mean."

"'Course I do," Phoebe smiled. "But I appreciate your concern. I've pitched a tent on the outskirts of the grounds. There's a couple of families that have done the same thing. Being near them makes me safe enough."

"Well then," Ki sighed. They rode on, keeping a comfortable sort of silence between them. After a bit, Phoebe asked Ki just what kind of Indian he was, and the samurai briefly explained his Japanese origins.

Phoebe watched him out of the corner of her eye. "You aren't married, are you?"

"No, I am not married," Ki replied.

"That's good," she laughed throatily. "Damn, here's where I turn off for my camp site."

Ki reined in his mount. "I must go on," he explained, feeling

91

true regret. "I promised the marshal I would patrol the fair-grounds—" He glanced up at the position of the sun in the sky. "Rather a long time ago, I am afraid."

Phoebe nodded. "If you have to. . ." Her sad expression brightened. "Will you come to watch me win the target match tomorrow?"

"Tomorrow is only the elimination part of the contest," Ki pointed out.

"Then come to watch me eliminate everybody!" Phoebe replied impatiently.

"I think you need more confidence in yourself. . . ."

"Huh?" She cocked her head, puzzled.

"Nothing."

"If you come, I'll win tomorrow's match just for you!" Phoebe boasted. "I'm real glad I met you." She rode a few paces, and then wheeled her horse around to face the samurai. "You promise you'll come?" she pleaded, her big, blue eyes suddenly grown wide with concern.

"Do not worry," Ki called to her.

"But promise!" Phoebe begged theatrically, clearly enjoying her own performance.

"Enough," Ki chided her gently. "You are much too pretty to need to show off in such an undignified manner."

"I *do* like you, mister." Phoebe's grin stretched from ear to ear. "See you tomorrow!"

"I like you, as well, Phoebe. See you tomorrow."

The girl colored. She waved and then rode off.

A slight smile played at the corners of Ki's mouth as he watched her go.

Chapter 5

About the time that Ki had been enjoying his swim, the Star-buck wagon carrying Jessie and her guests was making its way through the first of many strands of shade trees, toward the path that led up to the Starbuck house. Jessie's home was built of stone, with the main, middle section of the house standing three stories tall. One-story wings jutted out from either side. There was a bunkhouse for the hands, and a stable nearby.

The buckboard stopped in front of the veranda. Hired hands unloaded everyone's luggage and carried it up to the guest rooms on the second floor. Though the main part of the house was three stories high, there were only two floors. The second-floor bedrooms opened out to a hallway, one side of which was a railed balcony that overlooked a huge combination dining area and living room. Dark-stained roof rafters accented the soaring ceilings of this magnificent interior, which had polished hardwood floors, bright scatter rugs, and a massive, gray slate fireplace. Comfortable leather furniture was arranged about the living room portion, while a mahogany dining room set commanded a generous space of its own, near the double doors that led to the house's kitchen.

Jessie suggested that her guests rest in their rooms until dinner that evening. Longarm took a nap, and then awoke in time to shave, change his shirt, and make it downstairs to the living room, where he found Barston, Thorn, and Tompkins all formally dressed in black velvet suits, and all enjoying before-dinner sherry with their hostess.

Jessie poured Longarm a glass, and the deputy marshal spent a fidgety quarter-hour sipping at his wine and listening to Barston dominate the conversation with an unending series of excruciatingly boring anecdotes about life in the Capital. Was it Longarm's imagination, or did Jessie send a look of relief his way when they were summoned to the dinner table?

Barston somehow managed to keep talking and still polish off several helpings of the delicious meal prepared and served by Myobu, the elderly Japanese housekeeper. By the time the dishes were cleared away and coffee and brandy were served, Longarm was more than ready for a good, stiff drink.

"I know Jessie has no objections to men smoking at the dinner table," Barston said expansively. He took a leather cigar case from the inside pocket of his silk-lined velvet dinner jacket, and offered it to Longarm. "Care to try one of mine, Deputy?"

Longarm nodded. "Thanks, don't mind if I do." He'd been about to light up one of the bent and battered cheroots he carried in the breast pocket of his frock coat, which was just now serving as his dinner jacket, and tomorrow would serve as his breakfast and lunch jacket, as well.

"Don't suppose you get much opportunity to smoke fifty-cent cigars," Barston chuckled, winking at Jessie as Longarm puffed his smoke alight.

Longarm felt no need to dignify Barston's condescension with a reply. The fool was only trying to impress Jessie. It was Barston's hard luck if he had never learned that the best way to impress a lady was not to try so hard. He offered the cigar case to Thorn, who shook his head. Tompkins, meanwhile, had fired up a briar pipe.

"Well? What do you think of that cigar, Deputy?" Barston demanded loudly.

Longarm leaned back in his chair and exhaled a perfect blue smoke ring. "Not a bad smoke, Congressman," he announced, and then peered at the cigar's paper ring. "Although I'm sorry to say I believe you were overcharged by about two bits. Last time I checked the tobacconist's display in Denver, these Broadleaf Specials were selling for twenty-five cents."

Thorn shot Longarm a twelve-gauge, double-barreled dirty look, while Barston found himself speechless for the first time that evening. Watching him, Longarm knew that the congressman was trying to decide which was worse: to appear a fool for being overcharged, or to admit to lying about what he'd paid for his cigars?

"Well," Barston finally harrumphed. "I'll certainly look into this matter on my return to Washington."

Longarm nodded as he thought, *The right choice for a politico. Maybe Barston is White House material, after all.*

Jessie, meanwhile, was hiding her smile behind her napkin. Even Tompkins had let loose a chuckle over his boss's discomfiture, a chuckle he hastily turned into a cough as Barston glared at him.

Just them Myobu returned to the dining room, bearing a plate of sweets. Longarm took the opportunity to compliment the diminutive, gray-haired woman on the meal, addressing her by name, much to Barston's surprise. After Jessie translated Longarm's comment into Japanese, Myobu offered him a slight bow. The housekeeper uttered a sentence in her own tongue, her lilting voice reminding Longarm of the chirp of a songbird. Then she scurried from the table.

"What'd she say?" Longarm asked as Myobu disappeared through the double doors that led into the kitchen.

Jessie looked stricken. "Tell you later," she hissed from behind her napkin.

Longarm was about to ask more, but her pleading look silenced him.

"Just how did you two get to know each other?" Barston asked pointedly.

Hugely relieved to bring an end to the awkward silence that had followed Myobu's exit, Jessie enthusiastically launched into her reply. "Longarm was assigned to investigate the murder

95

of my father." She smiled at Longarm. "At first I didn't trust him, but as soon as we realized that we really were both on the same side, we made a great team."

"Along with Ki," Longarm added, smiling back at her. He couldn't help thinking about how lovely Jessie was looking tonight. Her long, tawny hair was pinned up, and she was wearing a low-cut dress made of silky material the same shade of green as her eyes. "Ki is a terrific fighter," he muttered thickly. Sitting there so close to Jessie, it was all Longarm could do to resist the urge to reach out and stroke her delicate bared shoulder.

Jessie had been watching Longarm all the while he spoke. In her eyes was the kind of look a woman usually reserves for a special sort of man. She kept her eyes locked with his as she continued in a mesmerized tone, "Together . . . Longarm and I . . . discovered that it was the cartel that had been behind my father's murder. . . ."

"You mean to say Long knows about the Prussians?" Barston asked, astounded.

Abruptly, Jessie tore her gaze away from Longarm. She gave herself a little shake, and then nodded.

"Jessie told me everything," Longarm cut in. "Many years ago the Prussians tried to coerce her father into using his clipper ships to transport Chinese slaves from the Orient. When he refused, the cartel began to send hired thugs out to raid his ships and business concerns, both here and abroad. When that didn't intimidate him, the Prussians tried to assassinate him. They failed, but Jessie's mother was killed in the attempt."

"How dreadful!" Tompkins gasped.

"*I* knew all *that*." Barston assured Longarm anxiously. "I was just curious to know what *you* knew, is all."

"Please go on for my sake," Tompkins begged. He peered at Jessie with concern. "If it's not too painful for you, my dear?"

"The killing of my mother took place while my parents were touring Europe," Jessie elaborated quietly for the benefit of the rapt secretary. "I was just a little girl then, so my parents had left me back in the States, under the supervision of a nanny. My father only had a few days before he was due to set off on the return voyage to America. He used all of his influence in a desperate attempt to get the European law-enforcement agencies to bring his wife's killers to justice. He knew that the cartel was responsible, of course, but the powerful Prussians controlled the police. The law would do nothing. So . . ." Jessie took a deep breath. "So my father took it upon himself to exact a form of justice. On the eve of his departure for home, he hunted down and killed the cartel leader's son in retaliation for that man's having ordered the attack that took my mother's life."

"Good Lord . . ." Tompkins had been about to relight his pipe. He flinched as his match singed his fingers. "What happened next?"

"My father returned to America and moved to Texas," Jessie replied. "He claimed it was because he wanted to get into the cattle business, but I suspect he felt he could more easily protect me away from a port city like San Francisco. He turned most of the day-to-day, routine operations of his empire over to his trusted employees, and devoted himself to building up the Circle Star herd. Ki had joined us by then. Ki is a Japanese samurai, Mr. Tompkins. That's a kind of professional soldier or warrior. Ki pledged to protect me—with his life if need be—and he has, to this day. My father fully expected the cartel to retaliate for the murder of their leader's son. To further protect himself, his business empire, and his only daughter, he hired private detectives to search out and identify the cartel's many operatives in America."

"What happened then?" Tompkins asked.

Jessie smiled. "Nothing. Years went by, and gradually my father began to believe that the war was over. A tenuous peace had sprung up between my father and the Prussians. It was as if both sides had come to realize that their violent feud would end up devouring everything they were battling so fiercely to protect: their business interests, their profits"—Jessie took a sip of brandy to steel herself—"and the lives of their loved ones . . ." Her voice trailed off as she became lost in private memories.

"Things stayed quiet until her father was ambushed," Longarm offered, wanting to allow Jessie a respite to compose herself. "It turned out that the man responsible for Alex Starbuck's murder was the son of the very man he killed to avenge his wife's death—"

"Incredible!" Tompkins exclaimed. "The cartel's leader killed Starbuck's wife. Starbuck killed that man's son, and then the son of *that* man killed him! What a story!"

Jessie nodded slowly. Almost to herself she murmured, "An eye for an eye for an eye—and it didn't end there. With Longarm's help, I tracked my father's murderer down." She smiled. "Longarm had taught me that killing was not the way to find justice. He and I tried to arrest my father's murderer, but he preferred to go out fighting. His name was Wulf Danzig, and he died by my gun—"

"And mine!" Longarm pointed out firmly. "He forced us to kill him! You did nothing wrong, Jessie!"

She nodded gratefully to Longarm. "Danzig's pistols now rest in my gun collection. Since then, Ki and I have taken every opportunity to search out and foil the cartel's schemes in America."

"You mean to say that these Prussians are operating within our national borders?" Tompkins asked, his brow furrowed.

"Indeed they have been," Barston declared. "At Jessie's urging, I have conducted some secret Congressional investigations into just how deeply entrenched this foreign cartel has become in American politics and business."

"Why haven't I heard about any of this, Wilson?" Tompkins sputtered. "This is news, man! Your efforts on your nation's behalf ought to be publicized!"

"I asked Wilson to keep his investigations a secret," Jessie interrupted. "The cartel's representatives would merely go underground if they were identified to the public. This way we can keep tabs on them and neutralize their efforts."

"And don't forget, there's no law that says a foreign power is forbidden to lobby in its own interests in America," Barston added.

"Wilson's absolutely correct," Jessie acknowledged. "More often than not, the cartel has bent the law so that it is on their side. They usually have the influence to keep themselves out of the papers. I certainly have no desire for publicity." Jessie smiled. "The one thing that the cartel and the Starbuck interests seem to agree upon is that our war is to be fought in private."

"No need to be so modest," Barston chided mildly. "Your actions have always been absolutely aboveboard and commendable." The congressman exchanged a quick glance with his bodyguard. "Thorn, seeing that the deputy knows about the cartel, I see no harm in revealing to him what you found up on that roof this afternoon."

"Thorn!" Longarm grumbled. "You told me that you'd found nothing up there."

"I tell you what I want to," Thorn sneered. "I answer to Congressman Barston, not to you." He reached inside his silk-lined velvet dinner jacket, and then flicked something across the table.

Longarm picked it up off the linen tablecloth. It was a plain white calling card. Embossed on one side was an intricate design consisting of a stylized crown. Longarm turned the card over before handing it to Jessie. There was no other printing, nor any writing, on either side.

Jessie's eyes widened as she stared at the card. "This is the cartel's insignia!"

Barston nodded glumly. "You see, Deputy, ever since I began those investigations into the cartel's doings, I've been receiving threats in the mail. That's why I hired Thorn. When I announced my intention to run for the nomination of my party, the threats increased. I was warned to retire from political life, or else."

"You should have turned that card over to me this afternoon," Longarm said flatly. "Congressman, I can't protect you if you refuse to cooperate with me."

Barston waved him off. "I didn't want anything to spoil my visit here. Although I do think that you owe me an apology, eh, Deputy?"

"An apology?" Jessie asked, mystified. "From Custis? I *thought* you two were fighting this afternoon. What happened?"

"Nothing you need to be concerned with, Jessie, honey," Barston said fondly. "The deputy simply made some patently false allegations concerning what had taken place during to-day's attempt on my life."

"Longarm," Jessie sighed, shaking her head in consternation. "What happened between you two?"

"I thought today's shooting was staged," Longarm said. "That card proves me wrong. I admit that to you, Congressman, and I do apologize for my accusations. But you owe me an apology as well."

"How so?" Barston looked amused.

"Not telling me you had that card amounts to withholding evidence, and that's breaking the law. Nobody's above the law, Congressman, not even you," Longarm added meaningfully.

"Is that some kind of threat, Deputy?" Barston asked, his voice dripping with scorn.

"Nope, it's a promise," Longarm declared. "You withhold any more evidence and I'll clap the cuffs on you so fast you won't know what hit you."

"Why, I've never been spoken to that way by *anybody!*" Barston raged.

"Custis, really . . ." Jessie reproached him.

"You ever try to arrest the congressman, and I'll stop you dead—" Thorn hissed.

"Right," Longarm replied. "We saw how good you were at stopping me up on that roof this afternoon."

"What's he talking about, Thorn?" Barston seemed extraordinarily perturbed. "Answer me!"

"We . . . nothing, sir . . ." Thorn shook his head and then looked away.

"Look here, Deputy Long," Barston said. "I didn't ask for you to be assigned to me—"

Longarm nodded. "But I am."

"I don't need you—"

"Yes, you do."

"Dammit!" Barston seethed in frustration. "Damn your insolence! I've never met *anybody* like you! And I *don't* need you. I've got Thorn."

"Thorn's an amateur," Longarm said evenly. "He couldn't keep you safe in a schoolyard." He smiled at Thorn. "No offense, old son—I admire your taste in clothes."

Thorn turned white. He tried to say something, but no sound came out of his mouth beyond a sputtering noise that caused spittle to collect on his lips. He suddenly reached into the side pocket of his velvet jacket to come up with a derringer.

Longarm was vastly amused. "What's that, old son? Your dinner gun?"

Thorn pointed the little pistol at Longarm's face. "Keep playing with fire and you'll get burned!" he snarled.

Longarm grinned at Barston. "Where did you *find* this jasper, Congressman?"

"For God's sake, Deputy," Tompkins begged in fear. "Don't provoke him!"

"Wilson, how dare your man produce a gun at my table?" Jessie demanded icily.

"Put it away, you fool," Barston muttered to his bodyguard.

After a moment, Thorn lowered his derringer. His pale blue eyes were downcast as he slipped the pistol back into his pocket, though his jaw muscles were clenched in anger.

"Your man is extremely fortunate that Ki was not here to witness his horrendous display of bad manners," Jessie told Barston. "Ki would have taken his pistol away from him forcibly, and more than likely broken his arm in the process!"

"See that, Congressman?" Longarm said quietly. "See how I spooked him? That's what I meant about Thorn here being an amateur. The man—or men—the cartel has set on your tail are professionals. Like me, they'll go through Thorn like a hot knife through butter. There's a thousand ways to do it. Sending a decoy around to taunt and distract him, while another man blows your brains out, is just one of the easiest."

"Thorn can shoot accurately," Barston argued. "He's a fast draw—"

Longarm shook his head. "That's a common mistake. You think those things are important because when it comes to this sort of thing, you're an amateur as well. A fast, accurate draw makes for a good gunslick, but a lousy bodyguard. Think about it, Congressman! What's a bodyguard's job? To keep you alive, or to kill people after they've shot you?"

"*You—*" Thorn's fingers were like claws as they dug into Longarm's forearm resting on the table. "I'm going to *kill you!*" He said it like a prayer.

Longarm pulled his arm free, and then smiled sadly. "No you're not, Thorn. You just think you're going to, but that's

101

another sign of an amateur: big talk with nothing to back it up but big dreams."

"You're fired!" Barston said through clenched teeth. "Do you understand? *Do* you, Deputy? I don't want you around me anymore. You're through. Get out! Go back to Denver!" He sagged in his chair, out of breath.

"Sir, I don't rightly know that you *can* dismiss me," Longarm mused. "You see, I was assigned to this duty by my superior, Marshal Vail in Denver."

"But—but I never *asked* for you!" Barston stammered. "I don't want you now!"

Longarm brightened. "You know, sir, I believe you've hit upon the key." He paused to relight the cigar Barston had given him. "You admit that you never asked for me—that, in effect, you never *hired* me—"

Barston lowered his head into his hands. "Oh, my God," he moaned softly.

"I reckon you'd have to get ahold of Marshal Vail. He's the only one who can take me off this assignment."

"I don't believe it. I just don't believe it," Barston was muttering.

"And until Marshal Vail does relieve me of this duty, I'll just have to keep you alive whether you want me to or not, Congressman."

Barston looked up to fix Longarm with his stare. "Denver? You say Vail's in Denver?"

"That's where his office is," Longarm said.

Barston nodded gleefully. "Tomorrow I'm going to send a lengthy wire to Marshal Vail. And when he reads it, you can bet your badge that he'll take you off this case, Deputy. And if I were you, I'd bet that badge while it still belonged to you!"

Thorn stood up. From where Longarm was seated, he could see a vein throbbing just beneath the bodyguard's thatch of blond hair.

"Congressman, may I be excused?" Thorn asked stiffly. Barston nodded wearily. "Ma'am," Thorn addressed Jessie, "thank you for dinner." He strode away.

"'Night, Thorn," Longarm called after him. Thorn merely hunched his shoulders and kept walking. "Gee whiz, I hope I didn't make him mad," Longarm said to Jessie.

"Custis, please!" Jessie implored. "Wilson," she called sweetly, "why don't we take a nice walk in the garden? The fresh air would do us wonders, don't you think?"

Barston's mood lightened instantly. "Why, sure. I'd *love* to go for a private little stroll." He hopped up to pull back Jessie's chair. "Good night, Tompkins." He glared at Longarm as Jessie led him away.

Both men had stood up as Jessie left the table. Longarm and Tompkins now found themselves staring awkwardly at each other across the linen. "A little more brandy?" Longarm asked.

Tompkins smiled shyly. "Won't say no." He scratched at his balding scalp with the stem of his pipe, and sat back down, as did Longarm, who poured a generous dollop of spirits into both of their snifters.

Longarm took his now cold cigar from the crystal ashtray by his elbow, and stuck it into the corner of his mouth without lighting it. "I was watching you handling those reporters this afternoon, Mr. Tompkins. You really know your business."

The little secretary beamed with pride. "Thank you, sir. I must say that I've been at it a long while. Twenty years in the newspaper trade before I started my own public-relations business."

"Uh-huh," Longarm murmured. "Have you been with the congressman long?"

Tompkins drained his snifter in one swallow. He was beginning to look a little flushed. "You don't think Miss Starbuck would mind if I had a bit more, do you, Deputy? It helps me get to sleep, don't you know."

Longarm grinned. "I think Miss Starbuck would be terribly insulted if you didn't help yourself."

"Ah . . . good!" Tompkins poured himself another drink, and then busied himself refilling his briar and firing it up. "Yessir, twenty years in Washington covering the political beat. And then six more years on my own. Do you know, Deputy—"

"Call me Longarm, Mr. Tompkins."

"And you call me Leo! Anyway, do you know that when I started out as a boy on the staff of the *Gazette,* I got to meet Abraham Lincoln himself?"

"No kidding, Leo?" Longarm poured a little more brandy into the press secretary's glass.

"Yes indeedy!" Tompkins boasted. "And then the poor man was assassinated!" Tompkins suddenly began to blubber. "I hate to admit it," he whispered, "but his getting assassinated was my big break."

"How so?" Longarm asked, enjoying himself. He knocked back his own brandy and helped himself to another shot. "Were you assigned to the White House so early in your career?"

Tompkins threw back his head and laughed uproariously. "Oh, that's rich!" he finally managed to gasp, wiping the tears from his bloodshot eyes. "No, Longarm, you see, I was the paper's second-string drama critic. The first critic was sick, so—"

Longarm's eyes widened. "Don't tell me you were—?"

"At Ford's Theater." Tompkins nodded, smiling. "I'll never forget the sound of that shot. I turned around in my seat and stared up at the Presidential box. Then all hell broke loose. I hightailed it back to the newspaper, and set to work writing up a profile of John Wilkes Booth. You see, since I was the second-string drama critic, and Booth was an actor, I knew where all of his biographical information was on file."

"Incredible," Longarm marveled.

Tompkins nodded. "My story appeared on the front page, with a byline! I did articles on Booth during those terrible days following the assassination, and pretty soon I built up a small reputation for myself. Another newspaper hired me on as a full-fledged news reporter covering the Capital." He shrugged. "And that was how it happened."

"That's a great story," Longarm said. "And you've been on your own for six years, you say?" Tompkins nodded as he raised his brandy snifter to his lips. "Have you been working for the congressman for all that time?" Longarm asked, pouring the now rather tipsy secretary another drink.

"Oh, my, no!" Tompkins laughed. "Congressmen rarely hire press secretaries, you see. No, I joined Barston's staff less than two months ago. It was then that he decided to enter the race for the Presidency." Tompkins leaned across the table as if to confide in Longarm, apparently forgetting that there was no one in the room to overhear their conversation. "You may not realize it, young fellow, but you can't believe everything you read in the papers."

"Really?" Longarm bit down on his cigar to keep his expression absolutely deadpan.

Tompkins nodded seriously. "When you've been around the big boys as long as I have, you know that you've got to be able to control the news if you want to succeed." He tapped himself on the chest. "That's where I come into the picture. A man like Barston wouldn't get anywhere if it weren't for me."

"I never doubted that for a moment," Longarm said wryly. "But since you've only been with him a couple of months, you really don't know very much about him, I gather?"

Tompkins shrugged. "What's to know? He's rich, handsome, educated at the best universities on the Continent, and well connected politically. I could handle this campaign in my sleep."

Longarm leaned forward. "You really think he's going to make it, don't you?"

Tompkins pursed his lips sagaciously. He looked sober enough, but when he spoke his voice was slurred. "Barston's a shoo-in for the nomination. Whether he can go all the way . . ." Once again, Tompkins shrugged. "Who's to say? I'll tell you this, Longarm. He's a favorite son of Texas. His political future is assured. If he doesn't make it into the White House this time around, he can always try again in four years. Sooner or later, Wilson Barston is going to be the President of the United States."

"Sooner or later," Longarm repeated softly, and then sighed. "I wish I didn't believe you."

Tompkins snickered appreciatively. "I've heard that before. Anyway, you should be asking Miss Starbuck about all this. She's the key. Her endorsement may well spell the difference between sooner and later."

Longarm looked rueful. "You're not as drunk as I thought."

"But drunker than I ought to be." Tompkins stood up, knocking over the brandy bottle in the process. "Dear me," he clucked. "We've drunk all of Miss Starbuck's frightfully expensive brandy."

"I wouldn't fret over it, Leo," Longarm comforted him.

Tompkins giggled. "She is rather well off, isn't she? So's Barston, you know. Their fathers were the best of friends."

"I know," Longarm said.

"They've been out enjoying the moonlight for a quite a while, haven't they?" Tompkins said. "Quite a lovely couple they make. Oh, how I wish they'd announce their intentions to get married!" He clasped his hands to his chest, overwhelmed with emotion. "What I could do with a story like that!" He leaned against his chair's back, and squinted at Longarm in an attempt to focus his eyes. "Well, I've chewed your ear long enough, young fellow. Thank you for keeping me company while I got drunk."

Longarm stood up. "It was a pleasure, Leo."

Tompkins shook hands with him. "That's one thing the newspaper business teaches you, how to get drunk." He stuck his pipe and tobacco pouch into his coat pocket and lurched off toward the staircase that led up to the second-floor bedrooms.

"Can you make it all right by yourself?" Longarm asked.

Tompkins waved reassuringly in Longarm's general direction. "I've had years of practice."

Longarm watched him make his way upstairs. He listened to Tompkins unsteady footsteps on the landing above, and then to the sound of the secretary's bedroom door shutting. Then Longarm was all alone.

He drained the last of his brandy, thinking that Tompkins had been right; Jessie and Barston had been out on their moonlight stroll for quite a while.

As he stood there ruminating, the double doors that led to the kitchen opened a notch. Myobu poked her head into the room. She glanced at the dirty coffee cups and brandy snifters on the table, and then questioningly at Longarm.

"I guess you never sleep, is that right, Grandmother?"

Myobu giggled, but still hesitated to enter until Longarm waved her into the room. She seemed to glide gracefully across the floor, rather than walk. Longarm wondered how old she was. He watched her gather up the soiled crockery on a tray. She was wearing a plain gray cotton kimono. Her white hair was tightly rolled in a bun. Her small round face, as delicate and translucent as the finest porcelain from her homeland, had a good share of wrinkles, but her sparkling black eyes were still those of a young girl.

Jessie had told Longarm Myobu's story during his first visit to the Starbuck spread, back when he was investigating her father's murder. In her youth, Myobu had been a renowned geisha, a courtesan of the highest rank, with a place of honor in the Emperor's royal court. Eventually she became young Alex Starbuck's paramour. It was to Myobu's sage business counsel that Starbuck owed his initial success. Many years later, after Starbuck's wife was murdered, he begged the recently retired Myobu to come to America as Jessie's nanny and teacher. With Starbuck's blessings, Myobu taught Jessie the Japanese art of negotiating in business, and the geisha's art of love. . . .

"Did Jessie's lessons include how to pick a husband?" Longarm sighed out loud.

Myobu glanced at him and giggled. That was to be expected, seeing that the old woman did not speak English.

"And I don't speak Japanese," Longarm told her. "The only other lingo I know is a bit of Spanish."

Myobu nodded and giggled.

"But I don't guess you've spent much time south of the border. . . ."

The housekeeper picked up her heavily laden tray and hustled it back to the kitchen.

Longarm watched the front door of the house for a few moments. He was tired, but somehow not ready to go upstairs to his room. He willed the congressman and Jessie to return from their stroll, but then thought better of his wish. What would he say to them? For all he knew, they were staying outside just to garner themselves a bit of privacy.

He trudged upstairs to his room, undressed quickly, and climbed into bed. The last thing he did before turning down his lantern was to stash his Colt underneath his pillow, assuring himself that it was in condition to fire. Longarm had not forgotten the trick he'd played on Bert the bank robber—wedging a bit of matchstick into his gun's mechanism. Thorn had gone upstairs earlier, which meant that he'd had the opportunity to tamper with Longarm's gun, which had been left in the room.

But nobody had tampered with his Colt. Longarm shoved it back underneath his pillow and dimmed the light. He tossed and turned for several minutes until he heard the front door open, followed by Jessie's silvery laugh. The fact that she was in the house safe and sound seemed to relax him. He was sound asleep in seconds.

Longarm's eyes sprang open. The house was deathly still. He could hear its timbers creaking, and the night's cool breezes whistling faintly in the eaves.

He squinted at his pocket watch on the nightstand beside his bed. The faint glow of the lantern was just barely enough for him to make out the time: 2:00 A.M.

Damn, Longarm mused sourly. *It's that time of night when there isn't a thing to do but sleep, and here I am wide awake.*

The wine and brandy he'd imbibed at dinner must have worn off, Longarm decided. What else would explain the sour taste in his mouth and the dull throbbing in his head? He swung his long legs out of bed and drank deeply from the carafe of water on the washstand, rinsing his mouth clean. Now that he was literally up, he found that he no longer had any desire to go back to sleep. He opened the window and inhaled a few gulps of fresh air, clearing the cobwebs from his brain.

The night was crisp and cool. Longarm spied a late-night sliver of moon, low behind the rustling leaves of a grove of hickory trees. Close by, the windows of the bunkhouse were dark; all the hands were sleeping. Longarm, his eyes grown used to the night, watched a good-sized, silvery gray shape slink across the clearing before disappearing into the trees.

A moment later, a doleful yowling reached his ears. *I guess there ain't a thing awake on this spread but me and the ranch's tom cat,* Longarm thought.

The tom's caterwauling song of longing continued. *And both of us are awake for the same reason,* Longarm concluded, shaking his head.

He decided to go out for a stroll and maybe a smoke. Being out in the open, beneath the sky, had a way of calming him. Being able to see mountains or rivers, or the moon and stars allowed him to put things in their proper perspectives.

There was a lot he had to chew on—for instance, his feelings concerning Jessie and Barston. Personally, he couldn't stomach the congressman, but if Jessie saw something in the man, that was *her* affair. What Longarm had to concentrate on was keeping Barston alive. Whether he liked the man or not, there now seemed to be hard evidence that the cartel was out to get him. Yesterday's assassination attempt was obviously calculated to scare Barston. But the congressman hadn't scared—Longarm had to give him that—which meant that the next time the cartel tried something, they'd be shooting to kill.

I'm the only one who can stop them, Longarm told himself as he dispensed with his longjohns and pulled on his trousers. *Thorn is worse than useless. His being around only makes Barston feel safe.* He shoved his feet into his boots, and his arms through the sleeves of his flannel shirt, not bothering to button the garment. Out of habit he reached for his Colt, but decided that it wasn't worth the bother of carrying it. Instead, he took his derringer from the pocket of his vest and tucked it into the top of his boot. Sure, the entire Prussian army—or Thorn—could be out there waiting in ambush on the off-chance that Longarm would wake up and take a walk, but somehow he just didn't think so. . . .

Longarm had survived a long time in a very dangerous job. He'd done it by keeping track of things, by being careful, by not thinking he was being silly when he kept his Colt beneath his pillow. He'd done it by trusting his instincts when they told him to crumple up balls of newspaper and scatter them between his bed and the door to afford him an extra moment of warning, should an intruder enter the room.

But there was a great difference in being a careful, prudent lawman and being a skittish, high-strung bundle of nerves. Longarm had seen it happen more than once: the sudden shootouts and tense, terse confrontations with armed fugitives got under the hides of some men. For some, there came a day when they just couldn't face that inevitable walk into a dark alley with nothing for company but a cocked Colt. When a man took on the job of upholding the law, shadows really did have a way of jumping out at him. Not all shadows, but just enough to get him dead and buried if he relaxed his guard a fraction too much.

The pressure drove some of them to the bottle, or made them so quick to draw and fire that they ended up murdering some poor fellow who just happened to be reaching for a smoke.

109

Longarm had made himself a promise that he'd quit if the job ever became too much for him. That hadn't happened yet, and he expected that it never would. Fear wasn't his enemy, it was his friend. Just now it had reminded him to take a gun along on his stroll. Deciding to take the derringer instead of the Colt kept fear in its proper place.

Longarm snatched a cheroot and some matches from his coat and left his bedroom, moving silently along the corridor to the top of the stairs. He was halfway down when he spied a huddled form wrapped in a blanket, sitting before the fireplace. Small flames crackled fitfully, casting tall shadows against the smoke-blackened walls of the great slate hearth.

One of the steps beneath Longarm's boots creaked, alerting the blanket-wrapped figure that somebody else was entering the room. The figure turned, letting the blanket slip, revealing a tousled mass of long blond curls, glinting with a coppery sheen in the lambent light cast by the little fire.

"I'd about given up hope," Jessie laughed softly. "I've been sitting here watching the flames, willing you to wake up."

"Here I am," Longarm smiled. "Although I must admit, my hangover had something to do with my being here."

"And I've got something for your hangover." Jessie reached down beside her and then held up a bottle. "Kentucky bourbon. Come drink your share." She tilted the bottle to reveal that it was only three-quarters full. "I've already had mine, I'm ashamed to admit."

Longarm walked over to the fireplace and sat down beside Jessie on the sheepskin rug. "All I brought was a smoke," he shrugged, grinning.

Jessie handed him the bottle in exchange for the cheroot. She struck a match against the stone hearth and drew deeply on the cigar. "Thank the Lord!" she groaned, exhaling. "All you men puffing away really got me in the mood to smoke. Of course, you're the only man I know who can watch a woman smoking without considering it a hanging offense. I never smoke, you know—except when I'm around you, it seems." She paused and sighed. "I'm babbling."

"Reckon so." Longarm took a sip from the bottle.

"We have to talk," Jessie said, fixing her big green eyes on him. "There are some things to be straightened out between us."

Longarm took a deep breath. "There ain't anything to talk about, dammit!"

Jessie flinched, surprised by the intensity of his reaction. "No need to get riled...."

"I *ain't* riled!" Longarm looked away. "All I mean is that I understand about you and the congressman. Hell, Jessie, you're both from the same station in life, if you know what I mean. Your daddies were best of friends. Hell, your father probably always had it in mind that you'd end up marrying Wilson Barston."

"My daddy thought Wilson wasn't worth the powder to blow him up."

Longarm glanced up to see an amused expression on Jessie's face. "But—"

"But nothing, Custis!" Jessie scowled. "Sure, my father and Wilson's father were good friends. After all, the two of them were among the first real cattle barons in Texas, and back in those days, good men were few and far between. When a friendship got forged, it got forged sound and true. If you knew anything about Alex Starbuck, however, you'd know that he'd never dream of trying to pick my husband for me."

"I'm sorry, Jessie," Longarm muttered. "I should've known...." He let his voice trail off.

"Should have known *what?*" Jessie demanded, exasperated. "Give me the bottle! I declare, trying to handle you could drive a woman to drink!"

"All I meant was that I should have known you'd picked Barston on your own, that's all," Longarm growled, his own temper on the rise. "Now, I said that I didn't want to talk about it and I meant it!"

"Wait just one damned minute!" Jessie ordered, silencing him. "Who said I was going to marry Wilson Barston?"

Longarm stared at her. "You're not?"

"I thought you didn't want to talk about it," Jessie murmured coolly, her eyes sparkling with mischief.

Longarm took her by the shoulders and gently but firmly shook her. "Don't you toy with me, woman," he said.

111

Jessie gazed up him. She saw the fire in his blue eyes even as she heard the husk of passion in his voice. "No . . . I guess I'd better not," she breathed. "Not that I ever meant to." She suddenly found herself trembling at the touch of his fingers upon her, but not from fear. No, the emotion that Jessie was feeling in response to Longarm's touch, the thick warmth radiating from her soft center, turning her arms and legs weak, had absolutely nothing to do with fear. . . .

A moment later, Longarm had her locked in his strong embrace. "Why, you're not marrying him at all," he said as he pressed his face into the fragrant mass of her hair. "Not at all." His tone betrayed his relief.

Jessie hugged him tightly. They stayed locked together in silence for a little while, and then both of them pulled away, chuckling nervously. Their faces were flushed and their hearts were pounding.

"You're not wearing anything underneath that blanket, are you?" Longarm asked. "It didn't feel like you were."

"No need to exaggerate," Jessie teased. "Actually I'm wearing a silk negligee." She held open the blanket. "See?"

Longarm saw. "You're right," he gasped. "There's no need to exaggerate."

The negligee consisted of a silken kimono-like top and a pair of loosely fitting, gauze trousers. The kimono was waist-length, and had wide sleeves. A red satin sash held it closed. The loosely tied bow and thin, flouncy silk material proved to be no match for the thrust of Jessie's firm breasts. The kimono gaped open to reveal the full extent of her cleavage. One of Jessie's pink nipples played a delightful game of "now you see me, now you don't" from behind the silken border of the kimono as her bosom rose and fell with her breathing. The gauze-like material of her pants revealed almost everything. The little the garment did hide only served to make the rest of her more enticing and delectable, if such a thing was possible. Longarm could see the barest hint of the golden patch between her thighs. He gazed at her soft belly, at the curve and swell of her slender waist and flaring hips, and then at the long, graceful lines of her flawless legs, accented by the soft folds of see-through fabric. The gauze was so delicate-looking that Longarm was sure it would fall away at the lightest touch. And how he felt like making that gauze part—right after he finished popping the straining buttons of his fly....

"As I said," Jessie smiled, "I was hoping you'd come downstairs. Slide over here and hold me for a while. I want to be close to the fire; this outfit doesn't exactly keep a person warm."

"Wouldn't know," Longarm cracked, wrapping her in his arms. "I never wore anything like that."

"Well, this isn't the sort of outfit you pick up in your average general store," Jessie agreed wryly. She snuggled against him. "Hmmm, this feels good." She hesitated. "Hey, something's bothering you, I can feel it."

"Of course you can feel it," Longarm joked. "It's only natural that a man gets hard like that when he's close to a beautiful woman—"

"No!" Jessie giggled. "Not *that* thing! Another thing."

"Well..." Longarm sighed. "I'm wondering how and why you let this rumor about you and Barston get started."

Jessie shrugged. "The *how* is easy. Wilson spread it around. He had his man Tompkins plant it in the society columns of the country's major newspapers. As to the why..." Jessie twisted around so as to be able to see Longarm. "I never intended to marry Wilson. God, I can't even remember the first time he asked me. But whenever it was, I knew instantly that I could never be his wife. Or even—" Jessie paused.

"What?" Longarm coaxed.

"*You* know," she said, blushing. "I mean, most women would consider him quite a handsome man, but there's something about him that keeps me from even wanting to kiss him, let alone make love to him."

Longarm showed his relief before he could stop himself. Jessie, still leaning against him, giggled in delight. "I knew you were concerned—"

Longarm nodded. "It wasn't exactly jealousy."

"I know it wasn't," Jessie replied softly. "We're both a lot alike, Longarm. We haven't seen each other in a long while, and we sure haven't been celibate during that time apart—"

"Jessie—"

"Hush, let me finish," she insisted. "I knew that you'd be concerned—more for my well-being than your own self-interest—if you thought I was romantically involved with Bar-

113

ston. Well, I'm not, and as far as I'm concerned, I never will be."

Longarm grinned. "I reckon I forgot that you're the only woman who has some idea about how I think, and—" He stopped, suddenly aware that he didn't know how to say what he felt.

"Hush," Jessie said. "That's how I feel about you, but I don't know how to put it into words, either."

"But if you're so certain you don't feel anything for Barston, why have you encouraged him by keeping mum the way you have?" Longarm asked.

Jessie fidgeted uneasily. "I guess I'd better start from the beginning," she said. "Wilson and I knew each other as children. The Barston cattle ranch is several days' journey from here, but we still managed to maintain our sporadic friendship, at least until we became adolescents. That was when Wilson was sent to Europe to continue his education. We lost touch with each other during those years when children become adults. The next time we saw each other was when I took one of my trips to the Continent, before the start of my final year at the university."

"You both must have done a lot of growing up by then," Longarm observed.

"Yes." Jessie smiled. "Physically as well as intellectually. We were both shocked. Wilson had been expecting to see a skinny tomboy of a girl with pigtails. For my part, I'd expected a gawky, clumsy boy with pimples." Jessie's eyes sparkled with the memories. "And we had so many things to talk about! Cultural things, as opposed to whose daddy had more cows."

"Reckon that university life does broaden a person," Longarm remarked dryly.

Jessie shook her head. "Some men don't need it," she told him with sincerity.

Longarm chuckled. "It's not that all folks don't need an education," he corrected her, "but some figure out a way to make up for what they can't get. Anyway, his being a young stallion, and you being—well, *you*—I reckon that soon enough Barston's mind moved off of culture."

Jessie blushed and nodded. "But even then, there was something about Wilson that warned me off. Wilson had hinted that

114

we might have a future together, and I couldn't get the idea out of my mind, despite my revulsion against his physical advances. Once again we lost touch. The next time his name came up was when he ran for Congress. My father supported his campaign out of friendship to Wilson's father. I remember Daddy mentioning to me that he had his doubts about Wilson. . . ."

"I know what your father meant," Longarm nodded. "There's a lot to doubt about the congressman."

"Oh, pooh," Jessie scolded. "You're that way with all figures of authority. You never willingly took an order in your life, Longarm. It's your natural way to lock horns with all the other bulls in the herd."

Longarm shook his head. "Only the ones that don't know what they're bellowing about," he told her firmly. "I don't go out of my way to buck my superiors, but life's too short to put up with fools."

"Well, there's a lot of the braggart about Wilson," Jessie was quick to agree. "But he's damned good at what he does."

Longarm relit the cheroot. "It doesn't ease my mind to think that Barston's typical of the sort of fellows we've sent to Washington."

"Believe me, he's not the worst," Jessie said grimly. "Anyway, I didn't hear from Barston until after it came out that the Prussians were behind the murder of my father. As you recall, Longarm, you and I were able to link the Governor of Texas into the cartel's scheme. . . ."

"Yep. I gather that Ki made good on his vow to persuade the Governor to retire from office, and in that way avoid a scandal?"

"That's how it happened," Jessie replied. "Barston, as a Texan congressman, found out about the cartel's doings. He wrote to me with a request for my help in his Congressional investigation into the extent of the Prussians' influence in this country. Barston was quite sympathetic to my desire to keep my family's name out of the newspapers. He allowed me to testify behind closed doors."

"His investigation never got very far," Longarm mused. "Seems to me that you and Ki have done more to confound the Prussians than our government has. . . ."

"You're very right, I'm sorry to say," Jessie shrugged. "But we mustn't blame that on Barston. One congressman, no matter how influential, can only do so much. Mobilizing federal might against the Prussians is something that Barston intends to do when he's elected President," she added quietly.

"Is that why you're backing him?" Longarm asked. "Because he's against your enemies?"

"That's why I'm *thinking* of backing him," Jessie said.

"Say, I'll bet your decision not to squash the rumors linking the two of you romantically has something to do with helping his candidacy?"

"That's true," Jessie admitted. "I figured that there was little harm in allowing Barston's secretary to get some extra publicity for the candidate. I assure you that I've planned all along to put a stop to the talk before it goes too far."

Longarm was quiet for a moment. "I had a talk with Tompkins earlier this evening. He seems to think that your support is what'll decide whether Barston makes it to the White House."

"Barston's father left his son a legacy of old friends, as well as great wealth," Jessie said. "Those friends are influential, but only in Texas. Starbuck has assorted business concerns stretching all across the country. Each of those offices has some people who are influential in their own home states. A Presidential campaign would find such support invaluable."

"You haven't answered my question," Longarm reminded her gently.

"What?"

"Can you get him elected if you choose to?"

Jessie pulled herself free of Longarm's embrace, and turned around to face him. "I don't know if I can," she said honestly. "And I don't know if I even want to try! I mean, on one hand, I have just as much right as any United States citizen to back the candidate of my choice. I'm not a king-maker."

"Nobody said you were," Longarm agreed.

"I mean," Jessie blurted, "it's the people who decide who they want to be President."

Longarm's eyes narrowed cynically. "Up to a point."

Jessie pouted. "You don't let a girl get away with anything, do you? Well, I guess I *could* help him get elected." She sighed in resignation. "What I'm unsure about is whether it's morally right for me to support somebody for such an important job on the strength of one issue, that being Barston's stance against the cartel. And that's as much as I've figured out about the whole question. I just don't know what to do, and Wilson needs my decision on this matter within the next couple of days. He told me that he wants to make the announcement of my endorsement of his candidacy during the fair."

"You haven't got much time."

"I *know* that!" Jessie scowled.

"What about your decision not to marry him?"

"Longarm!" Jessie scolded. "Don't start on that again, I can't bear it! For your information, during our stroll after dinner, I told Wilson that I could never marry him."

"You did?" Longarm asked, relieved.

"Yes." Jessie smiled slightly. "Satisfied?"

Longarm held up his hands in surrender. Jessie, laughing, laced her fingers through his and pushed him down so that she could stretch out on top of him. She ran her fingers through his thick brown hair, and began to nibble kisses along the strong line of his jaw.

"Jessie," Longarm whispered, "I'm glad to know the truth about you and Barston."

"I'm glad I've told you," she replied. "I hated the tension I felt between us. Now that you know everything, it's like a great weight off my shoulders."

Longarm slid his hands beneath the blanket wrapped around Jessie, gliding his palms down along her shivering spine, to caress the satiny mounds of her bottom beneath the tantalizingly sheer gauze pants. Jessie pressed her mouth against his for a lingering kiss. She giggled as she pressed herself against the rock-hard swelling at the front of his trousers.

"We'd better do something about that," she whispered, tracing his throbbing length with her fingers. "Unless, of course, you have some more questions?" she asked dreamily.

Longarm flipped her over so that she was lying on her back, cushioned by the thick sheepskin rug, with the blanket bunched beneath her. He nudged apart the silk kimono, so that Jessie's breasts were bared. "I've got just one last question," he murmured, flicking his tongue against her nipples, making her writhe with pleasure.

"Oh? What? What question?" she purred.

Longarm paused. "Just what was it that Myobu said to me in Japanese during dinner? Whatever it was, it made you blush as red as a beet!"

Jessie laughed. "That! She said that whenever Longarm comes, she is obliged to make up a special breakfast drink for me to replenish my strength."

"I see. An old geisha trick, huh?"

"From an old geisha," Jessie agreed. "Now would you get back to what you started?" She guided Longarm's head back down to her breasts. "Nobody likes a quitter, you know."

Longarm obeyed her command. Her nipples rose up hard and swollen as he sucked them. His tongue worked its way down her cleavage, a scent as fragrant as wildflowers made him dizzy.

"I dabbed myself with perfume, all over," Jessie murmured lazily while her fingers absently stroked the back of his head. "I wanted to be special for you. . . ." her voice trailed off, and her breathing became regular.

"Jessie?" Longarm glanced up. Her eyes were closed. "I'll be damned," he chuckled.

Briefly, Longarm entertained the thought of nudging her awake, but she seemed to be sleeping so soundly that he just didn't have the heart. Sighing, he scooped her up in his arms and carried her upstairs to her bedroom. Jessie hardly stirred all during the trip.

Longarm was just tucking her into her bed when her eyes blinked open. "What?" she mumbled sleepily. "Where am I? What happened? Oh, my! Custis, I'm sorry!"

"Don't fret," Longarm smiled down at her.

"It's just that it's been such a long day, and I've had so much to drink tonight, and I felt so relieved over our conversation by the fire, and it felt *soooo* good when you were kissing my breasts—" She pounded her fists against the mattress in frustration. "I can't believe I fell asleep!" She yawned. "And I still can't keep my eyes open." She shook herself. "But I will," she promised. "Pretty soon . . ."

"Go back to sleep," Longarm told her. "We've got plenty of time for lovemaking. Anyway, I want you when you're wide awake. I can't do *all* the work, you know."

118

"But we don't have time!" Jessie argued sadly. "Wilson's determined to wire Marshal Vail the first thing tomorrow morning, before the shooting match. By evening, Vail may well have ordered you back to Denver."

"No chance of that," Longarm told her. "You see, what I neglected to mention to the congressman is that Vail is out on a case of his own. He's trailing Wink Turner's outlaw band, trying to keep them from raiding this fair."

"Then you won't be leaving?"

"Nope."

Jessie nestled back against the pillows, pulling her blankets up around her chin. "G'night, Custis . . ."

Longarm stared down at her. He thought about the cool, slippery feel of her negligee and the warm resilience of her perfume-scented body beneath the silk. "Just promise me one thing," he sighed.

"Ummm?"

"Tomorrow morning you'll have a double portion of that drink Myobu's making for you."

Jessie smiled with her eyes closed. "Kiss me goodnight?"

Longarm bent to do as he'd been asked. Jessie twitched her nose in response to the tickling brush of his mustache, and then settled back into the rhythmic inhalations and exhalations of slumber.

She waited until Longarm had reached the bedroom door before calling out, "I love you," pretending to have said it while asleep.

Longarm pretended not to have heard. He stepped out into the corridor, shutting the door quietly behind him.

He stood indecisively at the railing, looking down at the first floor. He still wasn't sleepy. If anything, the thudding ache he now felt in his balls would serve to keep him wide-eyed for some hours to come. *Might as well stick to my original plan,* he decided ruefully, heading downstairs for his stroll out of doors.

He stopped by the fireplace to retrieve his half-smoked cheroot, and then continued on out the front door.

The cool night air refreshed him. Longarm grinned as he listened to the tomcat, which was still serenading the darkness with its plaintive wail.

"You can say that again, old son," Longarm quietly told the caterwauling tom. He himself was walking with a slightly bowlegged gait in order to spare his cramped and swollen balls. He headed toward the grove of hickories, and was just about to scratch a match against a tree trunk in order to light up his cheroot, when he was startled by the sound of doors squeaking open on rusty hinges.

Longarm bent to tug his derringer from his boot-top, and then glided as stealthily as any cat in the direction of the sound. He hunkered down behind a watering trough to watch Thorn exiting from the stables, pausing to shut the doors behind him. The bodyguard had changed out of his fancy dinner clothes and back into his leather jacket and black denims. *Riding clothes,* Longarm mused. *And by the dust all over him, he's just come back from a hard ride to somewhere. . . .*

Thorn was carrying his Winchester and a set of saddlebags. Longarm thanked his own good luck that he had been upstairs with Jessie when the bodyguard rode into the stables to unsaddle his horse.

Sure wish I knew where he's been, Longarm thought to himself. He stayed hidden and kept his derringer handy until Thorn had entered the house. *Be just like that jasper to swing around and peg a few shots in my direction, then claim that he'd thought I was a cartel assassin. I wonder if Jessie saw him go out?*

Longarm made a mental note to ask her about it tomorrow. He thought about Thorn's Winchester, and how interesting it might be to compare a slug from that long gun with the bullet he'd dug out of the Cattlemen's building this afternoon, the bullet supposedly fired from one of the cartel's guns.

Midnight rides to who knew where, cartel calling cards suddenly being produced—Longarm's head was spinning. There was so much to resolve, very little time, and getting to the bottom of things was going to be even tougher than usual. A federal marshal's badge served as a symbol of authority to most folks, but a heavyweight congressman like Barston had the ability to counter a lawman's badge with power of his own.

Well, we'll just eat this apple one bite at a time, Longarm told himself. He smoked the remainder of his cheroot in peace, and then went back to the house and upstairs to bed.

* * *

Jessie, hearing Longarm's footsteps as they passed her closed door, turned uneasily in her sleep. She'd been dreaming about the lawman, some crazy dream where he'd announced his candidacy for Mayor of Sarah, and was giving his speech in her father's study without a stitch of clothing on except for his gunbelt. . . .

Something was troubling her, but Jessie couldn't put her finger on it. Whatever it was, it was keeping her from relaxing totally. . . .

"Ki," Jessie said suddenly, her eyes springing open. "Ki . . ." She hadn't seen him since this morning. The samurai was all alone in town, and totally unaware that the cartel's henchmen could strike against him at any time!

★

Chapter 6

Ki opened his eyes, wondering what had awakened him. He held his breath, focusing his keen sense of hearing as he stared into the suffocatingly stuffy blackness of his hotel room in Sarah.

Everything *seemed* quiet. The darkness outside his window told him it was still a long while until dawn. He strained his ears, but heard nothing. Perhaps it had been his imagination. No, the samurai did not think that likely. Perhaps he had reacted to some fleeting dream. . . .

There! The sound! It *was* real, after all. Ki was more satisfied than frightened. It would never do for a samurai to start imagining things. As to the fact that there was indeed an intruder fiddling with the lock to his door—well, that intruder would find to his sorrow that it was exceedingly difficult to sneak up on a samurai.

And exceedingly dangerous, Ki grinned, anticipating a good fight. He reached down to pluck a *shuriken* throwing blade— a four-inch dagger without hilt or handle—from its place of concealment under the bed's mattress. He then sat up, letting his blanket fall away from his naked torso, and glanced around, trying to devise a strategy.

The room he'd been given was on the top floor of the hotel. Actually, it was more of a cupola stuck on the roof, than a room. The hotel had been booked solid because of the fair. The management had rented him this humble space strictly as a favor, seeing that Ki had volunteered to help police the unruly crowds that had flocked to Sarah. The cupola was so tiny that there was no room for furnishings other than a bed and a dresser. There was one large window, which did not open. It looked out over the eaves and gables of the hotel's sprawling roof. The door to the monklike cell was at the bottom of a short but steep flight of stairs that led down to the top floor's public corridor.

It was that door that was just now clicking open.

Ki wondered what to do. Anywhere he chose to stand in the tiny room, he would be backlit by the big window, making him visible to whoever was just now creeping up the staircase. Ki decided to pretend he was still asleep. He lay back, drawing up the covers and closing his eyes, but he kept his *shuriken* balanced for throwing on the tips of his fingers. He had more *shuriken*—both blades and throwing stars—secreted in his vest, but the garment had been put away in the dresser. No matter, one blade would be enough. The slight creaking of the staircase's floorboards told him that whoever was coming for him was all alone.

The samurai wondered who the intruder might be. The logical assumption was that one of the fellows he had beaten up at the pond was returning for another go at it. But why would just one of those louts dare to return? No, either all three would have come, or none at all. . . .

Well, whoever it was, he was certainly taking his time, Ki thought irritably. All this while, and the intruder had only managed to make it halfway up the short staircase. Ki was anxious for the relief from tension that some action would bring. He had been tense and restless ever since he'd parted from Phoebe at the fairgrounds this afternoon. Her sexy body and carefree manner had left him feeling quite randy. Ki was looking forward to seeing her tomorrow, and perhaps tomorrow evening as well.

But first things first, Ki thought. The intruder had reached the top of the stairs and was now approaching the bed. The samurai kept his eyes closed, charting the man's progress by the minute ticking of the floorboards. This fellow was good, Ki had to admit. The intruder was making very little noise as he walked....

A sweet scent in the air startled Ki. *Perfume?*

The realization made Ki want to laugh. Yes, this intruder was very good at moving quietly, or else this intruder was very light of weight—too light to be a man. That meant the intruder had to be either a boy or a woman, and unless Ki was mistaken, there were very few boys in Texas who wore perfume!

There came the sound of a match being struck, and then the candle on top of the dresser began to sputter as its wick caught. Ki decided to take a chance. After all, how many killers would pause to illuminate the room before striking at a sleeping victim? He kept his eyes closed and lay very still as a delicate hand stripped away his blanket. He heard a feminine gasp of surprise and pleasure, and then the wispy sound of a garment falling to the floor.

Ki opened his eyes. He did not have to pretend to be amazed. He stared at the extremely lovely, totally nude woman standing at the foot of his bed. She was close to six feet tall, with wavy, strawberry-colored hair that hung down to her waist. The flickering candle revealed her figure to be rather boyish, with small breasts, slim hips, and a high, well-rounded backside. Right now, her stance was rather bashful and a bit pigeon-toed. Her flat belly was showing its oval navel, while down below, her strawberry patch of pubic hair tufted out as sassily as a billy goat's beard.

The bedframe creaked as the mystery woman knelt on the mattress beside Ki. She did not wait a moment or say a word before she began to stroke his semi-erect member to full, throbbing hardness.

"Who are you?" Ki gasped. "What are you doing?" He paused. "Never mind that last question, I can figure that out for myself!"

125

"My name's Aggie Cling." Nervously she twisted a tendril of her hair with one hand, and nervously twisted Ki's turgid member with her other. "Maybe you've heard of my sister Dot and me? We're sharpshooters."

"Ah, yes!" Ki exclaimed. "The Georgia Peaches..." As he spoke, he found himself gazing at Aggie's breasts. Although they were smallish, they were exceedingly pert, with warm pink rosettes that were just now beginning to crinkle, causing her nipples to rise as he stared. "Yes, indeed, the Georgia Peaches..."

He realized that he was still palming his *shuriken* blade, and quickly slid it back into its place under the mattress. It seemed inevitable that this confrontation was going to end in close-quarters physical combat, but it was a different sort of combat than what the samurai had originally envisioned, and it certainly called for a different sort of dagger....

"We— that is, my sister Dot and I—saw you patrolling the fairgrounds this afternoon," Aggie explained. "We were cleaning our pistols in preparation for tomorrow's match, and Dot— she's the brazen one of the family—"

"This is beyond belief," Ki sighed happily.

Aggie smiled demurely while her fingers danced up and down Ki's erection. "Anyway, Dot says to me, 'Lordy be! But watching that fellow strut around in those tight denims of his makes me want to oil up and do an extra *fine* job on this pistol's six-inch barrel!'"

Ki reached up to stroke her nipples gently between his thumbs and forefingers. "Go on, Aggie."

Aggie's eyelids began fluttering. "W-we're kind of used to six-inch barrels, you see...."

"It is not barrel length that counts, but *caliber*," Ki remarked. "What is needed is enough power in the chamber to obliterate the bullseye."

"You don't know much about guns," Aggie sighed as Ki continued tickling her nipples.

"About guns, no," he chuckled. "But a warrior always hits the bullseye." His agile fingers now found their way to the space between Aggie's slim thighs, and began to caress and stroke her there.

"Oh! That feels good!" she whimpered. "Oh... I'm *soooo*

glad I tipped the night clerk a dollar to tell me your room number! You know, when my sister made that naughty remark, I said, 'There isn't anything we can do but try our best to meet that fellow and see what he's carrying in his holster. If we don't, that handsome stud is going to cause our minds to wander during tomorrow's match. There isn't anything worse than mixing up a *man's* shooter with a *six*-shooter!'" Aggie bent down to take Ki's erection in her mouth, and began sucking greedily.

"What she means is, you do that to a gun barrel and it'll rust...."

Groaning with pleasure, Ki twisted his head around to see a woman identical in face and form to Aggie, except that this one had long blond hair. As Ki watched, the newcomer shed her dressing gown to stand naked before him. *Yes, they were identical twins.* "Hello, Dot," he gasped as Aggie, perhaps wanting his attention back, gave him a little nip.

"I heard that slurping sound, and I knew I'd better get on up here before there was nothing left for me," Dot giggled. "I've shared enough meals with my sister to know she doesn't waste any time before helping herself to seconds!"

"You were down there all the time?" Ki asked.

Dot nodded as she watched her sister's head bobbing up and down. "Aggie and I did eenie-meeni-minie-moe to see which one of us could come up first, and which one had to wait down there at the foot of your stairs. I lost," she pouted. "And it was my dollar that got us your room number. Hey, Aggie! Slow down! I don't want you hurting your neck."

Things *were* happening a little too fast, Ki mused. Even for a samurai! If he was going to put a stop to all of this, now was the time....

On the other hand, what was the harm in indulging in an escapade with these two extremely forthright, extremely experienced sisters? He *had* been feeling randy, unable to relax, and looking to expend some energy. Meditation had not helped, but then Ki, being a samurai, had always believed that meditation was a practice more properly reserved to the old; a young man *acted,* he did not contemplate....

"Aggieee," Dot whined anxiously. "Don't wear him out." Her nipples were swollen, and beads of moisture had appeared on her pubic thatch, which was the color of spun gold.

"Not him," Aggie drawled. She had a glazed expression on her face as she gave Ki's glistening member a loving kiss.

"Oh, goody!" Dot cried. "An all-day sucker!" She hurried to take her sister's place as Aggie moved on up to the head of the bed.

"I don't suppose you've ever gone up against two sharp-shooter females," Aggie teased Ki as she guided his head toward her parted thighs.

Ki's almond eyes glinted with humor. "To my credit, I have surmounted even stiffer odds."

"Well, I haven't." Dot gave Ki's jutting length a little squeeze before straddling him, slowly lowering herself down until she'd engulfed him to the hilt. With her eyes closed and her head thrown back in ecstasy, she began to rotate her hips like an Arabian belly dancer. Whimpers of pleasure escaped her lips as she rode him.

Ki, although he was enjoying himself, was not content to remain idle. His tongue flicked between Aggie's strawberry-furred, strawberry-sweet inner folds.

"Oh, Lordy!" Aggie moaned. "Oh! Oh!" Her head slammed back against the propped-up pillows as Ki's expert tongue homed in with stunning accuracy on her very core. "It's too much, I—I can't!" Aggie begged for mercy. She tried to pull away, but Ki's strong hands took firm hold of the plump cheeks of her bottom, locking her in place. Aggie struggled for another moment before Ki had her paralyzed with pleasure. She shuddered, and then surrendered totally to wave upon wave of delicious sensation, all the while laughing and crying like a woman gone insane.

Dot, meanwhile, seemed totally oblivious to her sister's conquest at the hands and mouth of the samurai. She was shiny with perspiration wrung out by her ride upon Ki's shaft. Her blond hair hung in damp ringlets as she leaned forward to pinch his nipples with her trembling fingers. The flush of sexual abandon had reddened her fair complexion and spread down to bring a delicate tint to her bobbing breasts.

"I'm starting!" she whimpered between her gasps and grunts. "I'm sopping wet!" She pressed her face to Ki's chest and began to pump her hips like a piston.

Ki remained silent, content to give himself up to the feel of her scorching furnace gripping and stroking him. He hugged her tightly, pressing her supple body against the ridged muscles of his stomach, and began to buck his hips, grinding against her. His climax sprouted in the depths of his soul. He was like a man on fire as he exploded inside her.

Dot stayed plastered to his chest, grunting in response to her own melting spasms of joy. Her tingling fingers and toes scrabbled for purchase upon the twisted, sweat-damp sheets as she used the last of her strength to milk Ki dry.

Aggie was slowly recovering from her own, earlier orgasm. She leaned against the bed's headboard and ran her fingers through Ki's matted hair.

"It's a good thing they stuck you all the way up here," she told the samurai fondly. "Otherwise our noises would have woken up the entire hotel."

"I'm surprised we didn't, anyway!" Dot said, stretching languorously. She began to nuzzle Ki's neck. "But who knows, we just might make all the other guests come running before we're through tonight."

"That's just the way I feel," Aggie nodded. "What do you say, sister? Time to change places?"

"I think perhaps I should be consulted in this matter," Ki suddenly laughed. "I swear, you two make it hard for a man to get a word in edgewise!"

"We've always been like that," Aggie chuckled. "We're as close as can be!"

"We've gone to great lengths—if you'll pardon the expression—to arrange our lives so that we can be together even at times like this," Dot chimed in.

We just can't get satisfaction unless we can be together," Aggie said.

"Have you ever tried?" Ki asked. He was fascinated by the Cling sisters' confession. His training in the arts of lovemaking had exposed him to many novel ways of performing the act, but he'd never before heard of such a situation.

"Yes, we have," Dot replied.

"But it's no use," Aggie finished. "If a man wants one of us, he's got to take both—"

129

"Unless, of course, we happen to find two men who are willing to make love to us in the same place at the same time," Dot giggled. "But that's another story."

"Yes, it is." Aggie winked at her sister. "Don't be saying too much about *that!*"

Ki sat up in order to look at the two twins. "I have heard of good things coming in threes, but never in pairs," he teased. "Are you quite sure that you were not born triplets?"

Aggie and Dot laughed in unison. "Nope! No more at home like us!" they chorused.

"Mama always said that the two of us were more than enough," Aggie elaborated. "She was thankful that we had different-colored hair so that she had some way of telling us apart!"

"Are you really *exactly* alike?" Ki asked. "Except for your hair color, I mean."

"Well, there is *one* other way to tell us apart," Dot murmured shyly. "But a person would have to look mighty close to see it."

"Let's show him," Aggie chuckled merrily.

She and her sister positioned themselves side by side upon the bed. They took a kneeling position, angling their bottoms toward the samurai.

"Well?" Dot demanded, with her head resting upon her folded arms. "See the difference between us?"

Ki stared as those two shapely, upthrust female backsides jiggling and twitching in time to the nervous laughter of the twins. "Well, I notice the difference in hair coloring from this angle, but aside from that . . ." the samurai mused distractedly.

"Come closer and take a good look!" Aggie scolded.

"We're not going to bite you!" Dot added.

"Quiet!" Aggie tittered. "Else you'll give *him* ideas!"

"You both *do* look good enough to eat," Ki said, moving closer in order to peer at the proffered pair of posteriors. "Both of you appear to be identically shaped, and the same lovely shades of ivory and pink . . . . But what is this?" Ki exclaimed, his eyes narrowing. Gently he touched the small, dark mole situated just at the cleft where the top of Aggie's thigh swelled into the full, round curve of her left buttock.

"Ooooh!" Aggie shivered. "You found the difference. That's my love button—one of them, anyway," she added wryly.

"She's got a mole there, and I don't," Dot explained. "And I'd be careful about touching that button if I were you," she warned Ki. "My sister gets positively *lewd* when she's touched there."

"I see what you mean...." Ki watched as Aggie reached behind to grab hold of his jutting erection and then guide herself backward until she managed to corkscrew him deep inside the wet cleft between her legs.

"Ooooh!" Aggie sang softly. "Dot had *so* much fun. I was just *dying* to try this end of you," she told Ki, who was standing still as Aggie gently swayed back and forth while resting on her hands and knees.

"Hey!" Dot whined like a little girl. "I want some attention!" She turned to face Ki, reaching around him in order to stroke the hard, ropey cords of muscle beneath the moist, tawny skin of his buttocks and back.

Ki began to play with Dot's breasts. He was only mildly surprised when Aggie began to moan and twitch as if it were *her* nipples being teased. After all, Dot seemed to be experiencing her sister's pleasure. She ground herself against Ki's pelvis, her teeth chattering as she came.

"S-sometimes," Aggie moaned, still sliding upon Ki's marble-hard shaft, *"I* can feel what gets done to my *sister!"*

"A-and—" Dot began, trying to find words.

"I know," Ki growled as he thrust into Aggie. "And *you* feel what I do to Dot!" He arched his back, spasming into Aggie as she tried her best to muffle her screams of pleasure by pressing her face into one of the pillows.

Ki collapsed on top of her, and Dot belly-flopped across *him*. The trio stayed like that for several minutes, and Ki enjoyed himself as he was cushioned and covered by the two layers of warm, soft, and fragrant flesh. Eventually the samurai crawled free of the tangle of arms and legs. He pulled on his denim jeans, and gathered up the scattered dressing gowns of his two visitors while their whimpers of contentment gradually subsided.

The first faint gray glimmer of dawn was coming through

the tiny room's big window. The ghostly light turned the turrets, pitches, and cupolas of the seemingly endless hotel roof into a miniature, sleeping town.

"It's almost morning," Aggie sighed. "I suppose we'd better scurry back to our rooms."

"Where is your suite?" Ki asked as he pinched out the candle.

"Just down the corridor," Aggie replied happily. She gestured toward the flight of stairs that led down to Ki's door. "This little room is sort of like an attic to the suites on the top floor of the hotel."

Ki glanced down the short, steep staircase. A glimmer shining in from the gas-illuminated corridor told the samurai that his door had come ajar. He chuckled to himself, wondering at the picture that might have been presented to some nosy hotel employee investigating the noise. . . .

"How did you get a key to unlock my door?" Ki asked the twins.

"We didn't," Dot replied. "We've been in show business a long time, you know. Before our sharpshooting act we toured Europe as the assistants to a magician. He was quite famous. We played a lot of command performances for private audiences, as well as the best show halls on the Continent. . . ."

"Anyway," Aggie cut in, "the magician had an escape trick that was a very important part of his act. He'd lock himself into a trunk, and then have us wrap chains around it. There was a variation on the trick where one of us would get locked in, so we had to learn how to open padlocks and deadbolts with picks."

Dot giggled. "Your door was easy. We used a hairpin."

"And you forgot to relock it," Ki scolded her mildly.

"I thought we did," Aggie said. She and her sister burrowed under Ki's blanket against the chill in the room.

The samurai went down the stairs to shut and relock the door. He was halfway back up when he glimpsed movement about ten feet beyond his window, out on the hotel's roof. Ki dropped down on all fours. He crawled up the steps until his eyes were just above the top of the staircase. He watched as a man crouched behind a short, squat wooden chimney and drew a pistol. The man rested his arm across the chimney's top, and aimed his gun at the lumps beneath the blanket on Ki's bed.

He thinks the twins are myself, asleep, Ki realized. The samurai did not waste a moment speculating upon the identity of the would-be killer, or upon why the man might wish to murder him. Instead he concentrated on how he might save the two women. Ki knew that if he did not move quickly, the career of the "Cling Peaches" would end here and now.

He noticed that a corner of the bedsheet had come untucked during their spirited lovemaking. Ki sprawled on his belly across the floor and gripped the length of sheet with his right hand. He pulled back upon it with all of his strength. He managed to haul the mattress from atop the bed, toppling it and its precious contents to the floor before the cotton sheet shredded in his hand.

The twins tumbled out of the line of fire just as three quick shots exploded the window inward, scattering shards of glass around the room. The bullets slammed into the wall opposite the window. Aggie and Dot lay shrieking and cowering. The mattress had landed on top of them. That, and the blanket they'd been wrapped in, protected them from the shower of needle-sharp glass fragments.

Ki felt a hot, stinging sensation as some glass peppered his forearms, raised protectively across his face. The cuts were dripping blood, but the samurai considered them nothing more than minor scratches.

The rooftop killer, realizing his mistake, now stood up to pump two more shots into the room. He fired quickly, in panic. The shots went wild.

Ki spied his *shuriken* blade lying on the floor where it had fallen when he'd pulled the mattress from the bed. He snatched it up as he rose to his feet in pursuit of the shooter.

"We've got to get back to our rooms," Aggie gasped. "We can't be found here! It'll ruin our reputations!"

"It'll be a scandal!" Dot whimpered in agreement.

Ki ignored them. He was already climbing out the broken window and onto the hotel's roof. He was barefoot, clad only in his denim jeans, but the leathery, callused soles of his feet ground the jagged bits of glass into powder. He had only one *shuriken* as he chased the killer across the sloping, dew-slippery shingles of the roof, but the samurai intended to kill his attacker only as a last resort. The man had to be taken alive if he was to reveal the motive for his attack.

The would-be killer was dressed like a drover, in faded blue trousers, a brown flannel shirt, and a rust-colored corduroy vest. He wore a brace of pistols around his waist, a high-crowned Stetson on his head, and a pair of scuffed, high-heeled boots on his feet. Just now it was his boots that were giving the man the most trouble. High heels kept a fellow's feet in the stirrups, but didn't do very much to help him keep his footing upon a rooftop.

Ki's bare feet, meanwhile, securely cupped the treacherously slanted shingles, allowing him to close in quickly. The killer, seeing that Ki was catching up, pegged another shot over his shoulder, and then drew his second gun.

Ki flitted from gable to chimney as he pursued the man. The other's sporadic shots never came close to the samurai, but they served to keep him from overtaking the man as easily as he otherwise could have.

"Give up!" the samurai called. "You will not escape."

The man did not answer, but aimed carefully, firing just as Ki scooted around from behind the protection of a soot-blackened, corrugated-tin ventilation cowl. The tin cowl acted more like a tin can. It was jolted off its mooring by the impact of the bullet. Ki's ears reverberated with the noisy clang of the cowl coming loose, and then he saw stars as the sharp-edged metal housing struck him a glancing blow on the side of his head. He lost his footing and tumbled for several heart-stopping moments down the incline toward the roof's edge, before his fingers dug into the crevices between the shingles, thus preventing him from hurtling off the roof to his death.

The man, meanwhile, had used the time to reload his pistols before continuing his escape. Ki scrambled up the incline to catch sight of him cutting across the shingled ridges and valleys before hopping a low wall onto the front half of the hotel.

Ki followed on rubbery legs. His head was still throbbing where the cowl had hit him. As the samurai rounded a corner, he saw a crowd pouring out of the hotel's entrance, six stories below.

"There he is!" a man shouted.

"Open up!" came a roared command.

That was Marshal Farley's voice, Ki had time to think, just as a fusillade of shots sent him back down on his belly, hugging the rooftop for cover. *The fools do not realize that there are two of us up here,* Ki realized as another volley of shots chipped wood from the gutters of the roof. The samurai took some measure of satisfaction in seeing that the man he was chasing had also been pinned down by the fire from the street below. It occurred to Ki that the crowd shooting at him had no idea that the man they really wanted to blast had passed this way scant seconds before they'd arrived.

"Keep it up, boys!" Farley was shouting. "You got the bastard pinned down!"

"Farley!" Ki yelled as loudly as he could. "Farley! Stop!" But it was no use. Ki's mouth was just about pressed against the shingles. He didn't dare raise his head to make himself heard, fearing that some over-eager vigilante would take the opportunity to blow it off his shoulders.

Up ahead, his assailant was crawling toward where a rope tied around a turret dangled into the alley alongside of the hotel. Ki knew that if his man reached the rope, he could shimmy down and escape unseen from the dark alley. The problem was, the man had made it across the front of the hotel before the marshal and his armed posse arrived. Now Ki was going to have to make it across what had become a gauntlet of guns if he was to capture the shooter.

The samurai began to slither like a snake, hauling himself forward with his nose pressed into the rather ancient, brittle-looking gutter edging the rooftop. The dawn's light had not yet reached this front part of the hotel. Ki willed the sun to rise faster, so that the fools in the street below could see that they were shooting at the wrong man.

Gunfire echoed against the buildings lining Main Street as Farley and his men blasted away. It was no use, the samurai decided sadly. He would never be able to reach the fellow in time to stop him. The man was already almost out of the line of fire.

The samurai plucked his *shuriken* blade from the back pocket of his jeans. It would be difficult, but he believed he could hurl his blade into the other's back when the man rose up in order to grasp his rope.

It would mean not taking the attacker alive, but killing him was better than letting him escape to try his luck some other day.

Unless . . . The idea, when it came to him, seemed outrageous.

Ki smiled. Outrageous or not, it just might work. . . . The samurai tensed his arms and shoulders in preparation, and then used his sinewy muscles like springs to catapult him up onto his toes, and then *off* his flexed toes, to somersault high into the air. The shooters, unprepared for his leap, sent their deadly volleys exploding into the tattered shingles beneath him. Ki had only a split second before he began his descent. His eyes searched out the spot where Marshal Farley was standing, and then he snapped his wrist to send the *shuriken* blade on its desperate journey.

The posse below scattered as the weapon left Ki's fingers. They didn't know what was coming their way, but to a man, they figured that whatever it was, it would do them harm if it caught them.

An instant later, the glittering blade was vibrating in the earth between the toes of Farley's boots. The town marshal stared down at it and then, recognizing what it was, shouted, "Hold your fire! That's my deputy up there!"

Meanwhile, Ki had landed flat on his back upon the incline of the roof, in order to expose as little of his body as possible to the guns in the street below. He now slid down toward the roof's edge on his bare spine. He dug his naked heels into the gutter, listening to the old wood crack and splinter, and held his breath.

The gutter did hold, but barely. Ki sat up quickly, bending his knees to take his weight off the groaning wood. Now that the shooting had stopped from down below, the samurai was free to get to his feet and continue his pursuit.

The shooting *had* stopped from down below, but now it was continuing from the rooftop. The gunman had both of his pistols drawn. As he stood up to peg shots at Ki, his silhouette was visible against the brightening sky.

"We see you up there!" Farley called to the man. "Drop them guns! I got men in the alley to make sure you don't get away!"

The man stopped firing in order to see if what Farley said was true. He saw two men glaring up at him from the bottom of his escape rope.

"It is finished," Ki said, standing up. He held out his hands to the man. "Give me your weapons and you will live."

The man's head swiveled around, searching for a way out of the trap. Ki noticed him staring at the slanted rooftop across the alley.

"It is at least ten feet away, and a half-story lower than this roof. Please do not attempt it," Ki said quietly. "If you do, it will not end well for you."

"Throw them guns down or we'll shoot!" Farley called.

"Do not shoot him!" Ki shouted back quickly.

"Why're you doin' me a favor?" the gunman demanded.

Ki peered at him, but the man had his Stetson pulled down low to conceal his face. He took a step forward, but the man menaced him with his pistols. "I would like to know why you tried to kill me," the samurai said.

The man shook his head. "Just stay away," he ordered.

Ki held up his hands. "I am unarmed," he said. "If you intend to jump the alley, you will kill yourself. Before you die, will you not tell me why you tried to kill me?"

The gunman lowered his pistols. "All right, you win," he muttered. "Come get me." He sounded defeated, but Ki noticed that the hammers were drawn back on his revolvers.

"Please drop your weapons first," the samurai called out.

Swearing, the gunman swung up his pistols and fired. Ki crabbed sideways so that the gunman's lead plowed into the roof, sending shingles flying.

"Get him!" Farley commanded his men. As they fired up at the roof, the gunman crouched low, took a running leap, and sailed off the edge of the hotel. The men in the alleyway watched him swan-dive over their heads and shouted excitedly, "He's gonna make it!"

But Ki, watching from his rooftop vantage point, knew that the man would not. At last the gunman himself realized that he was going to fall short. He let his pistols fall as he stretched out his arms in a desperate attempt to hook his fingers into the building's gutter. He just made it, his body slamming hard against the building's clapboard siding. Dazed, he hung on out of instinct, and then began screaming for somebody to help him as his boot toes scraped uselessly against the smooth clapboard wall.

"Oh, shit," Ki sighed. The samurai did not often use American expletives, *but there were times* . . .

"Hold on, fella!" Farley encouraged the man. "We're getting a rope! We're—" The marshal listened as one of his deputies whispered into his ear. "We're getting the keys to that building!" he shouted. "Hang on! We'll be up there in two minutes!"

As Farley spoke, the wooden gutter from which the man was dangling gave way at one end. He wailed as he dropped down three feet in a sickening lurch.

Ki was at the edge of the hotel roof. "Listen to me," he said. His voice was as soft as a faraway wind, but somehow his tone carried the force to cut through the dangling man's hysteria.

"Oh, please," was all the man could say. "Oh, sweet Christ—"

"Quiet. Do not move. Do not even breathe," Ki warned him. "You are hanging there by the grace of a few inches of rotted wood."

"Don't do anything stupid, Ki!" Farley yelled. "We got a man riding for the keys to that place—"

"There is no time," Ki called back down to the ground.

As if to prove the samurai's point, another bit of the stressed wooden gutter came loose from the building with a loud *crack!* Once again the dangling man began to kick his legs in a futile attempt to gain some sort of foothold.

"Stop that," Ki scolded him. "Hold still, I told you."

"P-please!"

"Be brave," the samurai ordered. "I am coming for you."

He took several steps back as he prepared his mind for what his body was about to do. A samurai trained himself to be able to execute several types of *mae-tobi-geri*—the flying foot strike—but the leaps involved in those strikes emphasize height rather than distance. In a pocket of his leather vest he had a spool of cord approximately the thickness of fishing line, but many times stronger. Attached to one end of the cord were several razor-sharp hooks of tempered steel. The cord device had been perfected by the *ninja* of Japan to aid in scaling buildings. It would have been quite helpful in this endeavor, Ki knew, but regrettably the device was back in his room. There was no time to fetch it.

Ten feet away, and a half-story below. If you miss, a six-story fall to the hard, hard ground. . . .

"Then I will not miss," Ki murmured. A smile crossed his lips, and then slowly faded. The time for thinking was over. Now it was time to *do. . . .*

He ran smoothly to the edge of the roof and then launched himself into space. Midway across the ten-foot span, Ki curled himself into a ball to lessen wind resistance, and used his powerful stomach, back, and neck muscles to execute a forward roll, adding to his momentum. He hit the lower roof with his shoulders curled, absorbing the force of his landing by rolling with the impact.

Ki was on his feet and at the roof's edge in seconds. *Now for the hard part*, the samurai thought. The end of the gutter from which the gunman was dangling angled down more than three feet below the roof's ledge. Ki lay on his belly and stretched his arm down as far as he could, but he was still six inches short.

"Hurry! Do something!" The man stared up at Ki, his face pale and anguished. "I can't hold on much longer," he grimaced. "My fingers—numb!"

Ki looked around wildly. What he needed was something to extend his reach.

Across the way, Marshal Farley and his deputies appeared on the hotel roof. Ki watched them clamber carefully to the edge.

"Farley!" Ki called out. "Throw me your holster belt!"

The marshal seemed confused. "You want my gun, you mean?" He inadvertently looked down toward the ground, and swayed on his heels until his deputies grabbed his arms.

"No, keep your gun!" Ki demanded impatiently. "I need just the belt!"

Farley handed his pistol to one of his men and unbuckled his gunbelt. He wrapped the belt around the holster and threw the weighty parcel of leather and brass to Ki, who caught it in one hand and snapped it like a whip, unfurling the belt so that it hung past the dangling man.

"Grab on to the strap," the samurai instructed the man. "I will haul you up!"

"I'm afraid!" the man whined. "I'll fall!"

"Do it!" Ki growled. "Hurry!"

"But—"

Ki wasted no more time in useless persuasion. His foot kicked out against the still attached portion of gutter. The samurai's callused, stiffened toes were like steel chisels biting into the wood. The gutter gave way, cracking and popping like dry tinder in a fire. The dangling man screamed, but he let go of the falling gutter and wrapped his hands around the buckle of the gun belt.

"Knew you would see it my way," Ki muttered through clenched teeth as he began hauling the man up.

"Fingers cramped!" the gunman cried out. "Can't hold *onnnnn!*" The buckle slipped from his trembling hands and he began to fall.

Ki threw himself upon his belly and shot his right arm out with tremendous speed. If his hand had been clenched into a fist, or stiffened to deliver a knife-edged strike, the force would have proved fatal to a foe—

But this time the samurai was using the capabilities developed by his lifelong study of the martial arts to save a life, not take one. During the short while the man had hung on to the gunbelt, Ki had raised him at least twelve inches, well within his reach. Ki's fingers were curved into rigid hooks as his arm whipped down, snagging the helpless man by the back of his corduroy vest. The samurai's face twisted with exertion as he slowly flexed his right arm to raise the hundred-and-sixty-odd pounds of kicking, crying dead weight that was just now doing its best to snap the bones of his fingers.

The man hung like a side of beef inside his vest. As Ki slowly hauled him up, he began to babble.

"Thank you! Thank you!" he laughed hysterically. "You saved me. I know plenty of stuff you could use! I'll tell you everything you want to know. Why I was sent to kill you and—"

The man's torrent of words were abruptly drowned out by the hideous, rasping sound of tearing cloth.

"Noooo!" the man cried as the arm holes of his vest ripped

140

through. Ki lunged for another hold upon the man, but the samurai's best try only managed to knock the hapless man's Stetson from his head as he plummeted, screaming, to the bottom of the alleyway, five and a half stories below.

Ki, sweating and exhausted, stared down at the ragdoll thing lying in the dirt. Several men from Farley's hastily organized posse quickly gathered around the body.

"Neck's broken!" one of them called up to the marshal. "He's dead, all right."

A crimson stain was spreading out from beneath the corpse as Ki looked away. The door that led up to the roof from the building's interior swung open. A harried-looking man appeared in the shadowy portal. "Just got back with the keys." He held up a coil of hemp. "I brought my rope!"

Ki silently walked past the man, and started down the stairs.

"Hey!" the man demanded angrily. "Ain't you gonna try and save that guy?"

The samurai met Marshal Farley in the alleyway. Both men stared down at the dead man's face. The fellow had been young, no more than twenty. He had close-cropped brown hair, eyes that must have been quite blue when they could still see, and the smooth cheeks of someone who rarely had need of a razor.

"Ever seen him before?" Farley asked.

Ki shook his head. "A stranger to me."

"Well, I've seen him," the marshal replied. "At least I've seen wanted posters showing his likeness." He gestured at the body. "This here is—or was—Tommy Fitch. He don't *look* mean, but he was. Killed himself a whole train crew during a mail robbery. Just shot them down 'cause it was easier that way. He's one of Wink Turner's boys."

"The outlaw leader?" Ki asked, surprised.

"The one and only," Farley replied. "Deputy Long had mentioned to me that Turner and his outlaw army could be in the vicinity, but I didn't rightly believe him." Farley nudged Tommy Fitch's body with the toe of his boot. "But seeing's believing," he sighed.

"Why would Turner wish to bring his brigade of outlaws to these parts?" Ki asked.

Marshal Farley looked sour. "This danged fair has attracted

141

as many unsavory types as spilled honey does flies. Sarah Township is lucky that it's got an important politician like Barston paying us a visit. The U.S. Justice Department don't want anything to happen to the man who might be the next President of the United States. Longarm told me that his boss, Marshal Billy Vail, will be riding with a posse to intercept Turner before he makes it to Sarah." The marshal grew thoughtful. "'Course, Turner's gang has numbered as many as forty, and I don't reckon that old Billy Vail will be riding with anywheres near that many lawmen."

"Why would one of Wink Turner's men wish to kill me?" Ki wondered aloud.

Farley shrugged. "That's the real question, but I ain't got an answer for you. Maybe old Tommy here could've told you."

"And he would have," Ki remarked wistfully. "Marshal, I am quite concerned. While it is true that I have made personal enemies in my time, most of the violence directed against me has been the result of my association with Jessie."

"I follow you, son," Farley nodded. "Wink Turner sent this here boy to kill you, there's no doubt in my mind about that. And I agree that an attack against you is really an attack against Jessie. Why Wink Turner would be out to get Jessie is anybody's guess."

"Let us not mention this to Jessie or Longarm," Ki advised. "There is no point in causing either of them unnecessary worry. To my knowledge, she has never had a confrontation with Wink Turner or his men, in all of her battles against the cartel. It makes no sense that Turner would wish to do her harm."

"I won't mention it to anybody if you don't want me to," Farley muttered. "I just hope you know what you're up against." The marshal shook his head. "And I hope Marshal Vail and his posse can stop Turner's outlaw army before it reaches Sarah!"

The samurai gazed up at the lustrous bands of crimson, yellow, and blue suffusing the early-morning Texas sky. He sniffed the air, fresh and moist with the night's dew. "Somewhere under this day's sun, a battle will be fought," he murmured softly. "Marshal Vail, fight well...."

Farley was about to argue with Ki. He was about to point out that Ki had no way of knowing if Vail was going to intercept the outlaw army. Then he reconsidered; Jessie Starbuck was somehow involved in this puzzle, and where Jessie was concerned, Ki had an almost magical way of knowing things. . . .

"Some of you boys head over to Wilks's general store," Farley said irritably. "He oughta be opening up pretty soon. Fetch me a canvas tarp to wrap this here body up. Hurry now! I don't want this here corpse bleedin' all over our clean streets."

★

Chapter 7

Dawn broke as uncomfortably wet as a broken blister for United States Marshal Billy Vail and his nine-man posse. Broken blisters were pretty much on the marshal's mind just now; he and his men had been riding hard since midnight, following what they believed was the trail left by one of the small bands Wink Turner was known to send out to hunt game or steal cows to feed his outlaw army.

Vail held up his arm to slow his posse. He shifted painfully in his saddle, adjusting his holster so the heavy Walker Colt .45 could ride a different spot on his aching hip.

"You okay?"

Vail twisted around to glare at Talbot, one of his deputies. "Of course I'm okay! I'm sick and tired of listening to you men ask me if I'm okay! If I'm not okay I'll tell you!"

"Okay, boss!" Talbot removed his hat to run his fingers through his curly blond hair in consternation.

Vail took a deep breath, then nodded. "Sorry, Phil." He turned up the collar of his gray suit jacket against the morning dampness, and thought about what Longarm had said: *"You haven't ridden anything but that damned desk chair for a lot of years now...."*

"Tell the rest of the men we'll take ten minutes to rest," Vail said.

Talbot jammed his hat back on his head. "Whatever you say, boss."

Vail stared at him. Was it his imagination, or was Talbot eyeing him queerly?

Damn you, Custis Long, but you were right, Vail thought as he slowly and painfully swung a leg out of its stirrup and lowered himself to the ground. He clenched his teeth to stifle his groans as he gingerly rubbed at his backside beneath the baggy seat of his gray suit trousers.

I hurt, Vail told himself miserably. *I hurt from the top of my bald head to the bottoms of my swollen feet. I've got fingers swollen by rheumatism from the trail's cold damp, and a gut on fire from the bad food. What's happened to me?*

The federal marshal and his men had ridden the Texas & Pacific rail line to Grassy Bow, New Mexico, where they'd requisitioned horses at the army remount station. From there they'd ridden all the way to Texas, not resting for more than a few hours at any one time, desperate to come across some sign of Turner or his men.

"Want some beef jerky, boss?" Talbot asked, holding out a stick of the dried meat he'd taken from the pocket of his plaid wool jacket.

Vail was tempted, but he listened to what his sour stomach was telling him. "No, I'd better not," he said sadly. "I'm hungry, but I'd better not." He hauled out his pipe and tobacco, thinking to smoke away the gnawing he felt in his extremely empty but overly sensitive paunch. *What I need is a good warm bowl of the missus' buttered oatmeal*, he mused to himself. *Never thought I'd long for that slop....*

"Boss, it'd be better if you don't smoke," Talbot advised anxiously. "The smell of tobacco travels quite a ways out in the wilderness." The deputy looked away in embarrassment. "I mean, if Turner's men *are* somewhere in the vicinity..."

"What?" Vail asked blankly. He glanced down at his pipe. "Oh. Yes, you're absolutely right, Phil." He jammed the pipe back into his pocket. *Now, I knew that,* he thought. *I've got to quit acting like a greenhorn!*

The other men had remained silent during the exchange. Vail found that he could not meet their questioning eyes. Talbot, Hopkins, Glenn, and the rest—they were all fine deputy marshals.

I know what they're wondering, Vail thought. *They're wondering if I'm still fit enough to command them....*

The marshal looked around at the terrain, mist-shrouded and ghostly in the blue-gray light of dawn. "I ain't been in these parts for quite a long time," he began, and then chuckled, thinking, *They probably already figured that out.* "Anybody know where the hell we are?"

"Yep," Hopkins nodded. He was a tall thin man, with a taciturn manner that went well with his funereal black suit, but contrasted sharply with the brace of pearl-handled, double-action Colts he carried in a Mexican gunbelt studded with silver conchos.

"This here's the start of the Sagmaw Valley," Hopkins told the posse. "It runs on for a couple of miles yonder, I reckon."

"Ain't never heard of no Sagmaw River," Vail said dubiously.

"Ain't no river left, Marshal," Hopkins replied. "Sagmaw ain't the official name for the place, but it is what the locals hereabouts call it. The Indians have a legend that says the river itself dried up long before anything with two legs walked the earth."

"Injuns," Talbot spat contemptuously.

"There's still a lot of bogs and streams around," Hopkins continued. "That's where all this damned fog is coming from. As we ride into the valley, we'll find ourselves traveling what used to be the riverbed. There's lots of big boulders and clumps of oak trees growing where the water used to be. The walls on either side of us will rise up about a hundred yards, but gradually, more like hills or slopes."

Vail nodded. "Those slopes afford much cover?"

"Yep," Hopkins hooked his thumbs in his glittering belt.

"Shit," Vail sighed. "It sounds like a good spot for Turner's men to ambush us."

"We're not following more than four or five of them," Talbot interjected. "Leastways, not as far as we can tell from their trail."

"I know that," Vail said. "But we've got no way of knowing just where the main bunch of Turner's men are. Remember what happened to General Custer?"

The men nodded among themselves. "So what are we going to do?" Hopkins asked. "We can't reach Sarah without passing through here."

"I'm going to send two men ahead of the rest of us," Vail explained. "You, Hopkins, 'cause you know your way around this area, and Glenn."

"Lucky me," Glenn moped. He was a heavyset man dressed in denims. He carried no pistol, preferring a Winchester .44-40, its barrel sawed off to an eighteen-inch length. He carried the shortened rifle by means of a rawhide thong, so that the weapon hung down within easy reach of his right hand.

"I figure to have the rest of us stay well behind you two," Vail continued. "Maybe Turner's men aren't there. Maybe they are. If so, they may not know how many federal lawmen have been following them. And if they *do* know that there are ten of us, they might assume that we split up to cover more territory. In any event, I'm figuring that any outlaws lurking in that valley will show themselves rather than give up the chance to take potshots at a pair of lawmen."

"I *knew* I went into the wrong line of work," Glenn said sourly.

"Let's ride," Hopkins muttered.

The sun was a pale round disc as the main body of the posse entered the valley about a half-mile behind their two decoys. Vail rode in the lead, swearing furiously to himself as he squinted and peered through the wisps of fog that still shrouded the terrain.

"This stuff will probably burn off by noon," Talbot said helpfully.

"By noon I won't give a shit," Vail responded gruffly. "One good thing about it, we can't see anything, but neither can Turner's men."

"Boss?" Talbot called, his voice tentative. "We've got company."

"Where?" Vail asked sharply. Then he saw them. Two riders, coming down from the eastern slope. "Keep those pistols holstered, boys," the marshal told his nervous men. "Those two coming at us are riding *mules*. Unless I'm badly mistaken, there ain't no farmboy division of Wink Turner's band of outlaws."

The newcomers did seem to be right off the farm. They were gangly fellows whose legs came close to scraping the ground on either side of their stubby, barebacked mules. The two were dressed in faded blue overalls and worn flannel shirts of some indeterminate color, the cuffs of which were rolled up to reveal the bright red sleeves of their union suits. One of the men wore a straw hat, the other did not. Both had lengths of rope cinched about their waists to form makeshift belts, and each had a Colt Peacemaker tucked into the hemp.

"I'll be damned," one of the deputies chuckled. "You boys don't even have shoes!"

"We've got 'em!" one of the newcomers replied staunchly. "We're just not wearing 'em."

"That's right," the other said. "We got 'em in our possibles sacks, right here across our mules' asses," he explained, slapping his mule on the haunch until it turned sideways to reveal the burlap sack roped to its hindquarters.

"My name's Mike, and this here's my cousin Paul," the first man said as he doffed his straw hat to Marshal Vail. "We hail from Red Tick, Louisiana."

"Red Tick, Louisiana?" Vail scowled, and then shrugged. "Reckon you boys are a long way from home."

"Coming from a hometown with a name like that, who could blame them?" Talbot said under his breath.

"Yessir, we are," Mike said. He was a pleasant-looking man in his early thirties, with a wide, easygoing grin, a strong hawk nose, and long, lank brown hair which he wore bound into a ponytail. His cousin Paul was not as good-looking—his skin had been pitted by smallpox—but his wide-set eyes the color of sand held a look that was calm and intelligent. His short-cropped hair was black, but thinning on top. As if to compensate for his premature baldness, he wore a thick, bottlebrush mustache.

"We do miss home," Mike was telling Marshal Vail. "Seems

like we've been gone for a coon's age—"

"We're farmers," Paul cut in. "Partners in a potato farm—"

Somebody in the posse snickered. Fiercely, Paul searched the men's faces, trying to discover who it had been.

"Easy, Paulie," Mike soothed. "These here lawmen don't mean no harm."

"How'd you know we were lawmen?" Vail asked suspiciously.

"We've been following you for a couple of days now," Paul replied. "We've watched you tracking a gang of four men."

"You know for a fact there's only four up ahead?" Talbot asked sharply.

"Slow down! Slow down!" Paul exchanged an amused glance with his partner. "These here city fellows can pound a man into the ground with their questions. A couple of times we rode ahead of you, just to see what you were up against."

"My name's Billy Vail, and I'm the U.S. marshal for this district," Vail growled. "Now how many outlaws are we trailing?"

Once again the two farmers enjoyed some private joke among themselves. "You're trailing four outlaws," Mike began. "But you're going to run into ten times as many."

"Oh, shit!" Talbot moaned.

Paul cast a piteous glance upon the assemblage of law officers. "Ain't you boys never heard of Wink Turner?"

The sound of gunshots echoing in the valley kept Marshal Vail from replying. The whining staccato of a rapid-fire weapon came to them through the lifting mists.

"That'd be old Glenn's midget Winchester," Talbot muttered. "He can lever off rounds faster than a man can pull the trigger on a double-action Colt."

"I sent them into a trap!" Vail cried out. He pulled hard on the reins of his big bay gelding, causing the animal to show the whites of its eyes as it wheeled around. The marshal kicked the horse into a flat-out run toward the noise of the gun battle.

"Where the hell does he think he's going?" one of the deputies complained.

"We've got to follow," Talbot declared. "You two farmers stay here—"

"Now hold on," Mike argued. "You boys federal deputies?"

"Sure we are!" Talbot flashed the badge pinned beneath the collar of his plaid jacket. "Let's go!" The seven lawmen lit out after their superior.

Mike and Paul watched them go. "Reckon they're on the side of good, eh, Paulie?" Mike asked.

"Reckon," Paul replied. "And I reckon we oughta help out on the side of good. . . ."

"Reckon. . . ." Mike leaned forward and whispered into the rabbitlike, twitching ear of his mule, "We gotta hurry it up now, Sadie. . . ." When the mule ignored him, the Louisiana potato farmer clamped his teeth down hard on the stubborn critter's ear. The mule brayed its outrage, then began to run like the wind.

"Now, you don't want to get treated like Sadie, do you, Selma?" Paul asked his mount. The mule moved out fast.

Deputy Talbot, leading the men, noticed a brown shape flying past him.

"Goddammit!" he swore, staring down in disgust at his army mount. "Those two farmers on the mules are beating us!"

It was true. Paul and Mike, bouncing up and down the bare backs of their careening mules, had taken the lead. They were the first to reach Marshal Vail, sitting astride his lathered horse in the cover of a stand of oak trees.

The gunfire had quieted. Vail, his big Walker Colt in his hand, was peering cautiously through the foliage. "I thought I saw them a moment ago," the marshal told his men.

The sun overhead was increasing in intensity, slowly but inexorably burning away the ground fog. Soon the ancient, rock-strewn valley would be as clear as the Texas grasslands, and as hot as the desert.

"Sure wish they'd shoot at something, just so we'd know they're still alive," Talbot grumbled. He reached beneath his wool coat to ease out his Smith & Wesson.

"They're alive," Vail said. He glanced behind him. "What are those two potatoes doing here?" he asked.

"I tried to keep them out of this," Talbot said. "Guess they're volunteering."

"What the hell, I can always use a couple more guns." Vail chuckled dryly. "Assuming they can hit something. Swear them in as deputies."

Talbot nodded and turned his horse around, riding over to where the two men stood beside their panting mules. "Hey, you two gents want to be deputies?"

"Glory be!" Paul exclaimed. "Mikey, you hear what I hear?"

"Reckon," Mike grinned. "Just think on it, regular federal deputies. We're gonna be lawmen!"

"Yeah, yeah," Talbot cut them off. "We'll have the shindig later. Raise your right hands, gents—"

"We gonna get badges?" Mike asked hopefully.

"None extra," Talbot replied.

"Dang, then," the farmer moped. "Ain't that a gyp—"

"I see 'em!" one of the posse shouted.

The fingers of fog wafting along the valley floor had parted momentarily, revealing the whereabouts of the two deputies who'd ridden ahead. Hopkins was lying on the ground, his pearl-handled Colts glittering in the sun where they'd fallen. Glenn was crouched over him, his sawed-off Winchester at the ready, and pointed up at the eastern slope. Their horses had been shot out from under them. Both animals were lying in pools of their own blood, their thin legs twitching feebly. Glenn, his saddlebags and canteens over his shoulder, had managed to drag Hopkins halfway to the cover of a jumble of boulders before they'd been pinned down by gunfire.

"Glenn!" Vail cried out hoarsely.

The deputy glanced toward the grove of oaks. He had time to wave in Vail's direction before the fog once again closed in around him.

While the mists were still substantial where they'd pooled along the floor of the valley, they'd all but dissipated along the higher, warmer slopes. As Vail and his posse watched, a string of six outlaws popped up from behind the rocks. Rifles and pistols in hand, the six badmen began running and stumbling down the incline toward the two stranded deputies.

"Give me your horse," Vail ordered Talbot.

"Hold on now, boss. Just what have you got in mind?"

"I'm going to ride in and get my boys out of the predicament I put 'em in!" Vail thundered. "You men use your rifles to set up a covering fire."

"Billy, that fog keeps us from having decent aim," Talbot complained.

"Do the best you can, Deputy," Vail growled. "Now get off that horse!"

More outlaws hidden on the rocky slope had begun to fire down into the swirling mists protecting Glenn and Hopkins. Meanwhile, the original half-dozen badmen were approaching the valley floor.

"You can't just charge in there, Billy!" Talbot declared.

Vail planted one beefy hand against Talbot's chest and pushed hard, sending the blond-haired deputy tumbling to the grass. The marshal tugged Talbot's Winchester from its scabbard and tossed it to him. "You do what I tell you, son."

With Talbot's horse in tow, Vail kicked his horse into a fast lope. He quickly blended into the mists that had now lightened to the extent where they could no longer be counted upon to afford continuous cover from the outlaw snipers perched upon the slope.

Talbot got up, brushing the dirt and grass from his plaid jacket. "Crazy old coot," he muttered fondly.

Vail rode directly toward the spot where he'd last seen Glenn and Hopkins. He held the reins to his own and Talbot's horses in his left hand, and his Walker Colt in his right. The sound of gunfire was all around him now, but he paid it no mind, remembering that the shots a man could hear would never hurt him; it was the one he didn't hear. . . .

As Vail rode he forgot about his aching back, his sour stomach, and his swollen, rheumatic fingers; he forgot his age. All that was on his mind was the rescue of the men he was responsible for, the men who had ridden into what had literally become the valley of death, on *his* command.

The fog around Vail cleared to reveal riflemen squinting down their barrels at him. He just leaned low against his horse's neck and let Captain Walker do his talking for him.

The big Walker Colt .45 spat blue fire and gray smoke, its report echoing like thunder against the rocky walls of the valley. Vail saw an outlaw rifleman go down, blood spurting from his chest where the marshal's slug had hit him. Vail thumbed back the hammer and fired again and again, emptying his cylinder at the outlaws swarming down the slopes. At long last he reached Glenn and Hopkins.

Glenn stood with his sawed-off Winchester jammed against

his hip. He levered off shots in a steady stream. The spent cartridge casings being ejected from the smoking port of his little rifle pattered to the ground like rain.

"Come on!" Vail screamed as he reined in his mount. He hugged his saddle with his knees as he reloaded his pistol from the supply of loose cartridges bulging the pocket of his suit coat. "Get Hopkins across my saddle and mount up on this other horse—"

"Look out, Billy!" Glenn cut him off. The deputy shouldered his stubby rifle and levered off two quick rounds.

Vail saw a charging outlaw go down, gutshot, his knees plowing a furrow in the dirt. The man had not dropped his pistol, and now raised it for another try at the lawmen. Before Vail or Glenn could pull their triggers, Hopkins, who had been crawling toward his brace of Colts, raised his pistols and let loose with a double volley of shots, knocking the wounded outlaw flat on his back.

"Let's go, boys!" Vail shouted. The next thing he knew, he was blinded by a spray of hot blood as his horse's head took the impact of an outlaw's rifle round. Vail found himself nosediving through the air, pitched from his saddle as his mount's front legs crumpled. The marshal held on to his pistol for dear life as he landed hard on the ground, several feet away from Hopkins.

The wounded deputy was calmly squeezing off shots; first one pearl-handled Colt would fire, then the other. Hopkins kept up his steady barrage even while his left leg was involuntarily twitching in pain. Blood was seeping down, soaking his trouser cuff.

Billy Vail smeared the horse's blood from his eyes with the back of his sleeve, in time to see Talbot's horse go down. The animal screamed in agony as several shots stitched across its flanks.

The marshal rolled over onto his belly and gripped Captain Walker with both hands. A trio of outlaws was coming toward him, crouched low, their pistols cocked and ready to fire. Vail thanked the Lord for the blanket of fog as he sighted down on the first man and squeezed the trigger. The Walker Colt boomed, and when its smoke had cleared, there were only two outlaws left. They were no longer advancing, but were bent low, squeezing off shots in Vail's general direction just as fast as the actions of their guns could work. Vail fired twice more, riding up the recoil of his powerful handgun and then bringing it back down on target. The second outlaw clutched at his belly; the third was spun around as Vail's slug caught him in the left shoulder. The marshal swung his gun back upon the second man, who'd recovered from his belly wound sufficiently to fire his own pistol. Vail flinched as the man's slug kicked dirt into his face, and then shot the man in the chest, dropping him. The man who'd been winged in the shoulder was stumbling in retreat toward the sanctuary of the slope. Vail was about to blast him, but then changed his mind, shaking his head.

"I ain't ever been a backshooter," the marshal sputtered to no one in particular. "And I ain't about to start now."

Glenn flopped down beside him. "We'd best pull out of here, Billy," he said, feeding fresh rounds into the magazine of his Winchester. "Oh, shit, here come some more of Turner's turds!"

As they watched, a fresh wave of outlaws began leapfrogging their way down the slope. Some held their ground, firing to cover the men who were advancing. Next, the front line took cover in order to send down a volley while the men to the rear advanced.

"There's just too damned many for us," Billy mourned. "This is *worse* than Custer's last stand."

"You both make a run for it," Hopkins called to them.

"We ain't leaving you," Vail said sharply.

"Billy, my leg's broke," Hopkins replied. "I can't walk, and if you slow down to carry me, they'll get you for sure. Now you two make a run, and I'll keep you covered. What the hell," Hopkins smiled faintly. "Between my help and this here fog, you just might make it."

"Thanks, but no thanks," Vail muttered. "Anyway, we'd have one hell of a way to go before we reached the rest of the posse." He ducked as a bullet richocheted off a rock beside him.

"Where are the rest of the boys?" Glenn asked with mild interest as he aimed and fired his sawed-off rifle.

"Back yonder," Vail said. "They're sending up that covering fire you're hearing. Damn, I wish I had my Winchester," he added, gazing in longing at where his horse lay.

"You know something, Billy?" Glenn began. "I think that cover fire you mentioned is getting closer."

"Huh? What?" Vail scowled. He listened carefully, his jowls quivering as his face slowly contorted in helpless rage. "I told those bastards to stay put!"

A moment later the entire posse—Vail's seven men and the newly deputized Louisiana potato farmers—rode into the battle. Wink Turner's army sent down a rolling fusillade of lead, but for the most part they were firing blindly. The ground fog was still more or less swirling around Vail's position.

Talbot leaped off the back of the horse he was sharing with another deputy, and crouched down beside Vail. The other lawmen pulled their Winchesters from their saddle scabbards and began to send accurate fire up toward the dug-in enemy. Several outlaws pinwheeled down the slope, coming to rest in the assorted awful positions that only corpses can assume.

"We can see them, but they can't see us!" Mike the farmer laughed gleefully to his cousin Paul. Both men stood side by side, totally unconcerned by the spouts of dirt being kicked up scant inches from their bare feet. They pointed their Peacemakers toward the slope and blasted away.

"You two potatoes find yourselves some cover!" Vail roared. "Look at 'em!" he complained to Talbot. "Standing there, popping away with them thumb-busters like it was the Fourth of July!"

Two of Vail's men tried to ride toward the slope, hoping to cut off the outlaws who'd reached the valley floor. To execute the pincer maneuver, it was necessary for the pair of federal lawmen to ride toward the higher ground. The steadily shrinking blanket of fog no longer covered them. Vail watched in horror as the two men were knocked from their saddles in quick succession, victims of the withering rifle fire coming down from the slope. A moment later their wandering horses were shot down as well.

Many others of the posse's mounts had also been killed. The air was filled with the bitter tang of burnt powder, the coppery-sweet smell of blood, and the fetid stench rising from the exposed innards of the mounts that had been torn open by the bullets that were still pummeling them.

"Why'd you do it?" Vail demanded, glaring at Talbot. "You disobeyed a direct order!"

"Fuck orders," Talbot grinned. "Why'd you charge out here to rescue Hopkins and Glenn?"

"They're *my* men," Vail replied.

"Well, boss, maybe that's why we charged in to save you." The deputy winked at his superior. "We're *your* men."

Vail just shook his head, looking away.

"Anyway, boss," Talbot continued, "we didn't have a hell of a lot of choice. A whole shitload of Turner's men came down the slope toward us. We had to go somewhere, 'cause that grove of oaks wasn't safe!"

"You could've retreated," Vail began, but Talbot's sneer cut him off.

"They're pulling back!" one of the deputies called out.

"Then hold your fire!" Vail ordered. "We might be here for a while, and that means we can't afford to waste any ammunition."

"We ain't got a horse left," Glenn scowled, looking at the carcasses that littered the ground.

"Our mules are all right!" Mike beamed.

"We taught them to lay down on their sides," Paul explained as he shucked spent shells from his Peacemaker. "I led them around behind these here boulders. They'll stay put until we tell 'em to get up."

"Those damned mules." Talbot chuckled, shaking his head. "Well, I always knew a mule was smarter than a horse."

"Hell, it ain't nothing special," Mike scoffed. "Them mules only like to lie down on the job, anyway!"

"It comes natural to 'em," Paul agreed earnestly.

"How many men are hurt?" Vail asked.

"Lost two, and Hopkins here is wounded," Glenn answered. "Everybody else is okay...."

"Quick now, boys, get the saddlebags and extra ammo off those horses, and don't forget your canteens!" Vail instructed.

"We digging in, boss?" Talbot asked.

"Haven't any other choice, the way I see it," Vail said. "Two mules can't carry ten men—not even mules as special as yours." He smiled at the farmers. "Reckon you two boys got yourselves in some mighty hot water by joining up with us. . . ."

"Ain't nothing to fret over now, Marshal," Paul shrugged.

"All right then, boys!" Vail sang out. "Food, water, and ammo gets piled in the center of these here boulders. Move it! I want us all behind these rocks inside of five minutes! This here fog ain't going to last forever!"

"What do you aim to do, Billy?" Glenn asked quietly, as he and the marshal carried the groaning Hopkins to safety.

"Can't do much until nightfall," Vail shrugged. "Then I reckon we'll send a couple of men out of here on those mules. If they can reach Sarah, Longarm will lead back a rescue party."

Glenn frowned. "That means we've got to hold out all day today, tonight, and then, most likely, until tomorrow's dawn."

"There's no help for it," Vail said. "Those two mules are the only chance we've got. I don't dare risk them or any of my men until nightfall. The fog's all but lifted. There's no way a man could get through Wink Turner's gauntlet in broad daylight."

"Reckon so, Billy," Glenn was forced to admit.

"Now you supervise the rest of the men while they unload our supplies," Vail ordered him, sending him on his way with a pat on the back. "And don't fret! I've been in tougher spots than this."

In my dreams, Vail thought to himself as he watched Glenn hurry off to carry out his orders. Then the old marshal hunkered down beside Hopkins, to see what he could do to ease the man's pain.

★
Chapter 8

Longarm had wandered the parched sandhills of Nebraska, where a summer thunderstorm's ink-black clouds could blot out the sky quicker than spilled coffee could discolor a white linen tablecloth. The deputy had ridden the Colorado high country during early spring, when one day a meadow could be nothing but pale green grass, and the next morning it could be carpeted with a rainbow profusion of wildflowers.

He'd seen bees swarm out of what had looked to be empty logs, and bats pour from black caves. To his sorrow, Longarm had seen enemy soldiers spill from their Civil War trenches like water overflowing a dam. . . .

But in all his days, the deputy marshal had seen nothing to compare with the way the children of Sarah Township had massed to knock down the gates at the start of the big fair. Here it was only ten o'clock in the morning, and already the tykes had lined up at the concession stands to buy their caramel apples, sweet drinks, and paper sacks of rock candy.

Longarm watched the anxious popcorn vendors, worried that the kids would spend all of their pennies before noon, rush to fire up the little stoves beneath their gaily painted, glass-walled carts. Soon the air was filled with the fragrant aroma of popcorn swimming in butter.

But there was much more to the huge fairgrounds than food. Colorful canvas tents had sprouted in the fields like mushrooms. In a couple of hours, music and laughter would be spilling out from the entrance flaps as the first shows, exhibitions, and circuses began at midday.

Longarm strolled past a tent that proclaimed itself THE WORLD'S MOST FANTASTIC FREAK SHOW! The sides of the tent were painted with illustrations that depicted the fat lady, the dog-faced boy, the two-headed calf, and the bald cat that could be seen within. He passed an exotically costumed fire-eater who was just now settling down for a cup of morning coffee, a clownish juggler who was breakfasting on some of the apples he used in his act, and a loudmouthed concessionaire, the proprietor of a wheel of fortune. The fellow had a derby on his head, a cigar clamped between his teeth, and several days' growth of beard bristling his jawline. The concessionaire was alternately coughing and touting his game to the morning throngs rushing past on their way to claim the best bleacher seats for the target competitions.

"It's the early bird that catches the worm, folks! Who'll be the first to try for the hand of Lady Luck?" The gamester pointed a gnarled finger at Longarm. "How about you, friend? Care to try a spin on my wheel?"

"No thanks, old son," Longarm grinned. He walked on as the faint sound of calliope music began to be heard. A real, honest-to-god merry-go-round had been shipped in and assembled upon the fairgrounds, arranged and paid for by Jessie Starbuck, of course. Kids could ride on it free, but adults had to pay a nickel. The money went to a fund established to help pay for a new wing for the town's schoolhouse.

Longarm followed the crowds to the target-shoot area. That was where he'd agreed to hook up with Jessie and Congressman Barston. The congressman was inside the officials' tent next to the shooting range. Jessie, Barston, and Tompkins had been transported by wagon to the fairgrounds after a big breakfast at the Starbuck ranch. Longarm had ridden a horse borrowed from the Starbuck stables, and Thorn had also borrowed a horse, in order to ride to town and have the telegram Barston had dictated sent to Vail's office in Colorado.

"It won't be long now, Deputy," Barston had smirked as he buttered his toast during breakfast. "By this evening your new orders will have been cut and wired back to the Western Union office. Why don't you save yourself some time and leave now?"

Longarm and Jessie had exchanged glances over their coffee cups, but said nothing. Later, when the deputy had a chance to talk to her out of earshot of the congressman, he'd asked if she'd known that Thorn had borrowed a Starbuck horse for a midnight ride.

Jessie had been mystified. "He must have slipped out during the time I was in my bedroom, before I went downstairs to the fireplace," she'd guessed.

Jessie was wearing a gray wool skirt, a tan silk blouse, and a velvet vest the color of wine. A large leather shoulder bag hung at her right hip. She'd opened the bag to reveal her pistol. It was a .38-caliber, double-action Colt, finished blue-gray, with grips of polished peachwood. It was a beautiful weapon, and in Jessie's capable hands it performed beautifully as well. Longarm had seen her accurately squeeze off all five of her Colt's rounds as fast as any man he'd ever come across.

"I'd feel better if I could wear my holster," Jessie had confided to him. "But a gunbelt around my hips always provokes stares."

"Reckon it might be your hips themselves that are attracting all that unwanted attention," Longarm had smiled. "But if you want to go on believing that it's your gunbelt . . ."

Jessie had blushed. "Just as long as you keep noticing these hips of mine, I'm satisfied," she'd whispered shyly, and then immediately said, "But I think it's a good idea for me to have a gun handy. I don't intend to be as helpless as I was during yesterday's attempt on Barston's life, should more trouble develop today."

"You just make sure you do all your shooting in self-defense," Longarm had warned. "If trouble comes, keep out of the way!"

"Why, Deputy," Jessie had teased, her hazel eyes opening wide. "Don't I always stay out of trouble?"

"Jessie . . ." Longarm had growled.

"Oh, all right!" she'd surrendered. "I promise not to get involved in any shooting."

"Thank you."

"Unless it's absolutely necessary," she'd laughed. "And that's the only promise you'll get out of me, Custis Long!" She'd stood on tiptoe to give him a quick kiss, and then scooted off to see to the wagon.

Longarm could only sigh as he watched her go. He knew that as far as trouble and Jessie were concerned, he'd been lucky to get the headstrong girl to promise anything at all.

The Starbuck wagon had delivered them to the officials' tent around nine-thirty. Longarm had been in Barston's company for only a couple of hours, but already he'd had enough of the blustering, pompus congressman for one day. Since Barston was with Jessie, Marshal Farley, and the mayor of Sarah, and since Ki was keeping watch outside the tent's entrance, Longarm had figured it was safe to excuse himself for a while. He wanted to stretch his long legs and have himself an after-breakfast smoke during a stroll around the fairgrounds.

He'd had his stroll, but fought off the impulse to light up a cheroot. He'd been trying to quit the habit for years, never with any success. Recently he'd decided to cut back by not smoking before noon. He'd tried to hold to such a resolution before, but had never been able to stick with it. He supposed the *man's* thing to do was just to quit completely.

No chance. Longarm was brave, but not *that* brave. Besides, to do such a thing would be against the public good. Nobody got as ornery as Longarm when he ran out of cheroots. Why, if he quit smoking, he could end up *killing* somebody!

When looked at *that* way, Longarm mused, it was more like his continuing to smoke was a personal sacrifice he was making for the good of others. He was actually being *forced* to smoke in the name of public safety. Why, he was an unsung hero!

Longarm jammed a cheroot into his mouth and hurriedly struck a match. *It's good to think things through. Never pays for a fellow to go off half-cocked,* he reminded himself as he inhaled that first invigorating lungful of aromatic smoke. Just

162

the same, he would put that no-smoking-before-noon rule into effect in the name of moderation. Tomorrow.

He could hear Barston's droning voice even before he'd reached the tent. *Where are the cartel's assassins when they're needed?* he thought fleetingly, and immediately reprimanded himself.

Longarm did not wish death upon anyone, not even an asshole like Barston. Besides, he'd seen enough bigwig politicians in Denver to know that more often than not, a public servant's true personality was quite different from the sweetheart image he might project to the general public.

Longarm saw Ki standing outside the entrance to the tent. He met the samurai's long-suffering expression with a commiserating nod.

"That fellow Barston disturbs my tranquility," Ki muttered, shaking his head.

"He gives me a pain too, old son," Longarm replied, snuffing out his cheroot on his boot sole and putting it back in his pocket. "But not in my tranquility."

"Indeed." Ki held open the tent flap.

"You have those little throwing knives of yours on you?" Longarm whispered before entering.

Ki patted his leather vest and nodded. "But why?"

"I may want to slit my wrists before this day is over," Longarm grumbled.

"Quit jawing and get in here, Long!" Barston thundered.

Wincing, Ki let the tent flap close behind Longarm. "And I may want to slit a *throat* before the day is over," the samurai muttered to himself. "But not mine."

The officials' tent was roomy and furnished with several desks and chairs, lanterns, files containing duplicates of the licenses issued to the food-sellers and entertainers, and appropriately enough, a keg of beer resting in a trough filled with ice. The lanterns were unlit just now, as several of the tent's roof-flaps were thrown back to let in the bright sunlight. Jessie, Barston, and the town's officials were all seated around a long table.

"Congressman, I could hear you yelling a quarter-mile away," Longarm drawled, tipping back his hat and straddling a chair.

"Damn near drowned out the pretty music coming from the carousel."

"Has Thorn come back from the Western Union office, yet?" Barston asked meaningfully.

"Wouldn't know, sir," Longarm said politely. "As I'm sure you recall, Thorn doesn't answer to me."

Jessie's swiftly smothered chuckle did not go unnoticed by the congressman. "Make your jokes now, Deputy. You won't be laughing much longer."

"Yes, sir," Longarm sighed. "But what *was* all the ruckus about?"

"It's utter nonsense!" Barston said disdainfully, his handsome features twisting in anger. "Leo! Explain it!"

Tompkins nodded in resignation as Marshal Farley stood up, saying, "If you all will excuse me, I've got business to attend to." He tipped his hat to Jessie, and winked at Longarm as he ducked out of the tent.

Tompkins was pointing to a trio of elderly gentlemen grouped around the head of the long table. The trio were wearing outsized Stetsons upon which were pinned medallions that read OFFICIAL. "These three good fellows are Mayor Wilk, Councilman Hendricks, and the president of the Cattlemen's Association, Hiram Calhoun, Junior—"

"Senior, you nincompoop!" the elderly Mr. Calhoun cackled. "My boy's the junior, not me!"

"Sorry," Tompkins said, slightly flustered. "Anyway—"

"Never mind!" Barston suddenly exploded. "*I'll* tell him! Deputy, these three *officials* run the fair, and will judge the shooting match. They've scheduled the elimination trials to begin a mere half hour from now!"

"So?" Longarm asked. "What's the problem?"

"The *problem,* Deputy," Barston began, his voice dripping with contempt, "the *problem* is that after the initial round of mass eliminations, they've got me scheduled to shoot second—"

"That's right," Mayor Wilk nodded. "We've done it alphabetically. The second round begins with Deadeye Adams, then you, Congressman Barston. After you, Frank Butler."

"After Mr. Butler, we've scheduled the Cling Sisters, and then Leroy Kingsley," Calhoun added.

"That's *Two-Gun* Leroy Kingsley," Mayor Wilk corrected

164

him, consulting the sheaf of papers before him. "These show folk are a mite picky about how they're introduced."

"Gentlemen, I'll tell you this once and for all," Barston declared. "I cannot shoot second."

"The newspapermen won't be here until noon," Tompkins appealed to Longarm. "If the congressman shoots second, he'll be done before they get here to see it."

"That can't be helped," the mayor stated flatly. "Rules are rules. The schedule has been posted. There's nothing we can do to change the order of contestants at this late date."

"Jessie?" Barston pleaded. "Do something!"

"Mayor Wilk, couldn't you just delay the start of the match a half hour?" Jessie asked sweetly.

"Well . . ." Wilk looked at Calhoun.

"I don't like it," Calhoun decreed.

"What does the councilman have to say about it?" Longarm cut in. "Haven't heard a peep out of him." Longarm crouched down, trying to see the official's face. "Can't even see him under that wagon-wheel sombrero. Why are all you boys decked out in those things?"

"Nothing wrong with our hats, son," Calhoun replied, his tone ominous.

"He's right," the mayor said. "We look like toadstools, dammit!"

"These here are good old High Plains Stetsons!" Calhoun squawked. "Genuine Lone Star State, ten-gallon hats. The kind us *real* drovers wore back before there *were* any towns—or *mayors,* I might add!"

"We still haven't heard from Councilman Hendricks," Longarm pointed out.

"Maybe he died," Tompkins muttered.

"Nope, he ain't dead, sonny," Calhoun smirked. "He's just napping in preparation for the excitement to come." The old cattleman's laugh sounded like a rusty door hinge. "Hendricks ain't as young as he used to be!"

"*I'm* not as young as I was this morning," Tompkins sighed. He eyed the beer keg, licking his lips.

"Pardon me," Ki addressed the officials as he stepped into the tent. "There is somebody here to see you gentlemen."

"Send him in, then," Mayor Wilk replied.

"I think you had better come out, sirs," Ki replied. "There is quite a crowd gathering."

"Is it trouble?" Longarm asked with concern.

"Perhaps," Ki said noncommittally. "But not of the sort that would concern you, Longarm." The samurai turned back to the judges. "There is a latecomer who wishes a license to put on a show this evening."

"Impossible!" Calhoun shook his head. "We're filled up. No more licenses—"

From outside there came the sound of laughter, and then applause. Ki's almond eyes sparkled. "Perhaps it would be better if the officials told the latecomer that, personally?"

"Should I wake Hendricks?" Mayor Wilk wondered.

"Let 'im sleep," Calhoun advised. "We two can investigate this ruckus, and then come back and vote on what to do about Barston's complaint." The ancient cattle baron glared at the congressman.

"I really think you ought to settle the matter I've raised before you go on to anything else," Barston said.

"That's fine, sonny," Calhoun glared. "But you ain't President yet."

"Now, Hiram," Mayor Wilk cajoled. "Don't be getting cranky."

"Dadburn young fellow is just like my own son," Calhoun muttered. "They get their growth, they think they run the whole damned world. Come on, Mayor. Let's go see who thinks he's gonna get himself a show license at this late date!"

"We'll be right here when you get back," Barston warned.

"I think I'll step outside for some air," Jessie said quickly.

"I'll join you." Longarm stood up, waiting politely for the fair officials and Jessie to exit before leaving the tent. "Think we ought to wake the councilman?" he asked her once he'd caught up.

"I doubt the we *could* wake him," Jessie smiled, taking his arm. "Custis! Just look at that wagon!"

The vehicle was something, Longarm had to admit. It was twice the size of any old Conestoga he'd ever seen. Actually, it reminded him of the huge, ox-drawn Murphy wagons that once carried tons of merchandise along the Santa Fe Trail, back in the early part of the century. Like the awesome Murphys, this wagon had iron-rimmed wheels that stood as tall as a man, and eight oxen harnessed up front. Just now, the big beasts were tossing their huge horned heads and mooing loudly. A young lad was lovingly scratching their heads, and murmuring into their floppy ears as he checked to see that none of the wooden yokes was chafing the oxen's hulking shoulders.

The wagon box was painted blue, with big white stars. The wheels' spokes were painted in alternating barber-pole-style bands of red and white, to complete the Old Glory motif. A canvas curtain hanging from the wooden framework atop the wagon box shrouded the vehicle's interior. Spanning the breadth of the curtain was a painting of an enormous buffalo. Smoke puffed from the giant beast's black nostrils, while lightningbolts sparked from its pawing hooves. There was no lettering on the curtain, just that awesome bison's portrait.

As Longarm and Jessie watched, joining the small crowd that had gathered expectantly, the boy left his team of oxen to fiddle with several latches situated along the length of the wagon. Next he folded down an ingenious platform, which, when propped up by its swing-down legs, formed a rudimentary stage.

"Ladies and gentlemen!" the boy squawked, his adolescent voice breaking. "May I present Mr. Texas Jack Omohundro!"

The canvas curtain parted slightly, and out hobbled a bow-legged, gray-haired, leathery-skinned man of indeterminate age. The fellow was dressed in chaps and a black, twelve-button, bib-front shirt embroidered with what looked to be a meadow's worth of yellow flowers. He was holding a three-legged stool in one hand, and a five-string banjo in the other.

"Folks, my name is Texas Jack," the man said, setting down his stool on the right-hand side of the stage. He tipped his hat to give the audience a good look at the Stetson's Indian-beaded hatband. "I got this here band of beads, and my reputation as the meanest Indian fighter to ever have sighted down on a redman, by conquering the proud Apache—"

"What horse apples!" Longarm whispered to Jessie. She giggled and said, "I think that's the oxen you're smelling."

"—but there's one man even I look up to as an Indian fighter

167

bar none," Texas Jack continued. "I'd like to sing you a little song by way of introducing him," he finished, seating himself upon his stool, and perching his banjo on his knee.

"We're in for it now," Longarm grieved, provoking an angry stare from the people standing in front of him.

"I can't say for sure whether or not that's Texas Jack," Hiram Calhoun grumbled, "but I think that these here folks oughtn't to be putting on a show without a license that I, for one, don't intend to issue them!"

"Come on, Hiram," Mayor Wilk complained. "Let it continue. I want to see who's coming out. Besides, it ain't a show. It's—" Wilk thought hard. "It's a *presentation* for a show!"

"Politicians," Calhoun muttered, shaking his head, but he kept quiet.

Texas Jack, meanwhile, had begun strumming a doleful tune on his banjo. After a few introductory bars to quiet the crowd, he began to sing in the mournful manner of a coyote howling at the full moon:

"There's plenty o' tragedy in the West,
And folks, the Alamo ain't hardly the best;
Custer fell 'gainst savages on the warpath,
But here's what happened in the aftermath...."

Texas Jack stood up abruptly, whipping off his hat and clamping it over his heart. "Ladies and gentlemen!" he yelled. "May I present a grand tableau depicting the beginning of the long-overdue end of the redman, and one of the shining moments in America's history! I'm talking about *The Red Right Hand,* or *Buffalo Bill's First Scalp for Custer!*"

More or less on cue, the big wagon's canvas curtain more or less steadily rose. The audience gasped as they beheld a backdrop painting of a gory battlefield. Indian corpses littered the ground all the way back to a horizon stained with smoke and fire. Center stage, upon his knees, with his wrists bound before him, was an Indian wearing a loincloth, a buckskin vest, and an impossibly large headdress of mangy eagle feathers. From the stocky, barrel-chested look of the man, Longarm guessed that he was a Ute off the Ouray reservation near Wyoming Territory.

"I am Yellow Hand, one of the dastardly war chiefs who led his swarms down upon the greatly outnumbered American hero, George Custer!" the Ute wailed.

Of course, Yellow Hand was a Cheyenne, not a Ute, Longarm thought to himself. But if there was such a thing as poetic license, he supposed it extended to actors as well as scribes.

"Ha-ha! I laughed as I stood over Custer's body," the Ute said wistfully. "Little did I know that my heinous crimes would soon be punished by—" the Ute paused, gazing expectantly toward stage right.

"Ha-ha!" the Ute said a bit more loudly. "Little did I know," he shouted, "that my crimes would be avenged by none other than—" Once again the Indian paused, waiting for the appearance of somebody who was evidently just not coming.

Shaking his head, the boy who'd returned to tending his oxen now raced around behind the wagon. Texas Jack, seizing the moment, strummed a godawful banjo chord to get the audience's—and the panicked Ute's—attention. "Yellow Hand, you varmint! What was it that you didn't know?"

"Huh?" The Ute stared blankly. "Ha-ha..." he began stoically. "Little did I—"

"Lord," Jessie breathed. "I don't care *who* he's killed, he's been punished enough."

"—that my *terrible* crimes would be punished by—"

"By *me!*" called a deep baritone voice from offstage. Out strode a figure wrapped from head to toe in an Indian blanket. "Quake with good reason, Redman, for you face William Cody!" The newcomer let the blanket fall away from his head, revealing his hat, shoulder-length blond hair, mustache, and goatee.

"Holy smokes! I can't believe it!" Texas Jack said with what Longarm assumed was real sincerity. "It's Buffalo Bill himself!"

The star of the show dropped his blanket the rest of the way, to take a turn around the stage, acknowledging the audience's applause. He wore a fringed buckskin suit, palomino-tan in color, and high, black leather boots that rose up past his knees. Around his waist was a wide belt decorated with colorful Indian beadwork. A sheathed bowie knife rode his left hip, while a pistol butt protruded from the waistband of his pants. Buffalo Bill wore a Stetson with a wide brim, turned up in the front. He had several necklaces of bears' teeth and a knotted yellow kerchief around his throat. Turquoise-studded silver bracelets decorated his wrists.

"Here we are at War Bonnet Creek," Buffalo Bill told the attentive audience. "Mere days ago, the Sioux, under their leader Sitting Bull, and the Cheyenne, under Two Moons, defeated Custer and his troops at the Battle of the Little Bighorn—Custer's Last Stand!"

"The Indian race won that battle due to our superior numbers," the Ute playing Yellow Hand added. "But here at War Bonnet Creek—"

"During a fair fight—" Buffalo Bill insisted.

"—we were defeated!"

"And now, Yellow Hand, prepare to meet your doom!" Buffalo Bill snarled, drawing his bowie knife and holding it aloft. "This shall be my first scalp, for Custer!" He snatched away the Ute's headdress and placed his blade against the side of the Indian's head.

"Woe is me," the Ute moaned. Then both actors froze in place, as the curtain slowly lowered.

"This is our tableau," Texas Jack announced. "To see the whole play, and to witness Yellow Hand meeting his end, come to our tent show tonight at eight!"

There was a smattering of applause. Before the crowd could drift away, Buffalo Bill once more appeared upon the stage. He stood with his hands on his hips, looking quite the hero with that huge, painted bison tearing up the earth behind him.

"Men! Boys!" Buffalo Bill called out. "Don't forget! Tonight at eight! It'll be the darnedest blowout ever to hit Sarah, Texas—"

"*If* I decide to let you have a license, Freddy," Hiram Calhoun called out.

Buffalo Bill's eyes narrowed as he stared out over the audience. "I know that voice," he said, smiling.

"You ought to, Fred," Calhoun said, stepping forward, but still keeping his oversized ten-gallon Stetson pulled low to shield his face. "William Frederick Cody, alias Buffalo Bill!" The cattle baron laughed. "Why, if it weren't for me, you'd still be known as Freddy Cody!"

170

"Hiram?" Buffalo Bill blurted out. "Could it be, old son? Is that you, Hiram?"

Calhoun took off his hat. His wrinkled features were suffused with pleasure. "It's me all right, Freddy! How the hell are you?"

Buffalo Bill leaped down from the stage to embrace the old man. "Why, I haven't seen you since '68!"

"Easy, boy! Easy!" Calhoun laughed. "You'll break an old man's bones!" The elderly cattle baron glanced about in satisfaction at the number of witnesses who would later be able to report on his familiarity with the famous man.

"How's your boy, Hiram?" Buffalo Bill asked.

"Ah, I can't complain, I guess," Calhoun scowled. "He's only half as smart as me, but twice as big. What the hell, that's good enough. I was the one who got us all them cows. All he has to do is take care of them!" The cattleman's eyes fell upon Jessie, who was watching the reunion. "Come here, girl! Bill, you'll want to meet this little lady! This is Jessica Starbuck, Alex's daughter. You remember Alex, don't you?"

"Why, sure!" Buffalo Bill smiled. "And I see the resemblance in his lovely daughter." He took Jessie's hand and kissed it, much to the delight of the onlookers crowded around. "I learned all about hand-kissing from the Grand Duke of Russia, back in '72, when I took him on a buffalo-hunting trip," he announced grandly.

Jessie turned around to place a hand on Longarm's shoulder. "Sir, this is Deputy U.S. Marshal Custis Long," she said, introducing him to the famous scout.

Buffalo Bill nodded. "Pleased to meet you, Custis. I always support the law. And so should all the little buckaroos who want to be just like me!" he proclaimed for the benefit of the youngsters and their smiling, nodding parents. "Any mama and papa who want to teach their offspring that crime does not pay would do well to attend tonight's show with their entire family!" Buffalo Bill paused to wink at Jessie. "That is, if this old coot decides to issue me a license."

"'Course I will, Freddy," Calhoun snorted.

"In that case, I'd count it an honor if you sat up on the stage during the show, Hiram."

Mayor Wilk tugged frantically at Calhoun's sleeve and then whispered into the cattleman's ear. "The mayor wants to know if he can sit up on the stage with me," Calhoun cackled.

"Well," Buffalo Bill frowned. "It's going to be a mite crowded."

"Doesn't the mayor also vote on the license?" Longarm innocently asked Jessie.

"But I'd count it an honor if the mayor joined us onstage," Buffalo Bill said heartily, and then winked at Longarm.

"Hot damn!" Wilk exclaimed. "Maybe one of the boys at the newspaper could take a picture of us. It'd sure come in handy during the next election!"

"Speaking of elections—" Longarm said, and gestured toward Barston's secretary, Tompkins, who was just now stepping out of the officials' tent.

"The congressman demands to know the judges' decision concerning the target competition," Tompkins began, and then stared at Cody. "Say, aren't you—?"

Buffalo Bill nodded happily. "Yep, I am."

"Tell your boss that we've decided to delay the start of the match until noon," Calhoun said. "But it ain't for his sake I'm doing it. I just want a little more time to shoot the breeze with Freddy here."

"Just how did you two meet?" Jessie asked as Tompkins scurried back to Barston with the good news. "And you mentioned that you knew my father as well, Mr. Cody?"

"Why don't you and Hiram join me around back of my wagon?" Buffalo Bill invited them expansively. "We can sit in the shade and talk more privately. You come along as well, Deputy Long." As they walked, Buffalo Bill whispered to Longarm, "I owe you a favor for that tip you gave me concerning the mayor."

"I just figured this was one time that Buffalo Bill needed a scout to tell him the lay of the land," Longarm chuckled.

A canvas awning had been erected behind the wagon. A table and several chairs had been set out on the grass. A big pitcher of tea and a bottle of bourbon stood on the table, along with a plate of sandwiches. Longarm saw the Ute who'd portrayed Yellow Hand; he and Texas Jack were hard at a game of cribbage as they finished their lunch. Other performers and

172

a couple of roustabouts were nearby, either snoozing on the grass or munching on sandwiches.

Calhoun peered suspiciously at Texas Jack, and then whispered to Buffalo Bill, "That ain't actually him, is it? I mean, my eyes ain't what they used to be, but—"

"Your eyes are fine, Hiram," Buffalo Bill assured him. "Old Jack took sick. That there is a fellow I hired to portray him."

The Ute glanced up at the newcomers as they took seats around the table. He eyed them all indifferently until he came to Longarm, and his broad face lit up. "Greetings, blood brother!"

"Greetings to my friend of the mighty *Ho*,"" Longarm said. "How long have you been off the reservation?"

"It has been a long while since I cast my lot with Buffalo Bill," the Ute replied. "Do you have news of home, Longarm?" he asked eagerly.

"Afraid not, beyond knowing that Hungry Calf is still leading things."

"You two know each other?" Buffalo Bill asked, surprised. He grinned at the deputy. "Not many whites know that the Utes call themselves *Ho*. And did Dark Cloud, here, call you Longarm?"

"Longarm is known as an excellent law officer among my people," Dark Cloud said. "A long while ago he became a blood brother of the *Ho*."

"Longarm is his nickname," Jessie said. "It suits him, just like your nickname suits you, Mr. Cody. But please!" she begged. "I'm dying to know how you met my father!"

"There's not all that much to tell," Buffalo Bill replied as he poured them all glasses of tea. "After the War, I went to work for the Kansas Pacific Railroad, under contract to supply their workers with fresh meat. I was only twenty-two years old—"

"Your father and I had some money invested in the Kansas Pacific, Jessie," Calhoun cut in. "We decided to mosey on out and see how fast they were laying their track. One night we were all sitting around a campfire, sharing a bottle, and I said to young Cody here, 'You've killed so many buffalo, your name ought to be Buffalo Bill. . . .'"

"And it stuck," Buffalo Bill chuckled. "I ended up with a

tally of 4,280 kills to my credit," he boasted. "When Ned Buntline heard about it, it inspired him to write his first novel about me, *The King of the Border Men*. Well, after that, the nickname of Buffalo Bill was branded on me, right and proper."

"Why, Hiram Calhoun," Jessie teased. "You singlehandedly inspired a legend!"

The lad in charge of the oxen trudged past, lugging a large crate. "Cap'n, if we're going to set up the tent in time . . ." he warned.

Buffalo Bill nodded. "Thank you, Tim. Folks, you'll have to excuse us. We've got a lot of work to do to be ready to entertain the good citizens of Sarah this evening."

The lad stumbled beneath his heavy burden, prompting Buffalo Bill to reprimand him sharply. He then smiled in apology to his guests, saying, "The good folks who come to my stage show count it a convenience that I offer my own, personally written book for sale during the intermission and after the performance."

"You wrote a book, Freddy?" Calhoun marveled.

Buffalo Bill nodded. "*The Life of the Honorable William F. Cody, Known as Buffalo Bill, the Famous Hunter, Scout and Guide: an Autobiography.*"

"Is that the title or the whole book?" Longarm joked.

"Say! That's a good one," Bill said, though his expression did not strike Longarm as that of a man about to laugh. "Now if you folks will excuse me . . ."

"See you later, Freddy," Calhoun said as he stood up. "I'll send somebody over with your license. He'll guide you to a good spot to set up your tent."

Calhoun shook hands with Buffalo Bill. "Come along, Jessie, Longarm," the cattle baron crowed. "It's time to start the shooting match!"

The first heat of the elimination trials served to disqualify the amateur contestants, with the exception of Congressman Barston. Perhaps the reason was that target-shooting in a competition was a far different thing from plinking at tin cans out behind the barn, or taking potshots at squirrels. Perhaps it was that so many people were watching, and that during this first heat, so many contestants were firing simultaneously at their respective targets, positioned fifty yards away. In any case, it turned out that most of the nonprofessionals couldn't hit the broad side of a barn, let alone a bullseye a few inches across.

Barston, Longarm had to admit, was an excellent shot. The congressman was firing a custom-designed weapon. Both Longarm and Ki moved in close to examine the gun. It was a double-action Colt .32 with an eight-inch barrel, adjustable sights, and a sculpted wooden grip that fit its owner's hand like a glove.

Once the crowd of contestants thinned down, the competition proceeded to the timed-fire event. There were now few enough shooters to take their turns one at a time, which added to the suspense of the contest for the folks who were sitting in the bleachers. Each contestant had to fire five shots in twenty seconds. The top scorers in this event would compete in the finals the next day, and be within reach of the trophy, as well as the two-thousand-dollar purse.

Since the competition's start had been postponed until noon, the reporters had arrived in time to see Barston shoot in the first round of mass eliminations. He was still scheduled to shoot second, after Deadeye Adams in the upcoming round, but the congressman no longer objected to this, since the reporters were now present to attest to his skill.

When it was his turn, Barston marched up to the shooting stand, held his pistol in his outstretched right hand in the classic firing position, and smoothly squeezed off his five shots. Although his pistol was double-action, Barston used it as a single-action weapon, thumb-cocking the revolver before every shot. The accuracy he needed would have been impossible if he'd worked his gun's mechanism through its trigger. Longarm watched Barston critically, but he could find no fault in the way the politician held his pistol, cocking the hammer with a straight-back movement of his thumb while not allowing the weapon to rise, dip, or sway off target. By the end of the twenty-second period, three of Barston's rounds were in the small circle just outside of the bullseye, and two holes had been punched into the X ring, the absolute center of the target.

Only one hit in the X ring was required to make it through the eliminations. Barston got a standing ovation from the spectators when his score was announced by the judges. Longarm

175

watched the congressman smile and wave to the crowd, holding his arms clasped above his head in the victory sign.

"Damn," the deputy muttered to himself. "Right now, even *I* feel like voting for him. . . ."

The only other shooter to match Barston's score was Phoebe, the young farm girl that Ki had rescued yesterday at the swimming pond. As she made her way to the shooting stand, she anxiously searched the sidelines, looking for the samurai.

Ki waved to her. She beamed a dazzling smile his way, then took her place at the firing line. Today she was dressed in a much more modest fashion than she had been yesterday. A loose-fitting calico dress hid her sumptuous figure. With her clumpy work shoes, and her long brown hair plaited into no-nonsense pigtails, she looked like a schoolgirl. . . .

But there was nothing schoolgirlish about the way she handled a gun, Ki thought with admiration. Phoebe's pistol was a standard, factory-built Smith & Wesson. It certainly could not compare to Barston's target model. Still, this farm girl was the very picture of grace as she aimed her revolver with a fluid motion and let loose her five shots. She completed her round with three seconds to spare, and when the judges announced that she'd tied with Barston, the crowd went wild. Even the reporters deserted the congressman to get a better look at this extraordinary young lady.

Phoebe, however, was indifferent to the attention of the press and the cheers of the spectators. She made a beeline to Ki, throwing her arms around the samurai, and pressing her mouth against his for a sweet kiss.

"Did you see me?" she asked Ki ecstatically. "Didn't I tell you I'd win?"

"Yes, indeed!" Ki smiled in response to her wholehearted delight. His arms embraced her; he felt the warmth of her body through the thin cotton of her dress. "I do believe you're even a better shot than Jessie," he murmured.

"Jessie!" Phoebe grimaced. "Who is Jessie?" she demanded, pulling free of Ki's embrace and scowling up at him with her hands on her hips. "Is that your girlfriend?" she demanded in exasperation, and then shook her pistol at him.

Ki grinned. "Do not shoot me, Phoebe! Jessie is Jessica Starbuck!"

"You mean the woman who's paying for this shindig?" she asked, and them sighed in relief. "Well, that's okay, then," she giggled. "And Ki, I'd never shoot *you!*" she swore, her big, blue eyes growing round. "Except maybe just a *little.*" Her gaze dropped down to his crotch. "Nothing serious; just a scratch to keep you out of trouble until I could kiss it and make it better. . . ."

Ki felt himself growing very warm. "You are talking about a *crucial* level of accuracy."

"I can shave the whiskers off a fly's leg," Phoebe boasted. "And anyway"—she eyed the front of Ki's trousers speculatively—"even if my aim was a little off, you've definitely got plenty to spare."

"Young lady . . ." Ki growled, pretending to menace her.

Phoebe laughed, leaning against him. "Deadeye Adams, the Cling Sisters, and Two-Gun Kingsley were all eliminated," she murmured. "Tomorrow I'll only be up against the congressman and Frank."

"And who is Frank?" Ki asked.

"Why, Frank Butler, of course," Phoebe replied. "You mean you really have never heard of Frank Butler?" she demanded, astounded. "Didn't you see him shoot this afternoon?"

"I must have missed it," Ki replied. "I did do some patrolling of the fairgrounds."

"Oh, that's right," Phoebe nodded. "I forgot you're a deputy. Anyway, that's him, over there." She pointed out a middle-aged, dapper-looking man dressed in a blue suit, a red satin vest, and a black derby. Butler was clean-shaven and carried a gold-headed walking stick.

As Ki looked the obviously professional shootist over, the two men's eyes met. Ki was surprised to observe that Butler was definitely glaring at him.

"Now what did I do?" the samurai mused out loud.

"Huh?" Phoebe looked up at him.

"That man is angry with me for some reason. Do you have any idea why?"

"Oh, *no,*" Phoebe said quickly. "Why should I?" she added, with such elaborate denial that Ki was instantly suspicious.

"Phoebe . . ." Ki said warily. "Are you telling me the truth?"

"Why *shouldn't* I tell you the truth?" she replied. "Come

on," she pleaded, tugging at Ki's arm. "I'm thirsty. Will you buy me a lemonade?"

Ki nodded, letting himself be led away from the shooting field. He looked back just before turning the corner. Yes, Butler was still staring, and if looks could kill, Frank Butler would be one shootist with no need for a firearm!

Barston, watching Ki and Phoebe from some distance away, sneered, "She certainly seems lacking in morals."

"I wouldn't let Ki hear you say that," Longarm warned. "She seems to be a friend of his, and he takes nasty remarks about his friends real personal."

"Well, his 'friend,' if that's what she is, will lose this match to me," Barston vowed. "Tompkins?"

"Yes, sir?" the secretary replied meekly, worried that Barston was going to blame him for the reporters' desertion.

"Find out about that girl," Barston ordered. "Where she comes from, if her family owns any property under mortgage to a bank, things like that." The congressman's face took on an ugly expression. "We may need a little leverage if she shoots that well tomorrow. She is going to have to learn that her social betters are not without the ability to influence the outcome of important matters in her drab little life."

Longarm shook his head, muttering under his breath.

"What?" Barston asked sharply, whirling around to confront the deputy. "What did you say, Long?"

"Nothing."

"It had *better* be nothing," Barston smirked.

Longarm felt anger welling up within him. His pulse was pounding, and his gut was clenched with rage. "It's not necessary for me to say anything, because your lack of character speaks for itself."

"Now you've done it, Deputy!" Barston laughed triumphantly. "Tompkins, you're a witness to the way this government employee has insulted me."

"Sir," Tompkins cut in, grasping Barston's arm. "Miss Starbuck is headed this way."

"I don't care!" Barston snarled. "Let her be a witness to this bastard's insolence, as well!"

"Bastard, am I?" Longarm seethed. "Well, you'll have good

178

reason to call me that in a moment, Barston! I've made some reporter friends down through the years. I promise you this—you blackmail or interfere with that farm girl in any way, and I'll take my story to the papers about how you ordered Tompkins to do it!"

"Wilson!" Jessie gasped. "Is what Custis just said true? Did you intend to cheat?"

"Jessie, it's not cheating," Barston explained reluctantly. "It's done all the time up on Capitol Hill—" The congressman was quivering with hatred as he turned toward Longarm. "I'm not only going to get you fired, I'm going to have you thrown in prison for threatening a United States Representative with extortion!"

"Just you keep quiet, Barston!" Longarm thundered. "Else you'll have to prosecute me for busting you in the nose, as well!"

"Come on and try it!" Barston spat. He balled his hands into fists and took a fast step toward Longarm.

"Wilson! Are you *crazy?*" Tompkins whispered hoarsely. "Any moment now the press will notice! Do you want them to write that you got into a brawl?"

"Get out of my way, Tompkins!" Barston sputtered, bouncing up and down on the balls of his feet.

"Listen to your boss, Leo," Longarm smiled. God! How he was aching to take a swing at Barston!

"Longarm! Don't do this—" Tompkins begged, glancing over his shoulder at the deputy while he stood in front of Barston, blocking his way.

Much to his disgust, Longarm realized that Barston was making no real effort to shove past the little secretary. He relaxed, lowering his fists.

Barston seized that moment to renew his attack. He charged forward. Tompkins leaped up like a trout in a valiant attempt to keep his client from making a scandalous scene—

There was a shot. Tompkins had just reached the apex of his jump as he screamed, *What's happened to me?* He reached around in a frantic effort to plug the bloody hole that had appeared between his shoulder blades, then he collapsed to the ground.

Pandemonium erupted as two more shots were fired. A

woman wailed as her husband went down, clutching at his shoulder. The fairgrounds crowd milled about in panic, wondering where the next shot was going to come from, and who it was going to hit.

Longarm, his Colt at the ready, snapped a shot toward a rifleman sighting down at the congressman from the top row of the now deserted bleachers. The sniper was out of pistol range, but Longarm's shot sent him scurrying for cover.

Meanwhile, Jessie had pulled Barston to the ground. She had drawn her own Colt from her shoulder bag.

"Keep him here," Longarm ordered as he glided off in pursuit of the sniper.

"Where's Thorn?" Barston raged. "I don't want Longarm!"

"Longarm's all you've got," Jessie said coldly. "You're not worth it, Wilson," she declared in disdain. "But for your information, Longarm is the best there is!"

"N-not worth it?" Barston stammered in confusion. "Jessie? W-what are you saying?"

"Be quiet!" she ordered him, and turned her attention to Tompkins.

The secretary was lying on the grass. His face was ashen as he mumbled thickly, "Shot? Am I—?"

"Rest," Jessie soothed. "We'll get you a doctor."

Tompkin's eyes locked with hers. "Am I dead? It doesn't hurt. Am I all right?" He coughed. Blood, garnet-red in the bright sunshine, welled up out of his mouth to run down his chin. "Drank all your brandy," Tompkins mourned, just before he died.

"Keep down, all of you keep down!" Longarm shouted at the gawking bystanders. They all ignored him, rubbernecking like total fools for a glimpse of the sniper. Fortunately, no further shooting had erupted from the bleacher area. Longarm did not know why the sniper had stopped firing, but he was certainly grateful that it seemed to be the case as he ran a zigzag pattern toward the rickety tiers of wooden bench seats.

Longarm saw him sitting huddled beneath the bleachers. The man was old, and dressed in ragged clothing. He was clutching his rifle to his chest and crying so loudly that he didn't hear Longarm approaching. The deputy leveled his Colt at the pitiful figure and called out gently, "Give it up, friend. It's all over."

Startled, the sniper jumped to his feet. His tattered straw hat fell off of his head. "I didn't mean for any innocent souls to get hurt! You gotta believe me, lawman!"

Longarm stared. The sniper had to be over eighty years old! His scalp was as bald as an egg, crisscrossed with veins. There was not a tooth in the old geezer's mouth. The sniper's scraggly beard was more yellow than white, and his pale blue eyes were as rheumy as a bloodhound's.

"That little fella just jumped into my line of fire!" the old man blubbered. "I was aiming for that son of a bitch Barston! I swear I was!"

"But you missed him, and ended up shooting two other men," Longarm said. "Now give me that rifle before anybody else gets hurt."

The old fellow looked down in surprise, as if he hadn't realized that he was still holding his rifle. "Sure, lawman!" he replied quickly. Then he clutched the rifle to his chest again. "But first you gotta listen to me!" he begged. "I *did* mean to kill *Barston*, for what his daddy did to me a long time ago!"

Longarm nodded, and took a step toward the man. "Give me your gun and we'll talk about it, old-timer."

"Barston's daddy stole my land!" the sniper bawled. "I had me a right fine cattle spread back when I was a youth. I staked it out and built me a cabin all by myself. It was virgin land, I tell you son! Nobody owned it but me!"

"Give me the rifle," Longarm repeated, moving in on the man.

The elderly ambusher quickly leveled his rifle at Longarm. "Listen to me, *please!* Nobody ever has!"

It was the agony in the old man's voice that stopped Longarm, not the man's rifle. The deputy saw that the fellow's gnarled fingers were nowhere near the weapon's trigger.

Nodding, Longarm lowered his pistol. "Go on, uncle. I'm listening."

"Thankee," the man whispered. "What happened was that I built up a fine ranch in just six months' time. Then, one day in rides Barston's daddy with a lawyer fella and a bunch of

181

drovers. The lawyer said I hadn't filed the right sorta papers. 'Papers?' I said. 'Papers is for city folk. I'm a cowboy,' I told them. 'I never got the chance to learn reading and writing.'"

"What happened?" Longarm asked, although he already knew the likely reply to *that* sad question.

"They took away my land and scattered my cows," the old man wept. "They burned my cabin and sent me away with just my horse, my bedroll, and my sixgun. All that work, down the drain!"

"Didn't you complain to the law?"

"Sure I did, son," the man nodded. "But nobody would listen to me. I didn't have any money, and a fella needs cold cash to back his complaints when he goes up against a man like Barston's daddy. Everybody laughed at me. Barston's daddy had the gall to offer me a drover's job. Can you believe it? He wanted *me* to work for *him!* Ride the land that he stole out from under me! I knew then what I had to do. *I had to kill him!*"

Longarm shook his head. "You didn't get him, of course. And they sent you to jail for trying it, didn't they, uncle?"

The old man nodded. *"Thirty years—"* His voice was cracked and trembling. "Thirty years spent breaking rocks for trying to kill the man who ruined my life . . ." He swallowed hard. "When I got out, Barston's daddy had died—of natural causes." He giggled, a trifle hysterically. "Died in his sleep in his soft, warm, rich man's bed. I got me a job shoveling out the shit in a stable, and I listened right hard whenever young Wilson Barston's name got mentioned. I heard about how he was fixing to run for President—" The old man shook his head. "Can you imagine that, son?" he demanded fiercely. "A Barston for President? *I could never let that happen!* I was fixing to travel to Washington to get him, but then I heard he was coming here. So I—" Once more his tears began to run. They funneled down along the seams that life had worn into his cheeks long years ago.

"You've traveled a hard road, uncle, there's no question about that," Longarm said. "But today you hurt two people who never did you harm, and that's why I've come for you." He held out his left hand. "I don't want to shoot you, uncle, so I'm asking you for the last time. Give me that rifle."

The old man nodded. "I'll give it up. It's finished for me—" He began to lower the hammer on the weapon prior to turning it over to Longarm.

"Drop it, you bastard!" a harsh male voice commanded from behind the elderly sniper.

The old man turned in surprise, swinging the rifle around with him.

Thorn's short-barreled .38 Smith & Wesson barked three times, punching the old man back toward Longarm. The rifle fell from the sniper's fingers as he began to topple.

Longarm moved instinctively to catch him. The old man stared into Longarm's face in utter amazement, his pale blue eyes suddenly grown radiant. "Why, thankee, son . . . Thankee for caring about an old coot. . . ."

"Uncle—" Longarm began, but his voice failed him.

"But don't you fret, son," the dying old man whispered. "I was killed years ago. . . ."

He sighed pleasantly, like a man exhausted after a hard day's work. Then he simply dropped off to sleep, cradled like a babe in the deputy's arms. The fact that Longarm's hands were full was all that kept him from slaying Thorn at that moment. "You bastard!" he swore at the bodyguard. "You murdering, stupid bastard!"

Thorn's blond hair hung in his face. His blue eyes glinted redly as he glared back at Longarm with dumb hatred. "You care about that stinking old man, do you? He killed Tompkins, and he was trying to kill the congressman—"

Longarm lowered the old man's body gently to the ground. He straightened up, his Colt still in his right hand. "Let's do it, Thorn," he said evenly, angling his pistol toward the ground.

Thorn nodded quickly, licking his lips as he lowered his Smith & Wesson, pressing it against his trouser leg. "On the count of three, asshole. One, two—"

"Longarm! What's happened? Is everyone all right?" It was Marshal Farley, with an anxious-looking Ki right behind him.

Both Longarm and Thorn stared at the town marshal and his temporary deputy, and then both men slowly holstered their pistols. Thorn winked at Longarm. Longarm smiled thinly at the bodyguard. Neither needed words to tell what the other was thinking: *Another time, another place . . .*

"That old coot lying there murdered Leo Tompkins," Thorn volunteered. "He winged some other fellow from these parts, and was doing his best to kill Longarm when I got him."

"That so, Longarm?" Farley asked.

"He was surrendering to me when Thorn got trigger-happy," Longarm told the town marshal. "There was no reason to shoot him."

"Says *you*, Deputy," Thorn argued quickly. "Marshal Farley, I ordered this old man to surrender. He was still holding his rifle—the murder weapon—when I arrived. He turned fast toward me, aiming at me with that long gun." The bodyguard shrugged. "It's a clear-cut situation, as far as I'm concerned. I'll tell it to any jury . . . if that's what the congressman wants me to do."

Farley looked away. "Longarm, is it true that the old fellow was still hanging on to his rifle?"

"Yes, but—"

"That's it, then," Farley said quickly, and with obvious relief. "The old man shot two people and was trying for a third when Thorn dropped him. I'm satisfied."

"Marshal—" Longarm began, but Farley waved him quiet.

"It doesn't make a lick of sense to allow this to become any bigger a mess than it is already, Longarm. We've got reporters out there!" Farley exclaimed. "I've got my town to think about."

"It's not only up to *you*, Farley," Longarm replied. "Those reporters will listen to *me*, as well—"

"Longarm," Ki called softly. As Longarm glanced his way, the samurai shook his head. "Now is not the time, my friend. . . ."

Chuckling, Thorn headed toward the shooting range. Longarm stared after him, until Ki put his arm around the deputy's shoulder.

"Come, my friend," the samurai murmured. "Marshal Farley? You will see to it that this old man is cared for?"

"What?"

"While I take Longarm for a drink," Ki added quickly.

"Oh! Sure." Farley nodded. "That's a good idea. Get him a drink. I'll see to everything."

Ki led Longarm away from the bleachers. Farley, watching them go, suddenly grew miffed.

"Dammit!" he muttered, stalking away. I'm the town marshal. How come everybody tells *me* what to do?"

"I don't need a drink, Ki," Longarm told the samurai on their way across the fairgrounds. "I do thank you for your concern."

"Longarm, it is often very hard for an honorable man to stand by when an injustice is done."

"Thorn out-and-out murdered that old man," Longarm sighed.

"More than likely, the sniper would have been hung for killing Tompkins," Ki pointed out.

"A legal hanging is one thing," Longarm said dryly. "Being shot down like a dog is something else. Damn that Thorn! He only did it to get himself—and his boss—some extra newspaper space!"

"There was nothing you could do, Longarm," Ki said. "Tell me something. When Farley and I arrived, were you and Thorn preparing to shoot it out?"

Longarm nodded shamefacedly. "Dumb, huh?"

"Not dumb," Ki decided. "Thorn *needs* killing. It *was* foolish, however. Shooting him like that would have cost you your job as a federal law officer."

Longarm chuckled. "My job's hanging by a thread anyway, old son. If I've got to go, I might as well go out big. . . ."

"It is still not the time to bring down your enemies," the samurai insisted. "Vengeance, like fruit, grows sweeter the longer it is allowed to ripen on the vine."

Longarm stopped and stared at the samurai. "Now who made that up?" he grinned. "Confucius?"

"Shame on you, Longarm!" Ki scolded him lightly. "Why should I ever quote Confucius? First of all, he was Chinese; I am not Chinese. Second, he was a man of peace." Ki grinned, showing his teeth. "I am *not* a man of peace."

"Then what are you trying to tell me?" Longarm demanded, confounded.

"Only that Thorn *will* die," Ki vowed. "But not today."

The two friends resumed their walk back toward where Longarm had left Jessie and Barston. After a moment, Longarm asked, "How's your girlfriend?"

"Excuse me?" Ki asked politely.

"Come on," Longarm coaxed. "That sweet little lady who outshot everybody but Barston. I saw you two together."

"Ah, yes, Phoebe." Ki allowed himself a smile. "She is a delightful young lady. Extremely attractive, refreshingly forthright, and an admirable expert when it comes to firearms."

"Ki, level with me, you're sweet on her, right?"

The samurai rearranged his features into his usual impassive expression. "Longarm, these matters are not discussed by honorable men."

Longarm grew angry. "I know that! I mean, a gentleman never discusses his private relations with a woman, but dammit, Ki! I only asked if you *liked* her, I didn't ask anything about—"

The samurai shot Longarm a warning glance.

Longarm held up his hands in surrender. "Let's drop it. I forgot how you Japanese folks believe in keeping your private selves locked up inside."

Ki clapped Longarm lightly on the shoulder. "Your apology is accepted, my friend."

They'd reached a crowd of people clustered around the judges' platform. Ki craned his neck to see. "It looks like Congressman Barston is making a speech."

Longarm and Ki hurried around to the rear of the platform, where they found Jessie and Thorn listening to the congressman's orations. Thorn glanced at the deputy marshal and laughed.

"Listen to what the congressman has to say, Longarm. You should find it interesting."

"What are you getting at?" Longarm asked suspiciously.

"Hush!" Jessie quieted him.

". . . And today, my dear old friend, Leo Tompkins' died to save my life!" Barston proclaimed loudly. "Leo Tompkins— a man well known to you fellows of the press—bravely shielded my body with his own, to stop a bullet fired by a foreign assassin!"

A startled murmur ran through the assembled throng. "Congressman!" one of the reporters called out. "Are you saying you know for a fact that this attack upon your life was instigated by a foreign power?"

"That is correct!" Barston thundered. "Not only today's attack that took Tompkin's life, but yesterday's attack as well."

186

"That's not true—" Longarm began.

"You shut up," Thorn warned him as Marshal Farley joined their group.

"What's not true, Longarm?" Jessie demanded.

"I don't know about yesterday's attack," Longarm told her. "But today's shooting had nothing at all to do with the cartel." He was about to say more, but Barston chose that moment to resume speaking.

The federal lawman sent here to protect me could not do his job, but my own personal bodyguard managed to shoot the assassin before he could do any more harm." Barston suddenly held aloft a rifle. "This is the assassin's weapon!"

Longarm stared in disbelief. "No, it isn't, " he exclaimed. "The old man had a Spencer repeater. That weapon Barston is holding is a Winchester." He peered at the gun. "I do believe that's *your* rifle, Thorn!"

"So you say," the bodyguard shrugged.

"To prove that the same weapon was used in both attacks, I have here a rifle bullet dug out of the platform I stood upon yesterday," Barston told the crowd. "I believe this slug will match a bullet fired from this rifle. And to prove that both attacks were motivated by foreign interests, I offer this card, found at the scene of yesterday's shooting. It is the insignia of a Prussian cartel that has sworn to kill me if I persevere in my bid for the Presidency."

"Congressman!" a reporter shouted. "Why would these Prussians wish to see you dead?"

Barston stood tall as he surveyed the crowd. When he spoke, he carefully emphasized each word. "The reason is clear, ladies and gentlemen! I stand for America! The Prussians wish to see our nation weakened in the eyes of the world. They quake at the thought of a strong, determined man in the White House. The Prussians wished to interfere with the American democratic process; they wished to counter the voice of the American people with a bullet!"

The mesmerized crowd stood stock-still as Barston dramatically held aloft the rifle slug.

"Ladies and gentlemen, I put it to you," Barston continued, slowing his pace to allow the scribbling reporters a chance to catch up. "The choice is yours. Be dictated to by a foreign power, or defy their wishes. A vote for me is a vote for America!"

Barston basked in the whistling and stamping that followed his speech and continued for several minutes. Then, waving to the crowd, he stepped down to where Longarm and the others stood. His face was flushed and sprinkled with perspiration.

"Where the hell were you all morning?" he asked Thorn.

"I thought it would be best if I waited for Marshal Vail's reply to our wire," the bodyguard explained.

"I see," Barston said, mollified. "Well? Did a reply come?"

Thorn shrugged. "The marshal's office sent us back a telegram saying that Vail was on assignment. We'll have to wait for him to return before new orders can be cut for Long."

"Damn." Barston shrugged. "I suppose I'll be plagued with you for a few more days, Deputy Long."

Longarm ignored the jibe. "That Winchester you held up never belonged to the old man who shot Tompkins. I was there. The old man's weapon was a Spencer repeater."

"You're mistaken, Deputy," Barston said.

"Like hell I am." Longarm glared at Thorn. "Your bodyguard switched rifles."

"What junk!" Thorn laughed.

"Marshal Farley!" Longarm called. "You were there! You saw the rifle. You didn't leave the body, did you?"

Farley blushed. "To tell the truth, I didn't notice the make of gun the old coot had," he mumbled. "And sure, I left the body. I had to, to get some men and a wagon to transport the bodies of Tompkins and his killer back to town." He looked down at his shoes. "Sorry, Longarm."

"Then it's just your word against Congressman Barston's, Custis," Jessie pointed out quietly. "Wilson, you said you recovered a rifle slug from yesterday's attack?"

"I was the one who actually dug it out of the wooden platform" Thorn spoke up. He winked at Longarm. "I also carry a pocket knife, Deputy."

"Right," Longarm nodded. "But there's the bullet that wounded that bystander. When the doctor removes that slug from the man's shoulder, we'll see that it doesn't match up to a slug from that Winchester."

"How dare you question my veracity in this manner?" Barston demanded of Longarm.

"I'm not questioning anything, I'm calling you a—"

"Longarm!" Jessie cried out in warning. "Don't say it! Remember who you're talking to!"

"Indeed . . ." Barston hissed, his eyes mere slits.

"Folks, we're all whistling in the wind," Farley calmly interrupted. "I was with the doc when he treated that wounded man. The bullet went clear *through* his shoulder. The man will be all right, but the bullet that did the damage is lost."

"Well, then," Barston chuckled.

"You look relieved, Congressman," Longarm mused pointedly. "There's still Tompkins. There's a bullet in his body. When that slug is removed, we'll all be able to see that it doesn't match the slugs that Thorn and I recovered from yesterday's shooting."

Barston held out his hand, palm up. "As a duly elected official of the federal government, I demand that you turn your slug over to me, Deputy Long."

"Nice try, Congressman," Longarm chuckled. "But I'll hold on to it, for now."

"I'm warning you," Barston said. "In front of all these people, I'm ordering you to turn over that evidence so I can see that it safely reaches the *proper* authorities."

"But Longarm *is* a federal law officer," Jessie said, puzzled.

"Now he is, but in a few hours he'll be an ordinary citizen," Barston vowed. "Who knows? He might throw the slug away, just to foil my Congressional investigation. Farley? Can't you force him to give me this important piece of evidence?"

The town marshal shook his head. "If you get him fired, I'll get your evidence for you, but until then he has to guard it. Only person who can order him to turn it over is a federal judge, and only in person."

"You're going to wish you had cooperated, Marshal Farley," Barston said meaningfully.

"You keep on trying to bend the law, Congressman," Longarm said, "and pretty soon you'll break it clean in two. Why don't we all just head over to the undertaker's office to *see* what the truth is."

"Hold on," Farley sighed. He glanced at his pocket watch. "Undertaker's office will just be closing when that wagon carrying Tompkins gets there. We'll have to wait until tomorrow. I know for a fact that the undertaker is coming to the fair tonight."

"I reckon tomorrow will be soon enough to get to the bottom of this," Longarm said.

"Oh, of course," Barston said with elaborate sarcasm, addressing Jessie while glaring at Longarm. "He's more than willing to wait until tomorrow. That way he has more time to try to turn you against me!"

"Why are you so anxious, Congressman?" Longarm demanded.

Barston ignored him, turning to face Jessie. "That crowd is still out there is front of the platform," he said. "You heard my speech, Jessie. You heard how they loved me. Now is the time to endorse me! You can share the limelight! Get on up there!" he coaxed her. "Tell them who you're going to back for the Presidency!"

"Tomorrow we'll have the slug that killed Tompkins," Longarm said quietly. "We'll know who's been telling the truth, and who's been, uh, mistaken. . . ."

"I do believe I'm going to assign a deputy to guard that body," Farley said suddenly.

"That is wise," Ki nodded. "It seems that the unfortunate Mr. Tompkins has grown more important in death than he was in life."

"Don't get railroaded into anything," Longarm urged Jessie. "There's no need for haste."

"Tomorrow morning, every newspaper in the country will have my speech on the front page," Barston argued fiercely. "I've got the momentum to go all the way. Don't miss out, Jessie! The Starbuck business empire could use a good friend in the White House."

"There he goes with those threats again." Longarm said, shaking his head.

"You'd do well to back a winner, Jessie," Barston persisted.

"Tomorrow you'll be presenting the prize money to the winner of the shooting match," Longarm reminded her. "That's the right time to make a political endorsement."

Miserably, Jessie wavered between the two. Finally she said, "Wilson, before the commotion started, I was seeing a side of you I'd never known, and I didn't much like it."

Barston flashed her a pleasant smile. "Come on, Jessie, we've known each other since we were kids. I've helped you against the cartel. That's the reason they've been trying to kill me. Now admit it, honey. Don't you owe me this little old endorsement?"

"I'm sorry, Wilson. I owe Longarm *too*. If he's mistaken about this rifle-switching business, I'll endorse you tomorrow, probably while handing you the trophy for winning the shooting contest." She added brightly, "Now, won't that be fine?"

Barston was nonchalant. "Very well, I can wait," he said. "And tomorrow we'll find out that Longarm is more than just mistaken. We'll find out that he's a liar!"

"We'll see who the liar is, Barston," Longarm replied evenly. "You're going to look like an awful fool to those reporters tomorrow." He grinned. "I bet you don't even win the target shoot. I bet that little farm girl does. Hell, you as much as admitted you couldn't beat her fair and square—"

Barston rushed toward Longarm, his fists raised. The deputy blocked the congressman's roundhouse right with his raised left forearm, and drove his own right fist into Barston's stomach, doubling him over.

The congressman went down gasping for breath. Thorn had his pistol out of his waistband holster, but before he knew what had happened, Ki plucked it from his fingers.

The samurai nimbly emptied the revolver's chamber of its cartridges. He handed the useless weapon back to the livid bodyguard.

"You shouldn't have done that," Thorn snarled. "You're going to be sorry."

"Oh, be quiet," Ki scoffed.

"Marshal Farley—" Barston gasped as he slowly got to his feet. "I wish to press assault charges against Long."

Farley looked extremely unhappy. "I—sir—um—"

"You tried to hit Custis first!" Jessie declared hotly. "He was merely defending himself!"

"That's right, sir," Farley said meekly, smiling in gratitude at Jessie.

"You know that you're finished as a federal marshal?" Barston asked Longarm, almost gently. "It doesn't matter in the least who is wrong or who is right. It doesn't matter whether I win or lose." He clenched his fists in anger. "The fact is, I'm a congressman, and I can have your badge taken away. I have to wait for Vail to get back to Denver, and when he does, you'll be fired. Do you understand?"

Longarm nodded silently. "And you understand this: I know my badge is as good as gone. But with it or without it, I'm still going to be around, Barston. Either as a lawman or as a private citizen, I'm going to find out the truth."

"You're going to end up a bum, Longarm," Barston taunted.

Longarm thought about the old man who had long ago been ruined by Barston's father. *Rest easy, uncle. I was going to bring you to justice for killing Tompkins, but now I'll see to it that Barston is brought to justice for having you murdered.* "Just remember, Congressman. With or without my badge, I'm going to find out the truth."

He strode away from them. "Wait for me, Custis!" Jessie called, rushing after him.

"What do you know about that?" Barston remarked, glancing at his bodyguard.

Thorn shrugged and bent to pick up the cartridges Ki had spilled upon the ground. "Something tells me I'm going to need these. . . ."

★

Chapter 9

"Hold up!" Jessie demanded, tugging at Longarm's sleeve. "Dammit, I can't talk and run at the same time!"

"Leggo," he grumbled, lengthening his stride.

Jessie dug in her boot heels and leaned backward, the way her daddy had taught her to do when she was learning how to bring down a roped calf prior to branding. Eventually her dragging weight slowed him down.

"Jessie, I want to be alone right now," Longarm began.

"No, you don't!" Jessie shook her head adamantly. "What you want is to be with me, so that's that!"

Longarm stared at her, his scowl slowly turning into a smile. "Where'd you learn to be so bossy?"

"Custis Long, I've run a dozen different businesses and a cattle ranch since my father died!" Jessie informed him curtly. "I've also had my share of rough-and-tumble adventure. I've certainly handled harder men than you."

Longarm winked at her. "You have?" He frowned. "You certainly like to kick a man while he's down."

Jessie blushed scarlet. "Men," she sighed. "Come along, you. We're going for a ride. That ought to cool you down." She offered him a wry smile. "In more ways than one."

"That'd be nice," Longarm admitted. "I've got the roan gelding I borrowed this morning, but where will you get a horse?"

"I'll take the one that Thorn borrowed this morning," she said. "After all, it does belong to me!" They headed toward the makeshift stables that had been set up at the fairgrounds to tend to visitors' steeds. Jessie disappeared inside the proprietor's tent to have her horse fetched.

Longarm's still saddled roan gelding was waiting where he'd left it outside the canvas stables. He talked to the mount as he ran his scrutinizing fingers over its tack and then drew his Winchester out of the scabbard strapped to his saddle in order to examine it. His saddle and gear had been left untouched. He waited while Jessie had her horse saddled by the stable boy. At last she led out the dapple gray Virginia walker.

"I'm glad we're going out for a ride," Jessie said as she swung herself up into the saddle. "This one could use more exercise."

Longarm hoisted himself up into his saddle and followed her along the main road that led toward town. They were heading toward Goat Creek until Jessie led them onto a narrow turnoff that rose through the hills, where it dead-ended in a grove of walnut trees.

"Do you like it up here?" Jessie asked him, smiling. "When I was younger, I used to come here all the time to think and dream in private."

She and Longarm dismounted. Their horses did not wander far, content to whinny softly to each other as they grazed upon the sweet grass carpeting the secluded grove.

Jessie settled herself beneath the shade of a tree. "Just a few yards away you can look down upon the main trail," she said languidly. "You can watch everybody—the whole world—go by, but up here, things stay nice and peaceful."

"It is beautiful here," Longarm agreed, sitting down beside her. He stared up at the blue sky, and the sun filtering down through the leafy boughs. The grove was peaceful except for the fine, natural, soothing sounds of the horses grazing, the birds singing overhead, and the bees buzzing in nearby patches of flowers.

Jessie took his hand. "What are you thinking?" she asked.

Longarm shrugged, smiling bashfully. "About how peaceful it is here. Looking at the trees and the sky, listening to the breeze rustling the leaves, makes me forget my troubles."

Jessie nodded. "That's why I used to come here—to get a perspective on things. You know, it's funny. I've never known anyone else to come here, and I've never brought anybody here—not even Ki—before you, that is."

"Well, I thank you for sharing your hideout with me," Longarm told her, squeezing her hand.

"Custis, what's going to happen? Between you and Barston, I mean?"

Longarm was careful to keep his tone of voice flat as he replied, "Reckon I'm all finished as a federal lawman. There's no doubt that I'm going to be fired. Billy Vail may stand by me, but the orders to dismiss me will come down from *his* bosses. I'm through, and that's that."

Jessie eyed him. She chose her words carefully, remembering that Longarm was a proud man. "Wilson and I go back a long way," she began. "Perhaps I could talk to him—"

Longarm shook his head. "Won't do any good, Jessie. There's nothing you could say that might prevent Barston from having me fired, short of offering to trade your endorsement of him for my job." He shuddered. "Better that I get fired than that bastard gets elected to the Presidency." He grinned at her. "I do thank you for listening to me this afternoon, and not giving him your endorsement then and there."

Jessie leaned back against the tree trunk. "He no longer needs my vote of confidence," she sighed. "Oh, sure, the more groundswell for him, the better, but you saw how he handled the press and that crowd of voters. Wilson Barston is a shoo-in."

"Not if I can prove him a liar," Longarm pointed out. "And he is a liar, Jessie. That's what confounds me! The fact that he treats people like dirt, and threatens to crush anyone who stands in his way, is understandable. I've known other rich and powerful men who acted like the world belonged to them." He chuckled as he put his arm around Jessie and pulled her close. "As I remember, *you* had a streak of spoiled-brat stubbornness in you, back when we first met."

"What do you mean, *had?*" Jessie growled, playfully punching him in the belly.

"No . . ." Longarm laughed. "You may still be as stubborn as the day is long, but you lost whatever brattiness you had when you helped investigate your father's murder. You are a very rich lady who can have whatever she wants, but you don't think that you're better than anybody else—"

"Cut it out," Jessie protested shyly. "I don't like to talk about myself."

"All right," Longarm smiled. "But my point is made. The fact that Barston struts around like a king is hardly surprising. That he's acting peculiar and fudging the truth *does* surprise me! What's his motive, Jessie? Why would he lie about that poor old man who tried to shoot him today?"

"It would help if you'd fill me in on what you're talking about," Jessie suggested sweetly.

Quickly, Longarm sketched out what he'd learned from the old man who'd tried to kill Barston, and told her the circumstances surrounding the confrontation with Thorn beneath the bleachers.

"I must admit that the old man's story has a ring of truth to it," Jessie said ruefully. "Wilson's father *was* an imperious sort of man. Oh, he was delightful to my father and me, and to any other person he considered his social equal, but he had no remorse about crushing those who were too weak to confront him. He believed the world was divided up into winners and losers, that he was a winner, and that anybody who stood in his way was going to end up a loser. I still remember an evening when Wilson's father had come to our spread for a visit. I must have been no more than nine or ten. I was playing on the carpet by my father's chair while he and old Mr. Barston had one of those after-dinner, cigar-and-brandy arguments that old friends can often get into. I paid attention, because Mr. Barston was making all kinds of wolf-and-sheep, cat-and-mouse claims about the world, and at that time I was quite interested in animals. The next morning I asked my father what kind of animal he was. At first he didn't understand me, but when I explained that I'd heard Mr. Barston say he was a lion, and most other men were his prey, my father started laughing." Jessie's eyes grew bright. "My daddy said, 'Barston's no lion, he's a horse's ass, but don't ever tell him I said so.'"

Longarm laughed richly. "Well, now we know where his son learned how to behave," he said. "It sort of makes sense when you think about it. The congressman's father lorded it over him, and now the son lords it over everybody else."

"Custis, are you sure Wilson is lying about that rifle?" Jessie asked. "I mean, it just makes no sense. And it *is* logical that the cartel would hate him for the help he's given me."

"I know all that," Longarm frowned. "And while I still have my doubts that the cartel was involved in yesterday's shooting, I'm willing to give Barston the benefit of the doubt."

"Big of you," Jessie winked.

"That's the kind of sport I am," Longarm remarked jovially, but then his tone grew serious. "But I was *there* today, Jessie. I was an eyewitness. That old man had nothing to do with the cartel, and he was firing a Spencer, not a Winchester. Barston had his trained ape, Thorn, switch guns while Marshal Farley was away looking for that wagon. Or maybe Thorn switched the guns on his own hook; that's not important. The idea was to turn poor Tompkins's murder to political advantage."

"It makes sense," Jessie was forced to admit. "And Thorn shot down the old man to keep him from contradicting the story Barston gave the press?"

"That's right," Longarm said. "The old man acted on his own, but Thorn—and maybe Barston too—was quick-witted enough to concoct a scheme on the spur of the moment to make political hay out of the incident."

"But what about you, Longarm?" Jessie asked. "I mean, here you are with that slug in your pocket as evidence. They must have known you could prove them liars."

"I guess they did," Longarm shrugged. "Like I said, they just did their best to twist things to their advantage. I'm the fly in the ointment. The way they see it, I'm just trying to cause the powerful, successful congressman some embarrassment. To their way of thinking, I'm just like that poor old man who'd been crushed by Barston's father—a sheep, trying to get back at the lion for having had its tail nibbled off." Longarm's smile contained no hint of humor. "But Wilson Barston is going to find out that this time he's picked on a wolf in sheep's clothing."

"Longarm, I feel like such a fool," Jessie groaned. "I see it all now! Barston probably believed that I'd be swept along on the wave of outrage, that I'd endorse him on the spot in order to spite the cartel for trying to assassinate him."

"Now *you're* the one making sense," Longarm said in admiration. "Barston's little game is nearly foolproof." He ticked off the points on his fingers. "At best there was the chance that I wouldn't notice the switch. Second best was that I'd notice it, but being worried about losing my job, I wouldn't want to mention it. Third best was that I'd bring it up, but that the slugs in both the wounded man and Tompkins's body would be too damaged to prove my point."

"Oh, Custis!" Jessie gasped. "Could that happen?"

Longarm nodded sadly. "Yes, ma'am. There's a real possibility that the slug that killed Tompkins will be too bent out of shape to be compared. The fact that the bullet that wounded the other man has been lost forever only stacks the odds in Barston's favor. What I was mostly trying to do this afternoon was bluff Barston into admitting that he was lying."

Jessie shook her head. "What you forgot, Longarm, is that you can't bluff a man who doesn't believe he can lose."

Longarm smiled. "Fourth best for Barston would be that the slug from Tompkins's body would prove that I'm right, but that nobody—besides you, Jessie—gives a damn. It'd be a nobody ex-lawman versus the next President. The newspapers would be fools if they didn't ignore me and listen to Barston."

"But I'd believe you, Custis, just as you said," Jessie swore, pressing herself against Longarm and kissing him on the cheek.

"I know that, Jessie," Longarm whispered, embracing her. "But that only means your life might be in danger."

"Now you're being silly, Longarm." Jessie pulled away from him. "It's one thing to accuse Wilson of being crude in the way he deals with people, and to accuse him of coldly twisting a tragic circumstance like Tompkins's murder to suit his own ends, but when you accuse him of being capable of murder, you're letting your own personal dislike of the man carry you too far!"

"I'm sorry," Longarm said sincerely, accepting her rebuke.

"It's not that I'm naïve," Jessie elaborated, "I've fought too many battles against the cartel—and seen too many people die—ever to be surprised by what people are capable of doing to one another. It's just that I happen to believe a person is innocent until proven guilty."

"I know," Longarm said.

"As I remember it, you're the one who taught me that," Jessie pointed out keenly.

"You're right. That's why I apologized."

She smiled. "Then hug me some more, and let's, for goodness' sake, stop talking about Wilson Barston!"

They leaned back against the tree, watching the clouds for a while in silence. Eventually Jessie asked, "Have you ever thought about what you might do if you quit being a deputy marshal?"

"Not until I met you," Longarm said quietly.

Jessie giggled happily, closing her eyes as Longarm's lips planted kisses along her soft cheek. Eventually his mouth found hers. When at last they pulled apart, Jessie's face was flushed, and Longarm's heart was thumping wildly.

"You sure nobody ever comes up here?" he asked, his voice grown husky.

"Uh-huh," Jessie nodded, her hazel eyes wide.

"You reckon it'd be more comfortable if I went and got the blanket from by bedroll?"

"Uh-huh."

She undressed quickly while Longarm fetched the blanket. It was a silly game she played with herself: if she could get all of her clothes off before he returned, everything would turn out happily ever after—

Happily ever after? she thought. *And just what would that be, Jessica Starbuck? That he'd not mind about losing his badge? That he'd stay with you forever?*

She kicked off her boots and stood them up beside the base of the tree, next to her neatly folded garments. She rose and stretched, luxuriating in the feel of the hot sun upon her naked body. A soft breeze picked up the tendrils of her long, reddish-gold hair, whipping them gently against her face. She was standing like that, eyes closed, face tilted up toward the sun, hands on her hips, when Longarm returned with the rolled-up blanket on his shoulder.

"My Lord," he whispered, transfixed by the sight of her. He gazed at her long, shapely legs, the swell of her hips as contrasted with her narrow waist. Her breasts were alabaster globes, lush and large, slightly upturned where the dark rosettes culminated in her delicious, pink-hued nipples.

She looked so pure and innocent, standing there in the buff in that tranquil setting; she looked so sensual, so passionate, as she basked in the sun. To Longarm she looked like a goddess, like all the women in the world rolled into one.

"You look like Eve," he told her, taking pleasure in her giggle of delight at his compliment. "You look like Eve, and now I understand why Adam defied the Lord to do her bidding. Why he ate the apple—"

Jessie's eyes glinted merrily. She looked just then like some forest nymph out to tantalize and lure her man deep into some paradise from which he would never wish to return. "But Adam didn't eat the apple 'one bite at a time,'" she pointed out. "Isn't that your favorite expression, Longarm?"

"It is," he nodded. "That's what I say, and that's what I'm going to do." He looked her up and down, licking his lips. "One little bite and nip at a time . . . I'm going to savor it. I'm going to make it last."

Jessie had been moving toward him while he spoke. It was as if his words had formed a silken lasso that roped her and tugged her forward. Longarm let the bedroll drop as he embraced her. He let his hands trace the fluid, sculpted lines of her back until his fingers danced down to the cleft of her gently undulating buttocks. Then he cupped and stroked the silky, twin hemispheres of her bottom as she ground herself against him. He grinned to himself as her musky woman-scent rose up to his nostrils.

It had been a long while since he'd inhaled Jessie's fragrance. Once again he was forced to admit that it made no difference where he wandered or who he met; never would he be able to get the sight of her, the feel of her, the scent of her out of his mind.

Jessie wiggled like a puppy beneath Longarm's exploring hands. She gave herself up to the myriad sensations flooding her being. The masculine scents of tobacco, gun oil, and cowhide enveloped her, while her bare, soft skin rubbed against the rough tweed and supple leather of his clothes and gunbelt. Her hands burrowed beneath his frock coat to palm the sinewy muscles flexing beneath his sweat-damp flannel shirt. There was the stimulating rub of his close-shaven but bristled jawline as he kissed her, the tickle of his longhorn mustache as he dipped his head to lick and gently chew her turgid nipples, and always, overwhelmingly, there was the persistent, throbbing hardness barely reined in by the stressed wool of his trousers. His erection pulsed against her soft belly like a wild stallion kicking to be free of its stall. Jessie teased and tickled it; she goaded it on as if it were a raging bull confined within a chute. There was something marvelous in the fact that she could just now safely tantalize that shackled beast futilely lunging for her; there was something frightening, something that caused her knees to shake in the certain knowledge that soon that beast would be free.

Longarm released her in order to spread the blanket beneath the tree. Jessie reclined upon it, propping herself up on one elbow. Longarm kept his eyes fixed on her as he undressed, shrugging off his coat and unbuckling his gunbelt. He set his Colt down within easy reach of the blanket—just in case—and then quickly shed his boots, trousers, and shirt.

Once again, Jessie's nipples tightened and rose to meet Longarm's darting tongue, as he joined her on the blanket. His sighs of pleasure grew muffled as he buried his face in the warm valley of Jessie's cleavage. Strongly, insistently, Longarm pushed her over onto her back. He planted a line of kisses down her belly until he'd reached her first tendrils of golden softness. Then his tongue flicked and darted between her thighs, lapping at the sweet honey beading the warm, downy fur of her center.

Jessie tangled her fingers in Longarm's hair as he sent waves of paralyzing pleasure riffling up and down her spine. She tried to hold back. She was like a little girl presented with an ice cream sundae. She tried to make her sweet treat last by stirring the confection around and around until the frozen mounds melted away into a thick, warm syrup that trickled and ran, down and down—

Jessie arched her back, kicking and crying as Longarm's tongue whipped her into a long, shivering orgasm. "P-please, stop!" she whined, begging, but Longarm showed her no mercy. Once again she convulsed into a world where there was nothing but fire and ice, wrapping around and piercing through her.

Overhead and nearby, the birds chirped and the bees buzzed. Jessie's animal-like mewls and groans did not seem at all out of place in this unspoiled, private grove.

When she was able to form words, she pleaded, "Come inside me." Without a word, Longarm did as he was asked. His marble-hard shaft seemed to split her in two as he slid into her to the hilt. They moved in an easy rhythm, gasping and sighing as their bodies slid and sucked and rocked together.

Low growls came from Longarm's parted lips as Jessie's inner muscles squeezed at him, snugly hugging his entire embedded length. The coarse wool blanket bunched beneath her bucking, gyrating hips as each of his thrusts carried him deeper and deeper into her.

He tried to hold back; he desperately wanted to make good on his vow to prolong their pleasure, but there was no chance of that now; he'd been waiting too long! His body ignored the commands of his mind. His climax was relentlessly, inexorably overcoming him. He could not do a thing about it, and he knew it. . . .

Jessie knew it too. She laughed in delight, locking her strong thighs around Longarm's trembling hips, overpowering him in her luscious embrace. He cried out as he spurted into her, bucking uncontrollably. . . .

Afterward, they lay side by side, their bodies interlocked as perfectly as the pieces of a jigsaw puzzle. Longarm had lit up a cheroot, and every now and then Jessie would reach over to take a puff. They watched a hornet—the Texas kind, the kind that grew so big that its abdomen hung down like a ripe, bluish-black grape—hover and hum around their bare toes. The hornet was so big, it seemed to leap from spot to spot like a mountain goat, rather than fly, but neither Jessie nor Longarm was concerned about being stung. For one thing, their lovemaking had tranquilized them into sleepy happiness. For another thing, the insect struck them as friendly, almost a pet. They were not at odds with the creature; they were at one with it.

"I think I finally understand what Ki means when he talks about being a part of the perfect circle that is the world," Jessie drawled, her fingers lazily twisting curls in Longarm's damp, matted pubic hair.

The hornet bounced once or twice against Longarm's shin, and then whirred off to other pastures. "It'd be nice if folks could hold on to the feelings they stir up in lovemaking," Longarm observed. "There'd be a hell of a lot less meanness in the world, and a hell of a lot less need for lawmen—Oops!" He sighed wearily. "Sorry to bring up all that bad stuff we've been trying to forget."

Jessie nodded sorrowfully. "I had forgotten it all too . . . but it's all come back now. Oh, Custis! If only you and I could stay here in this grove, under this tree forever! We'd just watch the sky and make love."

"But we can't," he replied. "And to be honest with you, I wouldn't if I could."

"Why not?" Jessie asked, intrigued now by the serious note in his voice. "Why go out looking for trouble when there's all all the happiness the the world, right here?"

Longarm smiled. "Because looking for trouble is what I do best, Jessie. I've been a soldier in my time, and I've been a cowboy, but being a lawman is what I was born for. I'm good with a gun and with my fists, but outfighting a badman is only half of it. You've got to outthink him as well. Call it whatever you want, it's the kind of thinking I do best." He blushed, his voice becoming soft and hesitant. "I reckon all of us have something we're meant to do on this earth, some job we're best suited for. A man might be a banker or a cook, a rancher or a storekeeper or he might turn out to be a rogue. Well, Jessie, somebody has got to keep the rogues from preying upon all those other folks."

Jessie laughed softly. Longarm glanced at her anxiously, worried that she was making fun of him, but the tears in her sea-green eyes reassured him.

"It's like what Barston's father said," she murmured wistfully. "The world *is* divided up into sheep and wolves."

"No, ma'am," Longarm said firmly. "It's not that simple, and it never was. I've been a lawman long enough to know it's not black or white, but shades of gray. Most all of us have got the sheep and the wolf mixed up inside. We're neither one nor the other, but both at once, with different sides coming out at different times. There's some folks who feel it's not civilized to show their wolf sides. Other folks feel it's their right to show the fang-and-claw side all the time. That's what Congressman Barston believes, and that's where I come into the picture. What I do best is protect the mostly civilized ones from the ones who mostly think that the world's a hunk of beef, and they're a steak knife."

He nodded decisively. "Yep, looking for trouble is what I do best. For the last few years now, I've been drawing a monthly salary in exchange for finding that trouble, but I don't really do it for the money. No true lawman does. There ain't enough money in the world to pay a man for the risk of it. When we get old and gray like my boss, Billy Vail, when we can't hardly go out looking for trouble anymore 'cause it looks as if we won't be able to come back with our skins intact, they stick us with a desk job, and a few years later a pension. A lawman lives poor and he dies poor, but he's got one thing no other man can call his own, the knowledge that he's kept a few lambs from the slaughter. The knowledge that for a little while he's sort of been like a campfire out on the prairie. 'Cause of him, the wolves have hung back, and folks could sleep safe in their beds."

Longarm stopped abruptly. He chuckled to cover his embarrassment. "Reckon I've been hanging around the congressman too long. I've gotten the habit of making speeches."

Jessie hugged him tight. "And it was a fine speech, too, Custis Long. I don't think I've ever met another man like you, and I don't think I ever will! You know, I was sort of hoping that after you...handed in your badge..." She muttered quickly, "That you'd maybe want to stay on here with me, that maybe you'd end up wanting to get back into the cattle business and—"

"Hush," Longarm admonished her. "When the time comes,

woman—and I've no doubt that it will—*I'm* going to be the one to issue the invite, if you catch my drift."

"I do," Jessie said meekly, wishing devoutly that the question she was replying to was in fact the very "invite" that Longarm was talking about.

"All right, then," Longarm smiled. "Let's not bother worrying about the future just now. We're in each other's arms, under a bright blue sky with a soft breeze blowing. Let's just make love, and for a little while the rest of the world can be damned!"

Jessie threw herself upon him, purring like a cat as she tongued his nipples. Her fingernails scraped lightly along the ripples of his stomach before her nimble fingers found their way to his groin. She stroked his turgid shaft to full hardness, and tickled his scrotum until she had him twitching around like a man staked out over an anthill.

Longarm expected her to straddle him, but that was not what happened. *A man should only expect the unexpected where Jessie Starbuck's concerned*, he reminded himself as she sat up, swung around so that her back was to him, and straddled his chest.

"Hmmmmm, this looks like a delicious candy cane for a girl to suck on," she murmured, leaning forward. A moment later, her mouth had engulfed him.

Longarm's spine went rubbery as Jessie's hot, wet mouth wrapped his swollen, sensitized member in heavenly sensation. When he came, Jessie sucked him dry, swallowing every drop. She kept on sucking until he was flaccid, and only then did she release him. Then she swung around to lay her head upon his chest. She yawned deeply. In a matter of moments she was sound asleep.

Longarm stroked her hair, staring up at the sky. He thought about all manner of things for a while, and then gradually he thought about nothing at all, falling asleep himself.

When he awoke, the sun was a fiery stain below the hills to the west. The birds and the bees had given up their song-making for the day, turning the world over to the fiddling crickets. He woke Jessie up, and both of them stood and stretched, then smiled sadly at each other. No words needed to be spoken; both knew that like the original Adam and Eve, their time to leave paradise had come.

"Lord! If we don't hurry, we'll be late for Buffalo Bill's show!" Jessie exclaimed.

"Reckon so." Longarm bent to gather up his clothes.

After they'd both dressed, they embraced for a final kiss. Then, somberly, knowing full well what they were doing, they mounted up and rode back into the world.

★
Chapter 10

For U.S. Marshal Billy Vail and his men, trapped among the boulders on the floor of the Sagmaw Valley, it seemed as if night would never fall. The ambushed posse watched the majestic sunset impatiently, and sighed in relief as the burnt-orange sky deepened to blue-gray.

The darkness was what they'd been waiting for. Now that it was night, the waiting was over. Billy and his boys could *act*.

"We'll give it until midnight," Billy told his handful of men. He had six able-bodied deputies, one man—Hopkins—who was badly wounded, and his two Louisiana potato-farmer volunteers, Mike and Paul.

"Why wait, Billy?" Talbot demanded, scratching at his blond curls. "I figure we've waited long enough. All damned day!" He turned up the collar of his plaid wool jacket against the night's cold breeze, and sulked.

"I know how you feel, but right now Turner's outlaws will be expecting us to make a move," Vail quietly persuaded Talbot

207

and the rest of his men. "For the next couple of hours they'll be tensed and ready for us. Maybe by midnight they'll have relaxed their guard."

"It's a point," Talbot conceded grudgingly.

"No," Glenn said. He gestured with his sawed-off Winchester toward where Hopkins lay moaning in a fitful half-sleep. "He's in bad shape, what with that busted leg of his."

"I know that," Vail snapped back bitterly. "But rushing into a fool plan, and getting some more of us shot up or killed, isn't going to help Hopkins any."

Glenn muttered something unintelligible. He slouched down against a rock, his midget rifle across his knees.

Bill Vail chomped down on the sour stem of his cold briar. He was feeling frustrated, angry, and more than a little scared, but not of Wink Turner's men. Vail was becoming nervous about the reliability of his own deputies. Why were they questioning his judgment? Did they lack confidence in his ability?

It is true that I haven't seen any real action in a hell of a lot of years, Billy mused, feeling the self-doubt begin to circle around him like a vulture patiently waiting for something badly hurt to give in and die. *And it's true that I'm old. . . .* He pulled his bedroll blanket tighter around his shoulders. Sitting still all day, first enduring the hot sun and now suffering the onslaught of the damp, cold night, had brought on a bad case of chilblains. He fought the impulse to scratch at his red, raw, inflamed skin, just as he did his best to stifle his traitorous body's shivering, and his teeth's chattering. Truth to tell, he was ashamed to let his deputies know just how keenly he was suffering.

They already think you're an old man, Vail told himself. *No sense making them think you're really an old woman. . . .*

Besides, his discomfort was as nothing compared to poor, wounded Hopkins. The bullet had smashed the deputy's knee, and Hopkins had lost a lot of blood. Right now Billy had a tourniquet cinched tightly around Hopkins's thigh. Periodically he loosened it, but each time he did, the blood gushed anew from the man's maimed limb. If they didn't get Hopkins to a skilled doctor, and damn soon, the leg would turn gangrenous. It was already looking as though he would lose it, but without care he would certainly die, either from infection or from loss of blood.

"You know, Billy," Glenn suddenly called out. "We're not even sure that Turner's men are still up there."

"They're still there," Vail insisted.

"You don't know that, Billy," Glenn responded.

The other deputies were listening silently to the exchange between the two men. Noticing this, Vail fought back his initial impulse, which was to pull rank. He addressed his comments not to Glenn, but to the attentive audience, realizing full well that he could no longer merely command his men to follow his orders. He now had to *persuade* them to do his bidding.

"We thought Turner had pulled back this afternoon," he reminded his men. "That's when we found out how tricky that one-eyed outlaw bastard can be."

The pinned-down posse had not seen a sign of the outlaw army since the bandits' earlier retreat back up the slope. Vail had sent one of his men—a volunteer—out from behind the cover of the boulders to lure the outlaws from their hiding places, if they were still there. Turner's men were good, Vail had to give them that. The outlaws held their fire until the last possible moment, probably hoping that more of the lawmen would join that lone deputy in trying to make a run on foot through the valley. When it became obvious that no other lawmen were going to show themselves, the outlaws popped up from their hiding places. Gunfire rained down upon the decoy deputy, who zigzagged like a jackrabbit during his flat-out run to regain the safety of the boulders.

"The marshal's right," Talbot chimed in. "There's no sense in playing into Turner's hands."

"I say that one of us should take one of those mules and make a try to get out of here," Glenn insisted. "If the man doesn't make it, so be it. One mule will still be left for some-body to make a try later on tonight."

"There's no point to that, Glenn," Vail declared. "Sarah Township is hours from here. Hopkins is going to have to hold on for at least another day, whether we send a man out now, or a few hours from now—"

"A few hours could decide whether he lives or dies," Glenn cut his superior off. "What's the matter, Billy?" he asked dis-dainfully. "Your memory failing you, as well as a few other things?"

There was a shocked intake of breath from the listening deputies. Mike and Paul, the two Louisiana farmers who'd volunteered their services as deputies, were sitting off to one side of the assemblage. They now glanced warily at one another.

"What do you reckon is going on, Mikey?" Paul asked, chewing worriedly on the ends of his bottle-brush mustache.

Mike's usually easygoing, handsome features were set in a frown. "If this was the navy, I'd say we was seeing a mutiny," he explained to his buddy in a hushed whisper. "Don't rightly know the label for it on land, but this here's a mutiny, all the same."

"I say we vote on it," Glenn declared flatly. "Billy, I mean no disrespect—"

"What you mean is insubordination," Vail growled, desperately looking to the others to side with him. "Do you hear this son of a bitch questioning my decision, boys?" He chuckled, although his laugh was more hopeful than heartfelt.

Glenn's eyes held real concern. "Truly, I don't mean anything bad like that, Billy. But our lives depend on what we decide to do. We ain't talking paperwork here, we're talking gunfights and strategy in the field." The deputy took a deep breath. "I vote that one of us should try to make a break for it now," he announced. "Who agrees with me?"

There was a moment of silence before anybody spoke. Then one deputy nodded.

"Reckon anything is better than just sitting here and waiting until midnight," the lawman muttered. "Sorry, Billy, but I side with Glenn."

"Well I stand by Billy," Talbot announced. "It makes sense to wait until later tonight."

"I reckon we can count on poor old Hopkins being an abstention," Glenn mused. "So far the voting's tied, with two saying we go now, and two saying we wait." He glanced at the pair of deputies who'd still not voiced their opinions. "Well? What'll it be?"

The two deputies shrugged, then looked at Marshal Vail. "Sorry, Billy," one of the men said. "I vote with Glenn."

"So do I," the last man said, avoiding the marshal's gaze.

"That's it, then," Glenn nodded brusquely. "Four to two, the men agree with me—"

"Well, hold on, now," Mike suddenly drawled. "You ain't heard how we vote."

"You don't get to," Glenn replied, busying himself checking the action of his sawed-off Winchester. "This here's a matter to be decided by professionals."

"You professionals ain't been doing so hot, so far," Mike observed.

"Now listen here, farmboys," Glenn growled.

"And while it's true that we are farmboys," Mike said, looking to Paul for confirmation. "Ain't that so, Paulie?"

"We're farmboys through and through," Paul nodded somberly.

"Get to the point!" Glenn swore impatiently.

"While it's true that we're farmboys," Mike plodded along, paying no mind to Glenn's anger, "it's also true that we're the rightful owners of those two mules, one of which you aim to use."

"Well, I guess we're *requisitioning* those mules," Glenn told them. "Look, you two fellas are nice enough, but I ain't got time to argue with you, get it?" He levered a round into the chamber of his stubby rifle for emphasis.

"Hold on now, sir, hold on!" Mike said quickly, holding out his empty hands, palms up. "You don't have to go waving that half-pint cannon of yours at us. We ain't gonna question you requisitioning our mules."

"You don't have to explain *nothing* to us, sir," Paul added.

"All right, then," Glenn replied with satisfaction, lowering the hammer on his weapon.

"But who's going to explain it to Sadie and Selma?" Mike asked innocently.

"Who the hell are they?" Glenn demanded in exasperation.

"Why, they're our mules, sir," the farmer grinned. "And it's a funny thing about mules, they got minds of their own. . . ."

"You could probably shoot us dead, sir," Paul said, looking as serious as a deacon. "Though I hope you won't, but if you did, Sadie and Selma probably wouldn't pay no mind. They just won't allow nobody to ride them but us. They're stubborn creatures. Why, they're as stubborn as"—Paul shrugged—"as *mules, I guess. . . .*"

"They gotcha, Glenn," Vail smiled.

"Reckon so, Marshal," Glenn moped. "I don't suppose you two potatoes would care to voice your opinion concerning our plan?"

"Guess we get to vote after all, eh, Marshal Vail?" Mike asked.

"Guess you do," Vail nodded, amused and impressed despite the predicament they were all in. These two hayseeds had managed to defuse a potentially ugly incident between himself and his men. No matter what happened, he owed these two for their help in cooling things down.

"We vote along with Marshal Vail," Mike said. "We think it makes good sense to wait for them outlaws to get sleepy before riding past their gunsights."

"Four against four," Glenn said hopefully. "That means it's a tie. Maybe we could get Hopkins to say what he thinks we ought to do—"

"Hopkins is delirious," Vail scowled. "His vote doesn't count."

"And Sadie and Selma will vote with us," Mike offered. "That makes it six to four, don't it?"

"Sadie and Selma." Glenn nodded dourly. "How could I have forgot?" The deputy lowered his head in defeat. "We do it your way, Billy. I'll keep my mouth shut from here on in."

"All right, then, we'll let the matter rest."

"And when we're out of this, Billy, I'll hand in my resignation for insubordination," Glenn offered.

"Let's hold off on that kind of talk," Vail said gruffly. "Hell, it's an even chance that we ain't going to get out of this. Right now I'd like to hand in my own resignation—"

"You think Wink Turner would accept it?" Talbot cracked.

Billy and the rest of the men chuckled in appreciation at the joke, grateful for the opportunity to dispel the tension that had arisen during the challenge to the marshal's authority.

Talbot and Vail exchanged a wink and a nod, and then the marshal spoke up. "Here's what I want to do. A few boys will swing out of here and try to get themselves a position on the slope back the way we came—"

"*Back*, Billy?" one of the men asked. "I don't get it."

"There's some of Turner's men in that stand of trees by now, Billy," Talbot fretted.

"I *know* all that," Vail seethed. "All of you just shut up and *listen* for a change! We shot a mess of Turner's men—"

"About ten," Talbot interjected.

"All right, then," Vail continued. "He can't have more than thirty left, strung along the length of that slope, even assuming that all his men are here, and not out stealing cattle or robbing banks or the like."

"I still don't get it," Glenn frowned.

"I want three of us to take up positions back the way we came, in order to divvy up Turner's firepower," Vail explained. "Divide and conquer, boys! Say that a half-dozen of the outlaws shoot it out with the three I send back. Another fifteen or so trade shots with those of us still in position right here—"

"That leaves less than ten men shooting at the man we send out of here!" Talbot said excitedly. "Less than ten rifles, and under the cover of darkness, the dumb cluck just might make it!"

"That's *two* dumb clucks," Mike chuckled. "Marshal Vail? We weren't joshing about how Sadie and Selma won't let no one but us ride them."

"I didn't think you were," Vail said quietly. "But it don't seem fair that one of you civilians—"

Mike waved him quiet. "All the job calls for is the ability to ride, and the truth of it is, Paul and I can ride a damn sight better than we can fight."

"But you both don't have to go," Talbot interjected.

"Mike and I will stick together," Paul replied firmly. "And anyway, if two of us try to escape, there's an even better chance of one of us making it."

"Who wants to stay here with you poor suckers, anyway?" Mike joked.

"It's settled, then," Vail announced. He checked his pocket watch. "The three decoys will take their positions after eleven tonight. You two will make your break for it at midnight. We've got a few hours until it's time to start moving. Gather 'round. Let's work out the details of this scheme. . . ."

★

Chapter 11

Back in Sarah, it was just eight o'clock in the evening, and a half hour into Buffalo Bill's Wild West Show. Bill's big top held three hundred, and tonight's performance was strictly standing room only. The packed rows of backless benches stretched all the way to the apron of the elevated stage, which was backdropped with paintings depicting the various highlights of William Cody's eventful life.

Longarm and Ki were standing just inside the entrance to the tent. The deputy did his best to keep an eye on Jessie, Barston, and Thorn, seated sixth-row center, but not even a woman as lovely as Jessie Starbuck could stand out in that sea of twisting, bobbing heads.

Longarm sighed in frustration. "I'm probably the only body-guard in history who has to keep his distance from the man he's supposed to be guarding."

"I feel the same way," Ki confided. "I am worried about Jessie, now that I know the cartel may have assassins in the immediate area, but you and I have little choice in this matter."

Longarm frowned. "I still don't understand why Jessie wanted to sit with the congressman."

Ki chuckled softly. "You do not understand because you were not trained in the Japanese art of negotiation and diplomacy, as Jessie was," he replied. "She may sit next to Barston, but that does not necessarily mean she cares for his company. She may smile at him, but that does not necessarily prove that she is his friend. You have antagonized Barston to the extent where all relations between the two of you have ceased. Jessie is merely doing her utmost to keep the lines of communication open between you and your foe."

Longarm shook his head. "Old son, I swear, I never know when you're bullshitting me."

Ki nodded. "That is because you were not trained in the Japanese art of negotiation and diplomacy."

Longarm guffawed. "That's what I call shoveling the shit with chopsticks!"

Ki covered his mouth with his hand to hide his smile. "Let us watch the show."

The two friends gazed at the activities upon the stage. Seated in one corner on buffalo-hide chairs were the proud duo of Hiram Calhoun and Mayor Wilk. Buffalo Bill had gotten the bright idea of furnishing the two guests of honor with tonight's program, so that they could take turn announcing the acts.

The show itself was actually a vaudeville program comprising short melodramatic pieces interspersed with musical numbers and variety acts. Just now concluding was a knife-throwing exhibition featuring "Lucky Pierre, Blade King of the Canadian North Woods, and his assistant, Indian Princess Tall Smoke."

The princess had carrot-colored curls, freckles, and a show-stopping figure. Since she was wearing a rawhide dress that looked as if it had been soaked and allowed to shrink on her, the male part of the audience was willing to give the redhead the benefit of the doubt concerning her claims of royal Indian lineage.

After Pierre and the Princess took their bows, it was Mayor Wilk's turn to introduce the next act. The mayor had evidently forgotten to bring his spectacles. He squinted at the sheet of paper and fumbled his way through the introduction.

"The tent is stuffy and smoky," the samurai complained. "I am going outside for fresh air."

Longarm nodded. "Don't blame you, old son. I'll stay here and keep watch over things."

The samurai maneuvered his way through the other standees in the tent, managing to exit just as the audience gave a welcoming burst of applause to a fellow who claimed to be the owner of a nanny goat that knew how to count. . . .

The night was clear and cool. Ki took several deep breaths, and then began to stroll around the grounds. Other attractions were still open, but most of the folks around the fairgrounds had gone to Buffalo Bill's show, so the area was pleasantly deserted.

Ki moved easily through the darkness, his eyes quickly adjusting to the shadows that were only halfheartedly dispersed by the few torches marking the main paths through the grounds. He was contemplating heading over to the saloon tent to treat himself to a drink, when he heard a feminine voice softly call his name.

He stopped and turned. "Phoebe?"

She stepped out of the darkness, smiling shyly. "I saw you leave the show, so I thought I'd leave too." She wrinkled her nose. "Awful, wasn't it?"

Ki shrugged. "Most of the audience seems to be enjoying it."

"It just goes to show you how starved for entertainment folks are," she replied. "Being a sharpshooter is sort of like being a stage entertainer, more or less." Nervously she twisted one of her tightly braided pigtails around her fingers. "I've often thought about what it would be like to star in a show."

"You could, you know," Ki encouraged her.

"Oh, go on," Phoebe blushed prettily. "You're teasing a girl fresh off the farm, is what you're doing, Mr. Ki!"

"Not at all," the samurai protested.

"They don't want girls like me," she moped. "They seek out females like that there Princess Tall Tree." She glanced down at herself. "It's not talent, but the meat on a girl's bones

217

that they're looking to feature up there on that brightly lit stage."

"Well . . ." Ki kept his expression carefully blank. "You are not lacking in an appealing feminine form."

Phoebe giggled. "Are you kidding when you talk like that, or what? Never mind, don't tell me. I think it's cute, and I thank you for the compliment, if that's what it was."

This time Ki smiled. "It was," he said softly. "You are a very lovely woman." He ran the backs of his fingers along the sleeve of her loose-fitting calico dress. "Your clothes make you look tomboyish, and younger than your years, but I am not fooled. Do not forget, I have had ample opportunity to see the splendor beneath those modest garments."

Phoebe swallowed thickly. "Wanna see it all again?" She had to look away. The intensity of the almond eyes, set in Ki's handsome, hawkish features, was just too much for her to handle. She reached up to brush back a lock of inky-black hair that had fallen across his brow. When she spoke, her eyes darted this way and that, but her voice was firm and certain.

"There's a place we could go, you and I, to be alone for a while." She pressed herself against Ki. "I would very much like to be alone with you for a while."

Ki embraced her. Her warm, lush body was trembling. He felt his own desire rise up in him, insistent, heart-stoppingly powerful. "Show me," he said simply.

Pheobe took his hand and led him away from the public paths. Ki watched her sassy hips and voluptuous backside straining the thin cloth of her dress as she hurried. He himself was feeling as if his jeans had suddenly shrunk. "Where are we going?" he asked.

"My tent, where else?" Phoebe laughed. "I've got a sleeping bag, what more do we want?"

She put a finger to her lips as they reached the campsite area. "We'll have to be very quiet so that we don't wake up the folks bunked down for the night. But that's all right, isn't it?" she asked hopefully, her robin's-egg-blue eyes suddenly grown worried. "I mean, sometimes it's fun to have to be real quiet. . . ."

Quiet, indeed, Ki thought distractedly as he gazed at the closely pitched clusters of tents. *A ninja would have trouble*

*making love quietly enough to go undetected by these neigh-
bors....* He smiled at Phoebe. "In Japan, people must live
their lives in close-set houses with paper-thin walls. We shall
be quite discreet within our canvas cocoon."

"Woo-ee!" Phoebe sighed. "I do love it when you talk fancy
like that. Well, here's home," she said brightly, pointing to a
tiny pup tent wedged between a pair of family-sized canvas
shelters. Without further ado, she dropped down on all fours,
hiked up her skirt to expose her firm, honey-tan thighs, and
wiggled her way into the minuscule tent.

Ki gave her a moment to get settled, then followed her
inside. Phoebe was in the midst of shucking her dress off over
her head. Ki held the tent's entrance flap open for an extra
moment to allow a bit of the silvery starlight to enter. He wanted
a chance to feast his eyes on her abundant charms—on her
creamy breasts and dark nipples that so reminded him of sweet,
ripe cherries, and on the furry thatch between her legs, now
totally exposed as she sat cross-legged before him.

"Close that door," she scolded mildly. "You don't want
everyone to see us, do you?" she added teasingly.

Ki let the flap fall, plunging the tent's interior into darkness.
There were several ventilation openings along the sides of the
tent, but they allowed no light to enter. The samurai could hear
Phoebe's rapid breathing; he could almost feel the heat rising
from her naked body, but he could not see her, even though
she was only inches away from his eyes and fingers.

Phoebe was all over him as he kicked off his jeans and
shrugged out of his leather vest and cotton shirt. The tent had
been set up on a grassy knoll, so the ground, covered with a
blanket, was soft beneath Ki's spine as he lay back with Phoebe
stretched out upon his stomach. Her wide, wet, sensual mouth
was locked against his, her sweet tongue bold and thrusting.
Her hands fluttered along his muscular shoulders and arms.

Ki nuzzled her breasts, grinning happily as Phoebe popped
first one and then the other nipple into his hungry mouth. Ki
sucked at them lovingly. Was it just his passion-inflamed imagination, or were they as juicy and luscious as the cherries they
so resembled?

"Let's get into the sleeping bag!" Phoebe begged. "Can we?
Can we?"

"Hush," Ki chuckled. "I thought we were to be extra quiet?"

"Oh! Oh, yeah," she murmured, "I forgot. I guess you might have to *force* me to be quiet. . . ." she said dreamily. "There's not many men who could make me do anything, but you're one of them."

"Nobody is forcing anybody," Ki reminded her. "We are both here because we want to be."

Phoebe sighed. She took his head in her hands and helped herself to another long, lingering kiss.

Ki glided his hands along her silky thighs until his questing fingers could gently probe her moist, musky center. "I suggest you get into that sleeping bag," he growled. "For in another moment, I shall be getting into *you.*"

"Yes, sir!" she pulled apart the thick, quilted sleeping sack, and crawled inside.

Ki was right behind her. He burrowed down into the warmth of the bag, and then pulled Phoebe on top of him once again. Her agile fingers took hold of his erection and guided just the tip of it inside her. Then, slowly, lovingly, she straddled him, impaling herself until she'd taken in all of his considerable length.

"Ooooh," she moaned softly. "Ooooh, I've been dreaming of this moment since we met, haven't you?" She rocked back and forth, tensing her strong leg muscles so that she could rise and fall upon his throbbing, horn-hard member. "Ki?" she said. "Didn't you dream about me last night?"

"Of course," he said, thinking that in a way he was not *really* lying. Last night, while trying to fall asleep in that tiny cubicle of a hotel room, he had found his thoughts returning to the way Phoebe had looked, nude and dripping wet, at the pond. Of course, that was when the Cling Sisters had arrived, and those twin Georgia Peaches did have a way of turning a man's thoughts away from previous concerns.

"Last night," the samurai began, "if I had been given the choice of any woman, it would have been you." *There,* he thought. *That was certainly no lie.*

Phoebe laughed contentedly. She began to tilt and twist her plump, firm bottom until she'd set up a scorching rhythm that took her over the edge. She issued the tiniest scream of anticipation as she was overwhelmed by a climax that turned her from a woman into an animal. She cried and clawed at Ki as the waves of sensation washed over her. Just as her own orgasm was beginning to diminish, Ki began to flex his powerful belly muscles. He took a firm hold on her sleek hips, and began to lift and lower her upon his shaft. It was as though his pulsing erection were a glistening blade, and Phoebe's molten furnace were a velvety sheath for that awesome weapon. The intensity of feeling flooding her body soon had her whimpering and whirling into the vortex of another orgasm.

"Oh! Please stop, I can't stand it!" she hissed, but when Ki mercifully slowed his bucking hips, Phoebe immediately begged him to speed up. After that, the samurai ignored her pleas. He coaxed two more tearful, exquisitely torturous, multi-layered orgasms out of her sweat-wet, shivering body. Then she pleaded for a rest, and he let her have one. She collapsed in disarray upon his broad chest, like a half-drowned swimmer.

Phoebe's lips were sticky, and her breath hot in Ki's ear. "That was the b-best," she stammered. "W-when I was fourteen, I saw the bull doing it to our cow in the pasture. I've always wondered what that would feel like. Now I know. . . .

"You were not very quiet," Ki teased her.

"Wasn't I?" she asked. "I can't remember."

"I am quite surprised that none of your neighbors tossed their shoes in the direction of that yowling cat that so recently shattered the tranquility of the area."

"Oh, you!" Phoebe fumed. Her pretty face took on a look of sly determination. "You think you're so smart just 'cause you made me come three times, and I haven't gotten you yet. But just you watch out, Mr. Ki, 'cause now I've got you in my sights." She clenched her thighs against his sides, and leaned forward like a jockey mounted on a racehorse's saddle. Then she began to rock that pear-shaped backside upon his erection with the steady, unstoppable motion of a locomotive's piston. "And I *always* hit what I aim at. . . ."

She began to rub and gently pinch Ki's nipples between her thumbs and forefingers. Her inner muscles gripped and released him like a hundred tiny, grasping, feathery-soft fingers.

The samurai gave himself up to her marvelously expert

221

lovemaking. He could feel his orgasm slowly but unstoppably gaining momentum, rising up like water in a deep well as the pump handle is endlessly worked.

"I feel you swelling inside me," Phoebe whispered, her wet tongue darting fire into his ear. "Ooooh," she crooned, "I feel your balls groaning and grumbling like a dam about to burst...."

Ki could hold back no longer. His body went as soft as jelly as he shot into her.

"More, more!" she demanded, giddy with triumph as her body sucked every pleasure-filled drop out of his core. Finally she relented, cooling his fevered brow with sweet kisses while still taking care to cradle his softening, twitching member between her luxurious thighs.

"You do have excellent aim," Ki mumbled, as soon as he was able to talk.

"Now the score's *one* to three," Phoebe said contentedly.

Ki shook his head. "*Two* to three, at least," he sighed. "You just scored a double."

"Guess that's true," Phoebe mused. "Remember what I said about that bull a little while ago? Well, you were grunting and bellowing just like that old stud when he gave it to our milk cow."

"Was I?" Ki laughed. "I cannot remember."

Phoebe patted his belly affectionately. "Can I ask you something?" she begged after a few moments of silence.

"You can *ask*." He cursed himself for the slight warning tone in his voice.

"Uh-oh," Phoebe chuckled. "Don't you go getting proddy on me. It's just that I'd like to know a little something about you. I mean, this was wonderful, but I know it ain't likely that it'll ever have the opportunity of happening again. It would be good if I could know a little something to wrap up my memory of this night. You know, the way folks will wrap something precious in folds of cloth, so it doesn't get lost?"

"Yes, Phoebe, I do know about memories," Ki agreed. "They are precious, and they are easily lost. You may ask your question."

"It might be a hard one for you to answer, but it's important to me," she began. "Ki, just who are you? And what are you doing here? I mean, most folks have a home, even though they wander far and wide. Like I told you at the pond, my home's a farm in Ohio. But you were born in Japan, and it ain't likely that you'll ever find your way back there. What made you settle here in Texas?"

"Do you remember the woman I mentioned to you this afternoon? Jessica Starbuck?" Ki asked.

"Why, sure. Everybody has heard of her! I mean, she's so *rich!*" Phoebe sighed in envy. "Ki? You don't mean to say that you're hooked up with her in some way?"

"Phoebe, I am a samurai," Ki explained. "A professional warrior—"

"You mean like a sharpshooter?" she asked.

Ki smiled in the darkness. "Sort of, but actually more like a gunslick, I suppose. Traditionally, a samurai pledges his expert services to a family pursuing a cause or course that he believes in. Long ago, I pledged myself to Alex Starbuck, Jessie's father. Jessie and I were mere adolescents at that time, but Alex Starbuck, having lived in the Orient, knew that a teenaged samurai might be lacking in experience, but not in prowess. I was entrusted with the task of guarding Jessie, keeping her safe from harm."

"But who would want to hurt her?" Phoebe asked, confounded.

"I will say only that the family has enemies, and you must allow me to leave it at that," Ki said firmly. "I have agreed to reveal *my* past to you. I do not have the right to reveal Jessie's."

"I understand," Phoebe said, and kissed him. "So you and Jessica Starbuck grew up together. She's certainly pretty. Ki, are you and her sort of *engaged*, or anything?"

"Jessie and I are more like brother and sister," Ki murmured. "I could never allow myself to fall in love with her, you see, for it might compromise my ability to protect her life."

Phoebe kept silent. For a moment Ki thought she had dozed off while he'd been talking, but then she spoke.

"It's too dark to see your face, but I could hear the quiver in your voice, and the way your body tensed up while you were talking about her." Phoebe hugged him tightly. "It's bad when you have to carry a torch for someone."

Ki said nothing. What was there to say?

"I'm not complaining, mind you," Phoebe added quickly.

"I know enough about lovemaking to realize that while we were going at it before, there wasn't another woman on earth except me, as far as you were concerned." She paused. "I just want you to know that maybe I'm not all that different from you. We both made love to each other, and we meant it, but that doesn't mean we both can't also be in love with someone else."

Now it was Ki's turn to be intrigued by Phoebe's ambiguity. He would have liked to know more, but the woman was not offering the information. Curious as he was, the samurai's Japanese upbringing forbade his asking prying, personal questions.

"I promised a friend that I would return to Buffalo Bill's show," he confessed regretfully.

"Miss Starbuck?" Phoebe asked, trying to disguise her jealousy.

"No," Ki soothed. "A male friend. The deputy assigned to guard Congressman Barston."

"Then I guess I'll let you leave," Phoebe joked. "I'll even come with you!" She rolled off him, kicking her way out of the sleeping bag, as she reached for her dress. "Now that I've had my way with you, I can start wearing underthings again," she confided. "Yesterday, I soaked my way through two pairs of drawers just thinking about you! I mean, a girl can't be bothered with all that laundry!"

"Especially when she has sharpshooting on her mind," Ki responded merrily.

"That's a fact!" Phoebe declared. "Someday I'm going to have servant folks who'll take care of all that humdrum stuff like laundry for me. And when I travel somewhere to shoot, I'll stay in a fancy-dandy hotel, not a damned tent!"

Ki listened to the throbbing of emotion in her voice. Dark as it was inside the tent, the spark of determination and ambition revealed by Phoebe seemed to banish the blackness. For one moment, Ki thought he could actually see her defiant face looming out of the shadows as she prepared to take on the world—and win!

"I believe you will accomplish everything you set out to do," he told her sincerely. "I sense in you the quality of greatness."

"Don't tease me," she begged. "Not about that. My dream means everything to me."

Ki began to dress. "I am not teasing you, and I do not intend merely to flatter, but today, while you were shooting, I watched the crowd watching you. I cannot explain the why and how of it, but you have the ability to capture the hearts of the public. Today those spectators switched their allegience from Congressman Barston to you. They rooted for you, a farmgirl, because you share their origins. Because they have a share in your success." Ki fumbled for her hand, and squeezed it in the darkness. "Do you understand what I am saying, Phoebe?"

"Yes," she said, her voice small and meek.

"Good," Ki decreed. "Someday you are going to have all the things you are dreaming about."

Phoebe giggled. "Until then, would you buy a girl who's had every drop of moisture wrung out of her a lemonade? I'm powerful thirsty."

"My pleasure," Ki told her. "Are you all ready?"

"Yep."

He held open the tent flap for her, and then exited. Ki watched Phoebe smooth down her modest calico dress and check to see that her pigtails had not come undone. It was difficult to believe that she was the same wildcat he had just bedded.

She took his arm, and they strolled toward a vendor who was still open and bought two cups of cool, thirst-quenching lemonade. Then they headed back toward Buffalo Bill's big top. Their approach brought them to the back of the show tent, where the troupe's wagon was parked. Ki noticed several people standing in the shadows cast by the huge vehicle.

The samurai slowed, and put a restraining hand on Phoebe. "Stand still," he whispered.

"Why? What's wrong?" she demanded, perplexed.

"And be quiet!" Ki hissed. He pointed toward a scene being enacted in front of the wagon.

As they watched, a man was brought around from the wagon's side, and pushed roughly against one of the wheels. The leader of the group began to address this lone victim. Ki could not make out the words, but the leader's tone was definitely threatening.

Ki squinted against the darkness. "I count three individuals against that one fellow," he muttered. "Unfair odds, no matter who is in the right."

Phoebe shook her head, pointing as yet another individual tossed a box out of the wagon before joining the group encircling the one man. "That makes four against one."

A member of the group jammed a crowbar into the box, springing off its lid. The musical jingle of spilled coins reached Ki and Phoebe. They watched as two members of the group scooped up the silver and gold, and stuffed paper money into a pair of saddlebags.

"They're robbing Buffalo Bill's show receipts," Phoebe whispered. "What are we going to do?"

"You will stay here," Ki began, but then stopped to watch as the lone man who'd been surrounded broke free of his circle of captors to make a run for it. One of the robbers sprinted after him, caught up with the hapless man, whirled him around, and stuck a knife in the fellow's belly.

"Oh, God!" Phoebe gasped, clutching at Ki as the stabbed victim sagged to the ground.

Ki stared hard. The murderer had been forced to step out into the torchlight to catch up with his victim. The killer was Pierre, the knife-thrower, one of Buffalo Bill's performers!

Ki charged forward. Pierre, a small but wiry man with black, curly hair, shouted to one of his accomplices to head Ki off.

"Get rid of him," Pierre demanded. "But no guns!"

Ki understood the knife-thrower's injunction. Shots would alert the audience inside the tent. Pierre and his band needed time to make good their escape.

The robber blocking Ki was one of the roustabouts whose duty it was to cart scenery and put up the big top. He was a hulking, tough-looking brute, taller than Ki, and he weighed nearly twice as much as the samurai. The roustabout had thickly muscled forearms, and big, scarred hands ridged with calluses. He balled those hands into hamlike fists as Ki confronted him.

"Come on, *Deputy!*" he laughed contemptuously, noticing the badge pinned on Ki's leather vest. "You ain't got no gun, and I'm not using mine." He patted the revolver wedged in his wide leather belt. "I'm gonna kill you *quiet,* boy!"

Ki stared into the tiny, bloodshot eyes set deep in the roustabout's leathery face. The man's nose was a shapeless mass of scar tissue, that looked as if it had been broken dozens of times, and his ears were cauliflowered by the deforming impact of countless blows. Extremely agile for his size, he danced lightly on the balls of his feet, maneuvering easily to block Ki from going around him in pursuit of the rest of the band of robbers, who were just now escaping with their stolen loot.

Ki balanced himself and moved in fast, slicing out at the roustabout with a *shuto-uchi*, or knife-hand strike. The rigid edge of Ki's right hand chopped into the roustabout's neck. It was a good blow, one that would have felled most men, but the roustabout merely tensed his beefy shoulders and shook off the impact.

"Now it's my turn," the man huffed, driving his right fist into Ki's midsection.

The samurai doubled over, more in surpise at the man's speed than in response to the actual pain of the punch, solid as it was. He swerved backward to avoid the roustabout's left to the side of his head, and locked his fingers around his opponent's still outstretched right wrist.

"Leggo!" the man demanded.

Ki bent the man's hand back on itself and twisted hard. Usually, the pain this technique caused would put an opponent on the ground; if he didn't fall, the result would be a broken wrist or elbow, or a dislocated shoulder. Usually.

But not this time. The roustabout managed to balance himself on his massive legs to counter Ki's effort. Grinning all the while, the roustabout slowly straightened his wrist, despite all of Ki's effort to keep it doubled back on itself, and the pressure on.

"This ain't going to work, boy," the man laughed as he pulled free. "What *else* you got to show me?"

Ki delivered two lightning-fast punches to the roustabout's jaw. The left-right combination rocked the man's head from side to side. Blood welled up out of his mouth. He spit out a tooth, but his tiny eyes were still focused, and his smile, while bloodied, was still wide and amused.

His big hands shot out, his fingers stretched wide, to hook themselves around Ki's throat.

Just then, Phoebe darted in beneath the lumbering rousta-

227

bout's outstretched arms. She plucked the man's revolver from his belt and back-pedaled away. Taken by surprise, the giant was not quick enough to catch her, but he did manage to deliver a backhand blow that knocked Phoebe off her feet and sent the pistol flying.

Ki took advantage of the roustabout's momentary distraction to deliver a snap-kick against his kneecap.

There was a brittle crunching sound. The roustabout swore softly as his leg folded beneath him.

Ki kicked out again, catching the roustabout on the chin, but failing to hurt him much, or even attract his attention. Instead, the man concentrated on trying to stand up. Each attempt ended in his flopping back upon the ground.

The samurai decided to quit while he was ahead. He hurried over the Phoebe. The farm girl had regained her feet, and had retrieved the roustabout's revolver.

"Are you all right?" Ki asked her.

"Yep," she nodded, brushing the dirt from her dress. "He just knocked me off balance," she asserted gamely. "Although I wouldn't be surprised if I'm all black and blue tomorrow. Boy, that fellow is strong!" She gestured toward him with the pistol. "Aren't you going to knock him out?"

"I do not have the time," Ki muttered in disgust. "I could chop down a tree faster than I could knock *that* one unconscious." Ki checked the stabbed victim of the robbers. He was dead.

"Aren't you afraid he'll run away?" Phoebe asked nervously, watching the roustabout.

"Not likely," Ki observed. "I broke his leg."

The roustabout was sitting on the ground with his injured leg thrust out in front of him. He was prodding at his kneecap, flinching slightly now and then. "Damn, that smarts," he moped out loud.

"I am going after the rest of the robbers," Ki told Phoebe. "You have seen Deputy Long. Ask him to assist me."

"I'll help—" she began, but the samurai cut her off.

"Do as I ask, please!" he begged. "It is too dangerous."

Phoebe twirled the revolver around her trigger finger, tossed it up over her shoulder, and caught it behind her back. "The devil himself is no match for me, as long as I've got a gun," she said.

Ki knew there was no time to argue with the stubborn woman. Every instant he delayed afforded the robbers more time to escape. "Fetch Longarm, at least!" he pleaded, and then raced off in pursuit of Pierre and his accomplices.

Phoebe hurried back to the show tent. It was intermission, and the audience had left their seats in order to mill about outside the big top, or else line up to buy a copy of William Cody's autobiography, now being hawked by a young man. Phoebe craned her neck to catch sight of Longarm in the crowd. She caught a glimpse of him standing with his back to her as he conversed with somebody. Phoebe pushed her way through the mass of people until she could tap the deputy on his shoulder.

"Please, excuse me!" she began, but then froze. Longarm had turned to face her, revealing who he'd been speaking with. Phoebe found herself face to face with Jessica Starbuck! The farm girl's knees turned to water as she stared at Jessie. She tried to speak, but the words wouldn't come. All that kept running through her mind was the image of herself standing in her soiled, threadbare dress before this woman who was so very rich and well known. Phoebe fought off the insane urge to curtsy.

"What's wrong, miss?" Longarm chuckled. "Cat got your tongue?" His smile faded as he noticed the revolver clutched in Phoebe's trembling hand. "Little late for target practice," he observed.

Jessie was staring at Phoebe's pale, drawn face. "What happened?" she asked gently. "Don't be afraid, tell us."

"It's Ki," Phoebe began. "Buffalo Bill's box office has been robbed and a man has been killed—"

"What's that?" demanded Marshal Farley, who'd been standing nearby. "Robbery? A killing?"

"Get Cody and check around back," Longarm ordered the town marshal. "I'm going to help Ki."

"The crooks are Pierre the knife-thrower and four others!" Phoebe called after him. "Ki already got one of them—"

But Longarm was gone.

"Three left, eh?" Jessie frowned. She drew her Colt out of her shoulder bag. "Stay here," she told Phoebe, and hurried off.

Phoebe stared after the woman who owned so much, *including* Ki's heart. *"Me* stay back?" she scowled. "Not on your life, Miss Starbuck!"

Longarm headed toward the stables. He had no clue as to where the robbers might be headed, but it seemed reasonable to assume they'd be looking for transportation out of here.

As he approached the stables tent, he removed his silver badge from his wallet and pinned it to the lapel of his frock coat. There was a man standing in front of the entrance to the canvas stables, the reins to four saddled horses in his hands, and an anxious, impatient expression on his face.

Longarm remained in the shadows long enough to assure himself that the man was alone. Then he began to saunter, whistling a cheerful tune.

The fellow whirled around in a panic, letting go of the horses' reins to draw his gun. His eyes widened at the sight of Longarm's badge glittering in the torchlight.

Longarm smiled to himself. The fellow was dressed in old wool trousers and a tattered shirt. From the way the man's hand was shaking, Longarm doubted that he'd be able to hit anything with that pistol of his.

The deputy kept his own hands well away from his Colt. He took on a look of surprise, calling out, "Take it easy, old son, I didn't mean to spook you!"

The man looked puzzled, then smiled quickly, holstering his pistol. "But you did spook me. Yeah, that's it!" he nodded adamantly. "I'm not doing nothing, lawman."

Longarm nodded agreeably. "You haven't seen any robbers around here, have you, old son?" he asked, meanwhile narrowing the distance between himself and the nervous man.

"Gosh, no," the man blurted. "Well, goodbye!" He began to hurry away. Longarm snapped out his hand to grab the fellow by the collar of his shirt. The horses scattered as the man tried to pull away, fumbling for his gun. Longarm batted it out of the man's holster, and delivered a short jab to his chin, knocking him flat on his back.

"Reckon you're under arrest for robbing Buffalo Bill and murdering his bookkeeper," Longarm said. He drew his Colt and laid it alongside the frightened man's head.

"I didn't kill 'em, Pierre did," the man babbled. "Please don't kill me!"

"Where did Pierre and the rest of your buddies go?" Longarm asked, cocking his Colt in response to his prisoner's stubborn silence. His pistol being a double-action, it didn't require cocking, but Longarm had found that the metallic click of the .44's hammer being pulled back tended to focus a fellow's attention.

The man screwed up his eyes. "Don't do it!" he begged. "I'll tell you. Pierre and that woman of his was headed off toward the carousel. They're trying to lose some joker who's chasing them. Think he's an Indian, or maybe a Chinaman. . . ."

Longarm nodded. "Good enough." Reaching into his coat pocket, Longarm took out his handcuffs. He snapped one cuff on the man's wrist, rolled him over onto his belly, bent back his leg, and locked the other bracelet around his ankle, effectively hogtying him.

"You won't shoot, will you?" the man whimpered as he lay facedown, helpless on the ground.

"Take it easy, old son," Longarm said soothingly. "I've never shot anybody like you in my life. I'm no murderer, like your friend Pierre." He paused, waiting for the agitated, relieved prisoner to respond.

"He ain't no friend of mine," the man babbled. "Look at the mess he got me into. You be careful up against him, lawman. I owe you this warning, for not shooting me when you had a right to. Pierre don't carry a gun, but he's real fast with those knives of his. And that redhead he travels with packs a pair of derringers, and she knows how to use them."

Longarm chuckled. "I already noticed her pair, old son. But from where I was standing, watching her in that skintight leather dress she was wearing, they looked a damn sight bigger than derringers." He kicked away the man's pistol to make sure it was well out of reach, and then headed off in the direction of the carousel. "Don't you go away now."

"Very funny," the man grumbled. Now that he knew he

was not to be shot dead, his fear was turning to anger. He bucked and twisted, trying to get loose, but he had about as much chance of going anywhere as a fish out of water.

Longarm kept his Colt in his hand as he approached the merry-go-round. This first jasper could have been arrested by a truant officer, but something told him that Pierre and his lovely and evidently lethal lady friend were not going to be anywhere *near* as easy to catch....

Ki hesitated before entering the dark, seemingly deserted carousel building. He had trailed Pierre and one other of the robbers to this place, ignoring the man who had angled off toward the stables. For one thing, that man wasn't carrying the stolen loot. For another, that man hadn't done the killing. Ki wanted Pierre. And now it looked as if he had him and his comrade cornered.

The samurai began to edge his way around the edge of the open doorway. He had one of his *shuriken* throwing blades ready for action, balanced on the tips of his fingers. He ducked low as two shots were fired, chewing holes in the doorjamb, and then he instinctively crabbed sideways just in time to avoid being skewered by one of Pierre's hurled blades.

"Did you get him?" called an anxious feminine voice.

Of course, Ki thought. *The redheaded assistant to Pierre, the so-called Princess Tall Tree—*

"I don't know," Pierre growled. "Now shut up!"

The samurai's keen ears picked up the sound of spent cartridges being dropped to the floor. *So, the woman's gun only holds two shots.* He nodded to himself. The pistol's twin report had sounded to him like the bark of a double-barreled derringer. A furtive movement caught his eye. He sent the *shuriken* blade hissing toward it.

"My Lord!" Pierre gasped in amazement. "That was close!"

Ki heard the squeaking sound of his *shuriken* being pried from the wall. He palmed another one and made himself ready, doing his best to try to pinpoint the whereabouts of both of his foes, lurking in the shadows. It was difficult. The big building—one of the few all-wooden structures built for the fair—had a cavernous interior that distorted sounds, making them reverberate so that a noise seemed to come from all directions at once. Added to this was the nuisance created by the looming animal shapes of the merry-go-round itself.

By day, the brightly painted horses, lions, and bears were a child's delight, but in the dark of night the shapes took on a nightmarish aspect. Behind which wooden animal were the flesh-and-blood Pierre and his gun-toting accomplice lying in wait, Ki wondered.

"So, my friend," Pierre called out, his voice sounding ghostly in the darkness. "I see that you too prefer the sharp, clean cut of a steel blade to the messy hole made by a firearm."

"Stop jabbering and kill him, dammit!" the redheaded assistant demanded impatiently.

"I have your little knife in my pocket, friend," Pierre shouted.

"I see him!" the woman crowed in triumph, squeezing off another pair of shots.

Ki flinched as the bullets knocked wood chips off the pint-sized, prancing stallion he'd been hiding behind. He'd desperately searched for a glimpse of the muzzle-flash from the woman's gun, but he hadn't seen any. His ears had been set to ringing by the two shots. Accordingly, he did not hear the sound of Pierre's dagger whistling through the air. Something cold bit hard into his thigh. Ki grimaced in pain, clapped his hand upon the hilt of the knife embedded in his leg, and tottered sideways, to fall with a crash against the machinery that ran the merry-go-round, situated in the carousel's center.

"You did it," the woman gloated to her confederate.

"But he's not dead, my knife took him too low to have killed him," Pierre warned. "Take the money and get out of here."

"Come with me," she urged. "He won't follow. He can't."

"No," Pierre replied. "He throws a blade almost as well as I do. It was only luck, and the fact that we were two against one, that allowed me to wound him. I want to see his face. I want to kill him." The knife-thrower laughed. "Then I'll *know* that I'm the best!"

"That's crazy," the woman pleaded, but Pierre's snarl cut her off.

"Get out of here! If you can't get to the horses, do the best

233

you can. Shoot anybody who tries to stop you! We'll meet where we've planned."

Ki watched the woman flit out through the open doorway of the carousel building. For one moment she was silhoueted by the starlight shining in through the open portal. Ki saw that she was wearing a cloak around her shoulders to camouflage her considerable female charms, and a man's hat pulled low to hide her curly red hair. The hat and swirling cape made her look like a man, and also allowed her to keep her pistol palmed and ready to fire at anybody in her way. . . .

Well, there was nothing he could do about the woman, and precious little he could do against Pierre, if he didn't get the knife out of his leg and stop the bleeding. Ki clenched his teeth and yanked at the blood-slippery hilt. After several agonizing tries, he managed to get hold of the dagger and wrench it out of his thigh. Fortunately, no major blood vessel had been hit, but the leg was bleeding severely. Ki fumbled around in the machinery pit until he found a couple of oily rags. These he knotted together to form a temporary bandage, which he wrapped tightly around the wound to staunch the flow of blood.

Pierre was approaching cautiously and circuitously, well aware that Ki, like any cornered, wounded creature, was capable of striking back.

Pierre was right to be cautious, but he certainly had Ki at a disadvantage. Pierre had mobility, while Ki did not. Pierre could attack unimpeded, while Ki's responces were slowed by his injury. The problem was not that Ki was physically unable to walk. The wound, while painful, was relatively minor, especially for a man who possessed a samurai's fortitude. Walking would be possible, but walking with the stealth necessary to confound Pierre and take him by surprise was another matter entirely.

What was needed, the samurai decided, was something to erase these inequities—a distraction, but one that would also serve to pinpoint the enemy.

Ki searched amid the carousel's machinery for something to use. He did not have much time left; Pierre was fast gaining confidence and quickly closing in.

The carousel was run by steam, so Ki could not hope to set the merry-go-round moving. It would take far too long to light the fire and build up a head of steam in the squat iron boiler tank—

Light the fire? Ki smiled in the darkness. The chances were good that there was some sort of flammable liquid around to prime the kindling. He hauled himself painfully into the compartment where the carousel operator sat, and began to search the shelves that lined the cubicle, just as one of Pierre's daggers thunked into the railing by Ki's shoulder.

"Go on, try and run," Pierre taunted. "I'd *rather* get you that way."

Ki threw one of his own *shuriken* blades, this one a six-pointed star, in Pierre's general direction, to slow him down. The star made a whirring sound as it flew through the air. Ki nodded to himself in satisfaction as he heard Pierre belly-flop to the wooden floorboards in order to avoid being impaled.

He resumed his search along the dark shelves until he came upon what he was looking for—a small bottle of kerosene. It was used by the carousel operator to soak the logs, making them easier to ignite in the burner. Ki poured out all but a quarter of the kerosene—after all, he had no desire to burn the merry-go-round to the ground—and stuffed a scrap torn from one of the oily rags into the bottle's mouth. He lined up several of his *shuriken* blades on the wooden railing, and took a match from one of the pockets of his leather vest.

There. He was ready. All that he needed was for Pierre to put himself in approximately the right position. . . .

Pierre was very close now, and somewhat to Ki's left. The soft scraping of the man's boot soles against the floorboards told Ki that Pierre had not yet stepped up on the merry-go-round's circular platform.

A tarp was draped over the grease-smeared gears and leather belts that drove the carousel. Ki burrowed beneath the tarp to strike the match and light the rag hanging from the mouth of the bottle; he didn't want the tiny flame giving away his position. Then he took a deep breath, hoping that his injured leg would bear his weight, and threw off the tarp, leaping up into the air to toss his fire bomb directly at the feet of his enemy.

Pierre stumbled back, startled. He'd been expecting a halfhearted defense, not a fierce attack. The bottle exploded no more than a foot in front of him, sending fragments of glass and flaming spatters of kerosene in all directions. The knife-thrower cried out, shielding his eyes with his arms as his clothing began to burn.

Ki seized the *shuriken* he'd lined up on the railing and sent them flying. They darted through the air like an enraged swarm of bees, peppering Pierre's chest. The killer coughed up great gouts of blood as he crumpled to the floor.

The samurai exhaled wearily. A small fire was crackling busily next to the robber's corpse. By the fire's gleam, Ki saw a bottle of whiskey on the carousel operator's shelf. He tore open the seam of his denims to expose the knife wound, pulled the cork on the whiskey bottle, and poured the alcohol into the gash. The damned whiskey hurt more than Pierre's knife....

That done, Ki pulled the tarp off the machinery and limped over to the fire to smother it. The last tongue of flame licked out from beneath the tarp to cast a glimmer of bogus life in Pierre's glazed eyes. The corpse was staring up at the mechanism that dispensed brass rings to those fast enough to snatch them as they whirled past on the carousel.

Ki took one of the rings and slipped it into his pocket as a memento. "You were a worthy opponent," he murmured. "But you should have listened to your woman. You should have escaped with *your* brass ring while you had the chance."

The samurai prodded the blackened, smoking section of flooring with his foot. The fire had not burned through. The floor of the carousel's building was still sound—

Good, Ki nodded. *Later this corpse would be carried out, and the blood spilled in this place would be washed away. Tomorrow the sun would rise on a new day, and once more the children could come here to play....*

Jessie had been wandering around the fair grounds, looking for Longarm, Ki, or the robbers, when she heard a pair of gunshots, a pause, and then two more shots from the deserted carousel building. She ran that way in time to see a cloaked figure, wearing a hat and carrying a pair of saddlebags, exit the building.

Whoever it was began hurrying across the fairgrounds toward the saloon tent. Jessie figured the man was planning on losing himself among the drovers patronizing the fair's only hard liquor watering hole. She hurried after the figure, closing the gap between them until she was within pistol range. Then she gripped her Colt in both hands, aimed, and opened her mouth to demand that the figure halt—

Before Jessie could say a word, she saw Phoebe step out from around the side of the bustling, brightly lit saloon tent. "Hold it right there, *Princess*," Phoebe addressed the cloaked figure.

Jessie lowered her Colt and watched, surprised as a sudden gust of wind lifted the figure's hat from its head, revealing the curly red hair and attractive features of the woman who'd assisted the knife-thrower during his act.

"Guess I know what's in those saddlebags," Phoebe said. She was standing with her legs spaced and the revolver she'd snatched from the roustabout held loosely in one hand. She frowned as another gust of breeze swirled the cloak around the woman's form. "You'd better show me your hands," she warned. "Come on, put 'em up!"

"Why don't you come a little closer and make me, you backwoods bitch," the redhead spat.

Phoebe strode forward angrily. "I'll tear your hair out by the roots!"

"Close enough," the redhead laughed triumphantly. Her hands appeared from beneath her cloak. She had her derringers ready to fire, and aimed at Phoebe.

Jessie could only gape in disbelief as Phoebe fired twice from the hip. The redhead yelped as her two little guns went spinning out of her hands. Phoebe fired a third time, and the clasp that held the woman's cloak around her neck disintegrated. The cape fell away, showing that the full-figured woman was still decked out in her skintight Indian-princess stage costume.

"That's some shooting!" Jessie called out in congratulations.

"Thanks," Phoebe called back. "Will you just look at that hussy?" she laughed. "She's gonna pop right out of that dress."

The redhead, meanwhile, was spitting like a cat that had been dunked in a pond. She lunged first in one direction and then the other, trying to find an avenue of escape. The saddlebags slipped from her grasp. As they hit the ground, one came undone, spilling stolen loot.

Crying out in despair, the woman made a grab for one of her derringers lying nearby on the grass. Phoebe raised her pistol, but Jessie stopped her, calling out, "Let *me* try!"

She aimed her Colt and fired, her bullet knocking away the derringer just as the redhead was reaching for it. The woman groaned in frustration, chasing after her elusive gun just as quickly as she could run—which was not very quickly, since the narrow skirt of her dress didn't allow her ripe hips and legs much room to stretch out for a rapid stride.

By now the saloon crowd, attracted by the shooting, had come outside to see what was going on. They roared as the woman skittered after the pistol, which Jessie kept flying with well-placed rounds from her Colt. Finally the distraught redhead literally threw herself at her gun, skidding across the dew-slick grass on her leather-garbed belly.

Jessie and Phoebe were laughing, but they laughed even harder when the woman tried to get up. As she rose to her hands and knees, there was an awful ripping sound. Her skin-tight rawhide dress split neatly along the rear seam, from hemline to neck, fluttering away from her nude form in two useless scraps.

The redhead screamed, leaping to her feet and trying to do her best to cover her jiggling rear and bouncing breasts with the two halves of her ruined garment. One of the whooping drovers from the saloon tent dashed forward to snatch one of the leather pieces from the humiliated woman's grasp. While in possession of both halves of her dress, she had barely been able to conceal her attributes. With just one little piece, there simply wasn't enough to go around. The woman blushed as red as her curls from head to toe. She hopped from foot to foot in a semi-crouch, bawling for somebody to give her some clothes.

Jessie scooped up the whimpering lady bandit's fallen cloak. "I'll trade you this for that derringer you managed to grab," she offered, laughing.

The sobbing woman glanced at the pistol she'd been clutching. Losing her dress had completely wiped from her mind the fact that she'd managed to regain one of her guns. "Oh, yes! Please!" She tossed the derringer away, and hastily snatched the cloak from Jessie's grasp.

"Aw, come on, Miz Starbuck!" one of the drovers yelled. "Don't go spoilin' our fun, now!"

"She's had enough, boys," Jessie admonished them, shaking her head. "A little fun at her expense is one thing, Lord knows she deserved it, but enough's enough."

"I second that," Phoebe asserted. "I also think that Princess Tall Tree here will just skip along real nice and polite to jail. Isn't that right, Princess?"

Longarm appeared, with Marshal Farley and Buffalo Bill behind him. One of the marshal's deputies had in tow the robber that Longarm had subdued.

"Here's another one for you, Marshal," Jessie said. "And I see you've already recovered your money, Mr. Cody." She eyed the saddlebags across the showman's shoulder.

"With that redhead, all four are accounted for," Farley said while his deputy led away both prisoners. "Ki caught one and killed the ringleader—"

"Where *is* Ki?" Phoebe broke in.

"He's with the doc," Farley began nervously.

"The doctor!" Jessie exclaimed. "Has he been hurt?"

"Well, just a little, it ain't nothing serious," Farley assured her. "Don't get excited, Jessie. That damned Pierre fella cut him a little, is all."

"Cut?" Phoebe cried. "Quick, where can I find him?" she begged. "Wait, here he comes now—"

"Oh, my Lord," Jessie gasped. Phoebe began to cry. Ki was limping toward them. His clothes were torn and bloodied. "It looks much worse than it is," the samurai assured them. "The doctor felt it was necessary to stitch up a small wound to my leg."

Phoebe rushed to him. "You poor dear," she murmured, hugging him.

"Phoebe, really," the samurai blushed. He tugged affectionately at her pigtails. "I understand that you and Jessie put that redhead through her paces," he said.

"Did she ever!" Buffalo Bill exclaimed. "Young lady, I happened to come upon the scene just as you shot those derringers out of her hands." He pointed his index finger in the air as if it were a gun. "Bang! Bang!" he laughed. "Why, I can't even *pretend* to shoot as fast as you can *really* pull that trigger!" The showman beamed. "'Little Sure Shot,' that ought to be your nickname, darling, or *mine* ain't Buffalo Bill!" He tipped his hat in Jessie's direction. "Miss Starbuck, you're an expert shot as well, let me hasten to add."

Jessie laughed. "Well, that may be, but I'm certainly not in Phoebe's league!"

Buffalo Bill chuckled, his eyes twinkling. "I reckon not, ma'am. Phoebe? You saved me a fortune." He patted his saddlebags. "Those owlhoots would have been my ruination if they'd gotten away with all this swag."

"How did Pierre and his assistant ever begin working for you in the first place?" Longarm asked.

"Shucks," Buffalo Bill turned beet-red. The change in his complexion was made all the more striking by his shoulder-length blond hair and goatee. "I guess I sort of made a bad judgment there. You see, folks, I knew that Pierre had been in trouble with the law before, but he assured me that he'd reformed, and, well, once I saw how talented he is with those throwing knives of his—"

Jessie glanced at Ki inquiringly. The samurai winked at her and said, "How talented he *was,* actually . . ."

Jessie nodded. "Next time, Mr. Cody, I advise you to pay more attention to your employee's references."

Buffalo Bill bowed. "I sure will, ma'am, I sure will." He smiled at Phoebe. "That brings me to my next point. 'Little Sure Shot,' it seems there's an opening for a new act in my show. I'm thinking along the lines of a cute little miss who can shoot the pants off any man—"

"—or the dress off any woman," Jessie added.

"Point well taken, ma'am" Cody grinned. "Anyway, Phoebe, I'd like to have you in my show. I'll make you a star!"

Ki gave the astounded farm girl a hug. "What did I tell you?" he murmured.

"Gosh, Mr. Cody, sir, I—well, I appreciate the offer," Phoebe began. "But I just don't think I'm ready for the footlights. Not *yet,* anyway." Her pretty face grew serious. "I do intend to be famous, but I've got some things to straighten out before I start that part of my career. First, I intend to win that prize money tomorrow, and . . . well . . ." she trailed off.

"Well what?" Cody demanded.

Phoebe glanced up at Ki, and then looked away. "I'd rather not say right now. It's sorta personal-like."

"It's your decision, dear." Cody smiled kindly. "I'll tell you this much, and in front of all these folks, too. I owe you a favor, young lady. And I aim to repay it. If not today, then tomorrow, or next year, or whenever!" he vowed emotionally. "I'm going to make you a star. There will always be a place in my show for Phoebe—" He hesitated, frowning. "What *is* your last name, dear?"

"Mozee," Phoebe said shyly. "Phoebe Mozee, sir . . ."

Buffalo Bill's lip curled. "Mozee, eh?" he muttered. "Hmmm, no offense, child, but it's just not right." His fringed arm made a sweeping gesture. "It—it just isn't *show business*, if you know what I mean."

Phoebe shrugged. "I guess I don't, sir."

"Charming!" Buffalo Bill laughed. "Isn't she charming?" he asked Longarm.

"You took the words right out of my mouth, Mr. Cody," Longarm grinned. "Phoebe? You have a middle name?"

"Yes, sir, Deputy. Shucks," she laughed, shrugging. "My family didn't have much money, so I guess they figured they'd be generous to all the kids with names, 'cause they don't cost anything. Anyway, I got *two* middle names. My full handle's Phoebe Anne Oakley Mozee."

Cody nodded to himself. "There you go, child! There will always be a place in my show for Annie Oakley!"

"Well, if you're dead set on winning that shooting match tomorrow, Miss Oakley, you'd better get some sleep," Jessie told Phoebe.

"Yes, ma'am."

"I will see you home," Ki offered.

"Okay, but you'd better lean on me," Phoebe suggested slyly, slipping her arm around Ki's waist, as they walked off.

"Marshal, I do believe that I would like for *you* to escort *me* home," Buffalo Bill chuckled to Farley. "A representative of the law would serve me well until I have time to cache this loot"—he patted his saddlebags—"somewhere around my campsite."

241

Jessie and Longarm bade the showman and the town marshal good night. "Are you going back to your spread?" Longarm asked, once they were alone.

Jessie shook her head. "I'm staying in Sarah tonight, at the home of some friends." She looked apologetic. "With all the excitement going on, I forgot to tell you—Barston used his clout to commandeer a suite at the hotel for himself and Thorn. He told me that since I was having second thoughts about endorsing him, he'd feel more comfortable if he was no longer a guest at the Starbuck spread."

"Well, then, I reckon I'd like to see you into town," Longarm grinned. "A relaxing night ride into Sarah with you sounds like just the thing."

"Perhaps my friends could find a bed for you as well," Jessie suggested.

Longarm politely declined her offer. "If you'll give me the use of that roan gelding for another day, I'd just as soon head back to that grove we were at this afternoon."

"Really?" Jessie said. "You want to camp out?"

"Sure," Longarm replied. "I've got everything I need tied to my saddle, it's a beautiful night, and besides, that grove holds pleasant memories for me." He winked at her. "Seriously, I'd *rather* sleep under the stars than under a roof."

"All right, then," Jessie said. "But in that case, are you sure you want to ride all the way back to town with me? The grove's between the fairgrounds and Sarah."

"I remember," Longarm assured her. "Come on, I'll get you home. Unless, of course, you'd prefer to camp out, as well?"

"I would," Jessie sighed. "But I can't, Custis," she added wistfully. "When this is over—"

"When this is over, and the crowds are gone, we'll have us a fine time," Longarm promised. "But tonight, it looks like you'll be staying with your friends in town."

Ki and Phoebe were slowly making their way back to the farm girl's tent. The grounds were pretty much deserted by now, and many of the torches that marked the main paths had burned themselves out.

Ki limped along carefully, taking care not to stumble in the dark. A fall could tear open his stitched leg, and that would be a nuisance, he thought grimly.

The samurai was grateful that Jessie had made arrangements to stay with friends in Sarah. She was armed, and since the house she would be in was filled with people, it was highly unlikely that the cartel, if they were even around, would try to strike against her this evening. Normally, Ki considered it his duty to keep watch over the woman he had given his solemn oath to protect, but tonight he was hurt and tired. Jessie had Longarm to see her safely to her door. She would be all right.

"Are you going back to your hotel room in Sarah?" Phoebe asked shyly. "I mean, if not, you could certainly stay with me."

"I would like that, Phoebe." Ki's smile was worn and tired. "The thought of riding . . ." his voice trailed off into a sigh.

"Come on," she comforted. "We're almost home, and you can sleep."

Ki nodded. He stumbled and then apologized, saying, "I am beginning to feel a little dizzy."

"It's no wonder," Phoebe fretted. "You've lost a lot of blood. Here, lean on me some more, I can hold you up! I've carried sacks of grain that weighed more than you."

"In that case—" Ki put his arm around her shoulder and slumped against her. Last night's romantic interlude with the ravenous Cling Sisters, followed by the rooftop battle with Wink Turner's assassin, and today's varied activities, culminating in his blade-battle and leg injury, were enough to exhaust even a samurai. Ki was a very sleepy warrior. He found his head slowly tilting to rest against Phoebe's.

The farm girl tightened her hold around Ki's waist. "This reminds me of how I used to carry my oldest brother home from the saloon in town," she giggled. "Of course, I'm having more fun with you, Ki."

"Well, well, look at the lovebirds," a male voice growled from out of the shadows.

Ki started, pulling away from Phoebe.

"Don't you two quit your lovey-dovey hugging on *my* account," the voice spat sarcastically.

Ki shook himself awake. His hand moved to his vest pocket for a *shuriken* blade.

"Move real slow, mister," the voice warned. A moment later, its owner stepped out from behind the back of a closed popcorn stand.

"Stay still, Ki," Phoebe whispered. "It'll be all right. Trust me."

Ki nodded, willing to give her the benefit of the doubt if it meant he could avoid getting into another fight this evening. He hoped Phoebe knew what she was doing. The samurai had much experience in facing down angry foes. He knew for a fact that this stranger just now confronting them had the sound of killing in his voice.

"There's no need to cause trouble, Frank," Phoebe said quietly. "He's hurt, and I'm helping him, is all."

"*Where* are you helping him, Phoebe?" the man demanded. "Back to your tent, like this afternoon?"

"Frank Butler!" Phoebe scolded, stamping her foot. "You don't own me, so you've got no call to say things like that. And if you don't mind your mouth, you never will have the right to bird-dog me!"

Ki squinted. His vision had become blurred from lack of sleep, but the man confronting them seemed to be the same fellow he'd seen earlier this afternoon. Butler was still carrying his walking stick, and was still dressed in his dapper blue suit, red satin vest, and derby. As the samurai's and the sharpshooter's eyes locked, Butler transferred his walking stick to his left hand, and casually brushed back his coat to reveal a revolver riding high on his right hip.

"Frank Butler, don't you dare try and pull anything!" Phoebe bristled. "I'm warning you!"

Ki admired the girl for her show of spunk, but from his vantage point by her side, he could see that she was trembling. Phoebe had given Marshal Farley the roustabout's revolver so that it could be used as evidence. She was unarmed. Ki had his blades, but in his weakened condition he was not at all sure he could take a renowned shootist like Frank Butler, if it came down to a fight.

"I'm not going to pull anything," Frank sneered at Phoebe. "Except this gun of mine. And then I'm going to shoot off that randy Chinaman's pecker, an inch at a time!"

244

"Never happen, Frank, you'd only be half done by the time that six-shooter of yours is out of ammo!" she scoffed.

"Phoebe, please," Ki muttered, watching as Butler scowled.

"Sorry," she giggled. "I couldn't resist. Frank, I'll promise you this. I may want to have some fun now and again, but I've yet to meet the man who can replace you in my heart."

"Awww," Butler's angry stance seemed to soften. "Is that true, darling?" he asked hopefully.

"Yep," Phoebe said quietly, batting her eyes.

"Phoebe here is my fiancée," Butler declared hotly.

"What?" Ki groaned. "Phoebe, why did you not *tell* me?"

"Well, I'm only sorta his fiancée, actually, Ki, honey," she apologized. "You see, Frank's been after me to marry him ever since I beat him by one point in a shooting match back in Cincinnati."

"That's the truth," Butler nodded. "She won the trophy and won my heart," he proclaimed. "I've been bird-dogging her ever since. So far, I got her to promise to marry me, I just ain't got her to say when!"

"Well, sir!" Phoebe took a step toward Butler and stuck out her chin. "I'll tell you right now, Frank, the answer to *that* question will be *never,* if you harm one hair on this boy's head!"

"Aw, shucks, Phoebe," Butler pouted, kicking at the grass. "I wasn't really gonna hurt him. The Chinaman's not even carrying a gun."

"He's not Chinese," Phoebe said. "For your information, Ki is half Japanese!"

Butler nodded quickly. At this point he seemed interested only in mollifying his angry fiancée. "I see it now. Sure, fella, I've seen folks from out of the Japans in San Francisco. Fine people, fine people..."

"Guess what, Frank?" Phoebe asked dreamily. "Buffalo Bill offered me a spot in his show. Wants me to call myself Annie Oakley."

"And what did you tell him?" Butler asked anxiously.

"Well..." Phoebe looked away. "I told him I wasn't ready. I said that there was something I had to work out in my personal life first." She took several tenuous steps toward the sharpshooter. "I meant that I had to marry *you* before I began my *real* career."

"You did?" he asked. "You meant it?" He seemed astounded. His grin slowly began to stretch from ear to ear. "Little darling!" he crowed triumphantly, stretching out his arms to her.

Phoebe ran to him and they embraced. Ki quietly backed away, allowing the betrothed couple their privacy. Butler and Phoebe were so engrossed in their murmurings that neither one of them noticed the samurai's departure.

Which was just as well, Ki thought. There was no reason to embarrass Phoebe with a reminder that just moments ago, he was going to spend the night with her. Ki smiled to himself as he limped along. As of now, he had no idea where he was going to sleep, but one thing he knew—it was not going to be in Phoebe's little tent! If Frank Butler was anywhere near as fast a thinker as he was fast on the draw, he'd find himself ensconced in Phoebe's comfortable sleeping bag tonight . . .

Ki cut across the deserted fields, taking a shortcut toward the stable tent. He did not favor having to ride, but if he wanted to sleep indoors, it meant journeying back to Sarah. If nowhere else, he could snooze the night in a vacant jail cell at Marshal Farley's office.

As he passed the saloon tent, which was still going strong, Aggie and Dot, the Cling Sisters, emerged from the tent, drunkenly weaving their way towards their wagon. The twins stopped to stare stupidly at Ki. Both licked their lips and then tottered over. Each took one of the samurai's arms.

"Ladies?" Ki nodded politely, doing his best to stifle a yawn.

"We were jusht havein' ourshelves a li'l nightcap," Aggie slurred. Her nose was as red as her strawberry tresses, and her breath smelled like a distillery.

"I would have thought you two ladies would be on your way back to Georgia, now that you have been eliminated from tomorrow's finals," Ki said.

"Plenny of time, plenny of time to go home," Dot mumbled. "Home, and what's there, will still be waitin' for us whenever we arrive. Wanted to have a li'l more fun before we left." Her bloodshot eyes glinted with lust as she smiled up at him. "How 'bout you, handsome? Wanna have a li'l more fun?" she hic-cupped.

Ki had no desire to make love to these two. For one thing, he liked his women sober enough to know what they were doing between the sheets. For another thing, he was lately feeling a little used, or perhaps the word was *abused*.

"Ladies," he began, leading them in the direction of their wagon, "I fear that tonight I would disappoint you both."

"Well, then, if there's not enough of you for the *both* of us, forget it!" Aggie declared firmly.

"How 'bout Wilson Barston, then?" Dot giggled.

"Now, sister, you be *dishcreet,*" Aggie said in warning, but then she laughed. "What the hell! Ki, maybe you *could* introduce us to that handsome congressman? He looks like he could handle a double helping of female!

"You mean maybe Ki could *reintroduce* us," Dot said.

"You two have met the congressman?" Ki asked, intrigued.

"Long time ago," Aggie mumbled, swaying on her feet as they walked. "He wouldn't remember us. It was in Europe. Prussia, it was. You don't have a flask on you, do you Ki, honey?"

Instantly, Ki became alert, all his weariness and pain for-gotten. "How was it that you were in Prussia?" he asked sharply.

"We were showgirls back then, Dot and I," Aggie contin-ued. "We were assistants to a fellow with a trained-dog act."

Dot added with a giggle, "The slogan on our wagon says we were 'the toast of Europe,' but it doesn't say in what ca-pacity."

"Barston hadn't yet been elected to Congress," Aggie said. "He and some of these Prussian businessmen who had a private box at the theater were real chummy."

"You are certain?" Ki demanded.

"Sure, honey." Dot patted his arm. "You see, us and the poodles became a regular act at that theater, so these here Prussians kind of paid us a retainer to be nice to visiting business contacts, if you know what I mean...."

Ki nodded. "And you were 'nice' to Barston?" he inquired.

"Hmmm," Aggie yawned. "The Prussians paid us *extra* to be *extra* nice. Barston kept bragging about how a deal he'd made with the Prussians would someday make him an important man. . . ."

Ki looked at the two sisters skeptically. "You remember a detail like that after all these years?"

"Well, Wilson Barston isn't any ordinary fellow, you know." Dot replied. "I mean, he was back then, sure enough. But as soon as he got elected and famous, Aggie and I started following his progress."

"And aren't we proud," Aggie cut in. "How many women can claim they've slept with a United States President?"

"Don't forget, we both made love to him at the same time," Dot corrected her sister. *"That* certainly ought to put us in a class by ourselves!" She glanced at Ki. "Don't you think so, honey?"

Ki nodded. "You are certainly both in a class by yourselves," he said evenly.

"We're also back at our li'l old wagon," Aggie mumbled. "Sure you won't come in, Ki?"

The samurai was already taking his leave. "Another time, ladies," he called over his shoulder as he walked as quickly as he could back toward the stables.

The fact that Wilson Barston was once in league with the Prussians was a bombshell, Ki knew. Jessie had to be told about this immediately! He would get himself a horse and ride directly to the house where Jessie was an overnight guest. Longarm, as well, should be made aware of the information, the samurai realized, but his first responsibility was to Jessie—

A horrifying thought suddenly came to Ki as he limped past the darkened fairground structures and along deserted footpaths. Perhaps the cartel was not so far away, after all. Did the Prussians have some sort of hold on the congressman? Was Wilson Barston being blackmailed in some way?

It made sense, Ki decided as he entered the stable tent. It was completely in character for Barston to have made some foolish business deal with the cartel when he was a very young man. He'd probably spent the profits long ago. Then he got elected to the United States Congress, and to assist his old family friend, Jessie Starbuck, he began to investigate the cartel's activities in this country. How shocked Barston must have been to have his sordid business dealings thrown up to him by representatives of the cartel! Had they also threatened to reveal how the man who wished to be this nation's next moral and political leader had been debauched by the likes of the Cling Sisters?

Or perhaps Wilson Barston had debauched himself, Ki thought wryly. In any event, if such information was made public, Barston would doubtless lose his chance at the Presidency. No wonder the congressman was anxious to secure Jessie's political endorsement as quickly as possible!

The interior of the stable tent reeked of horseflesh. All of the mounts that belonged to those camping on the fairgrounds had to be stabled here, by order of the town's health inspector. Ki found a lantern just inside the entrance flap of the tent and struck a match to light it. The horses were separated by rope barricades to keep them from kicking at each other within the close confines of the canvas enclosure. The chestnut gelding that Ki had borrowed from Marshal Farley after he had been deputized was waiting in a rope stall at the rear of the tent. The samurai hurried to where a row of saddles were drying out on a long wooden rack.

After a few moments of searching, he found his saddle, then set down his lantern so he could lug it off the rack. He felt the stitches in his leg pulling as he struggled to get the heavy saddle down, but there was no help for that. The young stablehand had long ago gone home for the night. . . .

He dropped the saddle to the ground and leaned against the wooden rack as a wave of dizziness came over him. He had not realized how weak he was. He left the lantern where it was, so that he could use two hands to drag the saddle over to where his horse was corralled.

Halfway there, he thought he heard a strange noise inside the dimly lit tent. He stood still, listening intently, before dismissing the sound as nothing more than a skittering rat or a pawing, snorting horse, disturbed by the noise that he himself was making as he dragged the saddle along. He continued on, at last reaching his horse.

Ki thought about retrieving the lantern, but he did not want to expend the energy. What did he need light for? He had saddled and bridled enough horses in his life to be able to do it in the dark. . . .

He quickly smoothed the saddle blanket across the gelding's back. Now for the hard part, Ki thought grimly, bending down.He barely managed to hoist the saddle off the ground, and then lift it high enough to set it upon the suddenly nervous gelding's swaying back.

Ki paused for a moment and soothed the horse. Normally the gelding was as docile as could be, but the samurai's groans of exertion and sudden, unsteady movements had made it anxious.

Once again Ki was forced to bend, this time in order to cinch the saddle tight. His injured leg was trembling beneath him, and the blood was roaring in his ears as his fingers fumbled with the straps in the darkness. Finally it was done. As Ki was straightening up, he felt himself beginning to black out. He leaned against the gelding's haunch, but the nervous mount shied away, so that Ki felt himself falling forward. He stumbled against the single strand of hemp that separated this stall from the next, like a punch-drunk boxer against the ropes. Something hot and wet began to run down his bad leg.

Damn, Ki thought. *I have torn open the stitches after all. Well, if it had not happened now, it probably would have happened during the ride to town*, he decided philosophically. *And before I can begin the ride, I still have to bridle the horse.*

As he got to his feet, he heard a footstep behind him. He tried to spin around, but his injured leg refused to obey his brain's command. The samurai next heard harsh laughter, and then saw a blinding flash of light as something hard whipped down against the back of his skull.

Ki dropped to his hands and knees like a poleaxed steer. *Really torn those stitches open now....*

"Told you I'd get even," a gruff male voice snarled from far, far above the dazed samurai.

Pistol-whipped, Ki thought as he tottered on the edge of consciousness. *Jessie! The cartel! Got to fight back...* Suddenly it came to him who his attacker had to be—

"Frank," he whispered. "Do not do this.... Phoebe will—" He reached back, trying to snare his attacker's legs, but the samurai knew he was far too slow to succeed....

The tip of a boot crashed against Ki's ribs, knocking him off balance. He went over on his side and tried to curl up into a protective fetal ball, but before he could, that boot slammed into his stomach. A moment later, the man's boot heel ground down upon the slash in his leg.

Samurai or not, Ki would have cried out if he could, but the dual kicks to his ribs and belly had knocked all the air out of his lungs. The incredible pain he was suffering served to focus his consciousness, the way the sharp tang of smelling salts will bring one out of a stupor.

This time his arm snapped out with *proper* speed, to hook his tormentor behind the knee. Ki pulled hard, and managed to bring his attacker down.

The man cried out in surprise. For one brief instant Ki thought he was going to make it, that he was going to get a chance to strike back at this bastard who had ambushed him from behind—

But once again the man whipped the barrel of his pistol against Ki's head. Ki went limp. His last thoughts before fading into blessed unconsciousness were that he would never have guessed that Frank Butler would attack from out of the darkness like this—and that Phoebe would never forgive the sharpshooter, assuming that Ki himself survived to accuse him . . .

Chapter 12

"All right, it's time," Marshal Vail called softly to his small band of men. "It's a quarter of twelve."

"You sure, Billy?" Talbot gulped uneasily. "Hell, it seemed like midnight was never going to get here, and now that it has, I wonder where the hours went."

"Keep calm now," Vail ordered his deputy. "It ain't going to get any darker, nor are those outlaws going to get any sleepier than they are right now."

"Besides," another deputy cut in, "the longer we wait, the longer it'll be before help arrives to get us out of this mess."

"Amen to that," Glenn said. He, along with two other men, had volunteered for the risky job of leaving the relative safety of the boulders in order to divert some of Wink Turner's army. "I've been sitting here freezing my ass off and chewing on beef jerky for way too long, as far as I'm concerned."

Vail nodded patiently. "Well, you'll be getting some action now, Glenn. I hope you—and the rest of us—will be able to handle it."

"Sadie and Selma ready?" Talbot teased nervously.

Mike grinned reassuringly. "We've got them up and kicking, Paul and me. Our mules will move out quicker'n grease through a goose."

Vail was dour. "They'd better. They're going to have to outrun a hell of a lot of bullets. Glenn? Move out!"

The deputy nodded. He snicked back the hammer on his sawed-off Winchester and gestured for his two-man patrol to follow him. Like serpents, the men slinked and slithered over and around the boulders. Then they were gone, vanished into the shadows of the night.

Vail stared at his pocket watch. There was no moon, but the marshal's eyes had long since grown accustomed to the lack of light. There were plenty of twinkling stars in the clear sky by which to see the face of a watch—too many stars. Vail wished he could snuff them out like so many candles to cloak his men in protective darkness.

At exactly midnight, Vail nodded to Mike and Paul. "They're in position by now. Get your mules and—" The marshal looked down at his boot tips. "If we don't meet again I just want to thank you on behalf of my men, and especially Hopkins—"

"No call to thank us now," Mike cut him off. "You'll be buying Paul and me drinks in Sarah, soon enough."

Vail grinned. "And carrots and sugar for them mules of yours."

"Sadie and Selma will be right glad to hear that," Mike smiled.

"Good luck, Marshal. We'll be seeing you," Paul said.

Vail watched the two farmboys hurry toward their beasts. "Strange," he murmured to Talbot. "Our lives are in the hands of a couple of barefoot Louisiana potato farmers, and I don't reckon we could have done any better for ourselves."

Talbot nodded. "They're all right," he said admiringly. "Let's hope we can keep ourselves alive long enough to be able to buy them those drinks."

Vail put his hand on Talbot's shoulder. "Let's hope," he sighed. "All right, boys! Get into position, see to your guns! We've taken a lot, and now it's time for us to dish some of it back!"

The plan called for the shooting to start at twelve-fifteen.

At a quarter past the hour, on the dot, the three Winchesters off to Vail's left began pumping out lead, fire flashing from their muzzles.

Vail waited. As he'd hoped, a sizable number of Turner's men were unable to resist the opportunity to fire down at those provocative muzzle flashes. He signaled to Paul and Mike to make their dash. The two farmers cajoled their mules into movement. A moment later they were engaged in a flat-out run through the valley.

The high slope lit up with spurts of orange flame as the main body of Turner's army fired down upon the Louisiana farmboys. "Open up!" Vail shouted to his few remaining men as the valley filled with rattling thunder. On either side of him, Vail's men sent up round after round, doing their best to draw Turner's firepower down upon themselves or, at the very least, spoil the aim of the outlaws blasting away at the escaping farmers.

Vail levered off shots until the magazine of his rifle was empty. He put the Winchester aside and drew Captain Walker. He thumbed back the pistol's hammer and aimed, but before he could fire, Talbot seized his arm, shouting something hoarsely in the marshal's ear.

Vail looked the way Talbot was pointing, in time to see one of the galloping mules go down. "Oh, shit, I think that was Paul—"

He and Talbot watched, their hearts pounding, as Mike reined in his mount, wheeling it around hard to double back for his fallen buddy. Paul had scrambled out from beneath his dead mule. He now stood above his beloved Sadie, screaming his fury up toward the slope while squeezing off shots from his single-action Colt Peacemaker. Mike rode by him, grabbing him from behind by the rope belt twisted around Paul's waist, and laid him across the withers of his own mule like a sack of potatoes. Paul was still kicking and screaming, oblivious to everything but his grief over the loss of Sadie, as Mike kneed Selma into a fast run out of the valley.

Most folks believed that mules were smarter than horses. Selma certainly proved the theory to Vail and Talbot. The mule evidently knew what was happening, for it immediately flattened back its jackrabbit ears and made up for lost time. Bullets kicked up dust spouts all around Mike and Paul, but the darkness combined with the posse's cover fire, gave them just enough of an edge to make it through Turner's gauntlet of rifles.

"I think they're all right!" Talbot crowed. "They made it!"

"We're going to be okay!" Vail enthused to his men. Actually he was a lot more pessimistic, but he kept his private doubts to himself. The two farmers were riding double on one mule. It would take them twice as long to get to Sarah Township. Vail could only pray that Turner would feel too self-confident to bother sending some of his men after Paul and Mike. Riding double, they'd have no chance of outrunning pursuers. . . .

The marshal noticed that Talbot was scrutinizing him.

"You never could keep a poker face, Billy," the young deputy chuckled. "I know we ain't out of the woods yet, not by a long shot. But I've got faith in those two potatoes. Even if Turner sends some men after them, those two strike me as having the know-how to outfox their trackers."

Vail just nodded. "Right now our main concern is to stay alive long enough to get rescued! We started those outlaws shooting at us, but I don't have a plan to make them quit!"

"Glenn and his boys are in trouble," Talbot muttered, jamming fresh cartridges into the magazine of his rifle and rejoining the pitifully meager firing line.

Vail could only watch helplessly, feeling vexed and frustrated as Glenn and his two men fought back against the wrathful gunfire cascading upon them. The marshal and his men numbered only four; right now they were being hard pressed just to hold their own as bullets richocheted all around.

Glenn stood in a crouch, endlessly levering off shots as he swept the squat barrel of his little Winchester back and forth. He was like a man trying to put out a raging forest fire with just a single hose. Beside him, one of the deputies tottered backward, dropping his rifle to clutch at his chest.

"Fuck this!" Glenn told his remaining comrade. "Let's make a run for Billy and the others!"

"They're coming back!" Vail shouted. "Cover 'em, boys!"

As Glenn and the other deputy dashed for the relative safety of the main group of lawmen, Vail and his men sent up covering fire, taking some satisfaction as one of Turner's men rolled and skidded down the slope.

Vail ducked as shots whined off the boulder he was hiding behind. "Glenn and Halliwell are almost back," he muttered to Talbot. "Keep firing! Talbot? I said keep firing—"

Talbot didn't answer. Vail was angry, but his attention was distracted by the sight of the deputy named Halliwell being peppered by several shots. The deputy sprawled to the ground. Glenn nose-dived down beside him.

Vail began to scramble out from behind the protective boulders to see if either of his men were still alive.

Glenn, seeing this, waved his superior down. "I'm okay, but Halliwell is dead. I'm playing possum so they'll shift their fire."

"Look there!" one of the deputies called out. "It's Turner himself!"

Vail, along with his men, stared up at the slope's ridge. A pair of huge torches had been lit, and standing between them, like a demon-god, was Wink Turner.

There was no mistaking anyone else for Turner. He stood close to six and a half feet tall. He wore a Mexican serape over his massively muscled torso. A brace of pistols rode his hips, while two more were suspended from a pair of holsters strapped to the two bandoliers crisscrossing his chest. Turner wore no hat. His shaven skull—a style he'd taken to in prison—gleamed with sweat in the flickering torchlight. A red bandanna was knotted across the entire left side of that skull, to hide the hideous burns that scarred half of Wink Turner's face. The outlaw leader had suffered those burns in a fire that he himself had started in his own cell in order to escape from prison.

Vail stared, mesmerized, as Turner stood with his hands on his hips in the red glare of the torches. The outlaw looked like something straight out of hell. Vail's deputies were doing their best to knock Turner down with rifle fire, but to no avail.

"We just can't seem to hit him," one of the lawmen groaned, and then shuddered. "Billy? You don't suppose what they say is true, do you? That Turner made a pact with the devil, and now he can't be killed?"

"That's bullshit!" Vail said sharply. "Damned jailhouse superstition."

The legend around Turner had sprung up when a rebellious pack of convicts, fed up with Turner's prison-yard dictatorship, closed in around him all at once, stabbing at him with their razor-sharp, homemade shivs. Turner absorbed the attack, refusing to fall down, even though his would-be murderers had turned him into a pincushion. He managed to wrestle away one of the blades that had grown slippery from his own blood. He slit the first man's throat, and then calmly pursued his attackers around the yard, killing them one by one as they shrieked for help. The guards tried to stop him, but they were hauled around like so many scrawny hound dogs worrying at a grizzly bear.

"If it's bullshit, why can't we shoot him, Billy?" another deputy asked plaintively. "I wasted an entire magazine on him!"

"He ain't out of rifle range, that's for sure," another man added nervously.

"You boys are just not shooting straight," Vail replied in contempt. "That's the answer, sure it is! No man is bullet-proof!" He glanced at Talbot's huddled, still form. "Phil, you shoot that outlaw bastard! Go on, Phil. What are you saving your ammunition for? Phil? I said shoot him—"

Vail reached out and shook the deputy. Talbot's hat fell away to reveal his blond curls, and his bloodied face. The young lawman had been shot between the eyes. When it had happened, Vail could not be sure.

He stared, horror-struck, as Talbot's body slumped sideways. *Sorry, Phil,* the marshal thought. *Sorry I got you killed....*

"Look," a man whispered. "Turner's *laughing* at us!"

Vail stared up at the devil on the slope. *Can't see so good anymore,* he thought sadly. *Things are glittery and blurred....*

The marshal realized that he was crying.

The shooting had stopped on both sides. Vail stood up and climbed over the boulders, out into the open. Before his men could stop him, the marshal began to walk toward the slope, and then to stride up it, directly toward Turner's position.

"Marshal!" Glenn hissed as Vail walked past him. "Come back, Billy, you damned fool!" Muttering to himself, the deputy slung his sawed-off rifle over his shoulder, and began to belly crawl after the marshal.

Vail walked on up that slope, clutching Captain Walker

firmly in his right hand. He waited—feeling surprisingly sanguine—for a bullet to slap him down, but none came. He kept walking toward Wink Turner.

"Hold your fire, everbody hold your fire!" Glenn quietly ordered the other deputies as he wormed his way up the slope, one perilous inch at a time.

Vail stared up at Turner, who loomed before him bigger than life, bigger than all the years put together that Billy had been a United States Marshal. Sunrise and sundown, day in and out, he'd worn the star and enforced the law. In the beginning he'd put his own body and his own gun on the line. In recent years he'd been forced to exchange his saddle for a desk, his gun for a typewriter, and his own heroics for a band of young deputies. Still, his entire life had been devoted to the law. Tonight it seemed that everything he hated was now standing on two legs, just a few feet away.

Wink Turner. Let me just bring down Wink Turner, he prayed. *Then I can hand over the reins; then I can rest. Wink and I, we belong together. We're opposite sides of the coin. I've got to bring him down if it's all not to have been a waste....*

Vail thumbed back the hammer on his Walker Colt. He swung up his arm and fired, without altering his pace. The big gun's report echoed against the silent, rocky slopes. Vail's arm was forced up by his pistol's recoil. He walked ahead, squinting through the cloud of gunsmoke spewed out by his .45.

Wink Turner still stood, as timeless and enduring as the boulders planted all around the valley. *As timeless and enduring as the evil itself?* Billy wondered.

No! That can't be! Turner is just a man! "I'm U.S. Marshal Billy Vail! Wink Turner, do you know me?" Vail shouted at the outlaw leader.

"I know you, Vail," Turner called down in a flat, emotionless voice. "Plenty of my men have spent time behind bars because of you."

"You're under arrest, Turner!" Vail shouted. "Surrender! "Do you understand? You're under arrest!"

There was a pause before Turner replied. He cocked his bandanna-shrouded head to one side, fixing his single beady eye on the lawman like an owl about to swoop down on a mouse. "I understand," Turner said, almost gently, almost lovingly. "If you want to arrest Wink Turner, old man, you best come up here and get him."

Vail plodded on up the slope. He was now less than fifty yards from the outlaw. He swung up Captain Walker and aimed. The pistol boomed. When the smoke had cleared, Turner was still standing. "Surrender!" Vail called, his voice breaking.

He walked on. *Boom!* "Surrender!"

Boom! "Surrender!"

Boom! Boom!

On Vail's last shot, Turner seemed to flinch. "He's hit him! He's hit Turner!" the deputies below babbled excitedly.

But Turner was still on his feet. Vail, who had surprised himself with that last, seemingly lucky shot, tried hard not to let his spirits plummet now that he could see that Turner seemed unharmed. Captain Walker was empty, but Vail didn't care. He didn't even bother to reload his .45, but merely slid it back into its holster. It didn't matter that Turner could not be shot, the old marshal mused to himself. It was not the gun that would bring Turner down. It was the badge. . . .

As if locked in a trance, Vail continued his trek up the slope. He was now thirty yards from Turner. Now twenty. Glenn, lying on his belly down below, held his breath as he watched. The outlaw and the lawman seemed to be locked in a battle of wills. For just a moment, Glenn began to believe that old Billy Vail's spirit was such that he would be able to crest that slope and snap those handcuffs on Turner—

But that sort of thing only happened in legends. He watched in despair as Turner nodded once, in an awful parody of a judge ordering an execution—

Ordering Billy's execution, Glenn realized suddenly in horror. "Look out, Billy!" he shouted hysterically.

One of Turner's men fired a rifle. Vail was spun around. He lost his footing and began to roll and tumble down the incline as the sound of that single shot echoed and faded within the confines of the deathly still valley.

Glenn began to hurry to where the marshal was lying. The other lawmen rose up in order to help, but Glenn waved them down.

Vail stared up at the starry sky. He felt no pain, and could hear nothing. His tumble had been dreamlike and silent. He'd heard the beginning of Glenn's frenzied shout, but after that, nothing at all. He'd not even heard the sound of the shot that had laid him low.

He could feel his own blood bubbling up out of the hole somebody had put in his side. Lord, the blood felt alarmingly hot against his cold, clammy skin. Was a fellow always that hot inside? It was a wonder a fellow didn't just boil away over the years. . . .

His angle upon the ground was such that he could no longer see the crest of the slope. He wondered fleetingly if Turner was still up there, looking down at him. *Probably ought to draw old Captain Walker*, Vail chided himself, completely forgetting that he'd not bothered to reload the gun. He tried to move his right hand toward his holster, but he couldn't do it. Funny, he could see his right hand lying there on the ground, but he simply could not move it. . . .

He gave up the whole idea of drawing his gun, and resigned himself instead to staring up at the sky. All those stars shining brightly, coldly, like diamonds. It *was* getting colder, Vail mused. His arms and legs felt like ice.

So many stars, Vail mourned. *Too damned many. Too much light. If only I could have snuffed them out. Then Talbot and Halliwell and the others would be alive. Then Hopkins wouldn't be lying wounded and in pain. Then Sadie the mule would still be up and kicking. Too many stars . . .*

Ironically, it seemed as if he were getting his wish, even though it was now coming far too late to help his dead deputies. As he stared, the stars seemed to be blotted out by a solid wave of darkness. One by one they were blanketed, until there was nothing at all left for a tired old marshal to see. . . .

Glenn hunkered down beside Billy's still body. The deputy peered up at the slope. Turner had disappeared, and the torches that had bracketed him were now extinguished. The entire slope appeared dark and deserted. For some cockeyed reason, the outlaw leader was going to let him tug Vail's body back to the shelter of the boulders unmolested.

As gently as he could, Glenn dragged Billy's hefty shape back to the others. The two remaining men lent a hand.

"How is he?" one of the deputies demanded.

261

"How the hell am I supposed to know?" Glenn scowled. "I wasn't about to conduct an examination out there in the open. I'll tell you this much—from the feel of him in my arms while I was bringing him back, I do believe us three and Hopkins got another vote on our hands. This time we've got to elect a new marshal!"

★

Chapter 13

Jessie had been sound asleep until the hesitant knocking on her bedroom door caused her to open her eyes. For an instant, while staring up at the ceiling, she was unsure just where she was.

Then she remembered—she was an overnight guest of friends who lived in town. This was the spare bedroom. That light shining in through the curtained second-story window, turning the ruffled cotton translucent, was coming from one of the newly installed gas street lamps that Mayor Wilk was so proud of.

Again there came the sound of somebody tapping on her door. "Yes?" Jessie called, her voice thick with sleep. "What is it?"

"Miss Starbuck? It's me, Emily," a child's voice replied.

"Em?" Jessie was puzzled. She peered at the grandfather clock standing in one corner of the room. It was almost four o'clock in the morning! What was a ten-year-old doing up at this ungodly hour?

"Come in, Emily," Jessie said, meanwhile pulling her blankets up around her. The door opened, and in shuffled a barefoot little girl in a pink flannel nightgown. Her long brown hair was tangled, and she was clutching a rag doll to her chest. Jessie took one look at that sleep-puffed little face, and said, "You don't look to me like a very wide-awake little girl. What's the matter, honey? Did you have a bad dream?"

Emily shook her head. "Somebody's here," she mumbled crankily. "He wants *you.*"

"What?" Jessie shook her head. "You were dreaming, honey—"

"No!" Emily stamped her foot. "He's downstairs and he wants to see you! He says that I *wahsn'tshupposedtowahke—*"

"Em," Jessie said patiently. "Take your thumb out of your mouth so that I can understand you."

The little girl popped her digit out of her mouth, but held it poised and ready for another go-round, as if her thumb were a pipe. "The man said that he was sorry his knocking woke me, but that as long as I got up, and not Mommy or Daddy, I shouldn't bother them, but come get you."

"Where is this man now?" Jessie asked.

"In the parlor," Emily replied, yawning.

"Did he say his name?"

Emily shrugged. Then she switched her rag doll to the other arm and held out a small card she'd been clutching.

Jessie took the card. Embossed on one side was Wilson Barston's name. Scrawled on the reverse sight was the message:

Please! He needs you! I'm waiting downstairs.

It was signed by Thorn.

"Should I wake Mommy and Daddy?" Emily asked, concerned.

"No, honey," Jessie smiled. "Everything is all right. I want you to tell the man that I'll be right down, and then I want you to go back to bed."

The child scurried out of the room to deliver her message and then return to her warm blankets.

Jessie shrugged on a blue silk dressing gown over her nightdress, wishing that she had remembered to pack her slippers in her suitcase, and then tiptoed barefoot across the cold, wooden floor. She slipped quietly past the closed bedroom door of her hosts, and peeked into Emily's room to assure herself that the child was safely back in bed. Then she went down the stairs and into the shadowy parlor.

Thorn was sitting in an armchair, with a lit candle beside him on an end table. The bodyguard was wearing his brown leather jacket and black denims. His Stetson was on his head.

"It's a bit late—or should I say early— for a social call, isn't it, Thorn?" Jessie asked quietly.

"Miss Starbuck! Thank you for coming down!"

"Please lower your voice," Jessie told him. "There are people sleeping." She felt Thorn's eyes feasting upon her curves, accented by the thin silk of her dressing gown. She pulled the gown closer around her, realized that making it tighter would only make the situation worse, and then resolved not to let this uninvited caller intimidate her. "What's the meaning of this card you asked the little girl to deliver to me, Thorn? Why are you here?"

"It's, uh . . . " Thorn closed his eyes. "Just give me a moment." He got to his feet, only to stumble. The Stetson fell from his head to reveal his thick blond hair crusted with dried blood.

"My word!" Jessie gasped, hurrying to his side. "You're badly hurt! Thorn, you need a doctor—"

"No," the bodyguard insisted. "No time. They—they jumped me from behind, knocked me down, and took the congressman—"

"Who, Thorn? Who did this to you?" Jessie coaxed as she helped the dazed man back to his chair.

"Thugs sent by the Prussians. They jumped us in the corridor just outside our hotel suite. Knocked me on the head and pushed me inside the room. Tried to get up, but I couldn't. They had guns. Took the congressman."

"How do you know it was the cartel?" Jessie asked.

He seemed not to hear her question. "My hat," he mumbled, pointing at the Stetson lying on the carpet.

Jessie fetched the hat and handed it to him. Thorn clamped it down over his blood-scabbed thatch of hair. "Don't want a pretty lady to see me all messed up," he blushed, smiling.

Jessie nodded impatiently, thinking to herself that she couldn't care less about Thorn's appearance, although she was worried about the severity of his head injury. From the amount of blood that had dried in his hair, he must really have suffered a good crack on the noggin. As to his vanity, well, Thorn *was* good-looking. Jessie assumed that he was one of those males who'd found certain types of women easy pickings, and now thought himself to be irresistible.

"You were going to tell me how you knew that Wilson was taken by the cartel?" she reminded him.

Thorn nodded. "Well, they *said* so, Miss Starbuck!"

"Why would they reveal their identities to you before kidnapping your boss?" Jessie asked.

"They didn't actually tell me," Thorn explained. "They hit me, and I went down. They probably thought I was out cold. The congressman demanded to know who they were—"

"Hold on," Jessie interrupted, remembering what Ki had taught her about interrogation. "Let's establish the facts. How many of them were there?"

Thorn stared down at his lap in shame. "Just two," he muttered. "I guess Longarm was right. I *am* an amateur to get taken by two men."

"Hey, that's nothing," Jessie comforted him. "Anybody can get ambushed from behind."

Thorn looked up at her, his expression plaintive. "Even Longarm?"

"Sure," Jessie smiled.

"And that Japanese friend of yours? Ki? Could he get ambushed?"

"Yes," Jessie replied. *And I wish Ki were around right now*, she thought to herself. "So there were two of them, and the congressman demanded their identities?"

"Yes. They said that the cartel was following through on their warning to him. They said that if he behaved himself, he wouldn't be harmed." Thorn scowled. "Imagine! Telling somebody like Wilson Barston to behave himself!"

"Their decision not to harm him makes sense," Jessie mused aloud. "If they killed him, he'd become a martyr, a symbol that the country could rally behind against an overseas power. They probably intend to compromise him in some way. But how?"

"I know how!" Thorn frowned. "Think about it, Miss Starbuck! The congressman has established himself as a rugged Texan, a hard-riding, hard-shooting son of the Lone Star State. He was all set to win the shooting match tomorrow."

"I still don't understand," Jessie murmured.

"It's like this," Thorn said intensely. "The congressman wants the public to think that he's the kind of old-fashioned hero who can take care of the nation's troubles. How would it look if it became known that a couple of bullies kidnapped him, then maybe stripped him naked and force-fed him whiskey? He'd be discovered wandering around like a vagabond drunkard!"

"I see." Jessie nodded slowly. "Yes, it makes sense. People might feel sorry for Wilson, but they'd definitely lose their respect for him. Regardless of whether or not his predicament was his fault, Wilson Barston would no longer be a viable Presidential candidate." Jessie gripped Thorn's arm. "We've got to alert Marshal Farley," she began. "Organize a posse and set up a search—"

"No, ma'am! Please," Thorn begged. "Don't do that! Don't you see? If a posse finds him, the cartel will have succeeded in ruining his image. There's no way it won't leak to the news reporters that the rough, tough Wilson Barston had to be rescued by a bunch of drovers."

"I understand your concern about Wilson's political career," Jessie replied. "And your loyalty speaks well for you, Thorn. But the congressman's personal safety is our greatest concern. We *need* a posse. The more riders we have, the larger the search we can conduct."

Thorn's grin was as wide as a schoolboy's at the start of summer vacation. "But we don't have to conduct a search, Miss Starbuck. While I was lying there on the floor, I heard where they said they were going to take the congressman! Don't forget, they thought I was unconscious. One of the men said to the other, 'I'll feel better when we've got him stashed away at Castle Rock.'" Thorn looked concerned. "Since I'm not from around here, I was hoping you'd know where that is—"

"I do!" Jessie declared. "It's pretty far. About six hours' ride, out past Goat Creek." She winked at him. "But at least we know *where* to search. You've done very well. We'll get Marshal Farley and—"

"Excuse me, Miss Starbuck," Thorn said hesitantly, "I kind of hoped that you'd consent to just you and me rescuing the congressman."

"Well, I don't know," Jessie began, taken by surprise. "Um, you're hurt, Thorn, and—"

"Oh, I'm fine now, ma'am," the bodyguard replied quickly. "And I've heard how well you can ride and use a gun." He nodded firmly. "The two of us could take those two kidnappers, and once we move on them, the congressman would be sure to lend a hand. Don't you see? It would totally turn the tables on the cartel. The reporters would have to write that Congressman Barston got himself out of this predicament, just the way he's going to put the country back on the right track!"

Jessie was forced to admit that the bodyguard had a point. If she was willing to make the effort and accompany Thorn, Barston's career would suffer no setback.

"I want to level with you about this, Miss Starbuck," Thorn said shyly, looking away. "You know I want to do what's best for the congressman, but I'm also trying to look out for myself. I feel real bad about the way I got conked on the head. I was pretty useless to my boss. If I rescue him, maybe I won't lose my job."

"Come now," Jessie scolded mildly. "I really don't think that Wilson would hold you responsible for his being taken in a sudden ambush."

Thorn grinned wistfully. "We both know how short-tempered the congressman can be when his employees don't perform up to his expectations. Look at how he vowed to have Deputy Long fired, merely for talking back to him."

Jessie was again forced to agree. "Wilson *can* be insufferable," she said sourly. "Well, one good thing will come of this. When Longarm helps us rescue the congressman, Wilson will be forced to admit that he misjudged the deputy—"

"No, ma'am!" Thorn's face had grown dark with barely suppressed rage. "Longarm can't be involved!"

"Now, Thorn—"

"No!" he hissed. "I'd as soon go it alone, if that's your last word on the matter, ma'am! I've still got to look out for my boss's best interests. Deputy Long has good reason not to be fond of the congressman. If he helped rescue him, who's to say that my boss wouldn't be blackmailed by the deputy?"

"Now *I'm* getting angry," Jessie warned. "How dare you accuse Longarm of being capable of blackmail?"

Thorn hung his head. "Sorry," he muttered sullenly. "It's true that I don't know Longarm—" Thorn glanced at her with what seemed to be laughing eyes. "At least the way that *you* know him."

Jessie decided that it would be best to let *that* dig pass. "Make your point," she demanded.

"My point is that I can't take your word for the fact that Longarm won't use this whole mess to try and bargain with the congressman not to have him fired." He looked Jessie in the eye. "My point is that you can't give me your word that such a thing won't happen." Before Jessie could reply, Thorn pushed on. "I'm going to speak plain to you, ma'am, and let the devil take the hindmost. It's my feeling that you owe the congressman something. I know that you went to him for help against these Prussians a few years back. He's in this mess tonight because he agreed to lend you a hand." Thorn paused. "I'd always heard," he went on, "that the Starbuck family believed in paying back their debts."

Jessie thought about it. "We'd need horses."

"I've got two waiting for us right outside," Thorn answered quickly. "Woke up the stable owner and rented them before I came over here. Charged them to the congressman."

Jessie sighed and nodded. "You're right, Thorn. He's been kidnapped because he helped me. I owe it to him to try and get him out of this with his reputation, as well as his skin, intact."

"Yes, ma'am," Thorn agreed.

Jessie stood up. "Please wait outside for me. It'll only take me a few minutes to get dressed."

Longarm thought that the grove was just as pretty and peaceful at night as it had been earlier in the day. Of course, without Jessie on hand, it was a mite more lonesome. . . .

He'd turned his roan gelding free, confident that it wouldn't wander far from the meadow of sweet grass over yonder. He himself had supped on beans and bacon purchased from a provisioner who had set up shop at the fairgrounds. Longarm had cooked his meal in a skillet he always packed among his possibles, along with a battered coffeepot and a tin cup. Just now he was leaning against his McClellan saddle, waiting for his coffee to brew over a small campfire.

The coffeepot began to puff out little bursts of aromatic steam. Longarm used one of his leather riding gloves as a potholder, and poured himself a mug of strong black brew.

He sipped at it awhile, then lit up a cheroot to go along with the coffee. He'd already seen to his Winchester and Colt, cleaning and oiling the weapons by the bright light of the fire while he had it roaring and crackling.

So now his guns were clean. His supper had been eaten, and he'd rinsed his cookware in the water from one of his canteens.

There was nothing left to do but think—about the present, and about the future.

Longarm rummaged around in his saddlebags until he came up with the bottle of Tom Moore. He pulled the cork with his teeth and took a long swallow of the Maryland rye. Then he poured a generous dollop into his coffee.

What he had told Jessie earlier in the day was true. He had always thought he'd been born to be a lawman. He had his complaints about the day-to-day crap that he had to put up with, but hell, there wasn't a man on earth, employed or self-employed, who didn't have to deal with some kind of unyielding system. On the whole, his days as a deputy marshal had been the happiest time of his life.

But now those days were coming to an end. By this time next week, the badge pinned to his wallet would be a memory.

If he wanted, he supposed he could find some other law enforcement job. A town marshal's post somewhere, or at the very least, a job as a town marshal's deputy. Longarm sipped at his coffee and made a face—and not because of the taste of the brew.

Truth to tell, he was the sort of fellow who craved excitement. He'd just about go loco sitting behind a town marshal's desk, waiting for Saturday night to roll around so that he could go out and arrest the town drunk. No, local law enforcement was out. . . .

There were the private outfits, Pinkerton and the like; the problem there was that a fellow who wanted to last had to be even more of a toady than if he worked for the Justice Department. Hell, just about the only jasper in the world who couldn't give orders to a Pinkerton man was a crook. . . .

Longarm spilled the dregs of his coffee into the fire, and filled his cup with straight rye. All right, then. The private companies were out. That left becoming a private investigator, or a bounty hunter. Longarm had known a whole passel of PIs in his day. Some were good, and a whole lot more weren't worth shit. The problem with being a private eye was that there wasn't a whole lot of call for one outside of the big cities. Longarm felt comfortable in the wide-open spaces of the West. The hemmed-in, jampacked urban life wasn't for him.

Bounty hunting? Longarm had to laugh, just thinking about it. As he'd confided to Jessie, a real lawman didn't risk his life for money, but for the satisfaction of doing a job that few men could handle. When Longarm went after somebody, he did it in the name of the law, not his bank account. You couldn't generalize about bounty hunters any more than you could about private eyes. Some manhunters were good, and a whole lot were bad.

But even the good ones began to spoil inside, after a while. A badge-carrying man can always find a way not to take it personal-like if he's got to gun down a man, but a bounty hunter, well, he's got to admit to himself that he never would have confronted his quarry if it weren't for the price on the poor fellow's head. Pretty soon a bounty hunter has to start wondering whether he's gunning men just because it's easier to take them in that way. Of course, the same sort of self-doubt can overtake a lawman, but at least the question of personal profit can't enter into it.

No, Longarm thought to himself. Just about anything was better than being a bounty hunter.

That pretty much covered the possibilities of remaining in the lawman business. Longarm kicked off his boots, folded up his coat, vest, and shirt to make a pillow, and wrapped himself up in his bedroll's blankets. He stared up at the glimmering stars and thought about Jessie's unspoken offer.

He'd been down this trail before, of course. He and Jessie both sort of figured that they'd eventually hitch up together, assuming that both of them stayed alive. The thing was, marriage had always been in the future, and now Longarm's future seemed to have led him into a box canyon.

I've been a drover before, and I could always do it again, he thought as he watched the night sky. *Reckon I could marry Jessie and take over the day-to-day management of her cattle spread. Of course, I couldn't rightly complain if folks took to calling me Mr. Jessie Starbuck. After all, my marriage license would also be a meal ticket. . . .*

He grinned. If Jessie were a poor girl, he'd marry her in an instant, content to start a new way of life with a wife by his side. But no matter how he tried to rationalize the situation, he just couldn't come around to the idea of living off a rich woman's assets, and he couldn't rightly demand that Jessie divest herself of all her holdings in order to live the beans-and-bacon, second-hand clothing, saddle-sore life of a drover's wife.

A jumble of thoughts went through Longarm's mind as he fell asleep. He wished he could talk to Billy Vail about this mess. He thought about the bullet that had felled poor old Tompkins, and what it might prove. He'd never considered himself a vindictive man, but Wilson Barston was one bastard Custis Long meant to bring to justice before he lost his badge. . . .

Longarm came awake with his Colt in his hand. He wondered what it was that had disturbed his slumber, and then his attention focused on the dull thudding of horses' hooves approaching on the trail below the grove.

He kicked his legs free of his blankets and hurried over to the ledge that overlooked the main trail out of Sarah. There were enough stars out for Longarm to discern clearly that one of the two riders was Jessie Starbuck! It took him a while to recognize the man she was with. At first he naturally assumed that it was Ki, but a moment later Longarm realized that the other rider was Congressman Barston's bodyguard, Thorn.

Both Jessie and Thorn were riding hard. It was only a matter of seconds before their loping horses had carried them past Longarm's vantage point. He watched until they were out of sight around a bend in the trail, and then felt like pinching himself to make sure he hadn't dreamed the whole thing.

He made his way back to his campsite, noticing that his fire had burned itself out.

The embers had long ago grown cold, so he must have been sleeping for quite some time. He dug his pocket watch out of his folded frock-coat; it was five in the morning. The sun would be rising in another hour or so.

Longarm knocked back a cup of tepid coffee to wake himself up. He rinsed the taste of the stimulating but bitter brew out of his mouth with a swallow of rye. Then he quickly put on his shirt, vest, and coat, and stomped his feet into his boots.

There was no plausible reason why Jessie would be riding with Thorn before dawn. The congressman was supposedly staying in the hotel in town—why would Thorn be leaving him?

Of course, he didn't much care where Thorn went, but why would Jessie be traveling with him? Muttering to himself, Longarm strapped on his gunbelt and quickly stuffed his things into his saddlebags. He'd have to hurry if he wanted to pick up their trail.

He'd managed to get a good look at Jessie as she passed. She was dressed in denims and wearing her gunbelt. Longarm knew from past experience that Jessie Starbuck was the sort of woman who disliked wearing a man's outfit of jeans and a waist-length wrangler's jacket unless she expected a rough time. He knew that Jessie did not like to antagonize menfolk by wearing her gun on her hip unless she expected to have to use it.

As unlikely as it seemed, all the evidence pointed to the conclusion that Jessie, accompanied by Thorn, was riding to some kind of fight; Longarm figured that she was ripe for a spanking for not enlisting his help in the matter, but before he could spank her, he had to make sure she survived whatever she was getting herself into.

He shouldered his saddle and other belongings, and strode off to retrieve his horse. Jessie Starbuck was about to make some kind of play, and Longarm meant to be there when it happened.

★
Chapter 14

Ki wondered how long it would be before the stablehand discovered him. The samurai had come awake just as dawn broke—with his hands bound behind his back, his legs securely tied together at the ankles, and a gag stuffed into his mouth. He knew that day had come; it was heralded by the bright chirping of morning songbirds, and by the glimmer of light penetrating a split seam of the canvas tarp above his head. Ki assumed that he was near the stables because that was where he had been knocked unconscious, and because he seemed to have been stashed in a feed-storage tent. How else to explain the bales of hay upon which he was lying, and which were stacked all around him?

What Frank Butler hoped to accomplish by knocking him out, trussing him up, and sticking him in this tent, Ki could not imagine. The sharpshooter ought to have realized that it was only a matter of time before Ki worked himself free of his bonds.

The samurai flexed his strong stomach muscles and limber legs, curling himself into a ball. He rolled onto his spine, and then rocked back onto his shoulder blades. With a bit of stretching, he was able to slip his bound wrists beneath his drawn-up feet, so that his hands were no longer behind his back. He removed his gag.

Ki's leather vest was gone, and with it his assortment of weapons, including his *shuriken* blades. He would not be cutting these ropes. It was no use trying to snap them apart. The braided hemp was of fine quality. Cowhands brought down stampeding steers with just this sort of rope.

He gazed at the knots, testing with his teeth the tightness and complexity of the ones that were imprisoning his wrists. There were several of them, and all had been hitched tight, until they were as solid as rock. Ki could chew at them until his mouth was bloody, and he would get nowhere.

Speaking of bloody . . . the samurai gingerly probed his leg wound. There was a great scab of dried blood crusting his thigh. It itched a great deal, but Ki did not dare scratch at it. Right now the scab was acting as a natural bandage, sealing the wound closed.

The samurai turned his attention to his immediate surroundings, in case there was something inside the tent that might aid him in severing his bonds. It did not take Ki long to complete his exploration of the tent's interior. Less than a foot away from him in every direction were hay bales. It seemed that a space had been hollowed out in the stacked bales to contain him. It had been clever of Butler to choose this place. The thick walls of hay and the tarp that had been tied across the top would muffle shouts for help. There was no reason for anyone but the single stablehand to poke around here. Eventually that person would discover him, but would it be today, tomorrow, or the day after? If Ki wanted out, it was up to him to figure out a way to get himself loose, and without the use of a blade.

It was an interesting problem. His samurai training had included instruction in the use of *musubinawa,* a special rope made of braided horses' hair. The standard technique to counter being tied up called for the samurai to use his highly developed muscle control to literally swell his limbs and chest. Later, after his adversary had gone, the samurai would relax his body and the ropes would simply drop away.

Of course, Ki had been knocked out before he had been tied up; the only parts of Ki's anatomy that had swelled were the lumps that Butler had raised on the samurai's skull.

A samurai was also trained in *hojo-jutsu*, a technique by which to bind a noncombatant, such as a woman or a child, in order to take them hostage. But *hojo* taught no counter-techniques, since a samurai taken hostage would always be asked to give his word that he not try to escape. Such a promise, once made, would far more securely bind an honorable warrior than any rope.

Ki began to twist his bound wrists in an attempt to create a bit of slack. He ignored the way the coils of rough hemp cut into his skin. If he got desperate enough, Ki was prepared to reopen the wound on his leg. Blood-soaked hemp might stretch a bit. . . .

He paused as something hornetlike whizzed through the air. He listened intently, and heard what sounded like a distant gunshot, and then a repetition of that high-pitched buzzing noise.

Several blades of hay fluttered down to tickle his nose. . . .

Not hornets, Ki thought, as he again heard the faraway gunfire, and this time actually saw the outward explosion of hay as the bullet penetrated the bale that was scant inches above his head. This was no feed-storage tent! Butler never intended for Ki to live long enough to work himself free of his bonds. The samurai had been cached behind the targets being used in the shooting competition. The bales of hay were not intended to feed horses, but to act as a backstop for the sharpshooters' bullets.

Ki listened carefully. This time he heard a rapid succession of shots. He flattened himself as much as he could, and watched in helpless horror as more bullets whizzed through the small area where he lay bound.

He was sweating now. His body's own output of salt stung his leg wound and the areas on his wrists rubbed raw by the rope. He did his best to envision just where the target was situated on the far side of those bales of hay, and realized that Butler had placed him just about at bullseye level.

Ki brought up his legs and kicked out hard in an attempt to knock a hay bale off the stack. He grimaced in pain as his injured leg, bound to his sound limb, took its share of the impact.

The hay bale did not even shake, let alone topple. A portion of it shredded away beneath his stiffened toes, but the bale itself was far too heavy to be disturbed by Ki's weak and awkwardly executed kicks. He was about to try again, simply because he did not know what else to do, when a bullet burned a hole in the bale he was kicking against.

Ki quickly lowered his legs as he stared at the hole. If he had kicked out at that moment, the bullet would have taken one of his feet right off. . . .

All right, think hard, the samurai lectured himself. *Do not dwell on the ways in which you are helpless, but instead, concentrate on the ways in which you can turn the aspects of this situation to your advantage.*

Another bullet seared into the hay bale behind the samurai. This one passed so close above him that Ki instinctively sucked in his belly, in case a second round should follow.

But a second round did not follow for some moments, then there was once again a rapid series of shots. More holes appeared in the wall of hay before him.

That is another contestant's turn ending, Ki decided. This was a rapid-fire competition, which meant that each contestant could take a couple of practice shots, and then actually go for his score by squeezing off a series of rounds within a specified time period.

Ki began to shout for help. He reasoned that somebody must soon change the bullet-riddled paper target for a fresh one.

He shouted until his throat was hoarse, until the next practice shot chewed its way through the hay. *So much for that plan,* Ki sighed.

This time he watched exactly where the series of rapidly fired shots made their appearance in the wall of hay. It had occurred to the samurai that the people shooting were not common folk plinking away at tin cans, but this country's version of samurai. The sharpshooters were as proficient with their chosen weapon as any samurai was with throwing blade, sword, spear, or bow.

A new plan of action had occurred to Ki. The rapid sequences of shots had each time resulted in an extraordinarily tight grouping of bullet holes.

Ki peered at the groupings. None were more than two inches across. He stared at the bulge of knots between his wrists. The twist of rope was about two inches wide.

A skillful samurai could sever a thin rope with an arrow. It was quite logical to assume that any of the sharpshooters could do the same with a well-placed bullet. The problem here was that none of the sharpshooters just now firing had any idea that a rope target existed.

It would be up to Ki to maneuver his wrists into position so that the shots could sever the ropes. *A Zen master would be amused,* he thought. *The bullet cannot find the target; the target must find the bullet!* And there was another irony: the shot that freed him might also maim him for life, or might destroy his hands or wrists without freeing him at all. . . .

Once again he heard the practice shots, and watched the bullet holes appear. He readied himself, taking a deep breath and then letting it out slowly. He let all extraneous thoughts flow out with his exhalation, all self-doubts and fears about what would happen to him if this went wrong.

He could wait, of course—he could check and recheck his timing an infinite number of times, until finally one of the sharpshooters' bullets killed him. But in this particular instance he recognized his inclination toward prudence for what it was: that old demon self-doubt, creeping up on him with its seductive arguments.

Ki ignored the demon's cajolings. An expert in the martial arts spends long years developing total control over his movements so as to be able to spar without causing injury. Ki could hurl a punch full force and pull it at the last possible moment, to come within a scant fraction of an inch of hitting the target.

He would judge the probable placement of the rest of this shooter's bullets after the first couple of rounds, and then would position his wrists so that the knots binding them would be severed. He would not tremble or waver like an old woman. He would conduct himself in a steadfast and true manner, like an honorable warrior.

He would trust his years of training, and his instincts.

And his luck.

Gunfire, as the bullet holes began to appear.

One—two—three—

Thrust now! Ki thought. Quickly he raised his wrists—

There was a twanging sound, almost musical. Ki felt a jolt that numbed his hands to the tips of his fingers. A bullet had disintegrated the knots that bound him. Ki's hands were free.

The samurai waited for the shooting to end, and then made short work of the ropes around his legs. Painfully he stood up, tore open the already split seam in the canvas tarp, and wiggled quickly through the opening, anxious to show himself before any more shooting took place.

Ki looked around, totally surprised. He had expected to see a number of contestants, and a large crowd occupying the bleachers, but the grandstand was empty, and the only shooters at the firing line were Phoebe and Frank Butler!

Ki let himself carefully down to the ground. It was earlier in the day than he had thought. Now that he could actually see the sun's position, he estimated that it was no more than eight in the morning. Phoebe and Butler must have arrived early to practice for the day's official competition. That explained why there had been no target-changer present to hear Ki's shouts. The sharpshooting couple had been using the same target over and over.

The samurai noticed that his leather vest was lying on the grass behind the backstop. He picked it up, pleased to see that all of his *shuriken* blades and other devices were still inside the garment's many pockets. He put on the vest and strode toward Phoebe and Butler. Both shootists were staring at him in horror. Ki figured that Phoebe's shock arose from the fact that he might have been killed, while Butler's arose from the fact that he had not. . . .

"Ki?" the farm girl gasped. "What were you doing behind there? Why didn't you call out or something?"

The samurai ignored her as he lunged for the surprised Frank Butler. He gathered twin handfuls of Butler's lapels, holding the man fast.

"What do you want with me?" Butler gasped. "Get away!"

"Ki!" Phoebe demanded. "Stop it! Are you crazy?"

"Last night," Ki growled. "Last night, Butler attacked me

280

in the stables. He knocked me out and left me tied up in that backstop, so that I would be shot and killed during today's competition."

"Mister, I don't know how you got the idea that I jumped you, but you're wrong!" Butler sputtered.

Ki shook him the way a terrier shakes a captured rat. "You are lying!" he spat. "Admit it! Or I—"

"Mister, I ain't!" Butler cried out in fear.

"Ki, listen to me," Phoebe begged. "Frank isn't lying. He couldn't have jumped you last night. I know, because"—she blushed—"because he was with me, for the entire night."

Ki stared at her, and then into Butler's panicked eyes. "It's t-true," the sharpshooter stammered.

Ki thought back upon the previous evening's events. He had never actually *seen* his attacker. He had just assumed that it was Butler because the man had threatened him earlier.

The samurai loosened his hold on the man. "If it was not you," he muttered to Butler, "then who *was* it?"

"Look!" Phoebe called out. "Somebody's coming toward us, riding fast."

Ki peered in the direction she was pointing. He narrowed his eyes. "Marshal Farley and his two deputies. The other two men I do not know."

One of them was riding a mule, while the other was straddling one of Farley's own geldings. The two strangers were dressed in denim overalls and flannel shirts. They were both covered with trail dust, but looked more like farmers than drovers.

"Ki, we got trouble!" Farley grumbled. "These two fellows rode into town early this morning. They say that Federal Marshal Billy Vail and a handful of deputies are pinned down by Wink Turner and his band at Sagmaw Valley."

"They ain't gonna last long," said one of the farmers, a good-looking fellow who wore his long hair bound into a ponytail.

"We would have gotten here sooner, but those outlaw sons-of—bitches shot my mule out from under me," grumbled the other farmer, the one who wore a mustache.

"Where is Longarm?" Ki asked wearily.

Farley scowled. "That's what I'd like to know. I figured to

ask Jessie. She's staying with folks in town, but when I got there, it turned out that she was missing as well."

Ki felt something like a cold wind blow through him as he realized that whoever had incapacitated him last night had done it to keep him out of the way so that they could get to Jessie. *Where was she?*

"I came to fetch you before we ride out to the Sagmaw," Farley was saying. "I need your help on this, Ki. After all, you are my deputy, for a little while, at least."

Ki nodded. That was true; he had accepted the job. He was honor-bound to help Farley. But what about Jessie? Ki shrugged helplessly. He could do nothing for her if he did not know where she was. He could only hope that Longarm, who was also missing, was by her side.

"I will go with you," Ki told Farley. A small band of valiant men were battling an evil foe who greatly outnumbered them. That battle was the place for a samurai to be.

"We'll lead you there," offered the mustached farmer. "We were traveling toward Sarah, and the county fair, when we came across Marshal Vail and his posse. Those deputies are good men. We aim to see this fight through to the end."

"Then we'll come back here," the other newcomer announced. "We're looking for somebody."

"And who would that be?" Farley asked. "Not lawbreakers, I take it?"

"No, sir!" the farmer with the mustache answered quickly. "It's nothing like that, sir. Home-wreckers is more like it."

"We're looking for our wives," the other farmer scowled. "We married a set of twins, rambunctious girls. They used to be in show business years ago, before they returned to Louisiana to settle down." He grinned. "That's where we're from, by the way. My name's Mike, and this is my cousin, Paul. We're the Cling boys, from Red Tick—"

"And your wives are named Aggie and Dot?" Ki asked.

"Now how did you know that?" Mike wondered.

"Your wives are here," Ki chuckled. "Does Dot belong to you?" he asked.

"Nope," Paul cut in, his bottle-brush mustache bristling. "Aggie's the one that belongs to me. As long as we know where those two wandering women are—and wherever Dot is, Aggie ain't gonna be far away—we can leave 'em be until Marshal Vail and his boys are rescued."

"Well spoken," Ki complimented them. "But the five of us can accomplish little to rescue Vail from Turner's outlaw army. We need more volunteers."

Farley shook his head impatiently. "We haven't got any more. And who would dare go up against Wink Turner and his gang in any case?"

Ki smiled. "I think I know of some likely candidates." He turned toward Farley's brace of permanent deputies. "Here is what I want you two men to do."

★
Chapter 15

Billy Vail was greatly disappointed when he emerged from his dream. In it, he was back in Denver, officiating at the hanging of Wink Turner. He groaned aloud when he opened his eyes and realized that he and his men were still pinned down in the Sagmaw Valley, and that from the way things were going, if an execution was to take place, it was Wink Turner who would be doing the officiating. . . .

Billy gritted his teeth as he tried to sit up. His torn shirt was stiff with blood, and his side felt as if somebody had massaged it with a white-hot branding iron. "Hello?" he called out. "What's happening?"

"Well, well, look who's back with the living," Glenn chuckled. He crawled over to where Vail was lying. "Stay low, Marshal. Turner's boys have been taking potshots at us ever since dawn."

"Dawn?" Vail squinted at the sun blazing bright in the flawlessly blue sky.

Glenn nodded. He used his sawed-off Winchester to point

toward the slope where Turner and his men were sequestered. "You blacked out after you were hit by that rifle shot."

Vail nodded. "I remember, but how'd I get here?"

Glenn shrugged, and smiled. "Hell, it was on my way, so I picked you up. The fact that you stayed unconscious was a blessing. It allowed me do dig that slug out of the lard over your ribs without having to listen to you holler. I poured some whiskey over the hole, and taped you up with some sticking plaster I carry in my saddlebags. At first I thought you were dead, but that pot belly of yours stopped the slug before it could do any real damage."

"Thank you, Glenn," Vail said softly. "Reckon I owe you."

"Nah," the deputy shook his head. "Let's just say we're even for the way I backtalked you yesterday afternoon. I was wrong, and you were right, Billy, because if we'd tried our plan in daylight, we'd have ended up even worse off."

Vail frowned, remembering the night. "Oh, damn. Talbot and Wallace and—"

"Hush now," Glenn cut him off. "We lost a lot of men, but you ain't hurt bad. Hopkins is still holding his own, I'm okay, and Mack Spry and Todd Lennon over yonder are both as fit as fiddles."

Vail looked behind him. Spry and Lennon were sitting behind a boulder, tending their weapons. "Howdy, Marshal," Spry grinned. "Glad to see you back with us, boss."

"Glad to see you," Lennon agreed. His grizzled, normally taciturn visage split into a wide smile. "That was a mighty brave thing you did, walking toward Turner and throwing down on him like that. I ain't never seen nothing like it."

"None of us have, Billy," Glenn agreed. "We're all proud to serve with you."

"How about Phil Talbot?" Vail murmured. "Think he was?"

"Now, Billy!" Glenn scowled. "Don't turn weepy on us, like some old woman. Every deputy takes it into account that the odds are good that he won't live to collect a pension."

Vail nodded. "Reckon so." He found his rifle by his side, and used it as a crutch to push himself up into a sitting position. "Boy, that hurt," he groaned. "But I'm so hungry I could eat that dead mule down yonder."

Laughing, Glenn went off toward a blazing cookfire a couple of yards away. "I took the liberty of having us a fire," he told the marshal. "Figured it wouldn't do us any harm, as long as it was put out by nightfall. We had some beans and flour, so I made us up a stew with dumplings, and floated some dried beef jerky in it to soften up into something resembling meat."

Spry nodded encouragingly. "It's good, Marshal."

"I managed to get some down Hopkins's gullet, as well," Glenn said as he returned with a plate of food for Vail. "He's sleeping now." The deputy gestured with his chin toward his still comrade. "That's good, it'll give his body a chance to build up some more blood to replace what he's lost."

"Hot food is what we all need," Vail said between spoonfuls of stew. "What time is it, exactly?"

Glenn checked the pocket watch he kept pinned to the inside of his denim jacket. "It's just high noon." His eyes met Vail's. "Reckon I know what you're thinking."

Vail set down his plate. He patted the pockets of his suit coat for his pipe and tobacco. "If you built a fire, I can smoke my damned pipe," he muttered. "And, yep, I guess you *do* know what I'm thinking." He puffed the briar alight. "Those two boys should be on their way back with help by now."

"If they made it to Sarah in the first place," Glenn said tiredly.

"*If* they made it," Vail acknowledged, puffing smoke rings. "But I think they did. Don't ask me why, but that's how I think. I've had the opportunity to judge a lot of men in my day, and those two farmers rank with the best."

"Marshal?" It was a worried Mack Spry who was summoning Vail. "Look yonder, boss. It looks like the big showdown."

Vail glanced over his shoulder, toward the slope. "Oh, shit," he muttered. "All right, everybody, get ready for trouble."

Turner's men had left the safety of their encampment. They'd fanned out to leapfrog their way from boulder to boulder, down the slope toward Vail's position. The outlaws had their guns ready as they picked their way down in ragtag groups. Smack in the middle of the approaching force was Wink Turner himself.

Vail loaded up Captain Walker. "I count fifteen of 'em, men," he said encouragingly. "Looks like we did a fine job of thinning out Turner's army."

Glenn scowled as he levered a round into his sawed-off Winchester. "Maybe so, but it's still fifteen against four, and we can't run, not unless we want to leave Hopkins behind."

"No chance of that," Vail said. "Spry, Lennon, you two position yourselves by Hopkins."

Spry smiled. "We figured to do that already, boss."

"They've got good cover until they reach the valley floor," Vail mused. "Then they'll be close enough to start setting up waves of fire to keep our heads down while they send men forward to overrun us."

"That's the way I'd do it," Glenn said. "Let's hope Turner ain't that smart."

"He's that smart," Vail growled.

"Spoilsport," Glenn replied dourly, watching the slope. "Oh, oh, here comes more trouble. It looks like Turner's got a line of reinforcements."

As Vail and his small band watched, ten more figures appeared at the crest of the slope. "I guess those fellows will give the fifteen attacking us some cover fire—" he began, but then hesitated. "Wait a minute," he said, squinting up at the line of newcomers taking up positions along the crest. "Those aren't Turner's men. Look, two of them are waving at us."

Glenn began to laugh. "I'll be damned!" he shouted. "It's those two farmboys, and they've brought help!"

A moment later the sound of gunfire filled the valley as the newcomers, secure behind cover along the high ground, began to blast away at the unprotected backs of Turner's bewildered men.

Ki was extremely worried as the posse left their horses behind at the base of the slope, and began to follow Paul and Mike Cling as the two farmers led the way up the rise. Hours ago, Farley's two deputies had rounded up and brought to Buffalo Bill's tent all of the professional shootists who'd been entered in the target competition. Ki explained the situation to all of them, and then the frontier showman himself made an impassioned plea for volunteers to ride to the valley to rescue Vail and his men.

Cody had stood on his stage, surveying the assemblage like Moses addressing the tribes of Israel before leading them out of Egypt. Phoebe Mozee had been the first to volunteer, with Frank Butler agreeing to come along right after her. Two-Gun Leroy Kingsley—resplendent in his red satin suit and silver-filigreed holsters—threw in with them after that, and several more sharpshooters followed quickly.

Ki, Farley, Buffalo Bill, and the rest of the newly formed posse rode hard to the site of the battle, led by Paul and Mike Cling. Leaving their horses in a grove, they crept up the slope, only to find that Turner and his men had just vacated the position the posse had been about to attack, in order to advance upon Vail and his men.

Now, as they took command of the high ground, Ki was wracked by doubt. He had orchestrated this entire plan, and he hoped he had done the right thing. It was true that the posse was comprised of the world's foremost sharpshooters, but target shooters and gunslicks were a breed apart. Wink Turner's men were comfortable with the notion of shooting at flesh-and-blood human beings, while Ki's shootists customarily blasted away at nothing more substantial than scraps of paper.

The samurai turned to Buffalo Bill, who was crouched behind a boulder at his right. Cody was checking the load in his rifle, a Creedmore rolling-block buffalo gun, .45-70 caliber. When its trigger was pulled, the massive single-shot weapon would throw out a piece of lead the size of a rock.

Cody caught Ki's eye and nodded. "I'm ready, son. Those varmints down there won't know what hit 'em."

To Ki's left, Farley signaled that he and the others were ready.

For the coming fight, Ki had brought along his Japanese bow, an elegantly curved instrument of dark wood, oiled to a handsome luster, and as long as a man is tall. In the black-lacquered quiver that accompanied the weapon, Ki carried a selection of arrows suited to a wide variety of lethal purposes. At Farley's signal, Ki slid one of the arrows from the quiver and notched it to the bowstring. It was a "death's song" arrow, equipped with a perforated ceramic bulb just behind the head. The bulb was so designed that when the arrow was launched, air would rush through the perforations, creating the high-pitched keening sound from which the arrow took its name. This hair-raising wail would be the signal for the others to begin the attack.

The samurai inhaled as he drew back the bowstring and took a bead on the broad back of one of the outlaws. As he slowly let out his breath, he released the bowstring. The arrow screamed down the hillside, its banshee wail ceasing abruptly as the arrow buried itself between the outlaw's shoulder blades. The man belly-flopped to the ground without uttering a sound.

"Nice shooting," Buffalo Bill complimented Ki. "But watch this." His big-bore rifle thundered, and an outlaw halfway down the rise was picked up and propelled down the remainder of the slope, to collapse in a bloody heap upon the valley floor.

By now the rest of the sharpshooters were firing down upon Turner's panicked men. A half-dozen of the outlaws were picked off as they stumbled and rolled down the slope in an attempt to get out of range of the withering ambush set up by Ki and his force. Another half-dozen, led by Wink Turner, made it to the valley floor, but now they were out in the open, at the mercy of Vail and his deputies.

To the federal marshal's credit, he did not order that the outlaws be shot down, but gave them the opportunity to surrender. All six were anxious to do so. They dropped their guns and put up their hands. Only Turner refused to give up. Vail and his men peppered him with rounds, but as before, he just seemed to shrug the bullets off like raindrops as he ran for cover behind some boulders.

"Looks like they got Turner cornered like a mad dog!" Buffalo Bill exulted.

"Everyone!" Ki shouted. "Down the slope to join the marshal and his men!"

By the time Ki and his sharpshooting posse reached Vail, two of the federal marshal's deputies had put the cuffs on those of Turner's men who'd given up. The old lawman himself was leaning on his rifle, using the gun as a crutch as he made his way towards his rescuers.

Vail nodded in recognition to Farley. He'd expected the

town marshal to be among the rescuers, but Vail was surprised—to say the least—when Farley explained that the mission had not been organized by the law, but by a part-Japanese samurai, aided by none other than Buffalo Bill Cody himself.

"Longarm told me about you," Vail said to Ki. The marshal was awestruck before Buffalo Bill. "How'd you ever persuade these other celebrities to come help?"

"It was easy!" Cody said expansively, spreading wide his buckskin-fringed arms. "I just promised every one of them a decent share of the profits I'm going to make from publishing this story! Can't you just see it, Marshal?" Cody's shoulder-length blond curls flew about his head as he hopped in excitement. "Led by Buffalo Bill, a posse made up of the world's greatest sharpshooters rides out to capture the West's most feared outlaw, Wink Turner." Cody rubbed his hands together gleefully. "Old Ned Buntline will want to slit his own throat when he reads this one and sees what he missed!"

Somewhere far away, a coyote disturbed by all the shooting set up a mournful yowling. Phoebe Mozee, standing with Frank Butler, smiled at Paul and Mike Cling while Marshal Vail gratefully shook the farmers' hands.

"That old coyote sounds just like your wives did when you took them off to the woodshed," Phoebe chuckled to the two cousins. "How come they didn't ride along with us?"

"Well, ma'am," Mike began, "after me and my cousin finished blistering their tails for all the bad things they done that we know about—"

"And all the bad things they've done that we *don't* know about," Paul added, while Ki, blushing, looked away.

"—their backsides were too sore to sit on pillows," Mike went on. "Never mind *saddles!*"

"They'd billed themselves as being from Georgia, but you boys hail from Louisiana, don't you?" Frank Butler asked.

"Yes, sir, but our wives are Louisiana girls, as well," Paul answered. "They just made up all that Georgia stuff because it went well with their idea of calling themselves the Cling Peaches."

Ki suddenly realized that in all the excitement, he had completely forgotten his conversation with the Cling Sisters late last night. He had never managed to alert Jessie to Wilson

Barston's connection to the cartel. Someone had prevented Ki from alerting her, and now Jessie was missing. Could it be that—

"Come on, Ki!" Vail said, interrupting the samurai's thoughts. "This ain't over until we bring down Wink Turner!"

The group headed over to where the sharpshooters and Deputy Glenn had Turner cornered. The outlaw leader had his back to the boulders and a gun in each hand, as he taunted the semicircle of armed vigilantes blocking his escape.

Turner was certainly an awesome sight. The tall outlaw's serape was pocked with holes made by bullets that seemed not to have harmed him. His bald scalp was sweat-streaked, and the half of his face visible beneath the red bandanna was twisted into a demonic grimace of hatred.

"Throw those pistols down, Wink!" Vail ordered.

"Nobody takes my guns!" Turner spat back, his single eye rolling wildly as he gazed in turn at each of his tormentors. "Back off, all of you!" he roared. "Or I'll shoot my way out of here!"

"Like hell you will!" Glenn raged, squeezing off a round from his sawed-off Winchester.

Turner began blasting away with both of his pistols. The sharpshooters scattered to avoid being hit, and then returned the defiant outlaw's fire.

Turner was rocked by the impact of the volley that peppered his torso, but he stayed on his feet, not crying out—or even bleeding—as he squeezed the triggers on his double-action Colts.

"Why won't he die!" Glenn shouted in frustration.

Vail, standing back, leaned on his rifle for support and pointed Captain Walker at Turner's head. He squeezed the trigger on the big .45, and watched as Turner's good eye disappeared in a shower of crimson mist.

Turner's pistols dropped from his hands. He fell back against the boulders, and then slid down to the ground.

Silence descended upon the valley, except for the murmurings of the men, and Phoebe Mozee's slightly muffled sobbing as Frank Butler embraced her. Glenn started to advance upon Turner's body, but Vail yelled, "Stay away!" freezing his deputy on the spot.

"Billy," Glenn soothed. "He's dead."

Vail shook his head. "Maybe, but *I'll* be the one to make sure."

Glenn nodded in acknowledgement. "Yes, sir, boss," he said softly.

Leaning on his rifle, Vail approached the still body on the ground. *Wink Turner, the outlaw legend,* he thought to himself, holding Captain Walker cocked and ready. *Wink Turner, the outlaw nobody can kill. . . .*

He wanted to hesitate, he wanted to turn the job over to Glenn, or Ki, or anybody—*that* was why Marshal Vail forced himself to move forward without caution.

Wink Turner . . . last night I saw you as evil personified, Vail thought as he reached the body. Slowly, painfully, the marshal knelt down beside the still form. His trembling fingers spread apart the outlaw's bullet-riddled serape. He tapped on Turner's chest with the barrel of his pistol. A clanging sound arose. "Here's why we couldn't stop him," Vail explained as the others closed in behind him. "Turner's wearing steel plates across his chest. Our slugs just bounced off this armor plating."

"I'll be damned," Glenn said, and then laughed nervously.

"Miss Mozee, you may not want to see this," Vail warned. He pulled the bandanna away from Turner's face.

A quite dead, pale blue eye stared up at Vail out of the outlaw's grizzled but completely unscarred face.

"It's not him," Vail said wearily, shaking his head. He pushed himself to his feet with the rifle. "We've been duped," he added, as his shoulders began to shake with laughter. *So much for slaying evil,* he thought.

Glenn shoved through the crowd to peer down at the body. "The oldest trick in the book," he fumed. "And we fell for it."

Buffalo Bill nodded. "Sitting Bull used to send out braves dressed to resemble him in order to confound the army," he explained. "The bluecoats never knew who the real chief was."

"If that is not Wink Turner," Ki wondered aloud, "Where *is* he?"

Vail shrugged. "Who knows? I've got a wounded man back at my campsite who needs medical attention. Let's get going! Glenn? Take some of these good folks and cut down some striplings for travois poles. We can stitch some blankets be-

293

tween the poles and haul Hopkins back to Sarah that way. Spry? Lennon? Get your prisoners organized. The rest of us can gather the horses you folks brought, and the ones that belonged to these outlaws. That ought to supply us with enough mounts to get home."

As the volunteers moved off to do his bidding, Vail glanced down at the red bandanna in his hand. He stuffed it into his pocket, determined to carry it with him for the rest of his days.

It'll serve as a reminder to a foolish old man, Vail thought to himself. *There ain't no devil but the one that folks invent out of their own fear. And if a lawman wants to rid the world of evil, the only thing he can do is what Longarm always claims is the best thing any man can do—just eat that apple one bite at a time. As for me, I ain't done so bad for a deskbound old bastard, after all. . . .*

Leaning on his rifle-crutch, Vail began to make his way back to the campsite. *And won't I just be glad to get back to that good old desk!*

★

Chapter 16

Longarm crouched in the woods, watching as Thorn and Jessie walked their horses along the narrow trail that led to the tall granite spire, surrounded by a clearing, that was known as Castle Rock. The federal marshal had left his own horse about a quarter of a mile back. He didn't know the area, but he'd gambled that since Thorn and Jessie were leading their horses, they didn't have far to go. As soon as Longarm had caught a glimpse of Castle Rock rising up through the trees, he'd figured that the stone spire was their destination.

A funny feeling in the pit of Longarm's belly had warned him to follow the riders unobserved. That meant he couldn't afford to bring his horse along with him on this last part of the journey. Mounts had a way of calling to one another. Jessie would have guessed instantly that someone was on their trail. That didn't concern Longarm, but he didn't know how savvy Thorn was about such things.

It was just high noon. The ride to Castle Rock had taken close to six hours. Longarm had been given plenty of time to think about why Jessie had come to this lonely, out-of-the-way place with Thorn. He still didn't have a clue.

But it looked as though he was about to find out. As Longarm watched, Thorn put a finger to his lips and motioned to Jessie to draw her gun. The bodyguard did the same. He gestured with his snub-nosed .38 to leave the horses behind, and then he and Jessie began to move toward the clearing, crouched and careful. . . .

Longarm shadowed them. He had his own Colt in his hand, even though he felt foolish about drawing it. What was all the fuss about, he wondered. Castle Rock was as quiet as a tomb.

He was glad to see that Thorn was concerned about Jessie's safety, at least. The bodyguard was making it a point to keep his eye on her. Longarm didn't trust Thorn, and he certainly didn't think much of his ability, but he couldn't think of a single reason why Thorn would want to hurt Jessie. After all, she was Wilson Barston's potential ally, not his enemy.

Thorn had slowed down. Jessie was creeping forward cautiously beside him. Both were intently scanning the area around the granite spire.

Longarm watched them, and then tried to figure out what the hell they were looking for. The clearing seemed empty, but for a few fallen logs. The spire itself was large enough to conceal somebody within a depression or behind an outcropping, he supposed.

Longarm was sweating now. That old tingle in the pit of his belly was back again, double strength. Call it experience or know-how born of long years at his trade, or call it a talent, plain and simple, but Longarm felt a fight about to happen. The threat of violence hung in the air as suffocatingly heavy as a summer thunderstorm before those first fat drops of rain begin to fall. . . .

Drops of rain, Longarm thought, as a gnat—which he didn't dare swat—walked along his moist cheek. *Drops of rain . . .*

Drops of blood . . . Without knowing exactly why he was doing it, Longarm removed his double-barreled brass derringer from his vest pocket, unsnapped it from his gold-washed watch chain, and tucked the little pistol behind the buckle of his gunbelt, where he could more easily get to it if he needed that particular ace in the hole.

As he watched, Thorn and Jessie rushed the base of the spire. Once they'd reached the clearing, Wilson Barston, calling out to them not to shoot, came around from the far side of the rock.

"Wilson?" Jessie asked as the congressman appeared. "Are you all right? Where are the kidnappers?"

Barston just smiled. He reached beneath his suit jacket to produce his long-barreled .38 target revolver.

Jessie stared as Barston pointed his gun at her. "Wilson, what is going on here?"

"Your death is about to go on here, my dear," the Congressman chuckled. "Thorn? Would you do the honors?"

The bodyguard plucked Jessie's Colt from out of her hand and tossed it into the woods.

"This was all a trick?" She stared at Thorn, who now had his own gun leveled at her. "There *were* no cartel agents?"

"Jessie . . ." Barston shook his head. "You pretty little fool . . . I *am* the cartel agent."

Longarm figured that he'd heard enough to justify shooting both of those bastards dead to save Jessie. Cold-blooded executions were not his style, but he didn't see any other way to get her out of this unscathed. If he ordered the two to give themselves up, they could quickly use Jessie as a hostage. No, he couldn't take that chance. He'd shoot them both, and suffer whatever consequences his actions might bring down upon him later. There was only one thing Longarm was concerned about, and that was seeing that Jessie was unharmed.

He was centering his .44 on Barston's torso when something metallic and very, very cold pressed itself against his ear.

"You pull *that* trigger and I'll pull *this* one," a quiet voice warned him. "And that'll mean your head will get blown all the way to kingdom come. . . ."

Longarm let a hand approximately twice the size of his own take away his .44. The pressure of the gun barrel against his ear abated enough to let him look back over his shoulder. The man who had taken him captive was well over six and a half feet tall. He was wearing a Mexican serape, and was festooned with enough pistols—not counting the one he aimed at Longarm—to be Sam Colt's idea of a Christmas tree. Longarm did not have to tilt back his head and see the shaven skull, and that red bandanna angled across half of the fellow's face, to know who this jasper was. . . .

Longarm didn't have to do any of that, but he did, because how often does a man get to meet a living legend like Wink Turner?

The visible portion of Turner's face grinned. "Let's us join the party," he told Longarm.

"And to think that I've trusted you all these years," Jessie mourned to a gloating Wilson Barston.

She and Longarm were sitting beside each other on the ground, their backs against the base of the granite spire. She had not been at all surprised when Longarm appeared, but she did seem glum over the fact that he was also a prisoner. Thorn, Turner, and Barston were standing in front of them, their guns in their hands. Thorn had wanted to tie the prisoners up, but Barston had said there was no need to bother. There was nobody left to rescue these two, and there were no surprises that Jessie could pull. Hadn't he known that she always carried a derringer, for instance? It was something she'd confided to him years ago, during a visit to Washington.

"Of course you trusted me," Barston now answered Jessie, not unkindly. "That is only natural. I am a respected United States congressman. Why, even Marshal Billy Vail trusted me," he added, glancing coldly at Longarm. "He told me that he was sending out a posse to try to keep Wink Turner's band of outlaws away from the fair."

"And you sent Thorn out to warn Turner," Longarm said. He glanced at Jessie. "That's where Thorn went when he took one of your horses, late that night when we all stayed at your spread."

Barston nodded. "Of course, I'd had no idea that Vail would be fool enough to lead that posse himself." The congressman shrugged. "Well, he's dead now. Turner here disguised one of his men as his double, so that Vail would be lured into an ambush."

Turner leered at the two captives. "That joker is as big as me, but nowhere near as tough. Reckon he's enough of a fighter to beat an over-the-hill federal marshal, though."

"How did a fancy-dandy politico like yourself link up with a jasper like Turner?" Longarm asked.

"You must realize that I've worked for the cartel since the beginning," Barston explained. "One of my professors at the university I attended on the Continent first put me in touch with them. Later they helped me in certain business matters, and still later contributed to my campaign to get elected to Congress. They asked for little in return." Barston moved away from Jessie and Longarm to take a seat on a fallen log. "The usual thing, what any member of my constituency might ask for—special legislation, or an investigation into an onerous problem." He grinned, pointing his long-barreled target pistol at Jessie. "Merely what *you* asked for, my dear—help in certain matters of considerable personal interest."

"What does Turner have to do with getting special-interest bills passed?" Longarm persisted.

Barston sighed impatiently. "There are some matters of great importance to the cartel, and to me, that can't be solved by legislation. Action is called for, and that's where my friend Turner comes in. Thorn searched him out for me long ago. I pay Turner, and certain problems go away," he chuckled. "For good!"

Longarm nodded. "Sure, that makes sense. You're a man of action, aren't you, Wink?"

"You'd better believe it," Turner grunted. "I make them problems go away. Nothin' stops me. Pain don't stop me. Fire don't stop me." He touched the bandanna masking his facial scars. "Nothin' ever did, and nothin' ever will."

"I believe it," Longarm said devoutly. "And it's a good thing that Barston here has you on the payroll." He snickered knowingly. "Could you imagine what would happen if he had to send Thorn out to do the dirty work?"

Turner snorted loudly. "That's a laugh."

"You just shut up!" Thorn growled. He took a step toward where Longarm was seated on the ground, threatening the deputy with his pistol.

"See what I mean, Wink?" Longarm chuckled. "A perfect example of Thorn's style."

"He's a nothin', all right," the big outlaw smirked.

"And you shut up, as well!" Thorn cried out in fury.

Wink's one good eye narrowed ominously. "Who are you tellin' to shut up, *punk?*"

"That's enough, both of you!" Barston ordered sharply. "Thorn, you come over here and sit by me," the congressman soothed his bodyguard, patting the log. "And you, Deputy Long, kindly keep your observations about the prowess of my men to yourself, or I shall be forced to put a bullet into you even sooner than I'd planned."

Longarm shrugged. "I don't know what everybody's so touchy about. After all, *we're* the ones sitting here on the cold, damp ground." He winced as he stuck his thumbs beneath his gunbelt on either side of its buckle, trying to adjust it to a more comfortable spot across his hips. At the same time he lifted his butt off the ground prior to settling down into a relatively more comfortable position. "After all, *we're* the ones who are going to be killed."

"Don't be too sure of that, Custis," Jessie said. "If I know Ki, he's probably aiming an arrow at one of these three jokers at this very moment."

Turner looked around anxiously. "Maybe I better check out the area," he said to Barston.

The congressman shook his head, laughing. "No need, my friend."

"That's right." Thorn smiled cruelly. He tapped himself on the chest. "I took good care of that famous bodyguard of yours, Miss Starbuck."

"I don't believe it," Jessie said flatly.

"I beat him to a pulp, and then put him somewhere he won't be leaving alive," the bodyguard insisted. "I did it last night, before I came to get you." He took off his Stetson to ruffle his fingers through his blood-encrusted blond hair. "This here blood I used for my little play-acting *came* from Ki."

"*Is* he dead?" Jessie asked softly, her green eyes growing wet.

Thorn just laughed. "Not bad for a punk, eh, Longarm?"

"Tell me!" she cried out, rising up to her knees so suddenly that both Turner and Thorn brought up their pistols.

"Easy, Jessie," Longarm warned her. "Calm down." He took her hand in both of his, slipping her the derringer he'd managed to remove from behind his belt buckle during his patter about getting more comfortable. Jessie stared at him, her hazel eyes wide and questioning.

"Calm down," Longarm repeated steadfastly. "This is *not* the time."

Nodding, Jessie leaned back against the rock. She folded her hands in her lap.

"You know, in a way, I'm sorry it has to end like this," Barston confided to them. "I can't begin to explain how the cartel delighted in the idea that it would be Jessie Starbuck herself who would unwittingly put their agent in the White House. If Jessie had married me, she would have had the most wonderful six months of her life—"

"Don't flatter yourself, Wilson," Jessie said dryly.

"Now, now, my dear," Barston warned. "Never insult a touchy man holding a gun on you. Anyway, what I meant was that your life would have been happy but short, for you would have met with a tragic accident. Then I, the grieving widower, would have been helped along to the Presidency by the Starbuck family's powerful friends." He frowned. "But you ruined all that when you refused to marry me, and then you really brought matters to a head when you began to have your doubts about endorsing me." He pointed his gun at Longarm. "I blame *you* for that, Deputy."

"My pleasure," Longarm smiled. "But I don't see what you're going to get out of murdering us both."

Barston laughed richly. "What will I get out of it? Let me see, where shall I begin? Well, first of all, that nonsense about what sort of bullet it was that killed Tompkins will fade from everyone's attention."

"Okay, so you weasel out of having to admit that you lied during your speech yesterday," Longarm said. "You're still cutting off your chance of getting Jessie's endorsement by killing her."

"I'm losing the endorsement, but I'm gaining so much more," Barston replied. "You see, the story that Thorn handed Jessie will still hold water at my press conference tomorrow. Jessie rode to save me from outlaws working for the cartel, and she herself died in the attempt. I intend to have Thorn very carefully put a bullet in my own shoulder for the sake of authenticity. I shall be presented before the press as a man who fought tooth and nail to save the woman he loved. A woman who fought beside her man in the tradition of the stalwart female pioneer stock that made this country great."

"You can save the speech," Longarm interrupted.

Barston nodded. "As long as you get the general idea."

"I do," the deputy said. "But it won't work. You won't look like a hero unless you can prove that you got the cartel assassin who killed Jessie."

"I *have* underestimated you, Deputy." Barston smiled in rueful acknowledgement. "You *have* hit upon a sticky point, I'm afraid."

"Thought so," Longarm replied. "Hey, Wink," he chuckled. "Pay attention to this part, it concerns you."

"What's he mean?" Turner asked suspiciously.

"I mean this, Wink," Longarm continued. "They need an outlaw corpse to prove that they've been in a big fight. They need some big, bad villain to pin Jessie's death on. They'll probably claim that you worked for the cartel, which is actually the truth."

Turner, a dumbfounded look on his ravaged face, turned to confront Barston. "What's he mean?" he grumbled once again. The gun he'd been holding on Jessie and Longarm had begun to waver.

"Nothing!" Barston snapped. "Get out of the way, Turner! I need to see around you to guard them—"

"I'll tell you what I mean, Wink," Longarm interrupted quickly. "They're going to kill *you*, as well, and pin our murders on your body. Corpses can't defend themselves against what the living say about them."

"Was you going to do that?" Turner demanded. "Congressman, we go back a long way." The outlaw began to glower. "Was that why you had me send one of my men to try and kill Jessie's Chinaman friend? To pin all this cartel stuff on me?" He rushed toward Barston, moving between the congressman and the place where Jessie and Longarm were sitting.

"Stay away from me!" Barston screamed. Firing rapidly as he stood up from the log on which he'd been sitting, he emptied all six rounds from his .38 into the hulking outlaw. As the shots smashed into his body, Turner staggered, but he still managed to swing up his pistol and squeeze the trigger twice before he fell. Both slugs caught Barston in the chest, knocking him back over the log so that only his legs remained visible to Longarm and Jessie. The legs kicked feebly once or twice, and then they were still.

Meanwhile, Thorn had leapt from his place on the log. He'd crabbed sideways to fire at Turner's sagging form. Longarm crouched low as Jessie brought up the derringer. "Drop your gun, Thorn!" she shouted.

The bodyguard managed to spin around and fire once, his bullet richocheting off the granite behind her. Jessie countered by letting loose with both barrels of the derringer.

The two .44 slugs doubled Thorn over. He let his pearl-handled, snub-nosed .38 fall to the ground. The dying body-guard sagged to his knees, clutching at himself as he stared at Longarm and Jessie with stricken eyes.

Longarm shrugged at him. "What can I say? You're an amateur."

Thorn looked as if *he* were the one who wanted to say something. His lips were moving, but no sound escaped before he collapsed to the ground.

Longarm quickly moved to Thorn's body. "He's dead," he told Jessie, who had gone to see to Barston.

Wink Turner was lying on his side, coughing up blood. Longarm knelt beside the outlaw, but a quick look told him that Turner was a goner.

"Don't say nothin', Deputy," Turner gasped. "I see it all in your face."

"I'm sorry, Wink," Longarm frowned. "I guess I kind of got you into this fix."

The portion of the outlaw's face not hidden by the bandanna seemed to smile. "Hell, you just proved that I was as good as dead anyway. I just hope I fixed Barston, right and proper. Did I?"

Longarm nodded. "You got him, Wink. He's dead."

"Good enough," Turner concluded. "Lawman, do me one favor?"

"Name it, Wink."

"You know that man I've got pretending to be me? Make him quit it." He laughed harshly. "Now that I'm about to die, I wouldn't want him spoiling my reputation."

"I'll see to it, Wink," Longarm promised. "But I wouldn't worry about it. There's only *one* Wink Turner."

Turner didn't answer. He was dead.

Longarm retrieved his Colt from Turner's gunbelt, and walked over to where Jessie was standing, gazing down at Barston's body.

"Let's get out of here," Longarm told her.

"In a minute," she replied, still staring at Barston's body. "I knew him for a long time. . . ."

Longarm went off to fetch her Colt from where it had been tossed into the woods. When he returned with it, she was ready to go.

"Do you think it's true, what they said about Ki?" she asked Longarm as they walked out of the clearing.

Longarm scowled. "Thorn could never take a man like Ki."

"But the blood," Jessie whispered. "He *said* he killed him."

"Thorn, Barston, and Turner said a *lot* of things," Longarm cut her off. "And now they're all dead. Come on, Jessie." He put his arm around her. "Let's go find our horses and ride back to Sarah. We'll find out for ourselves."

★

Chapter 17

The honeymoon suite at the hotel in Sarah Township was decorated with flocked velvet wallpaper that was a very delicate
shade of pink. The thick carpets were purple, and most of the
fixtures were carved out of ivory. Longarm felt as though he'd
somehow gotten himself inside the carcass of a butchered steer.
The suite's colors and its doodads, including the too-soft double
bed, with its heart-shaped headboard, represented everything
that Longarm disliked.

This also happened to be the only suite of rooms that had
not been booked for the duration of the fair, so the honeymoon
suite was where Longarm and Jessie were now sequestered.

"I'm so happy, I *feel* like a girl on her honeymoon," Jessie
giggled. She and Longarm were both ensconced in that large,
lurid double bed. "It was such a relief to get back here to Sarah
and find out that Ki was all right, after all!"

"Told you so," Longarm yawned. They'd checked into the
suite yesterday afternoon, right after they'd arrived from Castle

Rock. A very tired Marshal Farley and a very busy undertaker had promised to take a wagon out to the granite spire in order to fetch back the three bodies that Longarm and Jessie had left behind.

"How can you still be sleepy?" Jessie scolded him gently. "Lord! We slept around the clock, except for when we had room service, and except for when we were doing *other* things," she added languidly. She kicked away the bedsheets. Her long, reddish-gold tresses had come undone during one of their many interludes of lovemaking. Her lush breasts had a faint, pinkish tinge where Longarm's mustache had rubbed against them.

Longarm propped himself up on one elbow to gaze at her. She was just so damned lovely, lying there nude beside him. Again and again during the night, and all through today, he had found himself reaching for her to envelop himself in her warmth.

And when he wasn't reaching for her, Jessie was reaching for him. Longarm flopped back upon the bed, to stare up at the ceiling with a broad grin plastered across his face. His balls were giving off the pleasurable ache a man feels when his sexual equipment has been thoroughly exercised.

Jessie began to tickle Longarm's belly. "It's so nice to know that you don't have to run off to Denver," she purred.

"Yep. For once I don't have to go to Billy Vail. He's come to me." The chief marshal was recuperating from his wound at the Starbuck spread, which was the main reason why Longarm and Jessie had elected to stay in Sarah. There would be plenty of time later on for the deputy and his superior to compare notes. What Longarm wanted now was a little relaxation. He considered himself off duty.

The town was certainly safe enough. Longarm doubted that Sarah had ever had so many lawmen in the vicinity. Hopkins was on the mend at the doctor's office, and Glenn, Spry, and Lennon were having a well-deserved good time at the fairgrounds.

"We *will* have to get out of bed by tomorrow," Longarm moped. "You've got business to attend to at the fair."

"Yes," Jessie sighed. "We'll have to meet with the reporters."

"You sure about how you want to handle it?" Longarm asked.

"Yes, I'm positive, Custis. For the good of the country, we've got to keep Wilson Barston's reputation intact. He came within a hair's breadth of being our next President. He's dead now, he can no longer do any harm. I *do* want revenge for the way he betrayed me by working for the cartel . . ."

"Then why not tell the reporters what a lowlife he really was?" Longarm demanded.

"Because my revenge will not come from sullying a dead man's name," Jessie insisted. "Listen to me, Custis. If I destroy the Barston family's reputation, I've gained nothing and hurt innocent people, Wilson's relatives. If I go along with the story that Wilson originally concocted to explain *our* deaths—that Wink Turner did the deed in the service of the cartel—the country will rise up in anger against the Prussians."

"You'll be making a martyr out of your enemy, but a martyr to serve America's interests, and not the cartel's." Longarm stared at her in admiration. "My God, you won't even be lying about Turner's role in the whole affair. He *did* kill Barston, and he *was* indirectly working for the cartel."

Jessie blushed. "You'll probably think me silly, but I wouldn't want to lie about Turner's role. I know that he was a bad man, but his straightforward evilness somehow pales when compared to Barston's treachery."

"I don't think you're silly, honey," Longarm told her. "I know just what you mean, and I agree with you."

There was a moment's tender silence between them, and then she said, on a businesslike note, "I'm going to have copies of all the newspapers covering the story sent to the cartel's headquarters in Europe. I'm going to include a handwritten note expressing my condolences on stationery that carries the Circle Star insignia. I think I'll write something like, *'How do you fellows like the Jessica Starbuck version of the facts?'*" She winked at Longarm. "What do you think?"

Longarm roared with laughter. "I think they'll be able to read between the lines."

"Me too," she said, satisfied. "We'll also have to hold the delayed finals of the shooting competition. I'm afraid there won't be much suspense now that Barston is eliminated."

"In more ways than one," Longarm added.

"Custis!" Jessie cast a disapproving look his way. "Don't joke about it like that! Anyway, with Barston—"

"Buried by the competition?" he quickly offered.

This time Jessie gave in. She collapsed, laughing, upon Longarm's chest. Once she'd regained her composure, she went on, "Since the only remaining contestants are Phoebe and Frank Butler, and since we already know that she's a better shot than he is, she's destined to win the prize money."

"Well, she deserves it," Longarm decreed. "The way that young lady has been stopping crime, I think that Phoebe Anne Oakley Mozee deserves an honorary badge."

"Speaking of badges, I'm glad yours is safe," Jessie murmured. "Even if it means you'll be leaving me once again."

Longarm reached out to cradle her chin gently in his hands. "I'll be leaving," he said softly. "But I'll be coming back, as well. You know that, Jessie. Hell, you've *got* to know it!"

"I know it," she agreed even as a tear escaped to run down her flawless cheek. "I know it, but sometimes a girl likes to hear it said out loud. I also know a few other things that you either can't or won't say, Longarm. Maybe I can't say them, either, but that doesn't mean they're not true."

"Then maybe we just better *show* each other," Longarm said. He pulled up the bed sheets to cover them, as Jessie took him in her arms.

Ki was downstairs, in the hotel's lobby, sharing a drink with Buffalo Bill, Phoebe, and Frank Butler. The happy couple had been discussing their wedding plans, and Cody had just repeated his offer to hire them both to star in an expanded version of his show.

"You won't regret it," Buffalo Bill was saying. "The stage presentation I've got in mind will be too important to play in small towns like Sarah." He stopped abruptly, coloring as he glanced at Ki. "Sorry, my friend."

But Ki had not been following the last few moments of the conversation. His attention had been riveted by a suspicious-looking fellow whose left arm was cradled in a grimy sling.

The man was a stranger, Ki was sure of that. He looked as if he'd ridden a long way, judging from the amount of dust on his canvas pants, flannel shirt, high-crowned Stetson, and fancy-stitched Justin boots.

"Well, I think our samurai friend is bored with our company," Buffalo Bill jested.

"He's just jealous 'cause the best man won," Frank Butler said with a grin, gazing affectionately at a blushing Phoebe.

"I must take my leave," Ki apologized, rising from his chair. "That man over there bears closer watching."

He stepped out from behind the row of spindly potted palms that separated the lobby from the check-in desk of the cattle town's only hotel.

"I'm looking for a fella named Custis Long. Reckon he's staying here, if he's in town at all . . . " the man was telling the desk clerk.

"Deputy Long?" the clerk asked.

"Yeah, that's him," the man growled.

"He is registered here," the clerk said, eyeing the roughneck distastefully. "But you can't disturb—"

"Oh, no?" The man spun the desk register around, to run his finger down the inked columns. "Ah! Custis Long, room 312."

"You can't go up there—" the clerk began.

"Just watch me!" the dusty drover shouted back, already halfway up the first flight of steps.

The clerk looked helplessly at Ki, who put his fingers to his own lips to warn the man to be quiet. "I will follow him," the samurai whispered. He set off after the stranger, hanging back a bit to avoid notice.

When he got to the third floor, the stranger quietly entered the main corridor. He tiptoed his way to the door marked 312. He pressed his ear against the paneling, smiled to himself, and then took a step back in preparation for kicking the door open. As he lifted his right leg, he reached for the Peacemaker in his holster—

Only to discover that it wasn't there. Ki, now standing just behind the man, had plucked it deftly from the stranger's holster.

309

"Gimme that!" the man squawked, grasping at the weapon, which Ki kept out of his reach. "I need it. I'm going to kill 'em!"

"Suppose you just calm yourself and tell me what this is all about?" Ki suggested.

"I'm warning you," the stranger blustered.

"Pardon me," Ki said. "But your left arm is in a sling, I have your gun, and if you will notice the badge pinned to my vest, I happen to be a deputy in this town." *For a little while longer, anyway,* Ki added to himself.

"You're a deputy, eh?" A wicked gleam appeared in the stranger's eyes. "All right, *Deputy.* My name's Bert, see? And I'm charging Custis Long with trying to blackmail me!" He laughed. "Yeah, that's it! Go in there and arrest Long for blackmailing an honest citizen." He stamped his foot impatiently. "Well? What are you waiting for? Do it!"

"Not so fast," Ki told him. "Just why would he blackmail an honest fellow like you, Bert? What could he possibly have against you?" *The more I talk to this man, the more I feel that I ought to recognize him,* Ki thought. There was something about Bert's appearance that jarred his memory. Ki was quite certain he had never seen the man before, so why did he seem so familiar?

"Never you mind *why* Long would want to blackmail me," Bert gulped. "It's my own business," he muttered, looking down at his boots.

Ki followed the man's gaze down to his footwear. *Those boots! Of course!* "Could it be that Longarm is trying to blackmail you because of your nasty bank-robbing habits?" Ki inquired politely. "You had better come with me, Bert. You see, the town marshal's office has received a wanted flyer for a man answering your description. Just come along quietly. We are supposed to bring you in alive, so that you can tell us where all that loot is hidden."

Bert paled. "Who sent out the flyer?"

Ki had to laugh. "Why, Deputy Long, of course."

"Give me that gun!" Bert yelled, leaping into the air in a desperate attempt to regain his weapon. "I'm going to kill him!"

Ki was forced to pop the hysterical bank robber gently on

310

the chin to quiet him. Before Bert could slump to the carpet, Ki bent over to scoop him up over his shoulder. Then the samurai trudged off to carry his burden to the town jail.

Longarm would want to interrogate Bert himself, but not today. Today, Ki thought, Longarm and Jessie deserved their privacy. . . .

Watch for

LONGARM AND THE BOUNTY HUNTERS

fifty-seventh novel in the bold
LONGARM series from Jove

and

LONE STAR AND THE DENVER MADAM

thirteenth novel in the hot new
LONE STAR series from Jove

both coming in August!